PIECE *of*
MIND

A Novel of Medicine and Philosophy

Robert H. Bartlett

FERNE PRESS

Bartlett, Robert H.
Summary: When four seriously ill patients are admitted to his
care, acclaimed neurosurgeon Donald Ingram—along with his
patients and their families—grapples with serious questions of
love, life, and death. As the story unfolds, the philosophical considerations of mind, body, and soul intersect with the practical
reality of brain function.

ISBN: 1-933916-01-X
ISBN 13-digit: 978-1-933916-01-9

I. Bartlett, Robert H. II. Piece of Mind: A Novel of Medicine
and Philosophy
Library of Congress Control Number: 2006932668

FERNE PRESS

Ferne Press is an imprint of Nelson Publishing & Marketing
366 Welch Road, Northville, MI 48167
nelsonpublishingandmarketing.com
(248) 735-0418

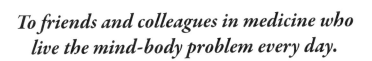

*To friends and colleagues in medicine who
live the mind-body problem every day.*

PROLOGUE
Leyden, 1641

The breathless boy pounded on the door to the St. Cecelia Gasthuis. "Help! Please help!" The two men behind him were carrying a young woman, unconscious, blood draining from her hair onto the cobblestones. Sister Houjke opened the door, murmured "dear God" at the sight of the woman, and guided them to the courtyard.

They laid her on a bench near the pump. Those in the courtyard—nuns, novices, kitchen helpers, and a few patients—gathered around her, murmuring. The woman was breathing but had no other signs of life. The right side of her head was smashed in. Her right eye was prolapsed from what had been its socket. A large laceration in her scalp bled with a steady ooze of dark blood under her blond hair. Soaking her apron from the pump, Sister Houjke tried to wash the blood from the young woman's face while Sister Marguerite pressed a cloth into the wound to slow the bleeding.

Dr. Sylvius, attending the bedded patients up on the first floor, heard the commotion and hurried down to the courtyard. Taking her cool hand, he felt her pulse at the wrist. It was slow—about forty—but strong. Stronger than he would expect for a young woman. But he had noticed this in fatal head injury before. Slow strong pulse, then death.

"What happened?" he asked of the men who had brought her, still sweating and breathing heavily from having carried her at a run all the way from the Burcht.

"Kicked by a horse," said Hans matter-of-factly. "Over by the Burcht. She dropped a biscuit, it rolled behind a horse. She bent over to pick it up and the horse kicked her."

"Not five minutes ago," said the other man.

The doctor raised the woman's left eyelid to examine her pupil, which was widely dilated despite the bright sunlight. "Who is she?" he asked.

"The widow Schippers," said the boy. "I run errands for her. Her husband was lost at sea last year, sailing with Tasman to the southern Pacific."

"She's the prettiest woman in all of Leyden," said Hans. "All the young men follow her about."

"Aah, so," murmured Sylvius, with a barely perceptible nod. He turned to the boy. "Go fetch Dr. Descartes. He will probably be in the university library on the Rapenberg canal. Bring him immediately."

"Is he her doctor?" asked Sister Houjke.

"No, but he is an expert on the brain. And he is her . . . special friend."

* * * *

Rene Descartes was sitting close to the window to take advantage of the light, reading Plato. The Plato dialog was titled Cebes, a thick folio, in Latin, with XXIX on the cover. It had been printed as a test run by Elsevier in Leyden in 1610. The library of the University of Leyden was said to be among the best in the world. In fact the university was arguably the best in the world. During the war of Dutch independence from Hapsburg, Spain, the citizens of Leyden won the battle for their little town by gathering on the man-made hill called the Burcht, then breaking the dikes, flooding the town, and drowning the Spanish soldiers. The battle was the turning point in the war, and in 1575 King William offered to the citizens of Leyden that they choose as their reward either lifelong freedom from taxes, or a university. To their everlasting credit the citizens chose the university.

That was why Rene Descartes—now forty-five years old, French physician, famous as an anatomist, more famous as a physical scientist, even more famous as a philosopher—was in Leyden in 1641. He was reading the dialog in which Socrates asks Cebes why men have to make up answers to questions which have no answers. Why are we driven to invent afterlife, spiritual energy, supernatural causes of natural events, Gods and God? How do the made-up answers become dogmatic truth? True enough to die for, to kill for? Descartes was pondering Socrates' question when the boy ran up to the window.

"M Descartes. Come quickly. To the Gasthuis. Come quickly. Dr. Sylvius says you must come to help with Mme Schippers. She's been hurt. Please come with me." Descartes did not understand the boy's babbling Dutch, but he did recognize Gasthuis, Schippers, and the sense of urgency. He put the folio in a drawer in the desk and hurried outside. (The desk was later moved to the Observatory where bored students carved their names on the top, then to the new Pesthuis north of town where it was used to hold the overflowing chamber pots, then in 1810 it was discarded. No one ever opened the drawer which held what was much later called "the lost dialog XXIX of Plato.")

"Where are we going?" asked Descartes as he ran to keep up with the boy.

"The Gasthuis. The Guest house. The hospital." said the boy between gasps.

The boy's felt shoes and Descartes' heavy boots clattered over the cobblestones, beside two canals, over two bridges, to the Gasthuis run by the Sisters of St. Cecelia. Sylvius met Descartes at the door, holding him back momentarily from the body in the courtyard. They spoke in French.

"Bonjour Rene. Thank you for coming. There is a patient with a brain injury. A young woman. She is near death. I knew you would be interested. I would like your opinion."

"And thank you for calling me," said Descartes, peering past the doctor's shoulder at the little crowd around the patient. "But I sense there is more . . . "

"Yes. The young woman is the widow Shippers. I believe you know her." Sylvius watched Descartes' eyes, then looked down. "Mon ami. Je suis desole. C'est domage. J'ai peine. I'm so sorry. Such a shame." He put an arm around the shoulders of his friend and brought him into the courtyard. She had been moved from the bench to a flat couch. She was covered with a flannel sheet, all except for her grotesque face. Heavy black swelling had developed around both of her eyes. She was breathing slow, shallow breaths.

Descartes was first the physician, first the scientist. He knelt at her side, touched her cheek with the back of his fingers, felt for the pulse in her neck. His eyes misted and he swallowed hard before speaking. "What happened? "he asked without looking up.

"Kicked by a horse," said Hans. "Not thirty minutes ago."

Widow Schippers stopped breathing altogether for what seemed a minute, then took a large gasping breath, then many, quickly. Then more slowly, then the breathing stopped again. Descartes leaned in close to her, whispering softly, "Katherine. It's Rene. Katherine." He shook her shoulder gently, an attempt to rouse her, but there was no response. For an agonizing moment he went from physician to man, burying his head in her chest, clenching the sheet, shuddering with sobbing. The others, feeling his grief, turned away. In time the sobbing stopped, he sighed into the sheet, wiped his face, and looked up at Sylvius.

"Two hours ago we were having morning coffee—this lovely, witty, charming woman and I." He remembered, but did not say aloud that twelve hours ago, and again four hours ago, they had made love. Rollicking, jovial, noisy, slippery, heart-pounding, hard pounding love. She with shrieks and giggles, he with grunts and exclamations, all muffled as best they could to avoid waking the neighbors in the next apartment. Life itself in the loving and in the melding of souls in the afterglow, her head on his chest.

"Two hours ago I left her laughing, humming, glowing with life," he said, partly to himself, partly to Sylvius.

"She is about to die, my friend," said Sylvius, hand on Descartes' shoulder.

"I know. Of course I know." He was back to being the physician. "Look here." He turned her face slightly to the right and wiped away gray goo from her left ear.

"Is it porridge?" asked the curious boy.

"It's bits of her brain." The boy blanched, turned aside, and retched. "Brain coming out of her ear. And where is she now? Her heart beats strongly. The skin of her neck is soft and warm." In his mind he added, but did not say aloud, "Under this sheet and her linen dress is the smell and feel of her slender waist, her bounteous breasts, her sweet succulence . . ." He spoke again, looking around the solemn gathering, "She seems alive—for the moment, at least—alive by any measure. But she is gone. Where is she now?"

"Surely her soul is here as long as her heart beats," said Sister Marguerite, as if she knew it was a fact.

Descartes hesitated, pensive, then said, "Surely." He wondered, but did not say aloud, "Where is her soul, her beautiful soul? Not here, I fear."

The next time her breathing stopped it did not start again. Her pulse became fast and hard. Then faster and irregular. Then faster yet, very faint, then not at all. No part of her moved, but her red lips and pink neck faded to a maudlin purple. The nuns crossed themselves and left to attend to the living. Hans shook his head and shrugged. The boy bent closer to see if he could hear the air come out—he did. Sylvius said again, "I'm sorry, Rene." He left Descartes alone, kneeling beside the body that had been Katherine Schippers—home to the soul of Katherine Schippers only minutes before. Two hours before, four hours before, twelve hours before, twenty-six years before.

Rene Descartes watched the lifeless mask of her face. Disfigured as she was by the injuries, he imagined her smiling, sleepy-eyed, kissing his fingers, her head resting on his shoulder. "Katherine, I love you so," he murmured quietly, although he, of all people, knew she did not hear. He said it as if she were close by. He actually looked around for her—looked up. But he saw only the pump, the tree, the sky. He reached out to lift the bloody, matted hair from her face, and to his surprise a part of her skull came with it. A little black blood oozed from the shards of bone and the tattered white parchment which had been the dura. Deep in the wound lay her brain. The once intricate folds and gyri now flattened, ruptured and interlaced with black clots. He watched it for minutes.

He remembered the anatomical dissection he had done in the amphitheater only a month before. A demonstration for the students and twenty townspeople who had paid a handsome fee. That man on the dissecting table had been fully conscious, screaming and proclaiming his innocence, right up to the instant the hangman's knot had broken his neck. Indeed for almost a minute after, judging by the look in his eyes and his attempt to speak as he dangled from the rope. At the dissection it could be seen that the spinal cord was torn in half at the level of the second cervical vertebra, but the brain was perfect. Descartes had spent twenty minutes pointing out the subtle anatomical details. Now he looked at Katherine's dead brain before him. And he knew that all the evidence of her soul had vanished the instant the iron-clad hoof of the horse had flattened her skull. But she had breathed and her heart beat on. Where was she then? Where is she now? He brushed away some hungry flies; they would have their chance soon enough.

Watching her ruined brain he remembered her voice, her laugh, her sighs, her tears. Her outward joy and her inward contemplation. The beauty of her self, of her soul. Where is that lovely soul now?

"Katherine, I loved you so," he murmured again, now in the past tense.

CHAPTER 1
Boston – 1986

Kathleen Dugan had a sense of joy about life which was unusual for a high school senior. To be sure, she enjoyed rock bands and driving to the Cape, but she also read Updike and sang songs with her father and talked to birds and trees. Every September, on the misty morning after the first frost, a single impatient maple took on a golden crown while the hundreds of other trees which rim Jamaica Pond were still relaxed in summer's green. The edge of every leaf in the crown was washed with crimson. Kathleen's father said that the tree was blushing like a choir boy who comes in two measures early, but she preferred to think that the crimson was the glow of pride and excitement, because it was always the same tree which led its cousins into the lusty hymn of New England Autumn.

Through the mist rising over Jamaica Pond, Kathleen could see that the herald maple was showing a yellow crown this morning. She shouted a greeting to the tree but didn't slow her brisk pace for fear of being late to her first class. She swung her pack of books to her other shoulder and wondered if Eddy would be driving his new Datsun to school.

The morning had started badly for Enrique Nobrega. He had slept too late—the result of too much red wine the night before—and still lacked his morning coffee. His first assignment was to deliver a load of cement blocks to a construction project in West Roxbury. Anticipating unloading the heavy blocks while the construction workers gathered around the silver-sided coffee truck annoyed him. The exuberance of the early-morning-drive-time disc jockey did not brighten his mood. He switched off the cab radio and tried to balance the map on the big steering wheel. Being from Charlestown, he rarely drove through Brookline. But the appearance of the big gray Boston VA Hospital on his left assured him that he was on the Jamaica Way.

1

He resolved to stop for coffee and a chocolate-covered doughnut at the next opportunity. The thought cheered him slightly and he pushed on the accelerator, as he reached across the seat to check the address on his clip board.

A familiar rhythm of horn beeps drew Kathleen's attention. A shiny, new, blue Datsun had pulled off the road on the center strip and Eddy Briggs was waving to her. She smiled and turned to join him. "Hurry up!" he shouted. The Datsun was only partly off the road, and the left lane of rush-hour traffic was angrily accumulating behind him. Hugging her backpack, Kathleen ran toward the Datsun. She was halfway across the street when she saw the truck. The driver was looking down at the seat beside him. He glanced up and their eyes met for an instant. He slammed on the brakes and swerved to the right. The impact was almost averted, but the fender grazed her enough to send her sprawling head first into the rocks on the center strip.

The first officer on the scene was Ed Flaherty. Traffic was stopped both ways on the Jamaica Way. Horns were blaring and a group of people were gathered around a body on the center strip. The girl's legs were covered with a man's suit coat, and Flaherty recognized her white blouse and blue blazer as the St. Cecilia's High School girls' uniform. A woman in a nurse's scrub suit was trying to feel for the girl's pulse while a tall boy in a St. Cecilia's football jacket was jerking from person to person, in the gathering crowd, alternately weeping and shouting, "Do something! Call an ambulance!"

Flaherty parked his motorcycle, squawked his siren to separate the crowd, and knelt beside the motionless girl. He brushed away the long auburn hair from the girl's face, observed she was breathing, and felt a strong pulse in her neck. "She's okay," he announced. "Give us some room now." He was already thinking about clearing the traffic jam. "Quiet that boy down. She's okay." Blood was matted into the hair on the back of her head but he saw no other signs of injury. "You're alright dear, can you hear me?" he addressed the girl, as he touched her cheek. Suddenly he caught his breath in recognition. "Mother of God," he said to himself, "it's Michael Dugan's daughter."

The paramedic van arrived within minutes of Flaherty's call. Two young men in blue jumpsuits expeditiously unpacked a box of emergency paraphernalia, made a quick assessment, and politely but abruptly dismissed the nurse and a doctor who had stopped to help. After a few minutes one of the paramedics returned to the van and picked up the microphone. "This is paramedic two calling base. I am on the Jamaica Way near the pond. I have a vehicle versus pedestrian, single victim, teenage girl, closed head injury with one slow pupil, breathing but shallow, pressure 140 over 70, pulse 110. Request permission to start an IV and stabilize." He was sitting on the passenger seat of the van with the door open, squinting toward the scene of the accident and talking louder than necessary. Flaherty thought he was performing for the crowd. The speaker crackled.

"Base to paramedic two. Negative on the IV, scoop and run. What's your nearest emergency center? Over."

"I am close to the Boston VA and the Brookline Women's but the nearest ER is at the Faulkner. Are you sure you don't want an IV?"

"Negative. Unstable closed head gets a quick trip. Load up and call back. Over." The attendant shrugged and pulled the stretcher from the back of the van along with a wooden board. He held Kathleen's head while his partner slid the board under her back. They pulled some straps around her body and wrapped a collar around her neck.

"Pretty girl," said the attendant who was holding her head.

"Hope she doesn't vomit," said the other. Flaherty assisted while they moved her onto the stretcher and settled the stretcher into the van.

"Pretty bad head injury, don't you think?" asked Flaherty.

"It's always hard to tell. Looks bad to me."

"Listen, this girl's father is a good friend of mine. I want her to get the very best, you know what I mean?"

"Sure," replied the more senior paramedic. "We all do."

"I know a neurosurgeon at the Longwood who's the best in the business. He took care of my uncle a few years back. What say we take her over there?"

"It will be tough in this traffic."

"I'll lead you there," said Flaherty nodding toward his motorcycle. It was very unusual these days for the police to offer more than cursory help to the paramedics. Years ago the police had directed the ambulance flow and had been the power brokers among the hospital emergency rooms, but the new paramedic system based in Fire and Rescue gave a minor role to the police department. The paramedics recognized the importance of Flaherty's overture.

"No problem," The paramedic smiled to indicate understanding. "Just lead the way."

Leaving his partners to talk to Nobrega, Flaherty crossed the middle strip with the van following, avoiding the bigger rocks and the oak trees. He switched his radio to the emergency band and picked up the microphone as he accelerated. "Mobile 18. Attention all units in the Mission Hill area. I have Captain Michael Dugan's daughter in ambulance and we are heading for Longwood Hospital from Jamaica Pond. Over."

In the van one attendant looked into Kathleen's vacant pupil while the other turned on the lights and siren and picked up the microphone. "Paramedic two to Base. Enroute to Longwood Hospital with a police escort." He paused to let it sink in.

"Base to paramedic two. Copy?"

The attendant grinned. "That's right. Police escort. Officer requests you notify Longwood Emergency, and a Dr. Donald Ingram."

* * * *

Through the small panes of his office window, Professor Benjamin Rothstein watched the noon-time crowd disperse along the diagonal sidewalks on the Harvard Yard. Two of his colleagues from the philosophy department, all tweed coats and sneakers and pipes, were having an animated discussion as they headed for lunch at the Yard of Ale. Rothstein sighed loudly and turned back to his cluttered office. He dropped the heavy book he had been holding onto the middle of the desk. The book was *Discourses* by Rene Descartes. Not just any Descartes, but the first edition in French, with a worn leather binding and stiff thick pages. Rothstein always led his seminars from a text in the original language, and he had quite a collection of first editions, most of which were gifts from his students. Over thirty years there had been many students who had gone on to great success in the business and professional world and who remembered this kindly and wise professor who challenged them to think, taught them how to think, suggested what was worth thinking about. He had come from the second meeting of his seminar, Philosophy 542: Descartes. Although he read from the French, he spoke in English and it was often weeks before the students realized that he was simultaneously reading and translating. Often months before they realized that he casually brought priceless first editions to class. For him this was more of a private joke than an exercise in showmanship, and when the students realized it, it simply added to the mystique of having studied with Rothstein of Harvard.

Unlike most of the other full professors, Benjamin Rothstein not only conducted his seminars but participated each year in the Introduction to Philosophy course. He had a series of six lectures on the mind-body problem—his specialty, if philosophers can be said to have a specialty. The lectures were always in the spring during the second semester course, which was oriented around ideas (rather than a chronological presentation of the famous philosophical writers, which was presented in the first semester). The room was always packed with students, auditors, and faculty colleagues. Even though the lectures varied little from year to year, professors of philosophy from Stanford and Paris and small colleges in Ohio would time their visit to Cambridge to include two weeks of Rothstein on the mind-body problem. He thought about that as he looked back into the Yard.

He gave up on trying to bring order to the stacks of books and papers on his desk and, once again, opened the folder which held the letter to his students. The letter was written in longhand, and he had composed it carefully over the last two weeks. It began, "Dear Friends and Students: The quandary of mind, body, and soul has come to rest in a very realistic way somewhere deep in my brain. It seems that a group of cells have taken it upon themselves to grow in a wild and uncontrolled fashion, causing changes in vision, and pain, which leaves no doubt as to the source of my particular problem."

His concentration was interrupted by a gentle knock on the door, and the entrance of Samesh Ravikrishnan.

"Hello Ben. I hope I am not interrupting." Ravikrishnan had the English school-boy accent of the native Indian, but years at Oxford and Harvard had mellowed the characteristic sing-song to a scholarly level. He was always the consummate gentleman, and gave the immediate impression of a thoughtful and kindly man.

"Hello Ravi, please come in. I have written a letter to my students but it reads more like an epitaph than a signpost to contemplative thought."

"How do you intend it?"

Rothstein smiled. Ravikrishnan often turned a comment back into a question, as any good teacher of philosophy would do. "I intend it, I suppose, as the last entry into an elaborate journal of preparation for the great adventure of the mind. The ultimate instruction to explore what lies beyond the edge of consciousness and the electricity of the brain. But, old friend, the sheer biology of my personal involvement keeps getting in the way." His smile indicated that he was trying not to take himself too seriously.

"And so it should," said Ravi. "But that little bit of electrical energy that causes you to ask the question is simply part of the universal energy—"

"The energy of the universe," interrupted Rothstein, "which you, as a Buddhist, would say lives briefly in my brain."

"As a Buddhist I would say it lives in your soul."

"And my soul is in my brain?"

"Perhaps."

"And the energy which makes up my soul is . . . ?"

"You know the metaphor," said Ravi.

"A dew drop in the shining sea," observed Rothstein.

"In the shining sea," agreed Ravikrishnan, a tear at the corner of his eye. They had argued over personal and universal immortality in an academic, even passionate, fashion many times, but now the discussion was emotional as well as theoretical. Silence, as they stared at the cluttered desk to avoid looking directly at each other for a moment. In the silence, cold reality was warmed by enduring friendship.

"Well, shall we go then?" questioned Rothstein, rising. "I've tried to make some sense of all these papers and notes but it seems hopeless. You could just dispose of them if . . . I don't return."

"Ben." Ravi's tone was more serious, "I'm glad to take your seminar, you know that, but in two or three weeks you will be sitting here

6

healthy as a horse and telling us about your adventure. Now there will be no more talk of epitaphs or disposing of your papers."

Rothstein nodded his head with a slight smile, and led the way to the door. "Ravi, I don't care about dying. What I am worried about is losing my memory, my mind, and my ability to think. If I can't think, I'm as good as dead. That's what I mean by not returning."

"Ahah!" said Ravikrishnan, searching for a way to ease the strain. "The contrapositive of the Cartesian argument! 'I do not think there-fore I am not.' Fascinating, absolutely fascinating." They walked downstairs to the parking lot and continued their high-level discourse as Ravikrishnan drove Rothstein to Longwood Hospital, where he was admitted on the service of Dr. Donald Ingram.

* * * *

Carol Rizzo sat on the gray, peeling stands behind the player's bench with one-year-old Matthew Jr. on her lap. She waved his mit-tened hand toward the players. "There's Daddy. Wave to Daddy." Doesn't he look funny in that big uniform? Wave to Daddy. Hi Daddy."

Matthew Rizzo Sr. took off his helmet so that his son might rec-ognize him, grinned, and waved back to his little family. The teams were lining up for the kickoff, and this was hardly professional, but no one took football—or any other sport for that matter—-too seriously at East Bridgewater State Teachers' College. Tonight's game against Manhasett Junior College, however, was the third game of the year and the East Bridgewater Blue Bombers (so-named when the school was organized shortly after World War II) had won the first two games, so interest in the team was greater than usual. There were almost four hundred people in the stands at Bomber Stadium when the lights went on and the Blue Bomber Band took the field for the pre-game show. The air was clear and crisp and smelled of smoke. "Just the night for football," thought Rizzo.

At twenty-four, Rizzo was unusually old for a sophomore at Teachers' College. But his performance at Natick High School had been mediocre at best, except for athletics, and after high school he had joined the navy to earn some money and consider his options. He had met Carol while he was stationed in San Diego. They had married six months later and quite quickly the priorities of life had come into focus for Matt. He was accepted at Bridgewater on a probationary basis but did exceptionally well during his freshman year. The steadying influence of his wife (now pregnant) and the generous dose of real-world responsibility that he felt were an incentive for studying. This year he had found time to go out for football, much to the delight of the coach. Suddenly there was the potential of a winning season, for the first time in many years.

There were only twenty-six players on the Bomber squad. Rizzo was a tailback (and the leading scorer during the first two games) and was also used on the kick-off team because he could get down the field faster than any of his teammates. His job was to contain the right side of the field and make contact if he could, to slow up the ball carrier so that his heavier colleagues could make the tackle. He put his helmet back on and dug his cleats into the fresh lime on the thirty five-yard line.

Although Matt Rizzo was an eternal optimist, tonight seemed to be the ultimate high. He glanced back over his shoulder at Carol, bundled up in his heavy navy coat, beaming. Matthew giggling and waving. An A on his Spanish quiz. The aroma of old equipment and tape evoking a non-specific memory of glory days in high school. How could life be better? Kevin Tracy (who was also the quarterback) lowered his arm, ran toward the ball, swung his foot through the leather, and the game was on.

Matt sprinted down the side line and was already at the twenty-five-yard line when the Manhasett receiver cradled in the ball and dug forward. The Manhasett plan was to sweep to the left, and the ball carrier gained momentum quickly, coming toward Matt. Matt never broke stride, slipped the only blocker, and nailed the big runner on the ten-yard line.

The game films would show that Matt started with his forehead up, but a last second change of direction, combined with an attempted stiff-arm from the ball carrier, forced his head down at the moment of contact. Matt never lost consciousness but heard a deafening crunch, like dry wood breaking, and suddenly felt as if his head were suspended and rolling through space. There was no pain. Just the incredible sensation of being freed from his body. His head finished spinning and found itself face down on the grass, with the ball carrier and other players on top of him. Whistles blew, the crowd roared, the drummers in the band played a cadence. The players climbed off the pile. Matt could see shoes and legs and freshly cut grass. But he couldn't move.

Kevin Tracy's face appeared in front of him a few inches off the ground.

"Hey Matt, are you alright? Jesus, what a tackle. The guy fumbled the ball and we have it on the five-yard line. Come on Matt, hop to." Tracy could see that Matt's eyes were open and he gave all the outward signs of consciousness. His breathing was shallow, and when he tried to speak his voice was very soft.

"Kevin, I can't move," he whispered.

"What's that buddy?" Kevin got closer so that the face guards were touching.

"I can't move, I think I broke my neck."

"Jesus!" Tracy's face disappeared, then his knee, then his feet came into Matt's line of vision. "Hey, get some help! Hey coach, get over here!"

Dr. Ed Crowe was in the stands because his daughter played alto saxophone in the Blue Bomber band. He watched the trainer and the coach as they log-rolled Rizzo onto the stretcher and none of his extremities moved. He made a mental diagnosis, hoping he was wrong. When the public address announcer asked for a doctor to come to the concession stand he was not surprised. (The First Aid Station, consisting of a cot and a white enameled cabinet, was part of the same cement block building that housed the concession stand and the field equipment locker.) Crowe waited several seconds after the announcement, looking over the crowd to see if anyone else would respond to the call. Crowe was a nephrologist, not a trauma surgeon, and his partner had once lost a major lawsuit stemming from his offer to help at the scene of an automobile accident. However his daughter caught his eye, and his wife, who had learned long before not to volunteer her husband's services, quietly commented, "Ed maybe you had better go."

As he entered the little first-aid room he felt the vague apprehension caused by the disconcerting combination of athletic equipment—all grass stains and dirt and sweat—with the sterile smell and white sheets of the surgical suite. The coach looked pale and the trainer was shooing Bomber teammates from the little room.

"I am a doctor. Can I help?"

"Oh yeah doc, thanks." The greeting came from the trainer. "Matt, the doctor is here. You're going to be okay, buddy."

Seeing that the patient was conscious and breathing, but not moving, confirmed Crowe's initial suspicion. "What's the problem son?" Crowe automatically assumed the in-charge role. His deep voice and air of confidence were reassuring to the small crowd in the room.

"I think I broke my neck. I can't move my legs," whispered Matt, looking scared.

"Can you feel this?" asked Crowe, rubbing Matt's little finger and trying to remember the dermatones.

"Feel what?" said Matt.

"Can you feel this?" asked Crowe, rubbing Matt's thumb.

"No, I can't feel anything," said Matt. His eyes implied, "Is that bad?" but he didn't say it.

"Do this," said Crowe, protruding his tongue and moving it from side to side. He had decided to work from the top down. Matt complied without difficulty.

"Do this," he shrugged his shoulders high. Matt did the same.

"Do this," Crowe raised his arms out from his sides. Matt's face showed concentration. "Am I doing it?" he asked. There was no motion.

Crowe didn't answer. He looked at Matt, thinking to himself "C-5." A look came and went from his eyes that only his wife would have recognized. "This poor kid." When he spoke he had to cough a little first, then he said "You hurt your neck pretty bad, son. It's definitely going to need some X-rays. I'm afraid you're going to need a trip to the hospital." He was speaking to Matt but looked up at the coach and the trainer.

"Do you think we need an ambulance?" asked the coach. "We can take the seats out of the suburban."

Crowe recognized this as a grasp at optimism, rather than ignorance, on the part of the coach.

"Oh no, we'll definitely need an ambulance. I'll be back in a minute," he said to Matt, and signaled to the coach to join him outside. "This is pretty serious," he said quietly. "You'd better take him all the way to Boston to the Longwood Hospital. This will probably be too complicated for the Cushing."

A girl in a navy coat with pretty dark hair and terrified brown eyes was just outside the door. She was carrying a little boy. "Is Matt in there? Is he okay? Can I see him? Are you the doctor? Coach, is he okay?" She pushed past them into the room. Dr. Crowe would return to talk to her soon. Just now he needed a moment to think. He walked to the pay phone behind the concession stand, pulled out his black appointment book and ran his finger down the list of consultants on the back page, looking for the phone number of Dr. Donald Ingram.

* * * *

"Five, four, three"—she signaled two and one with her fingers and pointed to Howard with a nod. Ellen Fletcher was working her way up the NBC production staff and this was her first opportunity at national television. She was, she reminded herself, only the local director for the Washington segment of an NBC white paper on "The Caribbean: Prelude to a Crisis." Through three monitors she watched three views of the two men seated in the studio, keeping the signal on camera two, Howard Mason.

"Thank you David. Howard Mason live from Washington with Senator John Bradford who has been kind enough to join us in our Washington studio." 13.6 million Americans were watching the telecast, if one was to believe the extrapolation from two thousand homes. 13.6 million Americans watched the camera angle widen to include most of Howard Mason, sitting in a vinyl-covered armchair, and Senator John Bradford, legs crossed, looking intently at Howard, hands resting calmly on his knee, nodding occasionally at Howard's preamble and initial question.

"Howard, my Committee on Central American Affairs is vitally interested in this problem, and I am delighted to have this opportunity

11

to share our findings with the American people." He had been looking at Howard, and camera two, closing in, was catching him in profile. Now he turned and looked directly into camera three with just the slightest hint of a glance at the control room. Ellen switched to camera three, and Bradford's next sentence seemed to be delivered very personally to each of 13.6 million Americans.

"What a pro," thought Ellen, pleased with herself for detecting his signal. She pulled back on camera three slowly. Mason waited for the senator to finish. He had learned from previous interviews not to interrupt this young republican senator from Rhode Island, for fear that his well-known wit would be turned against the interviewer.

"Senator Bradford, in light of the recent evidence linking organized crime to CIA activities in the Caribbean, would you comment on the point that President Rodrigo has just made in our Miami studio?"

"First of all Howard, although the evidence was recently made public, it concerns events which happened twenty-three years ago. And secondly—" Ellen Fletcher pointed at the camera to her right. Bradford looked toward camera one which was behind Howard Mason. The light went on, and 13.6 million Americans were listening to Senator Bradford from Howard Mason's chair, feeling very much involved. "—what General Rodrigo said, if I might paraphrase him, was simply . . ."

He stopped in mid-sentence and his face suddenly contorted in pain—eyes closed, lips pulled back. A little cry came from the back of his throat. This lasted only two seconds. He brought his hand to his right temple and pushed hard. "Excuse me," he said, and managed a weak smile at Mason. "General Rodrigo . . ." The look began to return "simply said . . ." His head jerked violently to the left and the left side of his body stiffened, forcing him out of the chair. He made a sound that oscillated with the seizure, "Arrarr, arr."

Howard Mason reached forward but not in time to keep Bradford from pitching out to the floor. "Senator! Senator Bradford! Senator . . ." The whole episode happened so quickly that Ellen didn't have time to react. Now she switched to camera two showing only Mason's face, white and trembling. Mason glanced from the convulsing senator to the camera, then to the control room.

Ellen spoke into her microphone. "Cutting to New York. Cutting to New York. Five, four, three." The New York production crew picked up the cue but the anchor man was not ready. He was caught looking aghast, with his mouth open, staring at the studio monitor. Gradually he regained composure.

"Apparently there has been some problem in our Washington studio. We will ask Howard Mason to keep us informed. Howard?"

Mason and other members of the crew were kneeling beside Bradford. A cameraman whose brother was epileptic wrapped a handkerchief around a pen and pushed it between Bradford's teeth. His shirt was spattered with a combination of saliva and blood, which filled Bradford's mouth. The senator's gray pants were stained with urine. Within thirty seconds, which seemed like an hour, the seizure subsided. His breathing became deep and regular, his limbs relaxed, and only his eyes twitched incessantly to the right.

Anne Bradford had been sitting in the back of the studio watching a monitor. The instant the convulsion started she rushed forward, arriving as the seizures began to subside. "Thank you. Thank you," she murmured, cradling her husband's head in her hands. As his jaw relaxed she removed the pen, flattened with teeth marks despite the covering, and gently wiped his face.

"This has happened twice before," she explained to Mason, as if some explanation was necessary. "I have been trying to get him to—" She interrupted herself, realizing that she was a politician's wife talking on the record. "He'll wake up in a minute."

"Mrs. Bradford, I am Ellen Fletcher, the studio director. What can I do to help?"

Anne thought that the girl seemed awfully young to be a director. It occurred to her for the first time that the entire television audience had seen what she had seen. It didn't matter now. "Thank you Miss Fletcher. Please call Dr. Harold Banks at Walter Reed Hospital. He has been seeing the senator." Bradford coughed and opened his eyes, looking at the faces hovered over him. Nothing seemed to register.

"John?" she whispered.

He stared vacantly. Slowly a look of recognition appeared. "Anne? Anne, this goddamn headache. Who—?" He struggled onto one

13

elbow, holding his head. No one spoke as he surveyed the TV studio, the pool of urine, the small, shocked audience. It took him half a minute to recall what had happened. He motioned to Anne to lean closer. "Did I have another seizure?" She nodded. "On television?" His tongue was still bleeding and blood dripped out of the corner of his mouth. She nodded again. "Damn! Let's get out of here," he said still holding his head. "Anne, in the morning, let's call that surgeon in Boston—Ingram."

CHAPTER 2

The oatmeal in the Longwood Hospital cafeteria was so thick and sticky, it was said you could patch tires with it. The new residents, who had grown up on Pop Tarts and Fruit Loops, wouldn't touch it—choking down the rubbery scrambled eggs instead. But the oatmeal was actually very good and, like the napkin rings in the Doctor's Dining Room, was part of the tradition of the place. Every morning except Monday, Ian McLaren came to the cafeteria line at six minutes after seven, thin and straight as a flag pole, his hair (gone from red to white ten years ago) carefully parted and combed. In his gnarly old voice he always greeted the attendant by name, and the attendant always replied (on instruction from the kitchen supervisor), "Good morning Mr. Mac. Would you like some Scottish oatmeal this morning?" And Mac would always say, "Thank you Sally (or Harry or Margaret), that would be very nice." Then Sally would fill the large heavy crockery bowl (left over from the '40s, white, with a dark blue rim and the old Longwood Hospital insignia in the bottom of it), fill the bowl with steaming oatmeal, put two pats of butter in the center, and offer it to Mac. The brown sugar was kept behind the counter just for him. No one at Longwood Hospital would have recognized the name of Ian McLaren, but everybody knew Mac, the night telephone operator.

Every nurse, resident, and medical student knew the raspy voice with the faint burr which came over the hospital speaker system in the lonely, uncertain hospital hours after midnight. "Dahktarr Em-ah-sahn, Dahktarr Em-ah-sahn call 465," and Dr. Emerson would promptly call 465, having learned early in residency that Mac would save you precious sleep if he could by checking out the problem with the nurse on C Main first, then trying the telephone in the call room, then resorting to a page only if he had to. Someone in Administration had suggested

15

replacing Mac when the beepers came in, in 1968. Someone in the university had insisted that he retire when he reached age sixty-five in 1976. But those administrators didn't understand tradition.

On Saturday mornings Donald Ingram ignored the Doctor's Dining Room to have breakfast with Mac at his customary table overlooking Shattuck Street. Today Ingram was already waiting.

"Good morning Mac," he smiled. "Did you decide to have the oatmeal this morning?"

"Well I had to have it Donald. See, the lass fixed it just like my dear mother used to."

". . . like my dear mother used to," Ingram joined in the last few words, which were always the same. Mac stuffed the corner of a paper napkin in his belt, closed his eyes long enough to murmur, "Bless this food to our use and us to thy service," and picked up the big spoon.

"You'd best be making rounds, Donald, for they'll all be waiting for you." Mac was the only person who called Dr. Ingram "Donald," and he did it because of a habit formed when Ingram was a resident and Franz Eastman, the prestigious Chief of Neurosurgery, had called him Donald. Ingram knew that Mac was referring to the two new patients in the intensive care unit. He always knew everything that was going on in the hospital.

"Yes, I know Mac. What's the word on the football player that came in last night?"

"I had to call Respiratory for Dr. Adams a few hours ago. He said it didn't look too good." Mac did not look up from his oatmeal as he made this report.

Ingram grimaced. "Must be a high lesion," he said, mostly to himself.

"Yes it must be. He needed Respiratory in a hurry." Mac rarely spoke unless asked a question, and never gave an unsolicited medical opinion. "But young Dr. Adams is a guud man, Donald."

"You're always a good judge Mac. And has your grandson started up at Tufts?"

"Aye. There is a lad . . ."

"Neurosurgeons are like hockey goalies and drummers," pronounced Randy Burleson, addressing the ICU night nurse. "They go through life on a different track than the rest of us."

"I suppose you're right" she said, remembering the drummer she had loved but had never really known. "I never thought of that combination."

"Well think about it," he said. "They're at the center of intensity with ice for blood, they smile when no one else smiles, and not very often. They're always good at what they do, they always know it, and they never flaunt it at you."

"I suppose so," said the nurse, trying to finish her progress note so that she could leave. Burleson was a new intern. He was talking to stay awake, as he had been up all night looking after Kathleen Dugan and Matthew Rizzo. He had some background for his analogy, having played hockey at Cornell and worked with a jazz quartet during medical school at Hopkins. But this rotation was his first experience as a hands-on neurosurgeon, and he felt very insecure.

"I mean, look at Adams over there." He nodded to bed three. "The guy operated until 9:00 last night and he has been in here off and on all night. The guy looks as fresh as a daisy. He looks like . . ."

"Like the drummer at the end of a long gig," she offered, with a knowing smile. "On the other hand, young Dr. Burleson, you look like Dangerous Dan McGrew. You'd better get cleaned up before Dr. Ingram arrives."

"Oh yeah, thanks." He'd already been reprimanded twice by The Professor for his appearance. He slipped out the door.

Donald Ingram took the elevator to the ninth floor, then walked down the back stairs to eight to avoid the Family Waiting Room outside ICU. He wanted to see the patients before facing the families, with their barrage of questions. He entered via the back door, away from the Nursing Station, close to the beds reserved for neurosurgery patients. Dan Adams was standing by bed three, scowling at the oscilloscope tracing, and adjusting a transducer which was connected by a piece of tubing to the skull of Kathleen Dugan.

"Good morning Dan."

"Good morning sir." Ingram had walked up behind Adams, who was concentrating on the monitoring equipment, but Adams did not appear at all startled. Rather, he turned deliberately and greeted his mentor calmly. His steady composure didn't come naturally. Adams had learned from Ingram to control any startle response, just as Ingram had learned it from Eastman. They had practiced it until it was automatic. Eastman used to say that you could always identify the neurosurgeons at the annual staff dinner. "We are the ones who don't jump when the waiter drops a plate of dishes." Ingram studied his chief resident. He was wearing a clean scrub suit under his starched white coat. He was freshly shaven and his eyes were bright.

Almost subconsciously, Ingram felt Kathleen Dugan's foot, as his eyes turned toward the monitor. He touched her with the flat back of his fingers first, and then cupped her toes in his palm and pushed them gently toward her head. He settled his hand on her ankle, the four fingertips lined up over the posterior tibial artery. Sometimes he actually thought about the sequence of his own physiology. From the nerves in his fingertips, electrical signals flashed to his brain and were translated into temperature, turgor, resistance, and three-dimensional space. Each of these sensations was modulated by information from his memory, as it became consciousness in the form of cardiac output, blood volume, pulse rate, blood pressure, and muscle tone, which—he noted—was flaccid.

"How much mannitol has she had?" asked Ingram, characteristically centering on the most critical issue.

"Fifty grams. I was just about to give her some more if her ICP is really that high." Both were looking at the calibrated screen which showed an irregular line fluctuating around the number thirty.

"It has a good respiratory fluctuation," observed Ingram, watching the tracing rise as the mechanical ventilator blew through the tube in her mouth into her lungs.

"Yes sir. Just wishful thinking I guess." He turned to the nurse across the bed. "Mary, let's give her another amp of mannitol." The nurse—graceful, with perceptive eyes and the smooth, tight skin of youth, still tan from the summer—swabbed the IV tubing with alcohol. She pulled off the plastic needle cover with her teeth and, holding it there while she punctured the tubing, thumbed the syringe. If she noticed that the men were impressed by her efficiency, she didn't show it. There was nothing more to say about Kathleen Dugan for now. Barbiturates, tubes, ventilator, monitors, and mannitol, there was simply nothing more to do but wait.

"How's the posterior fossa from yesterday?" asked Ingram.

"Mr. Harris," said Adams, pointing toward the corner bed. "He's fine. He was sleeping the last time I looked. Moved everything, talking, no nystagmus. He looks great."

"Then we won't wake him up," said Ingram. "Where's our intern?" Adams smiled. "Probably shaving."

As they moved to Rizzo's bedside, Randy Burleson appeared, hair wet from an unsuccessful attempt at its control, two small pieces of blood-stained toilet paper stuck to small cuts near his right ear, his new white coat rumpled and sporting the yellowish stain of some unidentifiable liquid. "Good morning, sir." He flashed a glance at Ingram, then looked aside, then at Adams, fidgeting with the cards in his pocket.

"Good morning, Burleson." Ingram knew that his presence made most new residents nervous, but he never eased up, preferring to see which of them grew into self-confidence without assistance. "We've already seen Mr. Harris and Miss Dugan. Can you fill us in on Mr. Rizzo here?" Ingram spoke in calm, unemotional tones which Burleson heard as challenging.

"We had to tube him a few hours ago. He has total complete quadriplegia with a high level, his vitals—" Ingram silenced him with a firm squeeze on his arm, holding up his other hand slightly as if to demonstrate a point. Ingram stepped to the head of the bed and leaned over, touching Rizzo on the cheek with his hand.

"Mr. Rizzo? Matt?" Rizzo opened his eyes immediately. He had not been sleeping, but kept his eyes closed to minimize the terror. His pupils were small from morphine and it took him awhile to focus, but he could clearly distinguish the tall, square-jawed individual leaning over him. "Matt, I'm Dr. Ingram. I'll be taking care of you while you are here, along with Dr. Adams and Dr. Burleson and the other members of our team. You're doing just fine. We've just stopped to talk about you a little bit." He smiled, leaving his hand on Rizzo's cheek. Ordinarily he would have held his hand, but there was no sensation there. Rizzo nodded and seemed relieved.

Burleson was dismayed. He had been told several times that the patient must always be addressed first during rounds on the neurosurgery service. Ingram and Adams had let him walk right into it again. He looked helpless, like a school boy who had failed to produce an answer on a direct question from the teacher. "Carry on Burleson. The vital signs?"

There was no getting off the hook in this small gathering. He found the big ICU clipboard and read from the last column of numbers, "Pulse 110, pressure 110 over 70, temp 36 respiration . . . well, he's on the vent. His PCO_2 got up to 52 and we had to intubate him a few hours ago."

"And what about his neurological status?"

"He's awake and alert with no signs of intracranial injury. He has a C5 sensory level and a C4 motor level. I thought he could move his left thumb when he first came in, but no one else did. The doc who saw him at the football game found the same thing, so his cord injury was immediate and complete. That means—"

Ingram silenced him with a subtle gesture, indicating that Rizzo was listening. "Did you put these tongs on, Dr. Burleson?"

"Yes sir," Burleson looked at the stainless steel bracket with its sharp points screwed into Rizzo's skull. "With a lot of help from Dr. Adams," he added sheepishly.

"Tell me about the use of tongs."

"Sir?"

"How do you go about it? How did you put these tongs on?"

Burleson was accustomed to this semi-Socratic method of teaching, but always felt intimidated when the questions came from Ingram. Adams had advised him to be more positive about what he knew, but never to guess. "The tongs are used to put traction on the cervical spine by pulling on the skull. The pins are positioned to pull the skull and spine in a line based on T-1, screwed into the outer table, under local anesthesia. If the pins are too far forward, the neck and skull extend too much." Burleson was reciting what Adams had told him only a few hours before when they put the tongs in.

"What's the difference between Crutchfield tongs and Stryker tongs?" asked Ingram.

Burleson felt uneasy. Adams had discussed several types of tongs while they were putting them in, but Burleson hadn't paid much attention.

"I think . . . I really don't know," he confessed. Adams looked relieved, as if he had passed a minor test. "Well, find out." Ingram said. Burleson nodded.

* * * *

The elevator doors closed and the Father John O'Reilly glanced at the other passenger, a young lady in white carrying a tray of what appeared to be blood-drawing apparatus.

"G'mawning Father," she murmured, smiling hesitantly, averting her eyes as if she had not been to mass for a long time and felt that somehow he knew it.

"Good morning. Looks like you have a busy morning." He nodded toward the thick stack of requisitions on her tray.

"It's not too bad," she shrugged, more relaxed. "Excuse me," she murmured, bowing slightly as she left the elevator on the fourth floor. The doors closed, leaving Father John alone with his thoughts of Kathleen Dugan. When he had visited the family last night he knew the news was bad, and he knew that they would still be waiting in the little family room outside the ICU. He had left his younger colleague to do the mass this morning; everyone at St. Cecilia's wanted him to be with the Dugans.

As he expected, Michael and Mary Dugan were sitting, puffy-eyed and disheveled from a sleepless night, in the little waiting room outside the intensive care unit. They murmured greetings and Mary pulled aside the rumpled hospital blanket to make room for the priest.

"Oh, it's good to see you; it's so good to see you Father." She kept her grip on his hand. John O'Reilly, just fifty-five, had dark black hair, quick blue eyes, and a ready smile. The ladies of the parish agreed, in very private conversations, that he was roguishly handsome. The only thought in Mary Dugan's mind this morning, however, was that the priest had come and would provide hope where there seemed to be none. He squeezed her cold hand between both of his, and addressed her husband.

"What's the news this morning Michael?"

"Nothing new Father." Big hands with thick fingers kneading each other. His tie pulled loose and his voice hoarse. "We saw her an hour ago." He nodded toward the direction of the intensive care unit down the hall. "She's not awake yet." He cleared his throat and looked aside.

A young woman in a ski sweater with dark, pensive eyes entered the little room and sat down next to Michael Dugan. "They said the doctors are making rounds and we can't go in until eight," she reported, as if she had been sent on a scouting mission. She glanced at the priest.

"This is Father O'Reilly, our priest from St. Cecilia's," said Mary Dugan to the younger lady. She turned toward the priest, still holding his hand. "Her husband was hurt in a football game. We kept each other company last night." She smiled briefly.

"God has a way of bringing people together in times of need," said Father O'Reilly. A look of cynicism flickered across the girl's face, but she said nothing. The priest was about to speak again when Dr. Adams entered the room followed by Dr. Ingram. The Dugans rose, expectant, fearful, trying to read something in Ingram's face.

"Good morning Captain, Mrs. Dugan." He glanced at the priest and felt they had met, but he couldn't remember where, only that it was not an unhappy memory. "Everything is status quo this morning. Her vital signs are stable. She's still unconscious."

"Doctor," Mrs. Dugan grasped his hand with a sense of urgency. "Will she—will she have any permanent brain damage?"

"It's much too soon to say—we just don't know. The question now is whether she'll survive."

"Of course it is," said Michael Dugan with a disapproving look at his wife for asking the question. He had been telling her just that all night. "Dr. Ingram, this is Father O'Reilly, our priest from St. Cecilia's."

"We've met before, Dr. Ingram" said the priest, rising. "You probably don't remember. We were on a panel at Boston College a few years ago."

"Oh yes, Father O'Reilly. I do remember. The discussion on the soul. An interesting session."

Ingram smiled inwardly. They had argued to a draw, as he recalled it. In theological dialectic with an academic Jesuit, a draw left a taste of victory with Ingram. O'Reilly had been a full professor at BC, and Ingram wondered to himself how he came to be a parish priest, but he knew enough not to raise the question in front of the Dugans.

"Thank you for taking care of Kathleen," said the priest. "Many people are praying for her. She is very special to us."

"I am sure," said Ingram. Mary Dugan had withdrawn her hand to cover her face as the sobbing began again.

"Dr. Ingram, this is Mrs. Rizzo, the wife of Matt Rizzo, the quad—" Adams caught himself before the word was out, "the wife of the young football player we just saw." Adams knew that Ingram would linger for more conversion with the Dugans, and they had many more patients to see before conference.

"Hello, Mrs. Rizzo." Ingram took her hand and put his other arm around her shoulder. She was about the age of his own son. "Can we talk for a minute?" He steered her toward the door. The only privacy was the anonymity of the hallway. Hospital staff in transit learned to avoid the intense little gatherings of surgeons and family members. Burleson backed out of the doorway where he had been making notes in the scut book. Ingram spoke softly.

"I just talked to your husband. He's awake and he's not in pain. As Dr. Adams told you, we had to put a tube in his throat to help his breathing, so he won't be able to talk with you, but he does understand. He's very scared and he'll need your help." As he went through a fairly standard speech, Ingram studied her reaction, subconsciously measuring the rate at which she could understand and accept the tragic information. "The breathing is just a small part of his major problem, which is injury to his spinal cord." He paused.

"Has his sensory level changed?" she asked in a firm voice.

"Are you a nurse?" asked Ingram automatically.

"Yes." She smiled at his instant recognition of familiar terminology. Under other circumstances she might have been offended that he hadn't asked if she were a woman surgeon, or a neurologist. But this morning just the recognition of some professionalism made her feel more secure. "I was a surgical ICU nurse before we were married."

"She's been helping us all night," said Adams congenially. 'Help' meant that she had stayed out of the way and let the ICU crew do their job, which was much appreciated.

"Dr. Adams has been great." She managed a brief grin.

"Dr. Adams and Dr. Burleson here have done an excellent job." said Ingram. Judging that she was well-informed and emotionally stable, he added, "We are going to finish our rounds, if that's all right." She nodded. "We have quite a lot to discuss. I'll be back at 11:15. Can you be here then?"

"I'll be here," she said, thinking that only a neurosurgeon would designate time to the minute.

* * * *

He could have stopped at the mailbox on the way in, but he chose to park the car in the garage and walk back down the winding driveway. It was an opportunity to savor the sensations of early autumn. The afternoon sun, shuttered by rolling clouds, lit but did not heat the chilly air. The leaves of the silver maple, turned bottom side up by the steady breeze, were showing gold rather than gray. Summer was going, no doubt, and Ingram was pleased, as he preferred the fall. Or more accurately, he preferred the change of season, for he would feel the same combination of relief and anticipation with the first snow and the first crocus. So he walked the length of the driveway, tasting the wind.

The mailbox, cast iron, built into the old stone fence fronting Walnut Street, held a few bills, the latest issue of Brain Research, and a postcard showing the central campus at Stanford. He walked back up the hill to the house, abandoning the driveway for the more direct route across a carpet of white pine needles that substituted for a lawn. He flipped over the postcard and read as he walked.

"Dear Dad. The first two weeks of classes successful. Inorganic Chem will be <u>tough</u>. Miss you. Love Janet. P.S. Happy Birthday."

He read it twice and smiled. Neither Janet nor James would have remembered his birthday when they were living at home. James wouldn't write, but he would call on October 1 when Ingram would be forty-six.

The house was set on the hill. It was a big, dark brown colonial house with black shutters and black ironwork and a huge brass lantern hanging over the door. The pillared porch and the formal entrance faced west, making it both easier and friendlier to enter by the back door. Inside, the feeling was not somber, but old and warm. He had been alone in the house for just a few weeks, but had already contracted his living area to the kitchen and the library, and, when he could no longer concentrate, the bedroom. He observed himself developing this pattern, and finding it practical, accepted it. And then, the kitchen had always been the center of activity in the big house, particularly when Emily was alive and the children were young. Practical, then, and comfortable too. The inside of the house, varnished oak floors with paneled or plain white walls, was outfitted in simple, modern furniture and fittings—dark blue and silver somewhere in every room. Properly tended, the unlikely wedding of an old colonial house and a simple modern interior made a pleasant union. He thought that his Pilgrim ancestors would have noted the beauty of simple lines and space.

Looking into the refrigerator, it struck him that the level in the milk bottle went down only when he drank it. Nothing in the house happened unless he made it happen. Tuesday's newspaper was still lying on the kitchen table. The bottle of Talisker single-malt scotch whiskey was still on the counter rather than in the liquor cabinet where Janet or Emily or somebody would have put it. Matters of fact to anyone who lives alone, but new to Ingram. He opened a bottle of Heineken, put a lobster Newburgh in the microwave, an English muffin in the toaster, and sipped at the beer while electronic cooks warmed his lunch. The sun had disappeared into the overcast. The house was absolutely silent, save for the ticking of the microwave. A sensation between apathy and apprehension began to grow in his gut which he attributed to hunger, refusing to acknowledge the possibility of loneliness.

Like a child saving the black jelly bean for last, he set aside the new issue of Brain Research until he had finished lunch, cleaned up the kitchen, and traded his three-piece suit for jeans and a sweater. Loading some Vivaldi in the cassette deck, he settled into the Eames chair, propped up his feet, and removed the brown wrapper like a jeweler exposing his best diamond. Ingram had written nearly a hundred scientific papers, but he felt the excitement of a new father each time one appeared in print. Nine months ago he had submitted his manuscript—three copies, precisely typed, accompanied by glossy prints of the seven figures labeled carefully on the back. All quite proper, but looking very much like a high school term paper. Now it would be published in dramatic typeset, figures perfect, an official recognition of a contribution to scientific advancement. His paper was the lead article.

This particular paper was his best work yet. It was titled: "Anatomic Localization of Value Judgment Memory." The report described five monkeys who had been taught to sit very still for one hour without picking, mugging, or fondling themselves. This behavior (very unusual for a monkey) remained after a right frontal lobotomy, despite an apparent decrease in emotional responses, but disappeared after the left frontal lobe was removed. The other aspects of memory remained, but the monkeys had forgotten, or could not bring to consciousness, the behavior pattern which they had learned. The strength of the paper was a clinical correlation with three patients who had bilateral frontal lobectomies—two following trauma and one for metastatic lung cancer. The trauma patients lost both frontal lobes simultaneously. When they recovered they could speak, think, recognize friends and families and recall events from the past. However, they took any object they desired; they said whatever wandered into their consciousness without reflecting for a second on the impact; they satisfied sexual and bathroom urges instantly and frequently. Their language ranged from highly intellectual to totally vulgar, with occasional memory seizures—a term coined by Ingram to describe rapid-fire unloading of associations related to a time, a place, a word, or some other trigger event. The lung cancer patient had her dominant frontal lobe removed first, resulting in the usual euphoria caused by this procedure, but none of the personality change. The second lobectomy was caused by a metastasis. The inability to make value judgments began slowly and progressed to totally inappropriate behavior. This patient died soon after of metastatic cancer, but the trauma patients were still living in isolation rooms at Metropolitan State Hospital. Patients were the key to the observation, because the status of their intellectual function (Ingram had avoided the word "mind" in the "Results" section of the paper), was known, measured, and intact before and after the brain lesion. After most of both frontal lobes were damaged, words and sentences came out sporadically, sometimes in response to stimuli, sometimes at random. The functions of emotions and social interaction were missing. The monkey operations served as prospective experimental evidence supporting the clinical observations. There was no coordination, or even evidence of value judgment memory. Ingram had avoided the words "personality," "self," or "soul"—but that's what he was writing about.

The empty feeling which had possessed him earlier evaporated. The empty house seemed to buzz with excitement generated entirely within his own head, from reading his own written words, and enhanced by the controlled intensity of the Vivaldi. He paused to refill his mug with coffee and light a long, narrow Cuban (via Canada) cigar before reading the "Discussion" section.

The Discussion which made it into print was not what he had submitted with the first draft. In his original manuscript he had begun the Discussion with a concept of mind, derived from Gilbert Ryle, which included intellectual, emotional, and judgment functions, each of which depended totally on a vast memory system in which all experiences and sensations of that individual were recorded from early gestation onward. The fact that removing one frontal lobe removed emotion from the personality was certainly well known. In his original manuscript, Ingram had pointed out that disconnecting a frontal lobe, after all, was an effective treatment for ablating the emotional seizures of psychosis, whether it be done by an operation or by Thorazine. Similarly the selective loss of those social patterns that differentiate humans from animals was well known to every one with a senile grandfather or a brain-damaged child. What was new in this paper was the idea that the ability to make value judgments was lost when the memory necessary for those judgments was lost. The monkeys and the patients could think, reason, remember, and communicate. But they had no concept of good or bad, virtue or evil, acceptable or unacceptable.

Granting the validity of these observations, Ingram had argued that values must be learned—and learned uniquely by each individual. Values are stored in bits of brain that can be seen, touched, examined, cut out and put under the microscope and into bottles of formalin. Values which define a person's behavior and character are stored in specific chemicals in bits of brain which can be extracted, distilled, separated on columns, and quantified down to the last molecule of carbon, hydrogen, oxygen, nitrogen, and phosphorus. If this be true, then the memories which are called "values" will be changed by injury or disease, diet and metabolism, electrical charge and recharge, and lost altogether when that bit of brain is destroyed by cancer or disappears down the neurosurgical sucker. Values for an individual, then, are specific for that individual. To think that an individual personal value is universal must be only wishful thinking. The uniquely personal combination of values, intellect, and behavior which we call "soul" must be the ultimate wishful thought. Moreover, it follows that the values of a society are therefore the wishful thinking of that society, and a creation of that society.

Ingram chuckled to himself as he read the printed version of the Discussion, which contained none of his original preamble. The first reviewer of his original Discussion had simply stated that the observations were interesting, but did not justify the leap to such a rambling discussion. The second reviewer took a more intellectual approach, arguing that the change in behavior patterns did not necessarily indicate memory loss, merely a loss of function, which may include memory. The third reviewer had rejected the paper outright, stating that it questioned the very tenets of moral and religious belief, adding that papers on deviant philosophy should be sent to the Journal of Philosophy, not to such a prestigious scientific publication as Brain Research. After the exchange of several letters and revision of the manuscript, the paper finally had been accepted for publication, but only because the editor was a friend of Ingram's who shared the same obsession with anatomical localization of brain functions. The final version of the Discussion was focused on the question of memory loss versus functional loss, with only a hint that the capability to make value judgments was individual, learned, and remembered. It didn't matter. His friend the editor had let the original title stand, so the information would be there for anyone who searched the Index Medicus or Current Contents.

When he finished reading and rereading his own article the ash on the cigar was an inch and a half long. A well-made cigar, he noted. Through the big bay window at the west end of the library he noticed that the sun was out again and two errant sea gulls were circling over the pond. He thumbed the rest of Brain Research, reading the title, the authors and the conclusions of each paper. Lots of neurochemistry and pharmacology these days. He traded the Vivaldi for some vintage Ellington, resolved to go for a run before dark, and opened the latest Mitchener novel to page one. He hoped it had the zest of early Mitchener; he had been bored by *Space* and never finished *Poland*. Midway through the fourth chapter, the telephone rang.

"Dr. Donald Ingram speaking."

"This is the office of Senator John Bradford. The senator would like to speak with you." Click. Brief silence.

"Dr. Ingram?"

"Yes."

"My name is John Bradford. I am a US Senator from Rhode Island. I have a personal medical problem which I am told needs the attention of a neurosurgeon. May I discuss it with you?"

"Of course."

"The bottom line is that I seem to have a brain tumor. Dr. Banks at Walter Reed tells me that it's probably a . . . menajoma?"

"Meningioma?"

"Yes. Excuse me, I'm just getting used to these high-powered medical terms. At any rate I've had some bad headaches and more recently some seizures. I guess I hoped it would go away. My committee is into some terribly important investigations now and, well, I've just put off this problem for awhile . . ."

"Have you had a head CT scan?"

"Yes."

"Have you had an arteriogram?"

"No, it seems that's the next step."

"Where is the meningioma?"

"Dr. Banks says its on the fox . . ."

"Falx"

"Yes falx, and toward the front, up here." Ingram could imagine the senator pointing to the middle of his forehead.

"When can you come into the hospital? Today?"

A long pause.

"Tomorrow. I'll have to make some arrangements. There is a security precaution. And then . . . I need to be anonymous. This is very confidential and I wouldn't want to let the press know that . . ."

"I understand." Ingram had cared for several dignitaries and celebrities in the past. Both he and the hospital were used to it. "I'll arrange for admission tomorrow under the name of John Jones. Bring all your X-rays and laboratory studies. And bring a note from Dr. Banks. Better yet, ask him to give me a call tonight. Is your health good aside from this problem?" Ingram was already thinking about OR time and the weekly schedule. He had time on Friday but he might be able to bump Wednesday's case.

"Yes, my health has been fine. I must say, I expected a lot more discussion and less action."

"There is no reason to wait and every reason to move ahead. We can discuss the operation and the risks and the effects on your mental function when we know exactly what the problem is." Ingram had anticipated the senator's most vital concerns.

Bradford chuckled. "Dr. Ingram, I like your style. And I look forward to meeting you tomorrow. Are you a Republican or Democrat?"

"I don't know, it's been awhile since I looked."

"Fair enough. By the way, I believe you know my wife, Anne."

"Anne Bradford? I don't believe I've had the pleasure Senator . . ."

"Anne Harrington. When you knew her she was in college. Well, she wasn't sure you'd remember her . . ."

"Anne Harrington? Anne Harrington who was in nursing school in Boston about twenty years ago?"

"Yes, so you do remember. I'll tell her."

Ingram was suddenly glad they were not talking face to face. "Yes, I do remember her. We became good friends. I was a resident at the Longwood Hospital."

"That's what she told me. Anyway she'll be along tomorrow also."

"That's . . . just fine."

"Thank you again, Dr. Ingram. We'll both look forward to seeing you tomorrow."

"Yes, of course. Goodbye Senator."

"Goodbye." Click. Dial tone.

Ingram returned the telephone to its cradle and walked over to the bay window. His pulse surged and his breathing became faster and audible. A warm sensation deep in his mediastinum. Stimulated not by the thought of operating on a prominent senator. Not by the inevitable intrigue in the hospital—everyone would know anyway. Not by the international political implications of a bad result or a good result. Stimulated, rather, by the flood of memory associated with the thought of Anne Harrington Bradford.

CHAPTER 3

The sermon was entitled "The Ghost in the Machine," and Reverend Pulver had made some metaphorical reference to a fleet of rental cars and the patrons who signed them in and out. George Jacoby wasn't paying much attention, concentrating more on the preparations required to take George Jr. to the Patriots game in Foxboro. At the door at the Dedham Unitarian Church he congratulated the Reverend Pulver on an inspired message, and then sent his wife to gather the family while he retrieved the station wagon from the back of the parking lot. As he put his hand on the door of the old Ford wagon a tall young man with close-cropped hair and sunglasses approached.

"Mr. Jacoby."

"Yes." George thought he was going to be mugged. On Sunday morning, right in the church parking lot. He looked around for help, but his brisk pace had carried him far away from the other parishioners. Another older man in sunglasses and a dark suit appeared behind him. The younger man reached into his pocket. Jacoby considered shouting.

"Mr. Jacoby, we're with the Federal Government." From his pocket the man produced a wallet which he opened to show a badge and identification card. He didn't flash it. He held it open, steady, until Jacoby was convinced. "You are George Jacoby, Administrator of the Longwood Hospital, are you not?"

"Yes, that's right."

"Mr. Jacoby, Senator John Bradford is going to be admitted to Longwood Hospital this afternoon using the name of John Jones. We're going to need your help with some of the arrangements."

"Senator Bradford! Of course. Anything we can do."

"The senator and his family would like to keep this hospitalization totally confidential. No press, no gawky hospital employees, no visitors unless we clear them."

"I understand."

"The senator has been working with some top-secret security material. There must be somebody with him at all times. There will be a federal marshal named James Flint. He'll be with the senator as an aide. And there may be others as time goes on. I assume all this is satisfactory with you."

Jacoby nodded assent. "What's—what's wrong with the senator? I mean—I have to know where to put him."

The men exchanged glances. "I don't know what's wrong with him," said the younger man. "His doctor is arranging the details—a Dr. Ingram."

"Dr. Ingram is a neurosurgeon. That sounds worrisome."

"Please don't speculate Mr. Jacoby. Just help us out."

"Of course," said Jacoby, feeling very important to be taken into the confidence of national security.

* * * *

From his hospital room on the fourteenth floor, Benjamin Rothstein could see two dinghies tacking back and forth on the Charles River Basin. His view included only the north side of the river, so with each tack they came and went from his field of vision. He passed the time by judging their speed, judging the width of the river, the direction of the breeze (which was stiff this Sunday afternoon, with dark cat's paws flicking the surface of the waves), and the skill of the sailors. With all of these judgments he estimated when and where the pair of sails would appear again. Thus he passed the time. He reasoned that the sailors were MIT students because they were near the MIT boathouse, and also because it was a dreary, chilly, windy, September afternoon. The serious sailors would be down on Quincy Bay; the novices and dilettantes would be driven inside by the cold wind, and the Harvard boys would spend such an afternoon in front of the fire with a young lady. Over a dozen tacks he perceived that the two dinghies changed positions on each tack, and the following boat came about into lee of the lead boat just before a collision occurred. It was a complex game, weaving an intricate pattern back and forth across the river. Further evidence that the skippers were MIT students.

It was totally out of character for Rothstein to intentionally waste time, but he could not tolerate the insipid television, the headache precluded reading, and if he dozed, he awoke thinking of the tumor deep in his head and what the morning would bring. So he watched the sailboats and the cars crossing the bridge. After lunch, a nurse from the intensive care unit, exuding a combination of cheer and arrogance reminiscent of a second grade teacher, had guided Rothstein and another patient who was scheduled for heart surgery through the ICU. This tour was intended to make his inevitable stay in the ICU better-understood and therefore more tolerable. Or at least, so said the nurse. ("So when you wake up you'll like have a tube in your throat, okay? So you won't be able to talk, okay? Like that man over there and the tube will be like hooked up to a breathing machine, okay? So you don't have to worry about breathing but it's pretty scary and that's why we like explain it to you ahead of time so you won't be too scared. Do you have any questions?")

Neither Rothstein nor his horrified companion with angina had had any questions. They had just wanted to get out of there. He concluded that no knowledge of these particular circumstances was better than a smattering of knowledge, particularly when translated to junior high dialect. So he watched the sailboats, putting his worries out of his mind as much as possible, waiting for Ingram.

* * * *

On Sunday afternoon Donald Ingram made rounds without the residents so that he could spend as much time as he wished with each patient, leaving the residents with their usual flurry of preparation for Monday morning. He examined Matt Rizzo in leisurely detail, and satisfied himself that cord level was high C5: total and presumably permanent quadriplegia. Fortunately, Rizzo was a veteran. As soon as his condition stabilized he could be transferred to the Boston VA spinal cord injury service. There he would spend the rest of his life. Kathleen Dugan's intracranial pressure had come under control nicely. She remained in barbiturate-induced coma, although Ingram was not totally convinced of the effectiveness of this "brain rest" treatment. She had some twitching of her right arm and leg. Probably a seizure, but then "it takes a lot of brain cells to make a seizure," as Eastman used to say. Probably a good sign. He left the ICU in good spirits.

He continued his trek through the hospital with a subconscious plan to end up in X-ray, leaving Rothstein and the senator for last. He changed the head dressing on Mr. Harris, who was reading the Sunday Globe and looking as if nothing major had happened. He saw half a dozen other post-op patients on the neurosurgical floor and a low-back-pain consultation on the orthopedic service. There were three shunts on the pediatric service and an infant who needed one in the neonatal ICU. In X-ray he found Dan Adams studying a chest film.

"Well Dr. Adams, it's Sunday afternoon. Why aren't you out playing rugby or doing whatever it is you do on Sundays?" asked Ingram, who had fully expected to find Adams in the hospital this afternoon.

"I might ask you the same, sir," said Adams, who knew that Ingram always made extended rounds on Sunday afternoon. "Actually I'm here to look after a man who looks very much like a United States Senator."

"So you've met Mr. Jones."

"Yes. Interesting guy. He brought a stack of records and X-rays, but they wouldn't show them to anyone but you."

"They?" An image of Anne Harrington appeared again in his mind.

"There's some sort of security guy with him. He wouldn't leave the room while I did my exam. It reminds me of when we had the sheik's wife in here last winter."

"Great," said Ingram. Now the memory of swarthy bodyguards, pudgy female courtiers, and five-pound jars of caviar seemed amusing, but at the time it had been quite annoying. "I'll see Mr. Jones later. How about Professor Rothstein. Is he all set to go for tomorrow?"

"Yes he's ready. I've been over his labs, orders are written, his CT scan is right here," said Adams, pointing to an X-ray jacket on the desk, "and I squeezed the blood myself." The latter bit of hospital slang referred to a personal trip to the blood bank to verify that the six units of blood were indeed cross matched for the Professor.

"I'll take the CT scan with me," said Ingram. He squinted at the chest X-ray. "This must be Rizzo."

"Yes. I got the film to check on this catheter placement," tracing a faint line over the middle of the celluloid, "but I'm worried about this patchy stuff down in the right base." More pointing at shadows on the film.

* * * *

The sailboats had docked and the cold, sunless afternoon had worn on to early evening when Ingram appeared in Rothstein's room, X-ray jacket under his arm. "Professor Rothstein?" he knocked gently on the already-opened door to announce his coming. It was always a little surprising to Ingram how a fairly healthy person was transformed into a sick person merely by donning hospital garb and lying in a hospital bed. Rothstein was a good example. When Rothstein had visited Ingram's office a month before, he had appeared the quintessential philosopher, looking very much like the Karsh photograph on the dust jacket of his books. Now, in a flimsy hospital johnny, unshaven, loose skin hanging under his chin, he had taken on the aura of patient. There was a book on his lap, but it was closed and he was staring out the window.

"Good afternoon Professor Rothstein, I hope I'm not interrupting."

"Oh Dr. Ingram. I'm glad to see you. No, I was sitting here waiting for your visit." He put the book aside and arranged the bed covers rather self-consciously.

"You are scheduled for eight o'clock tomorrow morning. That means you'll be going downstairs about seven fifteen." Ingram launched directly into the critical discussion. He knew that Rothstein was anxious and needed facts, not conversation. He took an X-ray film from the jacket which he was carrying. "This is your CT scan. I thought you might want to see the cause of all this problem." He sat on the edge of the bed and held the film up toward the window so that the small black-and-white panels were illuminated. Rothstein moved closer to get a better view. "This is an X-ray image through your head at about the level of the ears. This is the front. See, here are your eyes and the upper part of your nose. All this is normal brain— and the problem is this little round thing right here." He was pointing with the tip of a pen, inscribing small circles around one area of gray- ness which appeared to be discrete from the adjacent grayness. Ingram continued, "Usually we can't see anything here, or maybe just a speck of calcium, so this little lump—about the size of a grape—is abnormal. It's in the area of the pineal gland."

"The home of the soul," observed Rothstein softly.

"The soul?"

Rothstein looked away from the X-ray, directly at Ingram, as if the comment had not been meant to be heard. "I was thinking out loud I guess. Rene Descartes thought that the pineal body was the conduit between the body and the mind and the eternal universe. His writings have been somewhat oversimplified, saying that the soul was located somewhere in the pineal gland. Actually, it's the weakest point in some otherwise brilliant observations."

"With all respect, Professor, Descartes *wrote* that the pineal was the access to the soul. What he thought might have been quite different."

"So you know Descartes, Doctor? Then you know of his obses- sion for real truth. He wouldn't have written such a bold statement unless he believed it to be true."

"Agreed, unless he wrote it to serve some larger purpose, which is my theory."

"Please explain," said Rothstein, warming to the challenge and forgetting for an instant about the impending operation.

"Descartes was a good physician and scientist as well as a philoso- pher," said Ingram. "He dissected the brain. He was in that first gen- eration of men to realize that every thought, wish, memory, sensation, dream, mania, and passion is seated in that organ, rather than the heart or the pancreas or some mysterious circulating humor."

"Quite so. A revolutionary idea at the time."

"Now it follows that a bright and perceptive man, realizing that concept for the first time, and holding in his hand the brain of a person who had loved and cried and thought and argued—it follows that such a man would have to conclude that the person ended as the brain became just so much rancid fat."

"He thinks not, therefore he is not," said Rothstein, thinking aloud again. "I just had that conversation with a friend. Of course, simply stating the contrapositive . . . the opposite to a declaration is not proof, even if the declaration is true. It does not follow the precepts of logic. But Descartes did perceive that all thinking stops when the brain stops."

"Precisely. And realizing that, the same man would have to conclude that personal afterlife is impossible. Just wishful thinking."

"Granted. That would certainly be a possibility."

"So it follows that a person who presumes to know about afterlife is a wishful thinker who might wish up anything at all regarding those things we do not understand."

"A plausible conclusion, Dr. Ingram. Cynical, but plausible, and untenable for a religious man, or a man in religious times. But Descartes believed the axioms of his religion. He did not doubt the afterlife; that was accepted as true. So he had to match his observations to the axioms of faith. It was not difficult for him to imagine that the humors and vapors which he thought connected the body to the mind simply returned to the grand spiritual universe when the brain and body died. He knew nothing of cells or metabolism or neurons. He didn't even imagine electricity. Just the ghostly humors leaving the machine. How does that happen? The pineal body was a likely route, located in the brain where the brain and body intersect. "

Ingram was silent, thinking, Then he nodded and smiled a little, as if he had come to a realization. " You are right of course. I was trying to read Descartes with our modern understanding of brain function. It seems obvious to me that we exist only in our own mind, and only so long as the brain functions. In fact only as long as certain parts of the brain function. I was trying to read that into Descartes."

Rothstein looked at the neurosurgeon intensely for a moment. "An interesting theory," he said at length. Ingram couldn't tell if it was a tolerant rebuff or a genuine acknowledgment. "And does your theory acknowledge the existence of soul?"

"That depends upon how you define it, but the simple answer is yes."

"I see. And is there also a mind in your theory?"

"Very definitely."

"The mind and the soul—in your theory—can be located . . ."

"In the brain."

"In the brain? Located and dissected and touched and identified in the brain?"

"Along with consciousness, vision and love and memory—they're all to be found there."

"Then why, Dr. Ingram, is not M Descartes correct? It seems to me that you've just supported his argument."

"I would say he was not correct because he made definitive statements about the mind and body as if they were true. But stated to match the axiom, as you point out. He guessed, but he really did not know the nature of the soul."

"And you do?" His grin indicated a gentle gibe.

"I'm working on it." Ingram smiled in return. He always found mental exercise to be more exhilarating and more exhausting than any physical activity.

"Now, to get back to the immediate problem, this tumor is most likely not in the pineal gland itself, but next to it. And it's likely to be sensitive to radiation. In fact, some neurosurgeons would simply recommend radiating this area first to determine the response. Now the risks of the operation are—"

"Dr. Ingram. My friend. We've discussed this before. I want to know exactly what that lump is before we embark on a course of treatment. And I know about the risks and I trust your experience. I'm not afraid of an operation, I'm not afraid of the diagnosis, but I want you to promise me one thing."

"What's that Ben?"

"If I can't think clearly, I don't want to be alive. Descartes notwithstanding, if my mind goes into the atmosphere or simply to the pathologist, I would rather not continue to exist. If I can't think clearly you must help me die. No machines, no tubes. Can you promise that?"

"Ben, with a tumor in this area your thinking should be just fine. But I can't guarantee that. And I understand exactly what you're asking but I won't do anything to end your life. However, the extent of treatment is always your choice. We'll do as much—or as little—as you wish. I'll promise you that."

"That's all I ask." A firm handshake seemed the right and spontaneous thing to do. "And I thank you in advance, if necessary."

* * * *

Rooms 950 and 951 were opposite each other at the end of the corridor on the ninth floor, farthest from the nursing station. They were both semi-private double rooms, but the hand-lettered signs on the board at the nursing station showed that 950 was occupied only by Jones, J. and 951 was occupied by Flint, J. Room 949 and 952 were empty.

Ingram noted the familiar pattern of the VIP security arrangement as he stopped at the nursing station to pick up the chart marked "Jones." At the end of the corridor two linen carts had been set up to form an unobtrusive but significant barrier. A typical complete isolation warning served to deter any casual visitors or curious hospital employees. Ingram knocked on the door of 950, then entered. The curtain in the center of the room was drawn and Ingram could not see the bed next to the window. The first bed had been removed and was replaced by a desk and chair, facing the door. In the chair sat a tall, hard, unpleasant-looking man. There was nothing on the desk and nothing in his hands. It appeared he had been sitting still, watching the door, for some time.

As Ingram entered the man rose, one hand in his coat pocket. "Hold it right there please."

"I beg your pardon?" Ingram was not used to being accosted in his own domain.

"May I see your identification please?" The man had positioned himself squarely in front of Ingram. He was as tall as the surgeon, with a beak-like nose and relentless eyes.

"I'm Dr. Ingram and Mr. Jones is my patient. And who are you?" Ingram said icily.

"Dr. Ingram. Please come in. Come in. I've been waiting for you." The voice came from behind the curtain surrounding the bed.

Without a flicker of recognition the tall man stood aside and Ingram walked past him to the bedside.

"Hello, Senator. I see you got admitted without too much fuss." The senator had eschewed the hospital johnny and was wearing his own pajamas covered by a heavy velour robe. He sat on top of the undisturbed bed with a stack of folders spread out on the over-bed table. To Ingram he looked a little older than he appeared on television. His handshake was firm. "Please call me John. I am sorry about the security. This is Mr. Flint. He will be with me most of the time." He nodded at Flint who had walked up behind Ingram.

"All the time," said Flint. It was not said in a joking manner. "Dr. Ingram, government regulations require that a marshal be present with the senator at all times in the hospital. It's mostly to protect yourself and the hospital staff. Through his position, the senator has knowledge of top-secret security information. Anyone who learned this information could be in a very vulnerable situation, if you see what I mean. It's really a matter of routine. I'm sure you will cooperate."

"Of course," said Ingram. He had encountered the same regulation on previous cases. Turning back to the senator, "Has Mr. Flint been with you long?"

"Only for the last few days, since my seizure on nation-wide television." He smiled self-consciously. "Actually it's only been a week or two since I previewed testimony for my committee—"

"Excuse me senator, that's just what I warned you about."

Bradford glared at Flint. "—learned of the testimony which precipitates this interest in security. It won't be necessary to interrupt me, Mr. Flint." Silence hung heavy in the air.

"Well, let's get back to your problems, Senator" said Ingram briskly. "John."

"Okay John. Did you bring some X-rays and records with you?"

"Yes." He hopped from the bed and pulled some papers from his suitcase. "I didn't show these to young Dr. Adams. There were instructions to hold them for you. I hope he wasn't offended."

"Not at all, although the safest way for a VIP to survive the hospital is to let the system run at its usual pace."

He was looking at the CT scan and not the senator, so his remarks would appear casual, but the message was clear. He glanced at the senator. "You see what I mean. Professors shouldn't be starting IVs and that sort of thing." The senator was silent, as was Flint. "When did you first start having symptoms?"

"Looking back, I have been having headaches for about six months. But I didn't think anything of it until the first seizure. That was two months ago. Dr. Banks ordered the CT scan and he has been urging me to do something about it ever since. On Friday evening I had a seizure right in the middle of a TV interview. That's when I decided to call you."

Ingram had been leafing through the xeroxed papers from Walter Reed Hospital. "Dr. Banks was right. You have a tumor in the middle of your head toward the front. It's most likely a meningioma—a benign type of tumor. It won't get any better, and needs to be removed."

"Well," said Bradford with a half-hearted laugh. "They were right when they said you wouldn't pull any punches or waste any time." Bradford studied the doctor anxiously, hoping for some softer information. "Isn't there some other way to go about this? I read about stereotaxis . . ."

"If there were any other way I would suggest it to you. A more important question is whether it can be removed at all."

"You mean an arteriogram."

"I can see you've already taken the mini-course in neurosurgery."

"I'm only repeating what Dr. Banks recommended next."

"Dr. Banks was right again. We've actually reserved time on the arteriography schedule tomorrow."

"Tomorrow?"

"No point in wasting time."

"I know. I just haven't admitted to myself that this is happening. I have so much to do . . ." The anguish showed on his face and he looked away.

Ingram sought to ease the tension. "With a little luck you'll be back to work in a few weeks. By Christmas you will just think of it as an expensive haircut." A forced chuckle.

Bradford was the first to become aware of another presence in the room. He was looking past Flint toward the door. Anne Bradford had slipped in during the discussion.

"Just a haircut John? That sounds good."

Ingram turned toward the husky, cheerful voice. What he noticed first were the dancing, sparkling eyes.

"Dr. Ingram, this is my wife, Anne. She tells me you have met before."

"Hello Don. Or should I call you Dr. Ingram?" She stepped forward and offered her hand. "Thank you so much for seeing John. We've been so worried for the last month . . ."

"Hello Anne. 'Don' is fine. It's good to see you again." It wasn't that the iris of her eyes was so blue—although it was—rather that the white part was so white. Some luminescence between mischief and firelight reflected from the surface. She had set the tone. It would be formal.

He hesitated just a second before taking her hand, wondering how it would feel . . . "I'm very glad to help" . . . if current would flow when he touched it. Her hand was warm and she held on just a second longer than was necessary. Or so he thought.

"Did I hear you and John discussing an arteriogram? Dr. Banks had mentioned that to us." He heard her voice, but tried to read her eyes. He concluded that he was overreacting. "Yes, we planned an arteriogram for tomorrow." Outer self speaking calmly, mind humming, he turned back to Bradford. "It's a series of X-rays. It will be a little warm when they inject the dye, but it won't be bad."

"If that's what it takes . . ." said Bradford. "Do you have a date in mind for surgery?" If Bradford sensed Ingram's distraction, he didn't show it.

"We can schedule your operation on Friday, depending on the results of the arteriogram. I'll go over the results with you tomorrow evening. Can you be here then, Mrs. Bradford?"

"Please call me Anne, and I'll be here any time you say. I have arranged for an apartment in the Longwood Towers so I'll be close by." She smiled warmly at her husband. White teeth—one slightly twisted—and deep dimples in her tanned cheeks. He had forgotten the dimples. Suddenly Ingram realized that he was staring at her, holding his breath. Quickly he turned to the senator.

"Doctor, could I speak to you for a minute?" Flint's dispassionate voice brought him back from memory. Ingram excused himself and they stepped into the hall.

"Will this arteriogram require anesthesia?" Ingram disliked Flint already, but he couldn't decide why.

"Only local."

"Sedation?"

"Usually the radiologist orders a little Valium. Why do you ask?"

"I need to know if the senator is likely to . . . say anything . . . out of the ordinary. I'll be there of course but . . ."

"Mr. Flint, my comments were meant for you as much as the senator. It's important to let our team work according to our routine. I understand your situation, but you can't interfere with—"

"Dr. Ingram, I certainly wouldn't presume to tell you how to do your job."

"Good."

"Don't tell me how to do mine."

They stared at each other, neither willing to look away. After a moment, Ingram returned to the room. Anne Bradford was sitting on the bed, next to her husband.

"Senator . . ."

"John, please."

"John, I'll see you early in the morning."

"Fine, thanks very much for everything."

"Mrs. Bradford."

"Anne, please."

"Anne, I'll be driving past the Towers when I finish rounds. May I give you a lift?"

"No thank you Don." She turned her head slowly, dancing eyes level. Ingram thought she was being deliberately proper. "It's only a few blocks—"

"Yes Dr. Ingram, that would be very nice," Bradford interrupted. "Anne, it will be dark soon, I'd feel better if you'd let Dr. Ingram give you a ride."

She was quiet for a moment. "Alright then. Thank you. Shall I wait here?"

"I'll be back in twenty minutes."

Ingram returned to the nurses' station, wrote a note on the chart and, feeling a little like a sophomore, tried to busy himself for twenty minutes.

* * * *

The hospital parking structure was two blocks away, six stories of uninteresting concrete ramps and posts. If offered some protective advantage from both the elements and juvenile delinquents of Roxbury, but, because of his rank, Ingram was entitled to a named parking place in the alley behind the old section of the hospital. He preferred it because it was closer, practical, and had once been Franz Eastman's parking spot. After bidding goodnight to the senator (Ingram politely, Anne with a kiss on his forehead) they rode down the elevator without speaking and Ingram led the way across the lobby. He paused to speak with Carol Rizzo, who was sitting in the lobby with Matt Jr. while her mother-in-law was upstairs visiting the ICU. He didn't want to stop, but they had made definite eye contact and conversation was inevitable. As they discussed Matt's motor level and chest X-ray, Carol looked from Ingram to the striking blond woman who had exited the elevator with him and was now standing aside, waiting. She wondered if the woman was Ingram's wife, but he offered no introduction. As they left, she noticed that he started to take her arm, then didn't, pointing the way toward an obscure door in back of the lobby. Carol concluded that the woman was not familiar with the hospital, and therefore, not Ingram's wife.

Through the door, he led the way down a narrow corridor—new cement block merging into old brick—then down an old flight of stairs.

"I hope you don't mind the back stairs. I'm afraid it's the only way to my parking place."

"Not at all. Isn't this part of the old hospital?"

"Yes it is. Watch your step." The stairs ended abruptly at a door which he pushed open into the windy alley. He held out his hand to guide her. It really wasn't necessary, but she took it for the last step and held on as if the wind threatened her balance. The car was right outside the door, under a sign on the old brick wall which said "Dr. Ingram," in black letters stenciled on a small white board.

"Donald Ingram," she said with some amazement, "This can't be the same car."

He smiled rather boyishly. "I didn't think you would remember. No, this is a '72. I used the '61 for parts."

"I might have known," she murmured as he opened the door. He watched her reaction as he walked to the driver's side. The car was an MGB, factory green. It wasn't exactly a restoration. The gear shift knob and the steering wheel were beautiful walnut, not original issue. A black Blaukpunt radio nestled in the center of the dash. Not a restoration, just perfectly kept. The engine purred when he turned the key.

"It's an old car but it gets me around." The radio came on with the engine, filling the little car with a Chopin etude for the piano. He quickly reached to turn down the volume.

"And Chopin? I'm not surprised." To him, it seemed her eyes were sparkling again.

"I wasn't sure you would remember." He backed into the alley and soon they were on Longwood Avenue.

"It really is nice of you to get John admitted on such short notice. He has been under such pressure. . . . It's not like him to be so paranoid."

"Anyone with a brain tumor should be a little scared."

"I don't mean apprehension, I mean paranoia. About people following him and that sort of thing. Didn't he tell you about it?"

"No."

"He will. He's so worried. Could that be caused by the tumor?"

"All sorts of personality changes can be related to frontal lobe tumors. But he seems fine to me."

"Maybe I'm the one that's scared. But I feel so much better knowing that you're taking care of him."

She touched his arm. It seemed an impulsive gesture to emphasize her confidence.

They exchanged pleasant small talk. Ingram tried to drive slowly, waiting for the right moment in the conversation to make an overture, but the Longwood Towers was only a few blocks away. He pulled into the circular driveway and parked near the front door. He was trying to think of what to say next when she opened the door. "Thank you very much. I must say this is elegant service—"

"No wait." He sounded too anxious. "Just a minute, I'll get it." He jumped out and came around to her side, opening the door and offering his hand. Even a teenager has a hard time climbing up out of the MGB passenger seat, but she made it look incredibly graceful. Amazing legs, he thought to himself. She paused just a second, as if adjusting her shoe, then stood up so that they were standing very close. She reached down and closed the door.

"Look Anne, have you had supper? Maybe we could get a drink, or a cup of coffee. There's so much to catch up on . . ."

"Don, you're so nice to ask. But I'm just exhausted. Besides you must have family waiting for you on a Sunday night. And I'm really tired."

"No Anne. Listen . . ." They approached the Longwood front door, which swung open and a rotund little doorman stepped out.

"Good evening, Madam." He had already been introduced to the senator's wife and had been given appropriate instructions. He looked at Ingram suspiciously. She stepped back—more than arm's length between them now.

"Thank you very much for the ride, Dr. Ingram." She appeared to be on the public stage again, very formal. "We do have a lot to discuss and we must do it soon. Now good night." Her back to the doorman, she sounded very proper, but she concluded with a wink and a silent little kiss, just moving her lips and puffing in his direction. Then she turned and disappeared through the door, saying "Good evening Mr. Duffy," to the doorman.

Ingram was a little stunned. He nodded to Mr. Duffy, started the car automatically, and was three blocks down Brookline Avenue before he realized he had not turned his head lamps on.

CHAPTER 4

Dan Adams took one of the plastic-wrapped scrub brushes from the box and squeezed it until it popped. He slammed the plastic wrapper into the wastebasket and turned on the water with his knee. He looked calm, but Burleson could tell from his brisk moves and his controlled silence that he was furious.

"Dan, I'm sorry. I didn't know he was supposed to be sitting up. I didn't even know you could do an operation with the patient sitting up."

"How the hell did you think we were going to get to his pineal? Burrow through his third ventricle?"

"I didn't know, I guess I just didn't think."

"Well, that's the first intelligent thing you've said this morning."

Burleson was silent. Head down, he continued to scrub his hands.

"Then we get that jackass anesthesia staff who wants to put in an arterial line. Christ we're a half an hour late and Ingram will be here any minute expecting to see the flap turned."

"Yeah, how come we don't have Peterson giving anesthesia like we usually do?" Burleson was glad to divert Adams's anger to anyone else except himself.

"Oh the patient is a big honcho professor from across the river. So we get big honcho Chairman Graham. He watches the schedule and only comes out of his office when there is a VIP. You watch. He'll come in here and make an ass out of himself, then he'll spend the whole case reviewing manuscripts for the anesthesia journal and telling us how shitty they are."

"He sure complained enough about sitting him up." They continued scrubbing, Burleson splattering gobs of brown lather on his scrub suit.

"Tell me about Rizzo," said Adams. "No never mind," he added as Burleson dropped his hands, "you can't scrub and think at the same time. Just scrub. I'll prep the professor. Tell me about Rizzo later."

Adams donned the prep gloves and began washing Rothstein's shaved head with Betadine soap. The professor's skull was clamped into position with metal pins and the rest of him was rather clumsily strapped and taped into a sitting position. Graham was bustling about like a mother duck checking the padding under Rothstein's elbows and knees.

"Don't get that stuff in his eyes. Try to be a little gentle. If you had told us ahead of time that this was going to be a posterior fossa we might have been ready, you know." His voice was high and whiny. "There's a reason we have preoperative anesthesia rounds you know. We don't do it just to be sociable." Adams did not respond. He glanced at Kay Lawson, the nurse anesthetist who was adjusting the ventilator. She shrugged slightly as if to indicate that it was going to be a long day and there was nothing she could do about it. Kay had a great chest, which she emphasized by pulling the baggy scrub dress together in the back with a safety pin. It was cold in the room and her nipples made tantalizing little knobs under the dull green broadcloth. Adams decided to think about that, and tuned out Dr. Graham.

"Is there anything special you're going to need today, Dr. Adams?" Helen Tibbets, circulating nurse in the neuro room, was trying to interrupt Graham's tirade. She was a former army nurse who was hell on interns but the enduring friend of chief residents. "I put out Dr. Ingram's long-lighted retractor and the extra-long bipolars. Jimmy made some of the extra large patties he likes to put on the cerebellum." Jimmy Jones, the scrub tech, was clattering the instruments on the back table louder than usual. Adams did not need all the information but he appreciated Tibbets's attempt to detour Graham.

"That sounds good Helen. We might need the MADAT clamp." Adams said gravely. The instrument rattling stopped and Jimmy snuck a look at Graham. MADAT was OR slang for "mandatory anesthesia dicking-around time."

"I'll see if I can find one," said Helen. If Graham understood this jibe he didn't show it.

While Adams draped, Burleson got gowned and gloved. He had managed to contaminate himself only once. "Ready?" asked Adams, leaning over to get another look at Kay Lawson who was standing up to see the color of the blood.

"Any time you're ready, Doctor," she cooed, and Adams made a sweeping incision with a #10 blade, starting backhand and ending up forehand, bearing down hard to cut the scalp and galea with one stroke. Red blood squirted from the business end of half a dozen arteries.

"Ingram always says that if you cut the vessels fast they don't bleed," said Adams, as Jimmy handed up scalp clamps to both Adams and Burleson as fast as they could take them. "We're running so late that I'm going to do the drilling today." It was an announcement from Adams, not a question. Burleson nodded and took the syringe of saline to cool the whirring drill bit. Adams was on the third burr hole when Ingram walked into the room.

"I thought you'd be inside the dura by now. Is Jimmy slowing you down again?" Everyone knew that Jimmy was as slick as oil. He enjoyed the recognition.

Adams didn't appear surprised at the voice behind him. "Good morning Dr. Ingram." he said, continuing to drill. "We had a bit of a late start this morning."

"I'll say we had a late start. Good morning Don." Graham arose from the high stool on the other side of the drapes. "None of your loyal Indians seemed to know whether we were going to do this operation lying down or sitting up or just walking around—you know what I mean?"

"Well Gordon, I'm sure you were your usual helpful self. How did we get to be honored with your presence this morning?"

"Aside from a desire to enjoy your congenial company, Dr. Ingram, I have quite an attachment to Professor Rothstein. He's very famous in the university you know."

"Well, we are honored, Dr. Graham." Ingram opened the door, heading for the scrub sink. "By the way," glancing back at Graham, "this is going to be a long case, so be sure to tell us if you run across any particularly lousy articles for the Anesthesia Journal." He left the room. Graham was silent, for the moment rebuffed. A quick smile of the eyes circulated between Adams, Burleson, Jimmy, and Helen.

"Now that the professor's here, we can have some music," said Kay brightly. She dialed in the classical station on the big radio on the back of the anesthesia table. Adams relaxed, and the atmosphere in the operating room became palpably softer. "That was beautiful," said Adams very softly to himself and chuckled. Graham was silent. A Bach harpsichord concerto drifted up from behind the ether screen. The bone flap was wrapped in a wet pack and carefully placed on the back table. Adams started to work on the dura.

During the early stages of the dissection they made verbal rounds on selected patients. Kathleen Dugan was still snowed on phenobarbital. Rizzo would probably need a tracheostomy. Adams had put the baby shunt revision on the schedule. If they finished Rothstein in time they might get it done this afternoon. But as soon as Ingram said, "Okay let me have a look up there," and displaced Adams on the high stool, the conversation was over. Tibbets put some tape across the door to discourage visitors. Kay Lawson, who had just the right sense for the level of concentration in the operative field, turned off the radio. For two hours the room was silent except for "joker . . . patty . . . buzz my right hand . . . suck on the patty . . ." every few minutes or so from Ingram.

Once, Graham interrupted the silence. "Don, you wouldn't believe this article. This guy from New York is using a lidocaine drip in the epidural space for phantom pain. There are only four patients and no controls and this turkey wants us to publish—"

"Not now Gordon," interrupted Ingram without moving his eyes from the operating microscope. More silence. Finally Ingram spoke to Adams, who was holding retractors and watching through the viewing head of the scope. "There it is Dan. I think it's free all the way around. What do you make of it?"

"It looks like a real pinealoma. I thought it was one of those lymphoid tumors of the choroid but now that you have it out it looks like the real thing. I've only seen one before."

"Well, that's one more than most residents have seen." He leaned back and stretched. "Dr. Burleson, you've been doing a wonderful job. You're the most important man in this operation." Burleson, whose aching arms had gone numb half an hour ago, had never received a compliment from Ingram. He suddenly felt ten feet tall. Ingram got up from the stool. "Here Burleson, let me hold that retractor a minute and take a look through the scope here and tell me what you see."

Burleson settled himself in front of the oculars and leaned forward. "Wow! This is terrific!" Small arterioles looked like garden hoses. Spiderweb fibers of arachnoid looked like the rigging on a clipper ship. The brain was pulsing with each heart beat—it reminded Burleson of waves on a water bed. In the middle of the field something that resembled a giant pumpkin was settled into the brain tissue.

"The round lump in the middle of the field is the tumor. Can you see it?"

"Yes. It's so big. I thought it would be a tiny little thing."

"Well, it's probably a centimeter or two in diameter," said Ingram.

"I guess that's pretty big."

"Yes, thank you sir," said Burleson, climbing off the stool. "Now do we just take it out?"

"That's it," said Ingram. "Dan, why don't you see if you can lift it out of there."

"Yes sir," said Adams, who needed no further encouragement. He moved to the position in front of the operating microscope. "There's a lot of edema on the roof of the fourth ventricle here," he commented. "We must be up close to the aqueduct."

"Right on it, I'd say," said Ingram who was watching through the viewing head. "Easy now. That stalk is usually broad-based and sessile."

By 1:30 Ingram took over again. At 2:15 the marble-sized lump came out. They spent a half hour cleaning up the site, commenting on the closure of the roof of the ventricle. The music came back on softly, and no one recognized that it had been off for four hours. Tibbets brought in some orange juice and assisted each surgeon in turn, lifting the lower part of the mask and working a straw into his mouth. For Burleson, nothing had ever tasted sweeter.

As Adams put the bone flap back into place, Ingram quizzed Burleson on the anatomy and the postoperative orders. It helped Burleson to stay awake, and Ingram seemed friendlier than usual.

* * * *

Although it had been less than three days since his injury, Matt Rizzo felt that he had been in the ICU for a year. The lights never went off, the action never stopped; he slept in short fits and starts. He knew it was Monday afternoon because Carol had told him. In fact she began each visit by telling him the day and the time—a habit from her ICU nursing days. She was still here, sitting beside his bed. He knew because he could see her shoes and her feet, along with the feet of the bedside nurse as she came and went in the nursing routine. Other than that all he could see was the floor and the bottom of the ventilator and the base of the Stryker frame. The floor was dirty with bits of dried blood and other speckled fluids ground into the pock-marked vinyl. Since he had seen nothing but the floor and the ceiling for the last three days, he had become obsessed with the idea of improving the visual spectrum of patients lying in beds in intensive care units. He hated the prone position. In fact, he was terrified by it. The tube in his throat, attached to the ventilator, became even more uncomfortable. His forehead rested on a canvas strap, creating painful pressure points, and there was nothing he could do about it. Saliva from his mouth drooled in a steady stream onto the pool on the floor. The nurse had put a towel on the floor there to collect it and the towel became the focus of his attention since it was the only thing he could see all of. Besides, every time they turned him prone onto the frame his neck hurt terribly, as it did now, but he had no way to communicate this complaint aside from trying to shake his head and move his lips. He thought he had been prone for about three hours, so soon he would be turned to his back again.

Carol's face appeared as she crouched down to look up at him. "Matt honey, you're doing great. I know you don't like to lie this way but it's good for your lungs and your skin." He looked at her, mouthing the word "no" and "hurts," and trying to shake his head. She could not make out the words but it was obvious that he was unhappy. "Dr. Adams says they will put you in a halo as soon as your neck is a little more stable. Then you will be able to sit up and get in a wheelchair. I know you don't like lying face down this way, but it's so important. The skin over your tail bone was all red when they first turned you over. It looks better now."

"In fact, your whole bottom looks terrific," said the nurse, whose face now appeared in Matt's vision as she crouched down opposite Carol. They both giggled as if it were a good joke, but the thought of his bare ass sticking out in the air was not amusing to Matt. He just closed his eyes. He tried to shout—he had tried it hourly since the injury. But no noise occurred, except for a buzzing from the ventilator followed by a paroxysm of coughing. The coughing caused the connection between the ventilator and the tube to come apart, the ventilator tubing fell into his line of vision, a high-pitched piercing alarm sounded, and the feeling of being unable to breath began immediately. He experienced this feeling each time the ventilator popped off, and he had already learned to wait through the panic, hoping that someone would hook him back up before the dizziness started. This time the nurse hooked him back up immediately.

"That coughing is good for your lungs," she said. "In a few minutes we'll do our chest PT and suction some more of that stuff out of there." Suctioning caused a painful, burning feeling deep in his chest. He looked at Carol, hoping that she would understand.

"I know Matt. Nobody likes the suctioning. But it's very important to keep your lungs clear. Dr. Adams said that you might get that tube out of your throat in a day or two if your lungs stay as good as they are now." A day or two? "In a day or two I'll be dead," he thought. At the moment he was so uncomfortable that he thought that he would rather be dead. He had experienced this thought this morning for the first time. Before that he had worried that he might die. Now it surprised him to realize that he was hoping to die. A transient thought, of course, he rationalized quickly, convincing himself that soon he would feel his arms and legs and then begin to move them. Carol needed him and so did little Matt. And Carol seemed so optimistic. Nonetheless, it had occurred to him that he would rather die than continue on this way. Carol reached up with a cloth to wipe the drooling saliva from his mouth. She looked great. Tears came to his eyes and he resolved not to think about dying. He tried to form a kiss and she smiled.

"Hello Carol. How are things this afternoon?" A pair of black shoes and black trousers appeared in his line of vision. Carol's face disappeared and her feet turned toward the black-shoed feet.

"Good afternoon, Father John." Her voice sounded a little shaky. "Matt is doing just fine, thank you. He doesn't like to be turned face down."

"Is he awake?"

"Oh yes, he's very awake. Say hello to him." The black shoes moved farther toward his head and soon the face of a crouching Father John O'Reily appeared. "Hello Matt." There it was again. The forced cheerfulness paraded by each visitor. "This is some fancy contraption they've got you in. I guess I didn't realize that it turned over. It must feel good to get off your back now and then." Father John didn't realize that he couldn't feel anything below his collarbones. Matt just blinked his eyes. It was like having a conversation with a dentist— worse. Matt could tell that Father John was uncomfortable. "Well, keep it up Matt. You've got a great little wife here." He grinned and the face disappeared, then the shoes.

"Well he's certainly awake. He looks pretty good to me." They had gone back to conversing about Matt as if he were asleep—a pattern of behavior he had come to expect. In fact, he had learned the most about his own case from listening to these bedside conversations. "Any improvement yet?" The priest's question was meant for Carol but Matt heard no answer. Instead both pairs of feet disappeared from his field of vision and he was back to watching the spittle accumulate on the towel. What did he mean, improvement? Was there a problem he didn't know about? A problem in addition to the obvious problem? He would try to get some answers from Adams. Adams or Ingram. Young Dr. Burleson seemed inexperienced and never had the answers.

Carol had walked over to the nursing station with Father John. "His attitude is pretty good but there is no return of function yet. We're still hoping."

"Well, we're all hoping. And praying for you too. Mrs. Dugan lit a candle for Matt just this morning."

"Lit a candle?"

"It's a thing that Catholics do." He smiled. "It's a way of drawing attention to special prayers behalf of people in need."

"You mean all those little red candles near the statue in the Catholic church?"

"Yes that's right, that's exactly right."

"All those candles represent prayers for people? I thought it was just part of the decoration."

"No, people light them to emphasize their prayers. Wishful prayers. That's why they're called votive candles—wishful candles." He was pleased. She seemed to be showing some interest. "It's a very powerful thing, the miracle of prayer. God hears every one. In every Catholic church all over the world there are votive candles flickering, and God worries about every one." The thought was very satisfying to him.

"Oh brother." She said it to herself, under her breath, reflecting merely what she was thinking but she hadn't meant it to get out. Father John was shocked. She looked a little embarrassed.

"I beg your pardon?" He had heard her perfectly well.

"Forget it. I'm sorry. It's a nice thought."

"Well, it's more than a nice thought. It's a miracle. I mean, when you think about it, the fact that God cares and loves each of us is quite miraculous. Isn't it?"

Her eyes dulled and her expression flickered through disgust into tolerance. It wasn't a discussion she wanted this afternoon. "If you say so." She winced internally at her own cynicism.

"Well, it's not that I say so, my child . . ." He wouldn't let it drop.

"Look, I'm *not* your child. You *did* say so, and when I want advice about mystical theology, I'll ask for it, okay?"

He looked like she had hit him with a brick. He opened his mouth to speak but nothing came out.

"Look, I'm sorry. You're a nice man and I know you are trying to help. I'm just tired of hearing all of these little homilies from every-body."

"Little homilies?" It was inconceivable to him that this young woman could consider the rock of faith a little homily. A rather evangelistic rebuttal organized in his mind, but she cut him off.

"Just drop it will you? Just drop it." She turned and walked back to the bedside, shaking her head and muttering "brother" again to herself.

* * * *

"If you're going to insist on staying in here, Mr. Flint, you'll have to wear one of those lead aprons. Don't get close to this table, it's all sterile." Henry Peabody was obviously irritated by the deviation from routine. First, a new orderly, and now an unsolicited chaperone. Ordinarily, he didn't tolerate visitors in the angiography suite. Mostly he was irritated because no one had told him that John Jones, the last case on his schedule for four vessel cranial studies, was actually Senator John Bradford. He had even tried to call Ingram to register his displeasure, but Ingram was in the operating room. "Mr. Jones, we're going to freeze your skin then put in a catheter. Are you allergic to anything?"

"I'm allergic to penicillin, and to walnuts. I'm very allergic to walnuts. I had a really bad reaction a few years ago. My wife had to inject me with one of those epi-pens."

"Okay, we won't give you any walnuts." Peabody chuckled at his own little joke. "Have you ever had Novacaine? For your teeth or anything?"

"Oh yes, several times."

"Any problems?"

"Never."

"Okay, then we'll get started."

Peabody missed his initial attempt at puncture of the femoral artery, hitting the vein instead, and the new tech, who was helping Beverly, dropped the guide wire on the floor. It added considerably to his frustration that there was a stone-faced layman looking over his shoulder.

Flint put on one of the lead aprons. He set aside one covered in calico cloth and picked the yellow vinyl version. "Just go ahead with your business Dr. Peabody. Just pretend I'm not here."

"Wish to God you weren't," muttered Peabody. No response from Flint. Peabody stepped on the pedal for his first look at the chest on the image intensifier. The catheter was floating in the position he knew to be the aortic arch. He injected a whiff of viscous contrast agent and watched it disappear up the neck. Pleased with himself for a perfect placement, he addressed the senator. "Now Mr. Jones, everything alright so far?"

"Yes perfect. I didn't feel a thing after that local anesthetic. Dr. Ingram was right, you're very good."

"Yes, good old Dr. Ingram," said Peabody, reminding himself again to complain to the neurosurgeon. He maneuvered the catheter into the innominate and past the right subclavian, checking his position with another whiff of dye. He handed the end of the catheter to Beverly and addressed his patient. "Now, we're all ready to make our injection. In a minute you'll feel something warm on the right side of your face. It might give you a little headache. And you'll hear some whirring and banging as we take our X-rays. The important thing is that you don't move. Just concentrate on holding still. All set?"

"All set," responded Bradford rather grimly, bracing himself for the unknown. The syringe of liquid contrast material was loaded into the automatic injector. Flint moved closer, to see better, Peabody assumed. The Shonander was loaded and ready. Peabody preferred big cut films to the cine-angiograms his younger colleagues usually took. "Lights on," he said, arranging the foot pedals with his toe. He glanced around. "Lights off again. Everybody ready?" He started to say shoot, but held back, suddenly realizing that something was not quite right. The senator had his eyes closed, concentrating, awaiting the burning and the noise.

"Turn the lights back on a minute," said Peabody.

He checked the Shonander, glanced at the patient, glanced at Flint, checked the injector.

"Don't they usually mark your indictable?" asked Flint casually.

"We always mark indictable, thank you," said Peabody testily, examining the syringe and finding no label. "Beverly, what is this?"

"Angio-Conray," she said matter-of-factly.

"It just looks funny." Peabody took off his gloves and removed the syringe from the power injector. The blood which had been drawn into the syringe looked abnormal in the clear contrast material. It wasn't the usual billowy cloud of red liquid. As he aspirated, blood came back but immediately turned to black sludge. Peabody glanced at Flint, who seemed to be observing him closely.

"Beverly, get me another syringe of Angio-Conray please." There were four loaded and labeled 50-cc syringes on the back table. She handed him one which he attached and aspirated blood. It had the familiar red billowing appearance. He aspirated a little more. The same. Trying not to appear as disturbed as he was, he loaded the new syringe onto the auto injector, capping the first syringe and putting it on the X-ray table near the senator's knee. Peabody sighed. He felt his pulse surge and noticed a little tremor in his hand as he put on a new pair of gloves. Holding the catheter tightly where it entered the skin he said, "Okay, lights down." His foot was poised over the pedal. "Okay, hold still Mr. Jones . . . Shoot."

Compressed gas fired the syringe and drove the liquid into Bradford's carotid artery. An incredible, searing headache occurred instantly and disappeared after a few seconds. Machines above his head and at his side went ker-chunk, ker-chunk, ker-chunk every second. In twenty seconds it was over.

"Alright Mr. Jones, you can relax now. That wasn't so bad, was it?"

"Not too bad," lied the senator, hoping that the test was over. Peabody had seen a large tumor on the screen. He would wait for the films, but he knew the injection was a good one. And he was glad to hear the senator respond in a firm voice.

Over the next half hour Peabody maneuvered the catheter into two other vessels and took three more shots. If Flint noticed anything out of the ordinary he didn't give any sign. He stood behind Peabody, never speaking. When he was satisfied with the quality of the films, Peabody directed the new orderly to help Mr. Jones onto a gurney and they disappeared down the hall, followed by Flint.

When they were gone Peabody took the suspect syringe into the prep room. He squirted the fluid, which was now uniformly darkly stained, into a small metal bowl.

"Beverly, what is this stuff? It doesn't look like contrast to me."

"No, it doesn't," said Beverly swirling the liquid in the bowl. "It smells like airplane glue."

Peabody sniffed the bowl, then took some of the liquid on his finger and held it to his nostril. "This is acetone! What the hell are we doing with a syringe full of acetone?"

"I don't know," said Beverly. We used some on the last case to take off adhesive tape. That new orderly was setting up the tray."

"Do you realize we almost injected 50 cc of acetone into the brain of Senator John Bradford? Christ!"

"Senator Bradford?"

"Yes. That was the patient we just studied. Acetone, can you imagine?" Peabody was shaking.

"Senator Bradford. Oh my God. I'll call that orderly in here right away."

"No, don't say anything about it." Peabody poured the liquid down the sink, rinsing out the bowl. "There's enough trouble with that secret service man. It's just a lucky thing I caught it. Don't say anything to any one about this, understand?"

* * * *

Ingram didn't scrub on the baby shunt. He just came into the OR and looked over Adams' shoulder, contributing a few comments and suggestions. He left before the skin was closed. "Dan, would you mind talking to the parents of this baby for me?"

"I'd be glad to, sir."

"And there's a neonatal fellow over there. Ramsey or something like that. He seemed to be very interested."

"No problem," said Adams, starting on the skin sutures. Ingram left and Adams finished tying the first prolene. "Come on Burleson, cut. Keep your head in the game."

Burleson jerked into attention, and cut the suture a quarter inch from the knot. He had, indeed, been daydreaming. Or more accurately he had been thinking about this little patient and what they were trying to accomplish. Adams seemed to read his mind.

"You know, shunts for hydrocephalus are one thing, but these premies with the big bleeds can have a lot of brain damage. This kid should have a pretty good result. He doesn't have too much atrophy and the bleed was almost all in the ventricle." Both residents were tired, but doing most of the pinealoma had Adams on a high. Burleson's morning mistakes seemed to be forgotten. Burleson was pleased. It was unusual for Adams to volunteer conversation.

61

"Why do we do it if the results are bad? I mean, wouldn't it be better if these kids just died?"

"Probably, but that's the problem. They don't die; they just go on living with a great big head and seizures and squash for brains. So it's good palliation. And it's good treatment for most of them."

"Probably so." Burleson became quiet, thinking about this new responsibility. Three months into his internship, he was so concerned with the facts and the process of medicine that the practicalities still came as a surprise. As Kay extubated the baby he coughed and opened his eyes, then closed them quickly as if frightened by the bright lights. Burleson wondered what the baby was thinking, if anything. What did he make of the three masked creatures bending over him, huge in the baby's frame of reference, the glaring lights, the pain in his head. Was all this imprinting into a memory channel somewhere? What happens to all the input of infancy? Never recorded? Unlikely. But recorded in what language? Or accessible in what language? Sensations recorded without an identifying code. Like a book stuck in a library with no call number. You'd never find it unless you just happened to be looking through the stacks.

"Do you think this kid will remember any of this?" asked Burleson,

"No," answered Adams. "Do you remember being a neonate?"

"No, but maybe that's because I couldn't talk."

"What do you mean?" They were both helping Kay move the baby back into the isolette which had been plugged in in the hall to keep it warm. Burleson was protecting the precarious IV in the baby's hand.

"I mean, we think in words, so maybe I can't remember anything because I didn't know the language."

Adams paused, leaning on the isolette. Perhaps there was hope for Burleson after all. "Well, Randy, that's an interesting idea."

"I mean, maybe it's stored away and only comes out as a dream or a hallucination." Burleson was surprised that Adams took any interest. Or just a sensation." he added. He looked at the baby. "This would be a pretty frightening experience."

"Well I was born as a breech and I have a morbid fear that a doctor is going to grab me by my bare bottom" said Kay, looking at Adams.

"Freud said that fears are secret wishes," said Adams, nudging against her shoulder.

"Oh doctor," she said sweetly, and rubbed against his shoulder. "Can you help me work out my phobias?"

"I can young lady," Adams replied in a mock German accent, "but the therapy could take many sessions."

"Whatever you say, Herr Doctor." OR flirting was standard practice, especially for Kay, but as he watched her, Burleson remembered that he hadn't had a date for two months, and was definitely horny. Adams, who rarely revealed any external evidence of wit or emotion, murmured something to himself and smiled at Kay.

"Look Burleson, why don't you check on Rothstein and get the lab data. Miss Lawson and I will take this baby back to neonatal."

"Try not to frighten him," said Burleson, grinning, and thinking that Adams was basically human after all.

CHAPTER 5

Anne recognized the etude for piano as Chopin, distorted as it was through the small speaker of the hospital radio. Soaring high and settling gracefully. Jean-Christophe had described it as poetry. Parts like sentences which start and wind, weave and stretch, and then resolve. Two or three or five parts of different length and color and texture and taste. So transparent yet so full. Each word-note carefully chosen to be the one unexpected. Each phrase woven to the next to make a part, then a period. Then a breath. Then another part, until the idea feels complete. Hence not a paragraph or a sonnet but a free, form poem. Definitely Chopin.

In 1974, during her second year as a cardiac ICU nurse at Georgetown, Anne took care of the French ambassador after a mitral valve replacement. That was how she met his son, Jean-Christophe, and he was why she moved to Paris in 1975. They shared a lovely apartment on the Isle St. Louis. For the first two years they thought they were in love. Jean-Christophe was a cellist who studied at the Paris Conservatoire, and they lived in company of serious musicians—and serious musicians in Paris love Chopin.

When the new wing of the Longwood Hospital was built, the company selling the wall-mounted headboards included an FM radio in the electronic gadgetry, a bid to further woo a hospital buyer. It was the cause of considerable discussion at the Board of Trustees Meeting, but Anne Bradford didn't know that. To her it was simply an alternative to silence, waiting for her husband to return from Radiology. Some thought had gone into making this institutional hospital room seem like something else. Soft colors. Natural wood. Indirect lighting falling on a framed Utrillo print on the wall. Still it was a hospital room and she sat, uneasily, waiting anxiously and thinking about nothing in particular. Until the Chopin.

Because Chopin always reminded her of Donald Ingram, she chuckled at the irony of it.

How long ago was it? Fourteen, fifteen years? There was a fragmentary image of a young pianist who played Chopin all through their dinner at a little Beacon Hill restaurant. Notes in her diary recorded that the night of her graduation was the first time she received a dozen roses. The first time she ate sweetbreads, the first time she seriously considered giving up her virginity, and the last time she saw Donald Ingram. She had taken the job in Washington. She had spent a few weeks hurting, a few months tearing up unsent and unopened letters, and finally the whole episode became one of the coals that keeps a warm spot warm. Brought occasionally to consciousness carefully for analysis and re-filing, and occasionally unexpectedly, in a dream, or fanned by Chopin.

A memory—no, a pleasant memory, why not, she had convinced herself. But no more than that. Her marriage was very secure. Rumors of the senator's affairs were just political gossip. Trips away and lonely hours were worth it—part of the job. Their life had been on as much of an even keel as could be expected, until it had been turned upside down by the events of the last few months. The seizures, the paranoia, the security, the ever-present risk of brain damage, or death. The fact that the best neurosurgeon in the country happened to be Donald Ingram was just a happy coincidence. Friendly, but professional. He probably didn't remember it anyway. She thought about turning off the radio, then decided against it, trying again to concentrate on the novel in her lap.

As was his habit, Ingram knocked on the door as he entered, so that he was well into the room when she looked up. She seemed a little surprised.

"I thought your husband would be back from X-ray by now. I was expecting to face that insufferable bodyguard. What a very pleasant surprise."

"Hello Don." The smile, which Ingram thought incredible. "John's been gone for almost two hours. I hope everything is all right."

"I'm sure it is. It's just an arteriogram." A warm pause—long enough for two deep breaths.

"Did you arrange the Chopin?"

"Do you like it?"

"Very much."

"Then I'll take credit for it."

"Last night I . . ."

"Don, I wish . . ."

They started speaking at the same time, then paused, then started again. Ingram smiled and took a step closer.

"Anne, sometime I'd like to ask you about . . . about the old days. But the walls around here have ears, not to mention the nurses . . ."

"And the doorman," she added.

"Especially the doorman. He's taking his job very seriously." They were both amused by the protective portly Mr. Duffy.

"But I still have questions. Can we have dinner one of these nights soon?"

"Well, I suppose I owe you some answers. But Don I don't think—"

"Good. Tomorrow night then."

She put her hand on his arm to soften her refusal. "Sometime, maybe, but not while . . ." Before she could continue a nurse came through the door pulling a gurney, followed by Flint and an orderly. Anne pulled her hand back, and stood quickly.

"Oh good," said Bradford cheerfully. "My wife and my surgeon, all the people I need to see. Dr. Peabody sure knows how to give a fellow a headache." The gurney was rolled into position next to the bed and Bradford slid over, despite the protestation of the nurse who was trying to keep a heavy sand bag in position over the puncture wound in his groin. "You two look like you swallowed the Cheshire cat. Do you know something about the arteriogram? What is it?"

Anne looked aside and started a little gesture, but Ingram focused only on the mental connections indicated by the mixed metaphor. "Actually Senator, I haven't seen the arteriogram yet. You look like you survived it though."

"I did, but I certainly got a hot ache . . . hot . . ." He looked flustered and pointed to his head. "Hot headache I was trying to say . . ." He pointed again.

"Yes I know," said Ingram. "And how did the films look to you, Mr. Flint?"

"Good afternoon Dr. Ingram" responded Flint, ignoring the question. "Good afternoon Mrs. Bradford, is everything satisfactory at the Longwood Towers?"

"Yes thank you Mr. Flint. Quite satisfactory."

"Is it private enough?" asked Bradford suddenly.

"Why yes, John." She seemed taken aback. "It's fine."

"You can't be too careful Anne. You'd better check. You'd better check it out."

He pulled her close and said in a coarse whisper, "They're here too, you know. They've followed us from Washington." She appeared embarrassed, glancing about the room.

"John, we've been over this. Nobody is trying to—"

"Dammit Anne, don't correct me," he snapped glaring at her. He clutched at his head.

"John," she said with controlled irritation. "John, I'm not correcting you. I'm just pointing out—"

"Yeah, yeah," he cut her off with a wave of his hand. "Damn this hurts."

"I'll get you some medication, then I'll check your arteriograms," said Ingram, anxious to leave. "I'll be back later."

"Goob, good, goob" muttered Bradford, eyes tightly shut, grimacing.

"Thank you Don" said Anne, moving away from the bed and guiding him to the door. "John hasn't been quite himself lately. He could use something for pain." Now they were out of earshot.

"I'll order something right now. And tomorrow night?"

She hesitated again, and glared back over her shoulder at Bradford. "Well . . ." she sighed. "Okay. Sure. Tomorrow night."

* * * *

Paul Ramsey had a good case of the September resident doldrums. He had been hard at work for two and a half months learning

68

the new system, saving lives, losing sleep, and no one seemed to care except him. He recognized the symptoms, because he had lived through the same phenomenon as an intern, a resident, and two years in solo pediatric practice. Now, as one of the two neonatal fellows in the Longwood Hospital program, he was low man on the totem pole once again. Although he had known it would happen, the fact that he couldn't communicate with his patients was now starting to bother him. He had been drawn to Pediatrics originally because of a natural rapport with children, and he was a good pediatrician. He had applied for a neonatal fellowship because that was where the scientific action was in pediatrics, but he missed talking to kids more than he thought he would. The nurses and interns and students didn't recognize the September syndrome in Ramsey, because he was so friendly and such a good doctor that the worry didn't show through. But he knew what was going on, and he relied on his wife to cheer him up on the alternate nights when he was home. Besides, he knew the syndrome was self-limiting and he would feel his usual enthusiasm by Christmas.

Part of the problem was being the "boy" again. Last year, as Chief Resident in Pediatrics at Detroit Presbyterian Hospital, he had had his own office and shared a secretary. He had a parking pass and presided at conferences and held his own teaching rounds each week. His chief had given him glowing praise and personally arranged for the neonatal fellowship at the prestigious Longwood. Now he had to prove himself again to a new chief, gain the trust of other attending staff and residents, endure the skeptical looks of seasoned nurses, and the Harvardian perception that anywhere west of Route 128 was cowboy and indian country.

He was down, he realized, because the Wilson baby was dying and there was nothing he could do about it. He had been experimenting with ventilator changes for the last thirty-six hours but there were two steps back for every one forward. He examined a list of jobs on his three-by-five card to see how much he had to do before he could go home. The respiratory therapist handed him a small slip of paper.

"Here are the last gases on Wilson. The CO_2 is down a little bit."

"Fifty-two," he read from the slip. "Is this the first gas after the chest tube?"

"Yes. Do you want to go up on the rate? It's eighty now."

Ramsey knew that Hendricks, the neonatal staff on duty, pushed hyperventilation with zeal. But the mean airway pressure was already twenty-two and the air leak would only get worse with higher pressures. "No. Let's hold it there and check it again in an hour or so."

"You're sure?"

Ramsey recognized the condescending tolerance of the respiratory therapist and knew that he would ask Hendricks when he returned from supper. He stifled the impulse to be dictatorial, and then tried to explain instead. "Yes. If we go up on the rate the air leak will get worse and we'll never be able to blow off the CO_2. Let's wait for the post-tube chest X-ray."

The respiratory therapist shrugged, grunted, and put the blood gas slip in his pocket after making a note on the clipboard. Seeing the neurosurgery resident in the hall with an isolette, Ramsey left the ICU.

"That didn't take long at all. I thought this baby would be in the OR 'til ten. You must be slick."

"We do a lot of shunts," explained Adams, deadpan. He recognized Ramsey vaguely as one of the new neonatal fellows, but they hadn't formally met.

"He goes down here," said Ramsey to the shapely brunette pushing the isolette. Her name tag identified her as a nurse anesthetist. They rolled the isolette into the stepdown unit and made all the connections and adjustments without much conversation. After washing his hands, Ramsey reached through the port holes and checked the new IV, raising both eyelids with his thumb and palpating the fontanelle with his middle finger, reflexively, without really thinking about it. Adams noticed this, and decided that the new neonatal fellow knew what he was doing.

"His pressure's down now. We took a little fluid off," said Adams, looking up from the chart where he was finishing his note. "I've written the post-op orders. We'll keep up the antibiotics for two days. And Dr. Ingram likes to keep these babies well hydrated."

"Thanks. I'll check them over."

Adams closed the chart and handed it to Ramsey. "Check them as much as you want, just don't change them." It wasn't a joke or a challenge, just a matter-of-fact statement. Irritating to Ramsey, but nothing to generate a confrontation.

"Right," said Ramsey. "It's really a nice job," he added, looking at the two small incisions, neatly sutured and covered with collodion. In Detroit the shunt babies had come back with a big head dressing that always fell off or slipped.

"Would you mind talking to the family?" said Adams. "Tell them the operation went perfectly. The shunt will relieve the pressure but won't change any brain damage that's already occurred. Dr. Ingram will see them tomorrow."

"I'll tell them."

Adams nodded and turned to leave, followed by the brunette who had been going over sheets with the bedside nurse.

"Thanks a lot."

"Any time," said Adams over his shoulder.

Paul Ramsey checked the IV again, read the op note and reviewed the postoperative orders, which were perfect. "That looks nice, doesn't it?" he said to the bedside nurse, indicating the small incision.

"That's the way they always look," said the nurse. "Ingram is fantastic." She thought for a moment. "The residents are a little abrupt, but Ingram is fantastic."

"I see what you mean." Ramsey put his index finger in the miniature hand, trying to elicit a response. "Well little guy, your headache should be a lot better and if you don't bleed again, you might grow up to be a neurosurgeon. Would you like that?" If the baby was receiving and imprinting, he didn't show it.

* * * *

Although he didn't realize it, Randy Burleson was learning to be a good intern. It was not his grasp of facts and theories and drug dosages; he came equipped with those. Nor was it the experience to sense postoperative infection two days before the fever, or the confidence to give knowledgeable advice to cancer patients, or the global perception to conceive an operation from beginning to end; those would come later. But the ability to prioritize mundane jobs, to call

71

admitting and run the lab computer and write a workup all at the same time, the skill to get IVs into elusive eighty-year-old veins in twenty seconds—all of that he was learning, and learning well. Whatever thoughts he had about memory processes in the neonate were soon set aside when he left the OR and dug into his scut list, carefully detailed in the service notebook.

Teaching rounds were always held on Monday evenings, whenever they finished the schedule. Tonight it was 6:30—earlier than usual. Burleson had gobbled down two Almond Joys, but that only stimulated his hunger. He called down to reserve four late meals because he knew they would still be rounding when the dining room closed at 8:00. Waiting for Ingram and Adams in the 9 North nursing station, he collected the information from the three medical students, transferring it from their clipboards to the blue scut book.

"Now look," he addressed the students. "You can present the patients on rounds if you don't take too long, and I'll back you up. But don't gun me down in front of the big professors. If I say the hematocrit is thirty-two it's thirty-two. Got it?" The students nodded. Soon Mike Comstock, the third-year neurosurgery resident, appeared, followed by Adams and Sven Nordstrom, a neurosurgeon visiting from Sweden. Ingram walked up at 6:35, looking unusually cheerful.

"Good afternoon everybody. Did you get that shunt finished up all right?"

"Yes sir. Dr. Ingram, these are our new M3s, Roger Claypool and Lisa Raymond. They'll be with us for three weeks. And you know Paul Miller, our M4." He turned to the new students. "Usually you'll present the cases on rounds but since you just came on the service, Paul and Randy will do the presenting today, so speak up if you have a question. We'll do 9 North, then the ICU, then pediatrics and finish in X-ray. Let's go."

The group, along with Sally Robson, the charge nurse, made quite an entourage. In the first room Burleson greeted the patient first, then addressed the group. "Mrs. White is six days post-laminectomy for an L5 disc. She's afebrile, eating well, and her wound looks good. She's going home tomorrow morning."

Ingram turned to the third-year students. "Dr. Raymond, would you examine Mrs. White and tell us about the L5 nerve root?" The student looked terrified. It was her second clinical rotation. The first had been radiology and psychiatry.

"I'm not sure. Doesn't that have to do with the dermatomes?"

"In part. Did you study the nervous system in Anatomy?"

"Yes, but that was two years ago, I sort of forgot." Her lip quivered and her neck flushed.

Ingram turned to the M4. Paul Miller had been on the service for three weeks and had been well coached by Adams. "Mrs. White, I'm just going to examine your legs for a minute," Miller said promptly at the cue from Ingram. He took the sheet off her feet, covering her carefully at mid thigh. "Close your eyes please, and say 'now' when I touch you." She complied and responded appropriately as he rolled a little pinwheel over her legs and feet, first one side then the other. "Now hold your toes up for me." Mrs. White, who had been through this many times, was also well coached. She tried to raise her toes against Miller's grasp. The right went up easily but the left did not. "Now just relax your legs and let me test your reflexes." He pushed up on the ball of her foot gently and tapped behind her heel with a small hammer. The right responded briskly but the left did not. Miller, who knew what he was going to find because he had done the same exam a few hours earlier, declared, "There's still evidence of nerve root involvement on the left."

"So there is. Dr. Miller, that was a good exam. Mrs. White, you're still going to have some trouble walking, but it should get better over the next month or two."

"Can I still go home tomorrow, Dr. Ingram?"

"Of course. Now I'd like Dr. Raymond here to examine you also, alright?"

The patient nodded. Lisa Raymond had been so intimidated by the initial question that she had not observed the M4's exam very carefully. Her hands shook as she reached into her fresh white coat and produced a large reflex hammer. Adams looked at Comstock who closed his eyes and nodded, almost imperceptibly. The professor was in a mood to teach. It was going to be a long rounds.

By 8:00 they had finished 9 North and they followed Adams down the stairs and into the surgical intensive care unit. For the new students, this was the first visit to intensive care unit. The residents had forgotten how impressive and intimidating that first exposure could be. First, there was the smell. Neither a good nor a bad smell, but characteristic of ICUs. Some combination of Cidex and soap and tissue smells and the linen cart. You couldn't identify it exactly, but it was distinctly an ICU. Then the low hubbub of hushed conversation, the continuous beeps, the drones, the alarms, the whooshes and zephyrs of compressed gas—all combined to make the low roar that eventually became interpreted as silence in this big room. Then the atmosphere. A sort of controlled frenzy, calmer than might be expected, with a battalion of young women in blue scrub suits attending the twelve patients stretched out in cubicles along the far wall. They walked to bed 3, the wide-eyed M3s edging up slowly to the rest of the group. Kathleen Dugan's mother was standing at the bedside, as she had most of the time for the last three days. The bedside nurse, a chubby redhead identified as Michelle by her name tag, approached her.

"Would you wait outside for a few minutes Mrs. Dugan? The doctors are going to make rounds." Mary Dugan complied, but Ingram noticed that she was beginning to show the inevitable ambivalence of the ICU patients and families—grateful for the care, but sometimes resenting the caregivers.

CHAPTER 6

The comment about Captain Michael Dugan, whenever the subject was raised on the street or around the precinct or (more recently and more frequently) around City Hall was, "Mike Dugan is not your average cop." He was, first of all, a college man—graduated from Northeastern and the first of three generations of South Boston Dugans to have that distinction. Second, he was a singer of merit. Not just another tenor working at "The Rose of Tralee," but a member of the Handel and Haydn Society and twice a soloist with the Framingham Chamber Players. And then there were his three children. Pat, a senior at Dartmouth, was being discussed as a tight end of all-American potential. Meagan worked in Washington, on Senator Kennedy's staff. And Kathleen, smart and lovely, and the favorite of all of them—no one too proud to admit it.

Michael Dugan had a lot of sensitive side, but he was still a tough cop. Fair, honest, street wise, and intelligent, but tough. But coming into Longwood Hospital, early in the morning and late at night, he didn't feel tough. He had certainly spent his share of time in hospitals. In the carnival of the City Hospital Emergency Room with its smell of cheap wine vomitus and the unforgettable sounds of young men shot through the chest, old men gurgling to death, and women in labor. The waiting room of the old Lying-in, where he had paced nervously and smoked cigarettes while Mary, without benefit of Lamaze classes, and laced with doses of scopolamine and Demerol and Trilene, had managed to produce three healthy, well-adjusted children. The recovery room of the Beth Israel, where last month he had questioned the wounded proprietor of Kenmore Liquor, his pain measured in "Oi's." The Children's—so respected it was almost sacred—where Pat had spent two months in traction after his femur fracture. The old Brigham where, as a college student, he had been called to donate blood (for one of those rarely discussed radiated transplant recipients), and had slipped upstairs to get a glimpse of Robert Frost. That had turned out to be the day before the poet died. And of course the Longwood, where Mary had her thyroid operation, where he had visited the chief of police suffering from hemorrhoids, and where he had consoled bereaved families following accidents and assaults.

The consoling didn't seem to do much good now.

The familiar trip through the lobby, up the elevator to the eighth floor, and to the intensive care unit was a little more painful each time because the news was always the same, never good. Mary spent hours just holding Kathleen's limp hand. She had essentially camped out in the ICU waiting room, befriending the other families and sharing their worry. Michael, on the other hand, spent less and less time visiting, after that first tedious night. He found excuses to delay his visits and invented reasons to leave early. It wasn't that he didn't care—oh, he cared to the very center of his big heart—he just couldn't tolerate his own helplessness. He found Mary in the waiting room.

"Hello deary, how's it going tonight?"

"Michael, it's 8:15. Pat and Meagan both called. Where have you been?"

"I'm sorry Mary. Life goes on out there."

She shrugged. She looked haggard and sleepless. Some of her softness had eroded away, exposing the bones of impatience. "They just kicked me out of there again," nodding down the hall. "I stayed there all day so I could talk to the damn doctors and when they come, they shoo me out. This is the first time that Dr. Ingram has been in today, Michael, the first time. And the nurse this morning was so snippy. I have a right to be in there Michael. It's my daughter." Tears might have come if she were not so angry.

"She's my daughter too." Big hands holding her gently by the shoulder, trying to console her.

"Oh Michael, I know. It's just getting to me tonight." She sniffed, sighed, and looked in her purse for a fresh Kleenex. "Nothing's changed really. She looks like she's asleep, hooked up to all those machines and tubes. And people are doing the best they can, I suppose."

"What did Pat say?"

"Oh he's very worried. He talked about coming home again but I told him to stay at school. There is nothing he can do. There is nothing any of us can do."

"That's good. I'll call him back tonight." They lapsed into private thoughts, sitting now on the orange vinyl chairs. He wondered if the other families had overheard their conversation. By now he didn't care.

A nurse appeared at the door. "The visitors for Kathleen Dugan and Mr. Rothstein can come back in now. Dr. Adams said that he'll be back to talk to you as soon as they've finished their rounds." She left without waiting for a response. First to the door was Ravikrishnan, but he stepped aside for Mrs. Dugan, bowing slightly.

Kathleen looked, as described by her mother, to be asleep. The swelling around her eyes had subsided. The nurse had pulled her hair back into a ponytail and fixed it with a length of umbilical tape, which served the purpose well. (Among the many things Mary Dugan had learned about in the last few days was Umbo tape—a heavy twill ribbon used originally to tie the umbilical cord in the delivery room, now the universal fixit in the ICU—the baling wire of high-tech medicine.) A yellow plastic feeding tube entered her right nostril.

"She's lost weight," observed Michael, feeling the arm which had recently been so full of life.

"Yes." Mary bent forward, close to Kathleen's ear. "Kathleen. Your father's here. Kathleen, wake up and say hello to Dad." Michael glanced about, embarrassed by his wife's obviously nonproductive behavior. He said nothing however. "Kathleen, Dad's here. We're both here."

Professor Ravikrishnan had been sitting by the bedside of Ben Rothstein since he had returned from the recovery room two hours ago. Aside from his unusually strenuous breathing, Rothstein had not moved, and his friend was becoming anxious. He had said nothing except hello to the nurse, who seemed to spend most of her time helping to turn the young man in the bizarre-looking bed in the adjacent cubicle. So Ravikrishnan had said nothing, but now sought the young lady's attention. "Excuse me, Miss."

"Yes sir." She seemed pleasant enough. He was already embarrassed for distracting her.

"My friend here had a neurosurgical operation today. He seems to be very sleepy. Is that normal?"

"Oh sure." She shook the somnolent patient by the shoulder. No response. She rubbed her knuckle into his breastbone. "Mr. Rothstein?" He grunted slightly and pulled his arm toward his chest. "He's okay. Sometimes these cranies don't wake up for awhile."

"Cranies?"

"Craniotomies. Neurosurgical operations. His numbers are just fine," she volunteered, scanning the bedside sheet. "Why don't you go on home? You can come in tomorrow morning any time after ten."

"Thank you, Miss." He was much relieved. "I'll do that. Thank you again." She returned to helping her colleague with the quadriplegic. Buoyed by the good news, he stopped by the foot of Kathleen Dugan's bed on his way to the door.

"Excuse me Mrs. Dugan. I'm leaving now and I wanted to thank you for your directions earlier on. My friend is still sleeping." He looked kindly toward the old man in the first bed. "I hope the morning brings good news for both of us." Bowing again slightly, he turned toward the door. The Dugans mumbled their goodnights. They returned their attention to the girl lying in the bed. Their nurse was off on an errand.

"Come on Michael, sing again. I know she hears you. She squeezed my hand. Sing again."

He leaned over close to her ear, adjusting the makeshift ponytail.

"I peeked in to say goodnight,
then I heard my child in prayer.
And for me some scarlet ribbons,
scarlet ribbons . . ."

he faltered.

"scarlet ribbons for my hair," sang Mary Dugan softly.

* * * *

At 5:55 he awoke, as he always did, and reached up to turn off the alarm which would have rung at 6:00. The fog had the rosy glow of impending dawn. Ingram stretched and took inventory. No calls during the night. Laminectomy scheduled for 8:00, some meeting at noon, lecture to M3s at 2:00. Why did he feel like it was Christmas morning? Tuesday night! Dinner with Anne.

He pulled up the blanket and closed his eyes, letting his mind run the memory again. Over the years he had almost forgotten her. At first he had repressed the thought to prevent the pain. Then she appeared in his consciousness less frequently, then almost not at all. He had watched his own mind do this, grateful for the neurophysiologic mechanism by which time heals all wounds, and he let her go. Until last weekend, when her husband became his patient. Since then he had found himself recalling minute details. The first meeting of their eyes—those sparkling blue eyes—across the bed of a little girl. He was a junior resident. She was a senior nursing student. As if it were today, he imagined every crease in her blue pin-stripped uniform, the stethoscope resting on the white apron, the starched white student's cap on her perfect blond hair, the dimples (now he remembered the dimples). The rest of the world had stopped as they stared at each other. He remembered it as a full minute.

He played through long-forgotten scenes—kissing passionately on the stairwell; standing close enough to touch as Eastman and the senior residents examined patients on rounds; cuddling nervously behind the unlockable door of the call room; sneaking out to Jack and Marian's for lunch; clandestine one-ring phone calls. Clandestine because she had two curious, gossipy roommates in the dorm and he had a wife and two young children. His reverie was nudged aside by a full bladder.

He felt his way instinctively down the dark hallway, flipped on the bathroom light switch (outside the door, as they used to do in New England), and squinted at the bright light as his eyes tried to accommodate. In a series of automatic motions he turned on the shower to warm it up, flipped on the fan, loaded his tooth brush, and stood still, brushing with one hand and aiming into the white toilet bowl with the other.

He wondered if she was having any of the same thoughts. She had seemed so proper. Friendly, but proper. Of course her husband was always there, and the residents and nurses, and the ever-observant Flint. He rehearsed all he planned to tell her tonight, then wondered if he should. Would she be only tolerant, maybe even offended? Did she remember their affair—he had begun to think of it with that word—fondly or bitterly? After all, she had ended it without a word. Did she remember it at all?

In the shower he made practical plans. They would go L'Argent; would she remember? Should he send her flowers? Roses again? No, way too much. Should he dig out those returned letters buried in the back of a folder in the back of a file drawer in the bottom of a cabinet in the lab? Of course not. He decided that he would, however, drive via romantic Commonwealth Avenue rather than the more expedient Storrow Drive. And he would arrange for some Chopin.

Out of the shower he took stock of his trim body and the little roll at his sides. Not too bad, he thought, then rebuked himself for letting his thoughts get ahead of him. A married woman. Senator's wife. A patient's wife, for Christ's sake.

"Settle down, jerk," he said aloud, looking sternly at the face reflected in the shaving mirror.

CHAPTER 7

Musty! The odor was definitely slightly musty. A little mold combined with dust and, yes, a faint electric motor smell. He noticed it as soon as he walked from the kitchen into the main dining room.

"Simpson!"

A young man with a mustache the color of straw was folding heavy linen napkins in the shape of fans. He looked up. "Yes Mr. Galletti?"

"Did you vacuum the carpet this afternoon?"

"Of course. I just finished."

"You didn't change the bag in the vacuum cleaner, did you?"

"Well no sir, but—"

"Simpson, do you like working here?" Galletti's voice was low, and rich with an accent which seemed to be a combination of French and Italian (Du yu layk wearking heeah?). Simpson started to respond, but was interrupted. "These are simple steps, simple steps. You must be able to follow simple directions. Always put a clean bag in the vacuum cleaner. Always. Now, light two candles to dispel this awful odor and be sure to replace them with fresh candles before the guests come. Do you understand?"

"Yes sir. Right away sir."

Taking one of the napkins from the pile, Galletti polished the lids of the three huge silver chafing dishes against the wall near the door. Soon these were to hold the specially-seasoned Swedish meatballs, the fresh brandied peaches swimming in warm champagne, and the lobster bisque for which the restaurant was so widely known. The chafing dishes were set on a high sideboard of walnut-stained mahogany that was almost black. The same dark wood made up the wainscoting throughout the room. It would have been a dark and foreboding place were it not for the ivory-colored walls above the wainscoting and the brickwork which made up the serving areas and planters dividing the tables. Silver fittings were tastefully placed throughout the room, supplying both the trademark and the name of the restaurant for the past sixty years: L'Argent.

He completed his tour through the main dining room, small private booths, and the two upstairs board rooms reached by the staircase from the lobby. The banister spiraled around three quarters of the room, a swooping carving of the same dark wood which ended in the massive, silver-plated newel post covered with silver plate. As everything seemed to be in order, he returned to the kitchen to remind the sous-chef that the tarragon must be soaked before chopping, to add depth to the sauce Béarnaise. In the meat locker he squeezed the ducklings and found them firm and meaty, not too greasy. The salad cook, wiping his hands on his fresh apron, sought him out.

"Excuse me Mr. Galletti. Telephone call for you."

"Alloo?"

"Henri. This is Donald Ingram. I'll be dining with you tonight."

"Ah mon ami. Quelle plaisir! I saw your name on our list. I have just examined the board room and it's ready for you."

"Thank you Henri, but this is not my usual group. I'm coming with one special friend and we need some privacy. Is your little private room off the main dining room available?"

"For you, Dr. Ingram, I will make it available," said Henri, who had already scanned the reservation list and knew that there was no request for the private alcove. "Are there any special arrangements I can make for you?"

"Do you have a pianist tonight?"

"Mai oui, and the piano is just outside the private alcove. Shall I have it moved? It may be too noisy for you."

"Oh no, that's perfect. Perhaps you could just ask the pianist to play a lot of Chopin. Whatever he likes, but Chopin would be wonderful."

"Chopin it shall be. And do I detect that this might be a lady friend? Forgive my presumption, but we happen to have some extra roses and they are lovely this evening."

82

"It is an old friend, Henri, who happens to be a lady. Don't overdo it, but some roses would be nice. I shall see you about 8:00."

"Until then."

Henri Galletti took great pride in doing things well. Whether it was folding a napkin or serving a Grand Mariner soufflé, it pleased him to think that no one in the world could do it better. This attention to detail and personal compulsion to excellence had kept him in the very successful position of maitre d' and night manager at L'Argent for eleven years. He returned to the dining room where he made a few notes in the reservation book, left a message for the pianist so he would not forget, removed two of the four chairs from the private alcove and drew the red velvet curtain inside the window which closed the view from the other diners. He put the heavy silver ice bucket in the little room, checked for dust on the leather-bound books on the shelves (there was none), and put the remaining roses—six in all—in the silver vase on the table.

* * * *

Mabel Craig's glasses—proper reading glasses with metal frames—hung from her neck, suspended from an ornate cord, attached with silver clips, and perched on the large sloping shelf that was her matronly bosom, now covered by a crisp orange smock. She fetched the glasses to look at her watch, revealing the "Friends of Longwood" embroidered in blue thread where the glasses had been. She wore a small gold watch with no numbers, because she thought it made her look younger and sophisticated, but she needed the glasses to read the watch. Her white hair, lined face, and forty extra pounds bespoke her age, but her manner was undeniably Bostonian aristocratic. Peering through the glasses she determined that it was 4:35, then returned the glasses to her chest, holding them carefully all the while with her thumb and forefinger, little finger extended, the way she held her teacup. Being a shop clerk for salary would be unthinkable, of course, but volunteering a half day every week in the Longwood Hospital Gift Shop gave her a sense of fulfillment and dignity, although the irony of this situation never occurred to her. Dignity or not, 4:35 was close to closing time and, like any shop clerk, she had begun to look at her watch at ten-minute intervals.

Because of this, she knew that the tall, blond woman had been in the shop for twenty minutes, moving slowly from the silk scarves to the flowers in the refrigerated cabinet to the toiletries (she had sprayed a puff of "Night Song" on her wrist and registered distaste) to the novels with slick covers to the stuffed bears and rainbow stickers, and back to the scarves. The woman looked somehow familiar to Mabel Craig. She was obviously preoccupied and simply spending time—as people do in hospital gift shops—so, although they had exchanged properly sweet smiles a few times, Mabel did not interrupt her meandering. The woman was wearing a conservative beige silk suit with the hem cut low, narrow at the waist. Her shoes and purse, and the scarf sticking from her pocket, were exactly the same shade of copper, duly noticed by the portly Mrs. Craig. When the woman leaned over to pick up a newspaper, her skirt pulled tight against her long legs and round bottom, which so impressed the resident who happened to be buying candy at the counter at the time that Mabel had to regain his attention by reciting the price twice. Not at all embarrassed, and pursing his lips in response to a silent thought, he produced two wadded-up dollars for the Paydays and Lifesavers, and continued to admire the silk skirt again while Mabel made change.

Anne Bradford picked up *Yachting* magazine and *The Washington Post* and brought them to the counter, ignoring the direct and appreciative gaze of the resident.

"Two fifty," said Mabel, taking stock of the Gucci emblem and noting the sizable diamond on her customer's ring finger. They exchanged proper smiles again, and the blond woman left. Mabel watched her cross the lobby to the elevator, thinking that she looked very familiar indeed.

In the elevator Anne scanned the first three pages and the government news section looking for mention of her husband's disappearance from the Senate. There was none. Bracing herself for the unpredictable mood of her husband and the compulsory salutation to Flint, she walked into the room. "Good afternoon Mrs. Bradford. We've been waiting for you," said Flint.

"Mr. Flint," was her acknowledgment, holding up the magazine and the newspaper, knowing that he would ask to see them. "Hi John." Anne kissed her husband lightly and noticed that he appeared nervous. "I thought you might still be in the magnetic scanner, so I stopped in the gift shop." He nodded, taking the newspaper from her hand.

From his seat at the desk, Flint watched. Anne was perched at the edge of the bed, her gaze intent on her husband's face, as he impatiently rifled through the paper. She seemed tense, Flint thought. He was not surprised. Bradford's behavior was erratic. Flint realized that anyone would find it hard to make small talk for hours in a hospital room, avoiding discussion of the obvious, ominous problem. Harder still for a couple six years into a marriage, where there is little attempt at conversation at dinner, or in the car. Harder still with an observer—a stranger—silently listening and watching. Flint was obligated to spend time with the senator, it was his job, but he quietly admired Anne's efforts at pleasant affection.

"How did it go today?" she asked.

"Nothing to it. Not like that angiogram anyway. They just roll you into a giant magnet. Kind of interesting." He looked relieved as he put aside the newspaper.

"This might help get your mind off things." She smiled, putting the *Yachting* magazine into his hands on top of the newspaper.

"Oh yeah, that's great," he said enthusiastically. He flipped the pages, stopping at an ad on page twelve. "Anne, when I get out of here let's buy a set of these self-tailing winches for the boat. Remember how that genny sheet fouled last spring? I thought you were going to break your finger."

"And I thought we wouldn't lay the mark, but we did," she laughed. He took her hand, squeezed it, and kissed each finger. She seemed pleased at his attention, but she watched him closely. Bradford looked aside, not at her. Flint thought he observed a sheepish expression on Bradford's face . . . He wondered if Anne suspected this display of affection to be compensation for transgressions, small guilts.

"God, you're a great crew. Best damn crew on Chesapeake Bay. And the best looking too." Bradford held Anne's hand against his cheek and returned to the magazine. "We need some of these Harken blocks," he said. "That mainsheet squeals every time we get close-hauled."

"Maybe we need a new boat. I've been thinking about moving up to a thirty-eight." She quoted the phrase every boat owner recites driving home from the harbor. He laughed aloud. The first time in a week.

"I'll speak to the President about a little raise." They laughed again.

"Oh John, you look good this afternoon," she said, her smile full of relief, and she pulled the chair up to the bed and rested her elbows on the starchy sheet.

"I feel pretty good Anne. I've decided to not let this get me down. I'll just burn through this operation, we'll take a little vacation, and I'll be back on the hill before they ever missed me. I think they are going to ask me to give the nominating speech at the convention next summer, did I tell you that?"

"Several times."

"So it will all work out. But even if it doesn't, I'll just go back to practicing law, or maybe teaching . . ."

"At Harvard?"

"No, in some little town. Amherst, maybe, or Dartmouth. Dr. Ingram was in around noon. He said the arteriogram looked favorable. Apparently this tumor is just where he thought it was and the blood supply is accessible, or something like that. The operation is set for Friday morning. He said I should be home a week or so after that. That's assuming that everything goes alright."

"Oh John, that's great."

"I thought so." He paused, thumbing the magazine. "I like Dr. Ingram, and there is a reason why people say he is the best. At first he seemed a little stiff . . ."

"Like a regular doctor," she conjectured, smiling.

"That's it. I really didn't expect anything else. But he takes the time to explain things and doesn't treat you like a second grader."

"I know," she said. She paused and Flint watched her trying to formulate a question. Flint remembered suddenly the conversation he had overheard between Anne and Ingram, about dinner. "John . . . " she began.

"He's a sailor, did you know?" John continued.

"Who?" Flint thought she looked distracted.

"Ingram. Somehow we got talking about sailing and he turns out to be one of the group. I mean if someone has to be mucking around in my brain it might as well as be a fellow sailor. Maybe that's why I'm feeling better about this whole thing."

"It's good to see you looking more relaxed." She took a breath and looked more serious. "About tonight . . ."

"Oh yes, did Flint tell you? I have to get this done, and tonight seemed the best time to do it."

He smiled and squeezed her hand, somewhat self-consciously.

"Did Mr. Flint tell me what?"

"About the special counsel for the committee. Apparently there is some new information and I have to get a load of work done before the operation. I seem to be thinking more clearly today so I asked Mr. Flint to call . . . to call our special counsel for a meeting this evening. I hope that's okay with you."

"John, you were going to drop all that until this is over, remember?"

"I know Anne, but the world goes on. Besides, it keeps my mind busy. There's less time to worry. You must have things to do. Read a book, or call up old friends for dinner."

Flint watched her pause, start to speak, then pause again. "Which special counsel is coming?"

Bradford hesitated just a second. "Higgins."

"Sara Higgins? That lovely young brunette who kept whispering in your ear at the last hearing?" Her tone was distinctly sarcastic. She was more edgy than she had appeared, thought Flint, surprised that Anne had been able to conceal her feelings as well as she had. Flint's job success depended greatly on his acute capacity to gauge people's emotions—especially the ones they tried to hide.

"It is Sara Higgins, but I hadn't noticed that she was particularly lovely. Is she a brunette?"

"Now I see. You are sending me away so you can have a rendezvous with special counselor Higgins. That's it?" Anne's smile seemed forced, and the atmosphere had changed.

"Yes I am afraid I've been discovered," he said. The guilty smile again.

Anne did not appear nervous, Flint thought. Willpower, self-control, he decided. "Well anything that you and counselor Higgins can do in this hospital bed with Mr. Flint watching is okay with me. And I was thinking about having dinner with an old friend anyway," she said.

"I knew you'd understand."

The door opened and the evening dinner tray arrived. The attendant arranged the tray on the over-bed table and removed the plastic plate cover, exposing a leathery piece of pot roast, some canned peas, and a large glob of instant mashed potatoes. "Shall I pour your gravy, Mr. Jones?" asked the attendant, hand already poised on the little metal cup.

"Please," said Bradford, trying to contain a chuckle as some thick brown substance was unceremoniously dumped on the plate. The tension was broken, and when the attendant had left they both laughed out loud.

"It's plain to see that the kitchen hasn't discovered the identity of the important United States Senator," she commented. "Perhaps you could order a second tray for counselor Sara. Should I send up a bottle of wine and a candle or two?" She was not smiling as she stood and gathered up her purse.

"That would be nice Anne. Some Mogen David '84 should compliment this meal, don't you think?"

He tried to sustain the light mood. "You really don't mind, do you?"

"Of course not. Have a good meeting John. Don't stay up too late."

Outside the hospital the air was cool and smelled of fall but the evening sun was bright. She walked the few blocks back to her apartment. The sun had reached the angle at which the light turns to gold, and the old bricks on the facade of the College of Art seemed to glow like embers. She crossed Brookline Avenue—now packed with traffic all nudging and honking as it is customary to do in Boston. She was so deep in thought that she walked right into a pair of white-coated medical students.

"Oh, excuse me," she said. "My mind was somewhere else."

"No problem," said a student, looking at her intently, as if trying to place a familiar face.

Twice during the day she had picked up the phone to cancel the plans with Ingram. She had put down the phone both times. Now she sighed and walked more briskly.

Mr. Duffy greeted her and escorted her across the lobby. "Oh, Mrs. Bradford, there was a phone call for you this afternoon," he said as they reached the elevator. "You can pick up the message in your room."

Despite the flowers, the magazines, and the wine renewed daily by the Towers staff, after three days it still felt more like a hotel room then a private apartment. She kicked off her shoes and surveyed the few dresses hanging in the closet. She had packed for a week of hospital visits, and not for a social occasion. The beige suite she was wearing would be fine, maybe with the dark blue accessories. The only evening dress was the straight black silk which she always carried because it was light and never wrinkled. But it was bare-shouldered, somewhat revealing, and maybe it was too fancy. The suit would be fine. She flopped on the bed and pushed "message" on the telephone.

"Hello Anne, this is Don. I hope we're still on for tonight. I'll pick you up in the MG at seven thirty. I thought we would go to a little restaurant downtown. It's fairly private and we have so much to talk about—at least I hope we do. So . . . see you tonight. Seven thirty. Bye." The call had come in at four thirty. He had known that she would be in the hospital—no opportunity for rebuttal. It sounded rehearsed—a not too subtle hint of nostalgia, even romance. The MG has two seats, his wife was not invited.

Anne sat on the edge of the bed and listened to the message again. She showered and examined herself in the full-length mirror, standing straighter than usual. "Damn. This is not smart," she said to the face in the mirror. She opted for the black silk.

* * * *

"I suppose this is silly," he began, having completed the polite small talk about the crispness of the evening and about how nice she looked, "but I feel a little like a teenager on his first big date." He was driving on Commonwealth.

"I know what you mean," she said. "I started to tell John that we were going to dinner like two old friends but I felt a little . . . mischievous I suppose."

"You *started* to tell him?"

"Well, something came up. I never got around to it."

"Then perhaps you are anticipating some mischief," he said lightly with a grin.

"I was just telling you how I felt; don't get any ideas," she said curtly. "And I notice you didn't bring Emily along."

"Emily died two years ago."

"Oh Don, I'm sorry, what a terrible thing to say. I didn't know."

"There's no way you would have known. She died of breast cancer. It grows like wildfire in young women, you know. And I am totally adjusted to it now, so don't be sorry. It's just a fact of life." She was silent for minutes as he rounded the Public Garden, nudged in to the left lane, and drove into the underground parking garage.

"I am *so* embarrassed," putting her hands to the side of her head and looking at her knees. "I sounded like a . . . brat."

"It's my fault for teasing you," he said gently. She still looked somber. "And if you feel mischievous, then I'm delighted." He parked the car and opened the door. "Then we can call it a date." As he walked around the car to open her door, her embarrassment gave way to a feeling of sympathy. He helped her out of the car.

"Very well, it's a date. Do I look alright?"

"Fabulous."

The light was changing when they reached Beacon Street and he took her hand as if to help her hurry across, but she withdrew it as they approached L'Argent.

"I knew we were coming here," she said. "I didn't even have to ask."

"I wasn't sure you'd remember."

"I'd never forget. Even the door knocker is the same," she noted, fingering the heavy silver lion's head on the black door. He rapped it down and the door opened.

"Bon soir, Dr. Ingram, I knew it would be you. Always on time, and I see already that the lady is very special." Henri was always very tactful but direct with his observations. Henri and the regular staff knew it had been some time since Ingram's wife had died. In recent years he came to L'Argent only to host a group of stuffy doctors. Henri was obviously pleased as he ushered them in, and Anne nodded politely in acknowledgement of his compliment

Oak and cherry logs—small ones, about five inches in diameter, split once—were burning in the shallow fireplace in the lobby, the flames reflecting off the huge silver balls which topped the andirons. The aroma crossing the lobby was faintly scented with wood smoke and a hint of some dark spice, which was actually the perfume of the hostess standing by the guest book. The hostess was wearing long silver earrings and a silver necklace which emphasized her bare shoulders and the black taffeta gown. "Good evening, doctor," she smiled politely, making a little mark in the book. Henri pulled out the table in the secluded booth while they slid into the seat, which was real leather by the feel of it.

"The roses are lovely," Anne commented, caressing one of the large blooms with her finger.

"May your evening be as lovely," said Henri. "Paul will be your waiter this evening." He signaled almost imperceptibly to a handsome young man in a tuxedo standing nearby. All the attendants were in tuxedos, except for the busboys, who wore black ties and cummerbunds but a shorter jacket cut away above the waist. "Bon appetit mes amies," handing them the leather folders containing the menus. Prices were not listed on the menus. Henri's philosophy was that one should choose the meal for the sake of the food. In the menu given to the head of the party, there was a small card indicating that the prix fixe was ninety dollars per person, including the wine.

Paul signaled the busboy to bring water (with a very thin slice of lime in each goblet) and bread (freshly baked, encradled in a silver bread basket and steamy when he folded back the heavy napkin). There was no offer of cocktails, which would insult the palate— another of Henri's policies.

Henri himself brought a chilled bottle of Bernkastler Reisling which he opened and sampled from his silver spoon. "Very nice," he murmured to himself, and poured for his guests. He didn't offer it for tasting because he had selected it himself and he knew that it was excellent. The wine cellar at L'Argent was large, but the wine list was short. Henri took great personal pride in the wine selection. There were only one or two labels in each category, and the experienced guests soon learned to trust Henri's judgment. The Reisling had just enough fruit in the bouquet to introduce the meal, and it complimented all the hors d'oeuvres, even the Swedish meatballs, which were served next, in a small version of the huge silver chafing dish at the doorway.

"The lobster bisque and Les Peches L'Argent are specialties which come with your meal," Paul explained. "The veal is particularly good tonight and the salmon mousse we are preparing with a hint of dill and sour cream, and baking it in a shell of puff pastry."

"That sounds wonderful Paul. How are the sweetbreads?" asked Anne. Ingram was impressed that she didn't exclaim over the menu or the elegant service, apparently assuming that this is the way a proper restaurant should be.

"The sweetbreads are very light and tender. Fresh today, from Wisconsin. And we are sautéing them lightly with shallots and white wine and presenting them on a bed of wild rice this evening." Coached by Henri, Paul had developed the habit of discussing the menu in the present tense, giving the impression that the chef was, at this very instant, preparing the items of the diners' choice.

"Then I shall surely have to have the sweetbreads," she said to Ingram. "I hope they're as good as the last time we were here."

"Sweetbreads are said to be an aphrodisiac you know," Ingram warned, as he had said at the end of the meal many years before.

"I'll risk it." Bright eyes dancing in the candlelight.

"The sweetbreads for the lady," Ingram said to the waiter, "and I'll have the salmon mousse encroute. The spinach salad, the lobster bisque of course, and we'll begin with a half dozen oysters."

"Oysters are an aphrodisiac you know," she teased him.

"A dozen oysters please Paul . . ."

"An excellent choice, sir," commented the handsome young man who had been slipping glances at the elegant lady and now smiled at her broadly. She sipped her wine and nodded.

"Ask Henri to select a dinner wine for us please, Paul." Paul disappeared, and soon returned with the oysters mounted on a huge silver platter shaped like a shell. Apparently assuming that Ingram would approve, Anne dumped all the horseradish into the cocktail sauce and mixed it with an oyster impaled on a small silver fork. She raised the dripping oyster toward her mouth, hesitated briefly with the hint of mischief in her eyes, and swallowed it slowly. "Delicious," she said.

The dressing for the wilted spinach salad was prepared and flambéed personally by Paul, who brought a small cart with a gas burner and a selection of exotic bottles. The pianist arrived, and began to play just when the cognac and bacon flared up in the brass frying pan, a coincidence which gave a magical quality to the polonaise which followed.

After the lobster bisque—which always drew the comment that it was even better than the lobster bisque at Locke Ober's—the silver plates were borne away and replaced with a subtle lemon-ice sorbet in a small silver cup. They discussed his career, his children now away in college, the tragedy of Emily's terminal illness (he spoke of it with clinical detachment), his laboratory work and his reputation in the neurosciences.

"Now tell me what you've been doing," he said as the main course arrived, implying "since our last meeting" but not saying it. "I think I sent some letters—Georgetown, wasn't it?—but I never got an answer."

"Yes. I worked in the cardiac ICU at Georgetown for a couple of years." She did not address his comment about the letters. "I met a charming French cellist and moved to Paris. I couldn't get a permit to work as a nurse, so I took classes at the Sorbonne. I actually got a degree in International Studies."

"Did you . . . did you live with this French guy?" asked Ingram focusing on the one fact that bothered him. He was surprised at his own possessive reaction.

"Yes."

He looked at her seriously., then aside. "I'm glad I didn't know," he muttered. For a moment all he could imagine was young, innocent Anne and a debonair Frenchman sharing the pleasures of the bed.

"We never married," she said as he looked as if he was trying to raise the next question. "I loved Paris, but after a while Jean-Christophe—that was his name—spent more time with the cello, and with the ladies of the woodwind section, than with me."

"What an idiot," said Ingram.

"I got over it," she said casually. "I got a job at the American Embassy in Paris and came back to work in the State Department. That was in '77. I'm actually the assistant to the deputy undersecretary for health policy."

"Amazing," said Ingram, truly impressed.

"That was how I met John. He was a brilliant young senator—divorced, witty, fun—we've been married six years last July. We've mellowed into a very warm and comfortable, loving relationship."

Ingram noticed her choice of words. "I'm so glad for you," he said sincerely. "Glad for both of you."

"Well, that's the story," she smiled at him with gentle eyes.

An awkward little silence, with sipping of wine. Henri had selected a Concannon Petit Sirah. Robust enough to support the salmon but not enough to overwhelm the sweetbreads like a cabernet might have done.

"John likes you very much."

"And I like him."

"You'd like him better if you'd known him when he was normal. For the last few weeks he's been so edgy—paranoid almost. Effects of the tumor, I suppose."

"Possible, but that would be unusual. The tumor is growing between both frontal lobes. It could certainly have an effect on behavior. Actually he seems fine to me. He's scared about his condition and the operation and the future of his career, but that's normal. Some of the possibilities are frightening."

"Well I haven't been providing very good support, I'm afraid. It's getting so I don't even want to be with him. I shouldn't admit that, it sounds so selfish."

"No, that's normal too. You know him as one person—one set of behavior which represents the workings of his particular mind. A change in the mind causes a change in the person. You're getting some of your old husband and some of someone else. You shouldn't feel guilty about it."

"Today he was great. Back to his old self—laughing and joking and optimistic about the future. He's even back at work. He called a lawyer from Washington to go over some papers this evening."

"I noticed that too. It's probably because the tumor has shrunk a little bit. That can happen after the arteriogram."

"Then removing the tumor will bring him back to normal." It was more of a question then a statement.

"I hope so. It's always somewhat unpredictable." Both were quiet for a moment. She was clearly thinking over his last statement. Ingram had spoken like a doctor, appropriately conservative. Now he realized that she had never thought about the outcome as being anything but perfect.

"You mean it's possible that he could be worse." Another statement question.

"It's possible. It's possible that the tumor is unresectable. But those things are unlikely. He'll probably be just fine." Another contemplative pause. "How are the sweetbreads? As good as the last time?" Her mouth was full and she giggled a little bit, apparently relieved at the overt change the subject, with a reference to their past affair, which seemed to take on a naively youthful perspective.

"The sweetbreads are marvelous. The whole evening has been marvelous. The dinner, the Chopin, the roses, it couldn't be better. What's coming next?"

"Les Peches L'Argent, if Paul finds a break in the conversation. Some of Henri's famous coffee, perhaps a walk on the Common, moon-watching over the harbor, cognac in my library, other assorted mischief."

"Donald Ingram, you are a sentimental romantic and I am going to report you to the Neurosurgical Society. I'll start with Les Peches L'Argent."

The peaches—selected to be just slightly on the green side so as to be firm—were halved, pitted, and soaked overnight in good brandy. (Henri used Christian Brothers. He wouldn't serve it at the table, but for this purpose it was fine.) About four in the afternoon the peaches were drained, then floated in champagne in a big silver chafing dish. A low flame kept it just warm. From time to time he would use apples or pears, even strawberries, but peaches were the best. Paul brought the coffee—mostly French roast with some Colombian ground in— in a tall silver pot with an ebony handle sticking out from the side. Two silver bowls held fluffy whipped cream and little chunks of crystalline rock sugar which looked like diamonds and other gems. Henri served the peaches himself, scooping the treasures from the large chafing dish and bringing them to the table in two silver bowls on the flambé cart. He put a dollop of the whipping cream on a big silver spoon, added just enough high alcohol brandy to float it, ignited the brandy from the gas flame and settled it, flaming, on top of the peach.

"Henri you are an artist!" exclaimed Anne. "This is a truly elegant evening."

"Madame is as kind as she is beautiful," he said to Ingram. Paul nodded, agreeing, and they backed away. As if on cue the pianist returned from a break, and began one of the nocturnes.

Les Peches were better than ever. The warm brandied champagne seemed to be absorbed immediately. She put down her coffee cup, dabbed gently with her napkin, and leaned forward lazily, head down but looking up into his eyes. "I had great reservations about tonight, but it's been wonderful." He felt an engorgement deep in his chest and had to let it pass before he could speak.

"I'm glad you're enjoying it. I was worried about it too. Whether it's the right thing to do and all that. But it's not over yet."

"I know, I'm just giving you a report on the first half. Who says old lovers can't be good friends?" Her eyes were not sparkling now, but half-closed and velvety.

"Who says old *friends* can't be good friends? We were never really lovers." He smiled, looking somewhat embarrassed. She didn't move her head and spoke softly.

"I was a nursing student and you were a handsome, young, married doctor. We were very much in love; I'd say we were lovers."

"Yes but we never quite . . . got it all together, if you recall. Not very good lovers by modern standards."

She closed her eyes and smiled widely, even chuckling, "Yes. That, in retrospect, was a mistake." Eyes half open again with what he observed to be a very tender look. "But we were old-fashioned lovers. Maybe that's still the best kind."

"Old-fashioned lovers did a lot of pushups and took a lot of cold showers."

She chuckled again and sat up, shaking her head as if to clear it. "Well then Doctor, how about that walk in the cool air of the Boston Common that you promised me."

"At your service Madam," he said, signaling Paul who quickly appeared and offered after-dinner drinks, which they declined. Paul removed the peach bowls, poured another cup of coffee, carded the tablecloth clean, and soon Henri appeared.

"Thank you Henri. You were magnificent as always. Please thank Paul particularly for me, and also the pianist."

"I certainly will Dr. Ingram." Henri took the vase of roses and handed it to Paul who disappeared into the kitchen. There would be no bill, but Henri would give Paul thirty dollars and the pianist twenty from the cash register at the end of the evening, pocket fifty himself, and add the meal and the tips to Ingram's monthly tab. "And I thank you too Henri," Anne said sincerely. "It's been a memorable evening." Paul returned with the roses, stems wrapped in aluminum foil to cover the thorns, and Anne and Ingram stepped into the cold evening air.

They walked hand in hand around the Common, reminiscing freely about their youthful romance, now that the ice had been broken. They laughed and sighed and followed one "remember the time when" with another, recalling a flood of anecdotes that never had been spoken aloud since they became memories.

Their love affair had been sudden; "Remember that day we met in Children's Hospital? You were the handsomest man I ever saw"; intense, "Remember the time we ran aground and we didn't realize it for half an hour"; short, "It wasn't five months, it was three months and four days"; and bittersweet, "Too beautiful, but not right. Not for you or your wife or your children. That's why I had to leave. That's why I never read your letters."

With heads sufficiently cleared, and riding on a wave of nostalgia, they cut short the circumnavigation of the Common near the Park Street Church and returned to the car. He drove across the bridge to the Cambridge side in order to see the moon over the Charles, setting off the Boston skyline. They discussed the food and the moonlight, but not John Bradford. They reminisced over the old affair which seemed to Ingram now finally, pleasantly, resolved. He formulated the next question in his mind, trying to sound casual and impulsive.

"Would it be indiscreet to suggest that we go to my house for a little after-dinner cognac?"

"Yes, Don."

"Yes, you'll come?"

"Yes, it would be indiscreet. It's nice to be old friends. Let's leave it at that."

"I . . . I had no other intention."

She laughed aloud. "Of course you didn't, you're a very proper neurosurgeon who just happens to be spending what turned out to be a romantic evening with an old friend. I, on the other hand, admit that I'd like to know how it feels . . . just to touch . . . after all these years . . ." Still smiling, she took his hand. "But that's the wine and the nostalgia. Practically . . . this isn't practical. I mean, aside from being honest and faithful, it's just impractical."

"Fair enough. I'm sure you're right."

"I am." She moved close enough to touch shoulders between the bucket seats of the MG.

He left her at the door of Longwood Towers with nothing more satisfying than a handshake, under the scrutiny of Mr. Duffy, and drove home murmuring "damn" to himself every few minutes—a reflection of pleasure rather than disappointment.

CHAPTER 8

Life for Randy Burleson, like all surgical interns, had become focused on sleep. On the neurosurgical service, Wednesday was clinic day and Burleson looked forward to Wednesday as if it were Christmas, because there was no operating on a clinic day and rounds started at the civilized hour of 7:00 a.m. This meant an extra half hour of sleep, which he savored carefully, turning off the alarm at 5:30 and drifting between sleep and consciousness until 6:00, chuckling each time he glanced at the clock as if he were fooling Father Time himself. At 6:00 he put his feet on the floor, feeling entirely refreshed. He was learning to get along very well with four hours of sleep, even when it was interrupted by telephone calls. The general surgery chief resident had told him, "Sleep is a habit which can be broken." He was beginning to believe it.

The on-call rooms were still in the old part of the hospital, reached by a series of staircases or an archaic elevator which was never used. The rooms were small, like monk's cells, but they served the purpose well. There was a certain historical legacy associated with the names of former occupants inscribed on one painted wall of each room: proof that successful practioners and prominent academic surgeons had survived the rigors of the Longwood. Burleson grabbed his towel and his kit of toilet articles and crossed the hall to the bathroom.

The common bathroom had been built in the days when all the residents and interns were male. A small bathroom one floor down had been designated for female residents, but it was inconvenient, so some of the more independent women used the big central bathroom. Like the sleeping rooms, it was immensely practical. The sinks, showers, toilets, and urinals were set in long rows, but the room appeared wider than it was because of the many mirrors. It reminded

Burleson of his fraternity house bathroom because it was never quite clean, smelled of disinfectant most of the time, and served as an important equalizer. Chief residents, interns, even the occasional sleep-over staff man, all peed and shaved and showered in the same fashion. Burleson stopped at a sink and started to lather his face.

The shower stalls at the end of the room were reflected in the shaving mirror. One shower was in use. When the noise of the water stopped, a hand reached out and retrieved a towel. A moment later the curtain was pulled back, and there revealed was a stunning young woman drying her hair with the towel. Burleson was so shocked he cut himself below his right ear. When she finished drying her hair and stepped into the room he realized it was Kay Lawson. His back was toward her and she did not look his way. She wrapped the towel around her and calmly walked out the door toward the chief residents' rooms. Burleson had remained frozen the whole time, partly awestruck by her body, but mostly embarrassed because he was, himself, naked. Finally he resumed shaving, thinking perhaps that he had gone unnoticed. Ten minutes later, he passed her on the way down the stairs. "Good morning, Burleson," she said. "I think you cut yourself shaving."

He checked the floor and the ICU, drew morning blood samples from two patients that the blood team refused to try, got most of his orders written, and was sipping the dregs of the night shift coffee on 9 North when Adams arrived.

"Morning Randy. I heard you cut yourself shaving," said Adams with a knowing, complicit grin. Burleson grinned back without responding, thinking that Adams looked a little more relaxed this morning. As they walked down the corridor, Adams said, "Fill me in on the sick ones."

"Dugan's the same. Rizzo had a little blood from his NG tube. I tried him off the ventilator but he could only tolerate it for a few minutes."

"He's going to need a trach. Let's do it today, otherwise we'll wind up doing it on the weekend."

"Sounds good. I helped on a few trachs on General Surgery. Do you think I could do it?"

Adams remembered his promise to himself to be the type of chief resident who looked after the interns. If Burleson did it, the trach would take an extra forty-five minutes. But he said, "Sure. I'll help you with it right after the clinic."

They arrived at the room closest to the nursing station—Ben Rothstein.

"Mr. Rothstein is two days post-op," Burleson began. "He had some bad headaches last night but his vital signs are stable."

"What do you mean, bad headaches?" Adams was suddenly tense.

"Just real bad headaches. The nurse said he looked okay but was having pain. I gave him some morphine."

"What?" Adams looked anxious. "Two days after a posterior fossa and you gave him morphine for pain? What did he look like?"

"Well I didn't see him exactly. The nurse said—"

"You didn't see him? Jesus, Burleson. How much morphine?"

"Only eight."

"Damn. Let's go see him." They pushed into the dark room. "Mr. Rothstein!" Adams said urgently, shaking his arm. No response. "Turn the damn light on," he barked at Burleson.

Rothstein took two or three choking breaths, stopped, then breathed again. Adams dug a fingernail into his eyebrow. No response. He raised the old man's eyelids to check his pupils—both dilated. At the same time, with his other hand he had been feeling the femoral artery. The pulse was strong, about sixty. With both hands he felt the scalp over the bone flap. Full but not tense. "Damn," he said again, pushing past Burleson and the students to the door.

In seconds he was at the nursing staff lounge. The nurses were smoking and sipping coffee, having report. "Colleen, the guy in 901 is coning," he addressed the head nurse. "Get me the stat cart and a prep set. I'll get the twist drill." He left without waiting for a response and several of the nurses whirred into action. He returned to the room with the twist drill and a pair of gloves. Burleson was totally bewildered. "What's going on Dan? Did I give . . . did he get too much morphine? His discs are choked. I just checked them."

"He blocked off his aqueduct and his ventricles started filling up with fluid. His pressure above the tentorium must be god-awful high. That's why he had the headaches."

"I'm really sorry."

"Don't be sorry, just be helpful. We have to put in a ventriculostomy. Pull him over to the right side of the bed and turn his head a little bit. That's good. Now pour some Betadine on there. Then hook up an EKG."

By the time the nurses arrived Adams had the drill assembled and a towel with a small hole in it placed over Rothstein's head. He made a small incision in the scalp without local. Rothstein did not respond. He pushed his gloved finger down to the bone. The twist drill (it was exactly that, an old hand-cranked drill, once shiny, now the color of old pewter) had not been used in a while. The mechanism was sticky and the bit proceeded through the skull in fits and jerks as Adams turned the crank. Nonetheless he could sense when he was through the bone. It was just about the distance he had adjusted when he put the bit in. Colleen opened the sterile pack which held a long Teflon catheter. Adams settled it gently through the hole in the skull, checked his orientation, and then slowly advanced the needle, holding the shaft of it between his thumb and forefinger to increase the sensitivity of his tactile sense. When he felt a slight give he advanced it another centimeter and then pulled out the obturator. Watery fluid came squirting out, and he let several cc's escape before putting his finger over the hole and fitting it with a stopcock. He sutured the long catheter in place and attached the drainage set, letting off another ten cc's, until the fluid stopped squirting and just trickled out of the catheter. A few minutes later, Rothstein's pupils were small and reactive and he began to groan. Burleson watched this whole procedure—which took about five minutes—wide-eyed.

"Jesus, Dan, that was great. That old guy almost died."

"Yeah, no thanks to you Burleson. When a neurosurgery patient has a headache you have to get your ass out of bed and go see him. Are you ever going to learn that?" He didn't wait for an answer. Burleson hung his head. "Colleen, send Mr. Rothstein to ICU so we can measure his intracranial pressure and keep him drained until then, okay?" She nodded. "Come on, let's finish rounds. We have a big clinic today."

* * * *

The Neurosurgery Research Conference was always held on Wednesday at noon, fortified by chicken salad, mystery meat sand-

102

wiches swathed in Saran wrap, hospital-order potato chips, small warm cartons of milk, and tepid coffee. The initial conversation was all clinical—still exciting and new to Burleson.

"So I told the guy it's not unusual to have dilated pupils after a cardiac arrest and he probably didn't need a neurosurgical consult after all."

"Who was this genius?"

"A chief resident in medicine."

"Well, he should know better. He has had three whole years of training." This followed by the reserved neurosurgical version of guffaws. By the time Ingram arrived there were fifteen people in the room. Staff and resident neurosurgeons, two neurologists, two behavioral neurophysiologists, some med students, and visitors.

"What's the schedule for today?" asked Ingram, selecting a large orange and a carton of chocolate milk.

"Frank's going to review the pet rock study and Ed has some lab data to present," said Adams.

Ingram nodded and Frank Pearson put down his sandwich. "We have eight patients in the study so far. Three have finished and five are still on follow-up. So far we have a nice study of recovery from head injury. I'm not sure what to make of the PET scans. I think they're going to be too gross to focus in on what we are looking for."

"Even that would be useful information," said Ingram. "Frank, why don't you remind everyone what this study is all about."

"This is a study of the recovery of brain function—no—it's really mind function, after closed-head injury. We're using the PET scanner to localize areas of brain which look normal, and hope to correlate that information with return of function. It's part of our overall project to localize the functions of the mind anatomically. Head injury is a good model because both memory and behavior usually return in stages from the most basic to the most complex. So we hoped that the PET scanner, which lights up different areas of the brain associated with specific thoughts, would let us localize each phase. Patients have to be in deep coma to qualify for the study, and the initial PET scan is pretty dark—like scanning a rock—hence the name . . ."

"We must think of a new name for this study," commented Ingram. "Families might get a little upset if they hear that the dear one is part of the pet rock study." A few snickers. "Have you entered the Dugan girl into your study?"

"I have her name on the list. There's not much sense in starting her out until she shows some sign of recovery. What do you think Dan?"

"At the moment she is more of an organ donor than a pet rock study. It's a little early yet, though."

"The most interesting study so far," continued Frank, "is Bradley Wilson. He's the kid, remember, who rode his convertible into a tree a few months ago. He came back to what we call stage three, but hasn't gone beyond that."

"What's stage three?" asked Burleson.

"We set up an arbitrary scale of mind function ranging from zero—that's coma—to ten for normal. Three means that he can do some voluntary motions, can see and hear, does instinctive things like eating and scratching. He can say a few words but can't understand or communicate verbally, that sort of thing."

"Sounds like a dog," said Burleson.

"A dog is actually about five or six on this scale," said Frank. "Dogs can understand verbal commands, show emotion, and have memory. Dogs would be fourteen on the Glasgow Coma Scale."

"Even more important," interrupted Ingram, "dogs can learn to inhibit their impulses. They can memorize proper social behavior— what's acceptable and what's unacceptable, for example."

"That's really interesting," said Burleson. "You'd say, then, that a dog has a mind?"

"Six on a scale of ten," smiled Ingram. "What do you think Father O'Reilly? Does a dog have a mind?" Ingram smiled at Father John who was sitting in the back corner of the room, unnoticed by most of the conferees. "Father O'Reilly is an old friend who is interested in problems of the mind, like we are. One of his parishioners is in the hospital—Kathleen Dugan in fact—and I asked him to join us for our conference."

"I expected to listen and learn," said Father John. "I'm afraid I'm no neurophysiologist. But to answer your question, if, by the mind, you mean intellectual functioning and the behavior related to it, then I would say that a dog has a mind."

"And Bradley Wilson has a mind also?"

"Three on a scale of ten, I've heard," countered Father John.

"And does Bradley Wilson have a soul?" asked Adams.

Father O'Reilly sat more upright, sensing the beginning of an argument. "Every human being has a soul, Doctor, but you put me on the spot. It depends on the definition of 'soul,' which can be very personal."

"Fair enough Father O'Reilly. We won't ask your personal opinion, yet, but is there a generic Jesuit opinion about the soul?" The question came from neurologist Gloria Berkowitz.

"Of course. The young man surely has a soul. It is divine. Patterned after the soul of God. Part of the soul of God in fact."

Tatsaku Ichiba, PhD, interrupted. "That sounds like the Buddhist concept of each soul as a part of some grand energy—a dew drop in the sea, as I remember from a course on comparative religions."

"Similar," said Father John, "but it's not just energy. God has a personal interest in each individual soul."

"Then God has a mind?" asked Ichiba.

"Yes."

"And a memory?"

"Of course."

"You're sure?" he asked, not with wonder but with disbelief.

"If that's true," said Ingram, "You know my next question is going to be, does the dog have a soul?"

"Yes I knew that was where you were heading. You see," O'Reilly turned to the rest of the group with a sly smile. "Dr. Ingram and I have had this discussion before."

"And what's the answer Father?" The question came from Burleson. The way he said "Father" revealed that he was a Catholic. He expected the real answer.

"Animals do not have souls."

Burleson was satisfied. "And that is why, if I remember, Father John," said Ingram, "that if a mouse eats the crumbs of a wafer that has been consecrated with the body of Christ that we don't have to worry about whether the mouse goes to heaven or not." Ingram was obviously enjoying the repartee.

"That is correct Dr. Ingram. You have a good memory."

"Nine on a scale of ten, some would say."

All laughed, easing the building tension. Adams, however, couldn't accept the simple explanation. "Excuse me, Father John, but how can you just say that's true? There are no data and no verification. It sounds like a fairy tale."

"It's true because the Church says it's true and we believe in the Church. And it's not without data. Thousands of scholars have worried over questions such as this for centuries. The Cardinals debate these issues, the Pope settles the debate. The Pope is Christ's arbiter on earth. That's the way that truth is determined on matters of faith."

"And if there are data showing that the Pope is wrong?"

"There are no real conflicts between scientific data and religious dogma. Two and two make four in the space shuttle or in the collection box, you know."

"Is that what they told Galileo?" asked Adams in a sarcastic tone which he rarely displayed.

"Now we're getting on to angels-on-the-head-of-a-pin minutiae," said Ingram. "Let's get back to the central question. We're trying to understand where the mind is and how that relates to what we call memory. To analyze these issues scientifically, we have to quantify memory—which is fairly easy—and mind—which is what we are trying to do with our scale. Of course the two are intimately interrelated, so measuring the integration will be the next step. A fairly good analogy is to think of the mind as the conductor of a grand opera. There are soloists, musicians, stage hands, chorus singers, and dancers. Each one knows his part, but each part by itself does not make the opera. The conductor controls who does what when, how loud, how fast, how each part integrates with the others. The result is the opera. We could think of the mind as drawing from thousands of memory banks—each one a little group of neurons—and integrating the information. The result is a thought or an action."

"One problem with the analogy," said Berkowitz, "is that the conductor himself has to have a remarkable memory to read the score and create the opera. And someone had to write it in the first place, based on memory of how sound is made by a tenor or a piccolo—and how to write it down—and on and on. So, following the analogy, could we say that mind is just memory, or that a series of memories make up the mind?"

"That's where the PET scan comes in," said Frank. "For the first time in neuroscience we are getting close to locating those tens of thousands of memory banks, without destroying them as we do in animal experiments. With enough data and a big enough computer we can start to answer that exact question. That is why we are starting with coma—no obvious mind and no obvious memory—and working up."

Ingram turned to Sven Nordstrom, retired Chairman of Neuroscience at the Karolinska in Stockholm, who was taking a sabbatical in the Philosophy Department at Boston U. "Sven, what are we trying to do here? Is this science or religion? Physics or metaphysics?"

Nordstrom took a long draw from his pipe before answering. "To me, Dr. Ingram, the most interesting question is why we ask the question. Humans have a desire, in fact a compulsion, to have a personal answer for these vital questions. Whether the answer comes in a dream, or from a priest, or years of introspective meditation, or from the collection of hard scientific data, appears to be less important to most people than the act of gaining an answer itself. The more we study it, the more we question simple dogmatic answers, as you did Dr. Adams. On the other hand if we begin with an axiom we believe to be true, everything else follows, as it does for Father John. One person's axiom won't be true for everyone, as Dr. Ichiba implied, but humans have a compulsion to force others to accept their axioms for imponderable questions."

"Megaponderables," said Frank.

Nordstrom sucked on his pipe. "I like that term. Did you just coin it now? When we know the answer to the megaponderables, then the innate human unrest is solved and we achieve peace of mind."

Later, as they were leaving, Ingram said to O'Reilly, "Thanks for coming. I hope you enjoyed it."

"I did, and I particularly enjoyed your analogy of the conductor and the opera. It makes my point about the soul."

"Is the soul in the analogy?" asked Ingram.

"Oh yes," said Father John. "It's the music."

* * * *

"I have to go now." Carol Rizzo leaned over to get squarely in his line of vision. She was beginning to look very tired, he thought. "Dr. Adams is going to do the tracheostomy now." He raised his eyebrows and shook his head from side to side, as much as he could in the heavy tongs, to indicate a question. She understood. "The tracheostomy. The operation to put a tube in your windpipe right here." She pointed to the base of her own neck. "Then you'll get that tube out of your throat. It'll be much more comfortable." He mouthed the word "talk" several times. She had come to read his lips quite well, even with the tube in place. "No, you won't be able to talk. Not just yet anyway. You'll still need this breathing machine. But at least you'll have the tube out of your mouth. That'll be better, won't it?" He nodded agreement.

She disappeared and he was once again looking at the ceiling, aware of some clattering and washing, as if preparations were being made for cooking. He heard voices and eventually Adam's face appeared, covered by a mask and a paper cap. "Matt, you're going to feel something cold on your neck. This won't hurt, we are only cleaning it off. We'll tell you just what we're going to do each step of the way, so don't worry." Matt found this reassuring and didn't mind the cool liquid which was rubbed on the lower part of his neck and ran around his back between his shoulder blades.

"These towels are just to keep the operation sterile," said Adams, positioning four folded towels around the base of Matt's neck. This one will cover your face for just a minute, then the nurse will lift it up." A green towel descended over Matt's face and lay on his nose. It caused him to blink but there was nothing he could do about it. He was beginning to feel claustrophobic. He heard a series of four clicks, like ratchets being closed down. The towel pushed even closer to his face as a heavy sheet was added to the drape. Then Sally, his nurse on days, lifted up the sheet and towel and attached them with tape to the IV poles.

"I'll be right here Matt," she said softly. "If anything hurts just blink your eyes and I'll tell Dr. Adams. Okay?"

"Now Matt, you're going to feel some stinging while we put some anesthetic in here." The voice sounded very far away, on the other side of the heavy drapes. Suddenly an intense burning began at the root of his neck, like the sting of a wasp, except it continued and spread. He blinked his eyes vigorously. "I know that hurts Matt," said Sally. "That's the anesthetic. It will be numb in just a minute." He heard some mumbling from the other side of the drapes. Surely enough, the stinging stopped and was replaced with a numb feeling. At least he thought it was numb. He felt some pressure but no pain. He thought it was over, and was much relieved. Next he heard Burleson's voice.

"Does that hurt? Mr. Rizzo, does that hurt now?" He felt nothing. Next came Adams's voice.

"Burleson, that's a dumb question. How could he answer you? Besides, that's not the way to do an operation under local. Watch." Adams's voice now became louder and seemed to be directed through the drapes, to Rizzo. "Matt, we have good anesthesia now. You'll feel some pushing and pulling, but no pain. If anything hurts at all, blink your eyes and Sally will tell us to put in some more anesthetic."

Adams was right. Rizzo couldn't feel a thing. He tried to relax and concentrated on the towels, reminding himself that soon the dreaded tube would be out of his mouth. But he was still terrified. He heard a muted, one-sided conversation from the other side of the drapes.

"That's a nice scratch. Now make an incision. I'll get the capillaries, you just keep operating. That's the mid-line, pick it up. With the forceps, Burleson."

The feeling of pushing at the base of his neck became intense. He blinked his eyes hard. Sally was writing something in the chart, not looking. The pressure feeling became even stronger, soon becoming sharply painful. He blinked again and tried to move his head. No response. The pain was now overwhelming. He coughed, setting off the alarm on the ventilator. This brought Sally's attention.

"He's hurting a lot up here."

"Thanks for letting me know. Matt, we're putting in some more anesthetic. You'll feel that burning again." The burning followed but the pain subsided. Matt closed his eyes but felt more tense than ever.

"Just a minute. Let me feel. Don't drift off the mid-line. Feel the rings? That's the thyroid isthmus. We'll be able to go above it."

Rizzo wondered what they were talking about. Adams was obviously doing the instructing. He hadn't heard from Burleson since the beginning of the operation. He didn't worry about who did what. He only wanted it to be over. The pressure in his neck was beginning to bother him again.

"Okay that's where we want to be. Hold on a minute, let's test the balloon and rehearse this a little bit." The mumbled conversation got softer as it moved away from the drapes. Sally was cutting the tape which held the tube to his cheeks. The motion irritated his throat and caused him to cough. More pressure in his wind pipe.

"Now, this is all up to you because I can't let go of the retractors. Start with the hook, try not to break the balloon when you place it in. That's good. Now transversely right above the second ring. That's right. Do it, do it. I can't stand the suspense."

Suddenly Rizzo was seized with a relentless fit of coughing. His throat burned, as if he had aspirated an irritating burr. In the midst of the coughing Sally began to pull back the tube from his mouth. Coughing continued, ventilator buzzed loudly. His mouth was filling with some fluid that came up with the coughing. The taste of blood. He felt heavy pushing on the lower part of his neck. Adams was talking but Rizzo couldn't make out the words. Suddenly the pressure stopped but the coughing continued. The tube now came out completely, and Sally put the suction tube in his mouth, removing the blood, saliva, and sputum. Soon the coughing subsided. He moved his tongue around, feeling his palate for the first time in days. He swallowed. Painful, but everything worked this time. He managed a weak smile.

"That's it. Just bring the ventilator in here. We're contaminated now. Randy, put a skin suture or two on both sides. Hey, you did a great job, a great job."

"Thanks. You were right. It took more pressure than I thought it would to get the tube in."

"Yeah, you can never believe how hard you have to push at first. That's right. A little more medial." Soon the towel and drape was removed and Rizzo could see the players in the little drama which he

110

had only heard while it was underway. Burleson was standing to his right, still sweating heavily. Adams was on his left, leaning over in front of him.

"That's it Matt. I hope that wasn't too bad." Rizzo smiled. "You should be a lot more comfortable now. Sally, can you fix up these trach tapes?"

Sally passed the twill ribbon around his neck and tied it at the side. She disappeared for a minute and returned with a cherry popsicle. "Here Matt. This will taste good." He bit off a piece of it and held it in his mouth, his first taste of food in the five days since the accident.

* * * *

Flint sat facing the door, upright as he always sat, hands folded in his lap. During those lulls in daily life when there is nothing to do, James Flint did not scan magazines, do crossword puzzles, or play cards. He did not sip coffee, thumb the newspaper, or listen to the radio. He read avidly—no, he studied avidly. The first thing in the morning and the last thing at night. But only by himself when he could devote full attention to the author for twenty minutes. This often limited his reading to a few pages at a time, but Kierkegaard, Nietzsche, Aquinas, Toynbee Whitehead, and Einstein require a little reading and a lot of thought. So he sat still, looking at the door, thinking.

Behind the curtain, Ingram was talking to the Bradfords. They were discussing recreational sailing because discussing that topic postponed the inevitable talk of the operation. Flint listened to Bradford's conversation to be sure the information he was protecting did not leak out. But he considered sailing (and cards and crossword puzzles and golf) trivialities of life which did not deserve his attention.

Anne Bradford seemed particularly vivacious and attractive today. Her laughter and her surge of energy when Ingram arrived were immediately apparent to Flint, but would have been lost on a less perceptive observer.

Now Ingram was promising to return for a more lengthy visit. The conversation was drawing to a close. Flint stood and waited outside the door.

"Excuse me, Dr. Ingram. May I speak to you for a few minutes?"

He indicated the room across the hall.

The hospital room had been fitted out for Flint, but it appeared even more spartan than usual. The bed was pushed against the wall and made up drum-tight, like an army cot, with no pillow. A desk with a large reading lamp was placed next to the door. Ingram noticed six books—including Descartes and a neurosurgery text—precisely aligned between bookends on the top of the desk. Three suitcases filled one corner of the room—heavy aluminum cases, ribbed on the sides, with a brushed surface and black fittings.

"I once made the acquaintance of a neurosurgeon at the Children's Hospital," said Flint, offering one chair and sitting on the other. "Dr. Eastman, as I recall. Is he still practicing there?"

"Dr. Eastman was my chief. No, he retired about five years ago and died last year."

"An impressive man, Eastman." Flint seemed to be saying this more to himself than to Ingram.

The only other piece of furniture was a four-octave electronic keyboard resting on a small table with two Schirmer books of Bach sonatas on the back of the keyboard. There were no speakers, only a set of earphones.

"So, you're a musician Mr. Flint?"

Flint nodded.

"I wouldn't have guessed that."

"Why not?"

"I don't know. It just hadn't crossed my mind I suppose." Ingram was embarrassed, feeling that he'd underestimated Flint, and had been detected. But Flint showed no offense.

"Music is applied mathematics and physics," commented Flint. "It's fascinating to me how a series of tones and rhythms can elicit human emotional responses. Why does that happen with music but not at the recitation of differential equations or the drawing of exact parallelograms?"

"That's a very perceptive thought."

"Yes it is. But it's not mine, it's from Schopenhauer."

"Schopenhauer thought that music was the ultimate art form. He marveled at how the mind could create new ideas by synthesizing pieces of old ones. Drawing from a series of memories including, I suppose, that ill-defined inward memory of emotion. It all depends upon experience. I suppose there are people who get great exhilaration out of the resolution of a differential equation."

"Quite so. The response—emotion or otherwise—is conditioned on past experience which depends upon memory. And where do we find the music-emotion memory bank in the brain? Somewhere between the auditory nucleus and the frontal lobe?"

"So you've been studying neuroanatomy too?" asked Ingram, flattered by Flint's reference to his own work.

"I've been learning what I can about Senator Bradford's condition and what might result from it. Since you are a major controlling factor, I have been learning about you as well."

This did not come as a surprise to Ingram. "And what are you learning?" Surely this must be the reason for the meeting, thought Ingram. Flint hadn't asked him in to discuss the neurophysiology of music.

"Regarding your work, I'm impressed and intrigued. It's refreshing to see such a straightforward scientific approach to the grandest of questions. But it's Bradford's condition that is my responsibility, and that's what I want to ask you about."

"Specifically?"

"This meningioma involves both frontal lobes. It might come out very easily with no side effects—'shelling out'—as I recall it . . ."

" . . . or it may require removing part of the frontal lobes or ligating the anterior cerebral arteries," Ingram added, waiting.

"That would result in significant alteration of behavior, as I understand it—could mean something as simple as paranoia or change of affect like he's having now, to an animalistic or vegetative state. Isn't that correct?"

"You've done your homework well, Mr. Flint. Yes, those are the possibilities. You've left out the most important one, however, which is death."

"That's the least important, from my responsibility. My assignment is to be guardian to the information in the senator's mind. He just happens to be the focal point of the information. He's the carrier.

If he dies, my job is over. If that portion of his memory goes into your surgical sucker, my problem is solved. But even with your knowledge of the anatomy of memory, we will never be quite sure what's been erased and what remains. If he comes out intact we're at the status quo. It's only those intermediate possibilities that put the information at risk of disclosure."

"So you're not a bodyguard. You're not assigned to protect his life, throwing yourself in front of bullets and all that sort of thing."

"Not at all. I guess you could say I'm a mind guard." Flint smiled as if pleased at his turn of phrase. The first time Ingram had seen him smile.

"And his political career. His presidential aspirations, the potential philosopher king? They're not of concern to you?"

"An overwhelming concern, Dr. Ingram, but only as long as his mind is sound. If not—there will be others. There will always be Bradfords . . . and Ingrams, and Flints. Honesty and treachery, relative good and relative pain. Beginnings and endings. War, death, birth, the desire to know. Those are the absolutes. Only the players change—but you know that as well as I."

Ingram digested this analysis, and the two men studied each other. "And what about the stuffing of life between those ends, Mr. Flint? All the Bradfords have hopes and fears and joy and passion. You described the digital display. How about the analog? Isn't life worth preserving for the Mozarts and the Einsteins and the Monets and the . . . the . . ."

"And the Anne Bradfords?"

If Ingram was stunned by this insight his face did not reflect it.

"Normal life has its pleasures and pains and subjective riches, Dr. Ingram. I'm asking, what will happen if John Bradford's truthful, wise, and careful mind disappears into the specimen jar, and some lesser mind inside his head has access to my important information."

"You mean, would I kill him?"

"Let him die, I think is the proper euphemism."

"If you mean using life support systems to keep a carcass alive, that's contrary to my philosophy and my duty to my patients."

"Thank you. That's what I wanted to know."

"But it's not as simple as that. Altered mental states may occur in neurosurgical patients who are not amenable to . . . that is . . . the patient may not at all be dependent on life support systems."

"I'm well aware Dr. Ingram, and I thank you for answering my questions. I find your outlook as enlightened as your research."

"Thank you Mr. Flint."

Walking down the hall Ingram realized that he had misjudged Flint entirely. Cerebral, not automatic. Discerning, not intolerant. And rather than totally stoic—which was the impression he gave—Ingram realized that Flint had learned to compartmentalize his emotions. Like a surgeon. Like himself.

CHAPTER 9

Father John O'Reilly was the first to notice. He was sitting at her bedside, holding her hand in both of his, and pleading with God to reactivate his presence in the mind of this child. She squeezed his hand. It wasn't just one of her intermittent seizures—he had become accustomed to those. This was a definite, purposeful act. He kept his eyes closed and prayed for her to squeeze again. She did. He had not spoken a word aloud. With passion, he thanked God for this undeniable sign of divine communication.

He lifted his head, eyes filled with tears, and she was looking directly at him. "Hello Kathleen," he said. No response. "Squeeze my hand again." The nurse stopped what she was doing and watched. Gradually, Kathleen's fingers tightened on the priest's hand. She sighed, looked away, then squeezed again. Father O'Reilly was crying freely now and a little cheer went up from the nurses.

In fact, Kathleen Dugan had been steadily improving for three days. Two days before, her breathing and cough reflex were strong enough and she had been extubated. All of her IVs were out and she was being fed by a small tube which passed through her nose into her stomach. She had started tracking people with her eyes that morning. Neurologic recovery notwithstanding, the priest was convinced that it was in response to his prayer that she finally made a purposeful movement.

Father O'Reilly returned to his prayer, repeating sincere and profound thanks for what he knew to be divine intervention. Then he asked the bedside nurse to verify the fact that Kathleen could squeeze his hand on command. The nurse determined that Kathleen could do not only that, but could close her eyes, move her tongue, and wiggle her toes. Even the tough ICU nurse agreed it was a miracle.

Mary Dugan was in her usual place in the waiting room, writing a letter to Patrick. There was no mistaking the joy on Father O'Reilly's face. She knew the message even before he ever announced it.

"Come Mary. Kathleen is waking up."

"Jesus, Mary, and Joseph," she said. "Oh, excuse me Father."

"And all the saints as well, Mary. Come now."

To the casual observer, the young girl with the vacant stare and half-open, drooling mouth was anything but awake, but she slowly turned her head when her mother arrived, and slowly clenched her fingers. Four out of ten on the mind function scale. Mary Dugan squeezed back and cried.

* * * *

Dan Adams stood at the old man's bedside, gently holding the plastic drainage tube between his thumb and fingertips. Forty cc's of watery fluid had accumulated in the reservoir since he checked it last. He didn't need to hold the drainage tube, but he rolled it gently between his fingers while thinking intently, as one might roll a pencil, or drum on a desktop. He stood, rolling the tubing, for ten minutes, finding it a quiet and secluded time to think. And he thought mostly about the old man, wishing that he would show some sign of mental function, and wondering if he would. His eyes were open, his gaze was vacant. He breathed, now slowly, now rapidly, and grunted from time to time. "Professor Rothstein," Adams whispered, shaking the old man's shoulder gently as he addressed him. "Professor." Back to silence, rolling the tubing and thinking.

"My friend is very still, Dr. Adams. Very still." Adams turned to see Ravikrishnan, who had entered silently and was standing behind him at the foot of the bed.

"Yes. That episode yesterday set him back a bit." Adams didn't elaborate further.

"You mean the terrible headache?"

"Yes, that's it. The headache caused a lot of pressure on his brain. He seems to be coming around," he said lamely.

"You're working late Dr. Adams. It seems you're always here." The Indian, who always seemed so kind and gentle, settled into a chair.

"As you are, Professor. You must be very good friends," said Adams, glad for the change of subject.

"Yes, very good friends. Since Rachel died—Rachel, that was Ben's wife—we sort of look after each other. Old men, old friends, good friends." He slipped a little further into the chair, stroking the well-cut edge of his white beard with the back of his fingers. "Yes, good friends."

Adams, observing once again the clear fluid draining from the ventriculostomy tube, thought to himself that the professor should be offered an overly realistic appraisal of the status of his friend, a form of communication the residents called "hanging crepe." He turned away from Rothstein, and half sat on the foot of the bed, facing Ravikrishnan in the room's only chair. "Professor Ravikrishnan, you should know that your friend had an episode of very high pressure inside his brain. The area where the tumor was removed is right at the point where fluid normally drains away from the brain. That spot blocked off for a period of time—not very long, but enough to raise the pressure very high. It's possible that he . . . that he won't recover very quickly . . . or . . . at all." Hands pushed into the pockets of his long white coat, brow furrowed, speaking softly as if to ease the ominous message.

"What do you mean by 'recover,' Dr. Adams?" Ravikrishnan had taken this information calmly and focused on the part which was of most concern to his friend.

"I mean return to normal function. I'm just not sure what the outcome will be at this point."

Ravikrishnan looked aside, then at his sleeping friend, then intently at Adams. "I thank you for being honest with me Dr. Adams. After what period of time in this condition," nodding toward the figure in the bed, "will you determine that there is no reasonable chance of recovery?" Adams was not accustomed to such an articulate and insightful question from a lay person. It took him a few seconds to formulate an answer. "I'd . . . I couldn't put a number on it. Sometimes these things can go on for a long time."

"I'm sure they can," smiled Ravikrishnan calmly, "but what is a reasonable time in which to expect recovery?"

"If there isn't a major change in four or five days, perhaps a week, then . . . the chances get a little smaller each day . . ."

"I understand. And again I appreciate your honesty Dr. Adams. We shall hope for recovery within a week, then."

"God willing," added Adams to bring the conversation to an end.

"God willing? Are you a religious man Dr. Adams?"

"Probably not in the sense that you ask the question," he answered. "I meant it as a figure of speech implying . . . fate, I suppose."

"In what sense?"

Adams's crepe hanging was turning into a philosophical dialectic he had not expected. "In what sense am I religious?"

A nod.

"In the sense that I firmly believe what I believe, but that does not include all the dogmas of any of the conventional religions. Why do you ask?"

A flicker of a smile passed Ravikrishnan's face, as he recognized the defensive posture taken by so many of his students who had been taught that it was antisocial—if not sinful—to deny acceptance of a prescribed list of beliefs, with its prophets, sacred writing, holy One, fantastic promises, demonic curses, clergy, rights, and ritual. "I ask only because it may have some bearing on the treatment of my friend Rothstein. He would appreciate your answer, and he would be very interested to know the character of those personal beliefs you espouse, as would I, but my question simply sought to ascertain your perception of your responsibility in the event of . . . lack of recovery."

"You mean permanent brain damage?"

"Inability to think clearly, yes."

"That's not a religious question, that's a medical question."

"I'm relieved that you see it as such."

"And my responsibility, as in all things medical, is to fulfill the wishes or the best interests of the patient."

"Well said. Well thought and well said. And I thank you for taking the time, Dr. Adams. I know you have many things to do and I won't keep you. We must continue this discussion at some other time." He smiled in a fatherly fashion, and Adams, who would have liked to continue the discussion on the spot, was aware that he had been dismissed. One thing he knew with certainty, it is impossible to predict how someone will react to the hanging of crepe. He excused himself and continued his rounds.

CHAPTER 10

Despite the efficiency and apparent organization of the modern hospital, there often comes a time when, to the patient, momentum seems to be suddenly lost. Somewhat like the feeling of having the palate ready for after-dinner coffee and finding there is none, or missing the flight home from a faraway city, only to discover that the next flight doesn't leave for sixteen hours. This sensation had caught up with John Bradford although, like most patients, he couldn't specifically identify the source of his troubling uncertainty and dissatisfaction, nor did he realize how it came about. If the truth be known, this abrupt pause in activity for a preoperative patient is usually brought about by the availability of operating time, or more accurately the desire of the surgeon to operate at a specific time. Bradford had been ready for operation on Wednesday. The furtive admission, the immediate arteriogram, the final details of physical and psychological preparation, led him to prepare as best he could for the event on Wednesday. When he learned the operation was to be Friday, Bradford was initially relieved, feeling that he had gained an unexpected chance to attend to details. But by Wednesday afternoon he was bored, and by Thursday at four, although he didn't realize it, he had lost his emotional peak. He sensed that he was "on hold" in the system.

Complicating this state of mind was his conviction that his life was threatened by more than the tumor in his head, and the longer he spent at the hospital, the longer he was at risk. The inertia seemed to affect Flint, and even Anne. They argued over minor points. When he suggested that she—or someone—had replaced the apple juice on his tray with some toxic chemical she had been exasperated, and left.

At 4:02 (he said he would be in at 4:00) Ingram arrived, without his usual retinue. He noticed that Flint was not around, which pleased him because he planned to have a private conversation. "Hello, John. I think we're all set for tomorrow."

"We'd better be. I was all set yesterday." The hostile response did not surprise Ingram. It was common with patients who were accustomed to controlling their own complex schedules. It was the response he expected from engineers.

"John, I know just how you feel. It's terribly frustrating to sit around waiting for a big operation. For you, and for me too. But I need a whole day to do your operation, so we need to start the first thing in the morning, and then I had to arrange for the best anesthesia and the best scrub team. Believe me, it is all to your advantage." Bradford could not disagree with the logic of this argument and began to arise from his depression. The thought of having the varsity players on the floor appealed to him.

"Who will be giving anesthesia?"

"Dr. Peterson. You'll meet him this evening, if you haven't already."

"Is he good? I mean, isn't Dr. Graham the Chairman of Anesthesia?" Ingram smiled. He should have anticipated that Bradford would have done all his homework.

"Dr. Peterson is our best anesthesiologist for neurosurgery cases. And as it happens, Dr. Graham will be out of town tomorrow—in Bethesda as a matter of fact, right in your backyard."

"I see." Bradford smiled, more relaxed. "And was that part of your planning also?"

"I must admit it crossed my mind." Ingram returned the smile.

"Have you ever thought of going into politics Don? You certainly calmed me down and won me over."

"In this case it's not politics, it's just good patient care and that's what we intend to provide for Mr. Jones, who's scheduled for a craniotomy at eight o'clock in the morning."

"All right. I'm ready for it. I presume, seeing that empty form in your hand, that you're here to describe the gory details and ask me to sign my life into your hands."

"Something like that. Is Anne around?"

Bradford noted the familiarity and the warm tone. "No, she left at lunch time. I think we were getting on each other's nerves. It's probably better that she's not here anyway. I expect you'll give me the straight scoop, and I'm not sure she's ready for that."

Ingram handed the form, filled in except for the signature, to Bradford, and, in carefully arranged discourse, explained that the tumor was in all likelihood benign, but in a very difficult area. That he would do whatever was necessary to remove the tumor or, failing that, alleviate the symptoms. That, in addition to the ubiquitous potential of bleeding and infection, there was a significant risk of damage to brain tissue. And this, if it happened, might affect memory, thinking, personality, creativity, intelligence, and the like. That someone from the operating room would pick him up about seven o'clock and he would probably be asleep before Ingram arrived. That Anne should wait here in his room, but the operation would not be over until at least noon and might last into the evening. That now was the time for final questions.

Bradford signed on the bottom line, commenting that he considered it ridiculous to agree to item eight on the form: first aid in the event of emergencies. He had obviously read the form carefully while Ingram was talking. "I have only one request Don. We've been over this ground before—not so explicitly I might add—but I trust your skill and I trust your . . . integrity."

"What's the request?"

Bradford sat straighter in the bed and asked Ingram to close the door. His face was tense and serious.

"That business about permanent brain injury—it worries me. I can see that my personality is changing. I'm suspicious. I'm demanding. I mix up words. Is it likely to get worse after this operation?"

"Just the opposite. The whole intent of the operation is to remove the meningioma that's pressing on your brain, causing those symptoms."

"But if that doesn't happen. . . . My uncle had a stroke a few years ago. He couldn't walk, eat, or talk. He couldn't ever think as far as I could see. But they kept him alive with IVs and tubes going into his stomach and round-the-clock nurses. When he got pneumonia they brought him back into the hospital for intensive care and a respirator. Cured the pneumonia too, then back to the nursing home. I don't want that to happen to me. I want you to promise that I'll walk out of here as normal as I am now."

"John, I can't guarantee that."

"No, but you can promise not to do what they did to my uncle. No intensive care, no respirator, no futile or useless life."

"That I promise you."

"Thank you. I'm relieved."

"But it's not that simple. You're going to need the ICU and the ventilator and the IVs tomorrow. Defining 'futile' and 'useless' is a problem."

"My point is, I might not be in any condition to have the conversation. And what do I know about neurosurgery? How could I recognize futility? It takes a lot of experience to decide when brain damage is hopeless, and what to do about it. That decision I leave to your judgment. Yours and Anne's. We've discussed this, Anne and I. I trust her completely. She has power of attorney. We've discussed what to do in the event of . . . permanent brain tissue damage, as you put it. And she knows a lot about it—she was a nurse years ago. Well, of course you know that." Bradford said this casually. Ingram knew that Anne had told him nothing of their brief, passionate, whirlwind romance many years ago.

"Fair enough," said Ingram, who was accustomed to this type of instruction on the eve of a major operation. Then followed discussion of ocean sailing, postoperative pain medication, the residents on the team, all part of smoothing emotional peaks and troughs into conventional interpersonal behavior. Flint joined them, and reviewed the operative consent without comment. As Ingram took his leave Bradford said, "Thanks Don. I'll tell Anne about our conversation. She might call you if she has any questions. She is terrific. You should get to know her. Have a good sleep tonight."

"Have a good sleep yourself."

* * * *

There were three yellow three-by-five cards in the center of his desk, which was otherwise clear of paper: one for Sunday with a list of new admissions, one for Saturday with a list of all the inpatients, and one for Friday saying, simply, "8:00 craniotomy Bradford AKA Jones." There was a note attached to the cards with a paperclip, carefully typed: "Dr. Ingram, I told the Neurology Search Committee (12 noon) and the Dean's Executive Committee (3:00 p.m.) that you would be absent. Don't stay too late. Good luck tomorrow. D."

Ingram chuckled aloud. "AKA Bradford" was Miss Lewis's idea of a little joke. And she knew that he had been staying late in the office. It never occurred to her that he might consider this preferable to going home to an empty house, since she had lived her adult life in an empty house, and her phantoms there were dreams, not memories.

Dorothy Lewis had been secretary to Ingram for four years, and secretary to his chief, Franz Eastman, for eighteen years before that. She was aristocratic, aloof, often demanding, the quintessential Bostonian, and the best secretary in the world. That assessment had been made by Eastman but was not fully appreciated by Ingram until he had been the chief himself for a few months. His life, which he thought was organized, became truly organized. Everything was done on time and perfectly, and he came to rely on the yellow daily schedule cards which she insisted on preparing, until he was in the habit. She had called him "Dr. Ingram" on the first day of his internship, and he had called her "Miss Lewis," and it was still so today.

It was 7:30 in the evening now and he chuckled again at her admonition regarding the hour as he put the cards in his pocket. In his characteristically precise printing, which was instantly recognizable in hospital charts and memos to residents, he wrote her a note. "Miss Lewis, Please leave at 2:00 p.m. and enjoy the symphony. Wear your white gloves. D." A joke for a joke, and one that they often shared. She always went to symphony on Friday afternoon. He tossed the note in Miss Lewis's basket, along with a dozen other bits of work which he signed, sorted, or dictated over the next half hour. He left the manuscript on the chimpanzee project until last. It was Comstock's first attempt at a full paper. He had sent back the first draft full of red marks and arrows and suggestions for new paragraphs. It was always a painful process. Midway through the third page he realized that he was correcting his own corrections. He sighed, tossed the manuscript in his briefcase, resolved to finish it at home. There was a knock at the door.

"Don, may I come in?" Anne Bradford entered the office cautiously. "I thought you might be here. I just left John and he said that you had already stopped in to see him." She seemed to be trying her best at composure, but Ingram notice the tension in her speech and the tremor of her upper lip.

"Sure Anne. I was going to call you later on. I'm glad you came by." He rose and came around the desk, taking her hand. It was cold. "Are you okay?"

"I'm okay. John was so good tonight. Then he started on that paranoid kick. He finally told me to leave. His big operation tomorrow . . . and he told me to leave. I just . . . need someone to lean on."

"Literally or figuratively?"

"Both."

He could tell she was about to cry. He put an arm around her, as he often did with patients or family members in an emotional crisis. She relaxed onto his shoulder. "I'm sorry. I'll be all right in a minute. I'm just not as strong as I thought I was."

His first reaction, which was professional and familiar, evolved into his second reaction which was much more physical. He backed away his pelvis and his chest, leaving their knees and shoulders touching, like proper strangers dancing. He thought next how this might look to passersby, since his office was on the ground floor, and he edged her over to the door which he gently pushed shut and flipped off the light. In the darkness he became aware of her hand on his neck, and he allowed his hand to spread over the middle of her back. A deep breath, and he let his face rest against the back of her head. The faint odor of a spicy perfume. Suddenly he thought himself quite indecent to be experiencing such sensations, taking advantage of what he assumed to be her simple need for release of anxiety. He pulled away, just slightly, to a more conventional comforting posture and tried to calm his thoughts. He concluded he was reading more into the moment than was justified. She sniffed, wiped her face with her hand, and reassembled her composure. He let himself wonder if she pulled him closer, just for an instant, before she stood back.

"I'm sorry," she said. "I really did come down here for medical advice. I never . . . I didn't come here to . . ."

"Understood," silencing her rationalization. "What are old friends for?"

"Thanks."

He eased the contact, trying to bank the coals without putting out the fire. She wiped tears from her eyes with the back of a finger, trying to catch mascara before it ran down her cheek. "I'm so worried about John. He seems so distant."

"He's scared too."

He stepped back too, keeping one arm around her shoulder, as if one or the other might fall otherwise, and took the briefcase from his desk. "Let me take you back to your apartment. I had a good talk with John—an interesting talk. I'll tell you about it in the car."

"Fine."

They wound through the corridors to the place where the MG was parked. "What did John tell you?"

"To get a good sleep—which is what I plan to do as soon as I drop you off, and also that I should get to know you better."

"Really?" She was back to full composure. "Thanks for all your help. Will I see you in the morning?"

"No, I'll find you after the operation. Probably around noon."

On the way home he noticed the faint smell of perfume on his collar, but his mind was occupied with rehearsing tomorrow's operation.

CHAPTER 11

Staring at the yellowed plaster, Bradford became momentarily obsessed with the idea that something should be done about hospital ceilings. Here in the operating room, with its pervasive astringent vapors and ominous metallic clattering preparation, this last view of conscious life should provide some serene escape, like the Sistine Chapel, or the stars and clouds which drifted across the ceiling of Lowe's Theater between features when he was a boy. It was nothing like that though. Just plaster and conduit and blackened specks, which Bradford suspected was dried blood (in fact it was). He had become aware of the specks as he moved from the gurney to the barely padded, narrow table, trying unsuccessfully to shield his bare senatorial ass from the youthful and overly cheerful nurse who was coaxing him to slide over. (It occurred to him that this was a little silly since it was the business of this young girl to deal dispassionately with naked men and she, in fact, would soon be sliding a Foley catheter into his senatorial urethra. But he had not reached the state of illness where modesty evaporates.) The OR ceiling had been preceded by the OR hallway where there were chips in the plaster and burned-out light bulbs; the elevator ceiling which held two very bright lights and a latticework which was not meant to be viewed from directly below; and the hallway on 9 West which actually had a cobweb in the corner. This continued series of minor imperfections did not inspire a feeling of great confidence in the housekeeping or sterility of the system, and was unnerving to the perceptive preoperative patient. However, it kept his mind off the immediate activities taking place on his outstretched arms and around the top of his head, and he preferred to focus on the trivia rather than the ultimate reality he was about to experience.

"Good morning John. How are you doing?" The question came from somewhere above his head. He recognized the reassuring voice of Dr. Peterson. He looked over his head and saw the tall anesthesiologist, upside down, as he was bending forward.

"Your ceilings need some work. Other than that, I am doing pretty well." Peterson chuckled and gave him a reassuring squeeze on the shoulder. "I hope that's our biggest problem. Now, as soon as Miss Lawson gets that IV started, we'll have you off to sleep. What's your favorite ceiling?"

He felt a sudden stinging on the back of his right hand. Then the young lady in the tight scrub dress held his hand in her left hand, and with a remarkable efficiency of motion placed a large needle into his vein, popped out the metal trocar and attached a waiting IV to the plastic sheath. She secured the tubing with prepared pieces of tape stuck to the IV pole.

"Well of course the Sistine Chapel comes to mind. Actually I've never been there. The ceiling in the House of Representatives is rather nice. I've dozed off looking at it from time to time . . ."

Looking around the room as best he could, he saw Peterson checking a supply of loaded syringes and other paraphernalia, laid out on a fresh towel on a table adjacent to his anesthesia machine. A man in OR garb—gowned and gloved and apparently already sterile—was moving silver-colored surgical instruments from a large tray onto an even larger table. The young nurse who had moved him onto the operating table was preparing some plastic tubing, her back turned toward him.

"I stayed in a room in Las Vegas once with mirrors on the ceiling. I didn't ask for it you understand, I just got assigned there. It was at some political convention. It was interesting. I always wondered if they were one-way mirrors."

A matronly woman bearing the name tag "Tibbets" was popping sterile packages onto the big table faster than the scrub tech could stack them up. She looked up while carrying out this routine job, surveying the room, taking mental inventory. She seemed unhappy with Flint, who, in surgical greens, was standing calmly against the wall, out of the way. Flint had appeared early in the morning dressed for the operating room, witnessed the preoperative medication, and accompanied Bradford through the corridors to the room itself. He appeared oblivious to Tibbets's disapproving gaze.

"I like the ceiling in the bar of the Copley Plaza, now that I think of it. It must be twenty feet high, sort of a dark copper color. It has a Victorian pattern on it and it's reflected in those high mirrors that look like windows. Have you noticed that Dr. Peterson?"

"Can't say as I have, but I'll check it out the next time I'm there."

Dan Adams came through the door, followed by Burleson. They were holding their wet arms up and water dripped off their elbows onto the scrub suits. Adams nodded to Tibbets and picked up a towel from the table near the door. Bradford assumed that Ingram was close behind. He wondered if he would see Ingram before he went to sleep. He really didn't care.

"Most of all, I guess I like the ceiling in the forward cabin on my boat. There is a big hatch cover right over your head when you're lying there—it's the sail hatch for racing, you know." The back of his right hand and forearm suddenly felt very hot. He wiggled his fingers and it seemed to pass. "On clear nights I flip the hatch all the way back so that the ceiling becomes the entire sky. I try to imagine which constellation I'm looking at, past the masthead." A bitter taste in his mouth and a ringing in his ears. "Some times the jib halyard . . ." His own voice sounded distant and pinched, as if it came through a long, narrow pipe. His mental image of the stars and the masthead light spun dizzily clockwise, phasing rapidly from specks of light to bands of intense color accompanied by the roar in his ears rising rapidly in pitch and he flew spinning past the rigging, past the masthead, toward the spiraling stars themselves for an instant. Then all was black.

Flint was pleased with the induction of anesthesia. Swift and complete with no time for rambling thoughts or disclosure of unmasked memory. From past experience he knew that the greatest risk of random conversation would come in the recovery room. Knew enough to stand against the wall to avoid interfering with the sterile field or the sojourn of the circulating nurse. Knew that his presence in the surgical domain would soon be forgotten, consumed by concentration on the task at hand.

133

He watched with detached interest as the tone of the room rapidly changed from the serenity maintained for the awake patient to overdrive intensity as the patient went to sleep. If the OR staff were aware that this was Senator John Bradford they certainly did not show it. Effortlessly, Peterson slid an endotracheal tube through his larynx, taking care to protect the incisors which made up the famous Bradford smile. Kay Lawson taped the tube in place and released the lock on the table so that they could spin it around, leaving the Senator's head available for the surgeons. The younger nurse whisked off the hospital johnny and stuffed a Foley catheter into his penis while chatting about her aerobics class. Tibbets tied up the strings on Adams's gown while Burleson took the paper cap off Bradford's freshly shaved head and started to prep.

"Don't get that prep in his eyes," cautioned Tibbets, who kept constant watch on Burleson. He glared but did not respond, continuing to wash the bald skull with both hands. Kay Lawson turned on the radio, the room filled with a dazzling polyphonic processional march. She turned down the volume.

* * * *

Donald Ingram planned to come to the operating room a little earlier than usual. After twenty years of getting into the skull, the routines of early exposure had become rather tedious, therefore best left to the enthusiastic resident. And, following his own advice, he specifically planned not to interrupt the routine because of the importance of the patient. However, he wanted to be sure that the incision didn't wander in front of the hairline and that the head positioning was just right. So he had curtailed his rounds in the intensive care unit earlier than usual and walked into the surgeon's dressing room at 7:45. Soon the little lounge would be filled with the morning regulars waiting for cases to start, ruffling old journals just to keep busy, dictating and calling the office, discussing cases with residents or stock quotations with the anesthesiologists. But at the moment the first battalion of workers was already in the operating room and the lounge was relatively empty. Ingram passed through the lounge into the locker room, grabbing, by habit, a large scrub suit and loosening his tie as he went.

He had kicked off his shoes and started on his belt buckle when he heard a characteristic cough and a toilet flushed behind him. "Good morning, Bart," he said without turning around.

"Good morning, Don. You're here a little early this morning." C. Hobart Newton had had the locker next to Ingram for ten years. Every morning that he was operating (which was three days a week) he settled into the first stall in the surgeon's locker room for his morning constitutional. After a period of time measured by the theater section and the sports section of the Globe, he coughed, flushed, and, without ever moving his pipe from his teeth, crossed from the stall to the sink, then put on his scrubs. The new young residents, especially those whose upbringing did not include the squash court locker rooms of the Harvard Club, regarded Hobart as a museum piece, with his creased and ironed boxer shorts, shoulder-strap undershirt, and short black socks held up by garters, always with his pipe between his teeth.

"Big case this morning?" asked Hobart, trading his cordovan wing tips for his old white OR shoes.

"Yes Bart, I have a patient with a brain tumor who's a bit of a VIP, so I'm going to look in early on," said Ingram, pulling the scrub shirt over his head.

"Aye-a. Know whatcha mean." Hobart had not lost the lingual affectations acquired during his annual August sojourn to Bar Harbor. "Well, I'm doing a mastectomy so just let me know if you need some muscle to stop the bleeding." He chuckled so violently that he had to remove the pipe from his mouth. He used it to point at Ingram. "Did I ever tell you how Harvey Cushing used to come into my father's operating room asking for muscle to put on the bleeders?"

"Yes Bart, several times. Quite a man, your father."

"Aye-a."

* * * *

"Sounds like Berlioz," commented Ingram, as Tibbets tied his gown and Jimmy held out his gloves.

"Couldn't prove it by me," mumbled Tibbets.

"Rimsky-Korsakov." The voice came from the corner of the room. Ingram turned.

"Is that you Mr. Flint?"

A silent nod.

"I see Mrs. Tibbets has given you the visitors' instruction." He couldn't tell if Flint was smiling or not behind the mask. "I believe you're right. Procession of the Kings, or something like that." Flint merely nodded again.

Adams had finished draping and Ingram waved him ahead. "Don't you want to do this skin to skin, chief?" asked Adams, hesitating.

"You go ahead Dan. I'll take over in a little while. Just stay behind the hairline." He nudged Burleson over and took on the duties of the first assistant, putting the heavy clips on the bleeding scalp. "Looks great up here," he commented to Dr. Peterson, referring to the bright red color of the arterial blood.

"Looks fine down here too, Don" responded Peterson. "What's your guess on timing? Will this just shell out or will it take some dissection?"

"I hope for the former and fear the latter. We'll have a forecast for you pretty soon. Give that drill to Dr. Adams, Jimmy." The fact that the wet bone dust was that of the prominent senator from Rhode Island was now lost on almost everyone in the operating room except Flint. The initial importance of the person had given way to the routine of the operating room, which now settled into the quiet crescendo of suspense that inevitably occurs just before the pathologic lesion is seen. Like opening a perfectly wrapped Christmas present. When the last saw cut was finished and bone flap tenderly teased off, the displacement of the frontal lobe could be seen even through the investing dura.

"Dan, let's trade places," said Ingram, spinning back to back with Burleson and walking around to the right side of the table.

The senator was right-handed, so they approached the tumor by retracting the nondominant frontal lobe. The tumor was huge—golf ball sized. It was covered with small pulsing arteries and large veins filled with red blood which indicated the vascularity of the tumor. Only a small portion of the top of it was visible as the frontal lobe was retracted. Very cautiously Ingram explored the margins, at first with a joker, then with the tip of his finger. Kay had turned off the radio and the room was very quiet.

"That doesn't look like a meningioma, does it sir?" asked Burleson. The nudge from Adams and the full minute of silence which followed told him that the question need not have been asked.

Finally Ingram said, "No, it doesn't." He stood up to address Peterson, but he was clearly outlining the game plan for all players. "This tumor, Pete, grows across the midline and sits down on the corpus callosum, but it's arising from the right frontal lobe. It's probably a glioma. It's going to take a couple hours to see if it's resectable, and if it is you'd better cancel your dinner date." The realization that John Bradford's political career was at an end had become obvious to Ingram when he first put his finger on the hard, irregular mass. Now, slowly, the same realization became a thought in the mind of Adams, then Peterson, then Lawson, then Burleson, and—finally—in the mind of Flint. Jimmy knew it when he saw the color of the blood in the veins. They shook their heads slightly, or hunched forward as if they had been hit between the shoulder blades. Ingram knew the team well. He waited a minute for them to adjust, then said, "Well, maybe this will just shell out. It looks like there is a nice plane on top here anyway. Kay, what happened to the music? Tibbets, would you give me my loupes? We'll go along here in the old fashioned style for awhile. These vessels are big enough for an old man to see." Ingram pushed the microscope out of the way and settled back on his high stool, placing patties and retractors, and watching the blood in the veins.

They worked for two hours with hardly a sound except the quiet music from the radio and the occasional familiar instruction ("Suck on the patty. Buzz my right hand. Joker. Cushing.") Burleson recognized the skill of the dissection, but Adams felt the awe which he had experienced when first operating with Dr. Ingram. A small hole appeared in the spider web of vessels, then a crevice, then a cleavage plane began to develop in the brain tissue a centimeter away from the tumor. The narrow cavity between the tumor and the frontal lobe looked like it was intended to be there. When they finally came down to the anterior cerebral artery, Ingram nudged at the dense tissue between the vessel and the tumor for several minutes, then put down his instruments and stepped away from the table, stretching his back. "Take a break Burleson. You're doing a great job. The exposure couldn't be better." Adams waited for the next part of the game plan, which he knew would follow. "The tumor runs right onto the adventitia of the anterior cerebral. To get it completely out we'll have to take that vessel and it's going to be hard to find the origin. He'll lose the whole frontal lobe for sure if we do that. If this is highly invasive, it won't matter anyway. If it's low grade we might try to shave it off the artery and pick up a few cells with radiation." He was thinking out loud, Adams had already been down the same sequence of thoughts.

"We could do a frozen, but I don't think it would help us," he volunteered.

"I agree," said Ingram. "Let's see if we can carve it off there." They returned to the dissection, and gradually the tumor separated from the small vessel, as small bits of brain tissue (hundreds of thousands of neurons) disconnected from their circuits and disappeared into the surgical sucker or the vapor of the electric cautery.

Now Ingram switched to the operating microscope. Millimeter by millimeter he stripped the little vessel of its covering, along with the fleshy malignancy. By the time he came to the anterior communicating artery there was a core through the tumor one inch long. Although the tumor was still attached at its deepest point, he could roll it completely out of the cavity in the right frontal lobe. The bare artery hung across the space like a telephone wire, oscillating with each pulsation. At the junction with the communicating artery some of the muscular wall had been cleaned away, and a bulge appeared like a boot in an old tire. Ingram pulled some adjacent tissue over it with a 7-0 suture, but the repair looked tenuous to both Ingram and Adams.

Leaving the base of the tumor still attached, they incised a patch of the falx where the tumor was adherent. As they expected, there was no extension to the left frontal lobe, although the gyri were displaced and flattened by the pressure. They dissected as far down the left side as they could, feeling the left anterior cerebral artery, but unable to see it.

Flint had been up early and had three cups of coffee before the orderlies came to wheel Bradford to the operating room. By noon his bladder was complaining, and at one thirty, after standing against the wall for six hours, he slipped out of the room, noticed only by Tibbets. With the senator deep under anesthesia and his head open, Flint was sure that the information he was guarding was safe. Quickly he made his way down the tiled hallway, found the staff lounge where he had dressed, and, finding the urinals in use and needing the rest for his legs anyway, sat down in one of the stalls. He voided for almost twenty seconds, feeling a little light-headed but much relieved. Outside the stall he heard water running and voices.

"Hey Jimmy. You be wanting to stop at the Keg after work?"

"No man. I'm working late tonight. We're only half way through our case."

"Come on man, let someone else finish up."

"Not me Lionel. You know I always finish my man's cases. I shouldn't be out here now, but he's sending everyone out on a break."

"You do that Jimmy, but it makes the rest of us look bad. I mean, we look lazy if we leave on time, ya know?"

"Your choice man. That's just the way I do my job."

"Tell you what I be thinking. I'd stay late too if I could work with Kay Lawson all day. Ooo wee."

"Whatta y'all mean?" In a voice ringed with a smile.

"I seen her in there rubbing her big tits on the IV pole and smiling at y'all."

"She has big tits, and a special nice ass . . ."

"Amen."

"But she ain't flashing that stuff at me. She's making it with Dr. Adams."

"Dr. Adams be making with that stuff? Ooo wee."

Flint waited until the conversants had left the locker room to go into the lounge. He washed his hands and splashed water on his face. When he returned to the OR, he positioned himself in a different place, so as to get a better view of Miss Lawson. She did, indeed, wait until Adams could look over the drapes before she stretched or changed the IV fluids.

* * * *

By two thirty they had done as much as they could, rolling the tumor from side to side, but it was still firmly attached to the corpus down near the optic chiasm. Ingram and Adams discussed whether to

139

extend the exposure, remove the tumor piecemeal, or to continue the partially blind dissection. Ingram took advantage of this break to send Burleson out because he would need steady exposure for this last assault and Burleson was starting to fade. Burleson protested only mildly. He was getting a cold and as soon as he was outside the room he blew his nose, which he had been wanting to do all morning. He retrieved two candy bars from his locker, cached there for just this situation, and ate one while riding up the elevator to the eighth floor. He scavenged three cartons of chocolate milk from the refrigerator in the ICU and crashed on a couch in the smoky nurses' lounge, eating, drinking and getting supine all at the same time. The nurses began to gather for report. Sally took pity on the disheveled, ravenous intern and rubbed his shoulders professionally while telling him that Kathleen Dugan was taking clear liquids, Ben Rothstein was draining less and seemed more alert, and Matt Rizzo had some bright red blood in his nasogastric tube drainage. She recited the vital signs and the blood gases. Gradually Burleson's blood sugar rose and the tension in his trapezius receded. He thanked her warmly, and was back in the OR ten minutes after he had left with vital information for Adams (should he ask), refreshed, and ready to go another six hours. Burleson was learning.

* * * *

They had decided that the only way to get to the base of the tumor was to take it out in pieces, hoping that the remaining attachment to the anterior communicating artery didn't have any big vessels in it. As soon as this was decided the delicate procedure became relatively gross as chunks of the tumor were burned out with the electric cautery.

"Not a very satisfying cancer operation is it Burleson?" said Ingram between swipes with the cautery.

"Whatever works, sir. I still can't see how you managed to resect any of it. It sure looks good to me."

Ingram accepted this compliment quietly. It didn't look good to him.

Finally, there was just a raisin-sized mass at the bottom of the hole between the two anterior cerebral arteries. "What do you think, Dan?" Ingram asked.

"We could ligate both ends of that anterior communicating and resect the whole thing."

"Yes but there are probably some small branches going posteriorly and superiorly into the hypothalamus. We'd never see them if they retracted back into the brain. I think we should shave this down just a little more and finish off with some radiation when this is all healed up."

He brought the microscope back into position and focused on the last remaining bit of tumor, pulsating because of the vessel behind it. "We're going to be through pretty soon here people. Let's get some irrigation ready and think about closure. Kay, what happened to the music? Burleson, you're doing a great job. Just hold this retractor and bovie the sucker when I tell you."

With a delicate dissector in one hand and the sucker in the other Ingram set out to remove the last half gram of tissue. Adams watched through the teaching head of the microscope, irrigating occasionally and holding traction on the little lump. In the middle of the mass Ingram found the muscular coat of the artery.

"On . . . off. On . . . off. Very gently now. On . . ." The directions to Burleson were given softly.

Flint had expressed an interest in the anatomy of the operation, and had gained Tibbets's grudging approval by standing at attention for six hours. Seeing that he was craning his neck to see from the foot of the table, Tibbets brought a low lift, which allowed him to improve his view without having to move closer to the sterile field. Tibbets was now out of the room and the dissection had returned to the micro-scope. Despite the lift, Flint could not see, so he gathered another low lift from the corner of the room and stacked it on the first, as he had seen Tibbets do for Jimmy. One of the rubber pads on the steel legs of the lift was missing, and when Flint hoisted his full weight onto the platform the leg settled into the metal groove with a crack like the shot of a rifle. Ingram stifled his reflex reaction in milliseconds, as did Adams. But Burleson jerked violently, turning on the current with his thumb and pushing Ingram's sucker down into the communicating artery. Blood squirted onto the microscope lens, then on to Ingram's mask and neck. Days later, Ingram would marvel at the timing, and wonder if Flint had done it on purpose. But at the moment the head filled with red blood which ran down over the sides, and he thought only about controlling the bleeder.

"We've got some bleeding up here Pete," said Ingram. Jimmy had brought up two of the large patties on a bayonet forceps when he saw the gush of blood. Ingram took the forceps—he didn't have to ask—and pushed the cotton felt squares over the artery, almost stopping the bleeding. "I'll say," said Peterson, who was already spiking a bag of blood. His anesthesiologist's response to the loud noise had been to look into the field to see if any damage occurred.

"We need a big tonsil sucker up here," said Adams. Jimmy had already found the large steel tube and used it to replace the small neurosurgical sucker. Rapidly the pint of blood in the head was transferred to the suction bottle, and Adams scooped out the clots while Ingram held pressure on the hole. Red blood still oozed forth with each heartbeat because there was little solid for Ingram to push against. Through the microscope, Ingram had seen the end of the sucker burn a hole through the wall of the communicating artery and he knew there was no chance to repair it.

"I need some silver clips on long handles Jimmy. Better get a few up." Jimmy was already prepared. Ingram cautiously replaced his right hand on he forceps with his left, losing another two hundred cc's of blood in the process. Judging by the hiss of the squirting blood, the blood pressure was obviously much lower. Kay Lawson hung another bag of blood and pumped it in. Ingram slid the silver clip applier down beside the forceps and adjusted it until he imagined it was nestled around the left side of the artery. He clamped it down and eased off the pressure to examine the result. The clip was sitting astride the communicating artery and the hole in the vessel became visible, still squirting with each heartbeat.

"Good shot," said Adams with genuine admiration.

"You try to get the right side Dan. You have a better angle on it." Adams took the clip applier and eased it into the depths of the wound, placing it in a position opposite Ingram's clip. He squeezed it down and removed the long handle. "That felt pretty good," he said. Ingram withdrew the forceps slightly, followed immediately by another gush of arterial blood.

"Must not be it. Let's try again. Here you control the bleeder. Adams took the forceps without releasing the pressure, and with that extra bit of guidance, placed another clip under the pool of blood and clamped it down. This time the field was dry when he withdrew the forceps. The carefully dissected remnant of tumor now looked like hamburger. They placed two more clips on the artery, obliterating the defect. Adams's first clip had occluded the right anterior cerebral, but it was too firmly placed to remove it. The entire episode was over in a few minutes and it took another half hour to get the pulse and blood pressure stabilized.

"Goddamn it, I knew we shouldn't have let any visitors in here," said Peterson bitterly, looking at Flint.

"I'm terribly sorry," said Flint. "I just stepped on this platform and it seemed to give way."

Burleson, who didn't realize that he was the only surgeon who had moved, was still shaking. "Boy, I never saw so much blood in such a short time," he said quietly, mostly to himself. Ingram and Adams quietly cleaned up the wound, irrigating the debriding small bits of clot until the carnage began to resemble a neurosurgical operation instead of an accident.

Finally, Ingram said, "Well, let's close it up. That clip on the left side looks a little tenuous but there is no room to get another one adjacent to that anterior cerebral. This frontal lobe won't be much good along with anything else that was served by those collaterals. Perfection is the enemy of good. Let's quit."

"Right," said Adams. Jimmy supplied some sutures for the dura.

* * * *

There had been no Chopin on WGBH all afternoon. Anne Bradford started to write a letter, then put it aside. She picked up the novel she had been reading, turned pages, then gave up. She sighed, paced, and watched the clock. She had received periodic messages, as Ingram said she would, and had nibbled at the lunch tray delivered to the room. The last message, delivered at four thirty, was that the operation was nearly over and Dr. Ingram would be out soon. Now, as any lay person equates the time of an operation with severity of the illness, she began to think that there might be a knock at the door every few minutes.

At quarter to five Ingram appeared quietly, hunched forward and drained, lacking the authoritative stance which he usually conveyed. She rose to meet him and he managed to smile, taking her hand in his. Her eyes widened. She searched his tired face.

"I'm glad to see you. It's been a long day," she said uncertainly.

"John's okay. He's in recovery and everything is stable."

She sighed deeply and now smiled, sinking back into the chair. Ingram took the chair beside her, still holding her hand. "The tumor was not a meningioma. It's probably a low-grade malignancy—but it's all removed." He allowed himself this slight deviation from the truth. He would bring up the radiation later. "His major brain function should be fine—hearing, talking, moving . . . and that sort of thing." He stopped talking, watching her lip and her eyes.

Her face was tense. "And?"

"And we had some bleeding which required taking some of the blood supply to the frontal lobes," tapping on his forehead to indicate the area. "We'll just have to see how things are when he wakes up."

"When he wakes up?"

"In the recovery room. It was a long operation. It'll take a long time for the anesthetic to wear off."

She sighed again, and the small furrow between her eyebrows disappeared.

"Thanks Don," squeezing his hand, "you must be exhausted." For almost a minute they said nothing, each getting the new information in perspective. "When can I see him?"

"Right now. I'll take you."

CHAPTER 12

"Good morning Mac. Would you like some oatmeal this morning?"

"Thank you, Margaret. Some oatmeal would be very nice." Somehow the carefully knotted maroon silk tie seemed to go with the red plaid flannel shirt in a way that would not be acceptable on a younger man. The sleeves of the shirt were too long, and he held them back with large rubber bands placed just above the elbows. All the joints in his hand were heaped up into round balls by arthritis, making it appear that his fingers came off at odd angles. The stiffness of his joints affected the function, as well as the appearance, and it took him four tries to extract a paper napkin from the tightly packed dispenser. He put the napkin on his tray, along with a big spoon and, awaiting the oatmeal, tugged on the old watch fob (worn black leather with his initials in brass) and pulled out his big pocket watch. 7:13. He returned the watch to the watch pocket of his heavy, creaseless, gabardine trousers. If he had gone out in search of new trousers he would have been unable to locate a pair with a watch pocket, but he had not been shopping for trousers for fifteen years. Like his shirt, the trouser legs were a little longer than necessary and the greatest wear could be seen, if anyone cared, where the back of the cuff touched the ground. The trousers had fit perfectly at one time; in fact, they made up the lower half of the suit he bought at Filene's to attend his grand-daughter's wedding. (The same granddaughter who now lived in California and last Christmas sent him the plaid shirt he was wearing.) His black shoes—well shined—made it obvious that the joints in his feet were similar to those in his hands, the old leather having given way gradually to the pressure of bunions and calluses.

The big bowl of oatmeal—chunk of butter melting in the center of the steamy goo—was ready. "And here's some brown sugar to go with it," said Margaret putting both bowls on the counter top.

"Aye lass, it's just like my dear mother used to make it." She added two pieces of toast from the stack on the back of the grill put there to keep warm, but made cracker-dry despite the margarine painted on with a little bristle brush, six pieces at a time.

"Good morning, Mac," said Ingram as the old man settled his tray on the table, nodding a salutation. "You know Dr. Adams, and this is Dr. Burleson."

They exchanged greetings. Ingram had the look of being up all night, easily recognized by Mac after decades of breakfasts in the Longwood Hospital Cafeteria. Mac had obviously interrupted a conversation, so he set about stirring the brown sugar into the oatmeal quietly. Ingram didn't make his usual comment about the oatmeal, but turned instead to Adams. "Did Mr. Flint finally give up and get some sleep?"

"I think so. He sat down in the corner with his eyes closed. He made me promise to wake him up when we pull out the endotracheal tube. I think he's more concerned about what the senator—" he interrupted the sentence, glancing at Mac, "—what Mr. Jones might say, rather than his state of health."

"He's not going to say much in the state he's in, even when he's extubated," said Burleson, realizing mid-sentence that he was once again stating the obvious, and in this case, also offending the chief. "I mean, he still seems pretty sleepy. Probably just the anesthetic . . ." voice trailing off again, eyes cast down. No one responded. They sipped coffee and stared, not at each other.

"Sometimes when Dr. Eastman had been up all night he'd asked me to page him at 8:15—just after the Surgery Conference started." The mischievous twinkle in the old man's blue eyes brought smiles to the tired surgeons. "Not that I would suggest it, you understand."

"Of course not, Mac. Especially in front of these eager young residents." More smiles. "Dan, I was so involved with our friend Mr. Jones that I didn't look around the rest of the ICU. Any problems?"

"Professor Rothstein is stable as long as we keep his CSF drained. He's not waking up much though. The Dugan girl is responding to

146

commands—I hope it lasts." Adams was going through the stack of five-by-seven cards which he had pulled from his pocket. Each one held small, meticulous printing. The next card was filled halfway down. "Rizzo is worrisome. He's still febrile. He blows up every time I clamp his NG tube and the drainage is bloody from time to time. He has that waxy feel that some quads get. He just doesn't look good. His wife wants to see you, by the way."

"His wife is tough," volunteered Burleson. "She must be a great nurse. She's a fine, tough lady."

"Yes, she's been a big help," added Adams. "She brought their little boy in yesterday. I think she's worried too."

Ingram rubbed his eyes and leaned back in his chair. "I'll see her today," he said, realizing that he was in for some more direct questions from families that the residents had punted to him. He was quiet for a moment, thinking about Rizzo's spinal cord. Then he turned abruptly to Burleson. "Why is it, Burleson, that neurons in the peripheral nerves regenerate but those in the central nervous system don't?"

"I don't know," said Burleson after some reflection. "I always thought that's just the way it is—just a fact of life."

"That's what most people think. How about you, Dan?"

"In the brain that might be right. I'm not sure. But in the spinal cord—I realize that this is heresy—I think the neurons do regenerate. I mean, there is proximal neuroma if the cord is transected, and a lot of scar tissue. There was a Canadian surgeon a long time ago—"

"Gordon Murray. From Toronto," interjected Ingram, looking wide awake now. He couldn't remember if he had discussed Murray's work with Adams in the past, but if not he was impressed that Adams knew about it.

"His theory was that spinal cord neurons regenerated but were blocked by scar tissue. He did some experiments showing that if you blocked the scar tissue in some way, you got regeneration of the spinal cord. As I recall he even did a few patients."

"He did a lot of cats, but no patients," said Ingram, pleased that Adams knew as much as he did about the work from the early '60s. "The way he controlled the scar tissue was to resect a couple vertebrae and take the tension off the cord . . ."

"Wow, that's a big operation" said Burleson.

"Damn big operation," said Ingram. "But Murray was quite a surgeon. He did the first kidney transplants and the first cardiac surgery in Canada. He was a wild man. The right kind of wild man who didn't accept the so-called facts of life. He had recovery of function in a significant percentage of his cats."

"Why didn't he do any patients?" asked Burleson.

"Two reasons. He ran out of funding before he finished his laboratory work. And he got caught up in a sort of academic political battle. He was quoted in the papers as saying that he had repaired the spinal cord on some patients—he never said it actually—but every paraplegic in North America called the local neurosurgeon. There was sort of a nationwide ego contest with pompous neurosurgery professors proclaiming that Murray was dishonest. After all, everyone knew that the spinal cord didn't regenerate, and Murray wasn't even a neurosurgeon. Eastman actually did part of the official investigation and after a few months he said it was damn good work."

"That's fascinating," said Adams. "Did Murray go on with it?"

"No. He was an old man at the time he did those experiments. He spent his whole career doing things that the establishment said was impossible. The chief said he just lost enthusiasm. 'Disgusted with the establishment,' that's what he said. He left it there in the literature and it's still there waiting for someone else to come along who doesn't believe that it can't be done. I think he retired to fish for trout, or something like that."

"Hasn't anyone tried to reproduce those experiments?"

"Not as far as I know."

"But that's really important." Burleson was squirming in his seat. "I mean why doesn't someone do that?"

"Why don't you do it, Burleson?"

"Right! Why *don't* we do it, anyway? Why don't we do it to Rizzo? I mean the guy's cooked the way he is, what's there to lose?"

"What's to lose," injected Adams quickly, "is the rest of C5 and maybe C4. He could lose even more function. But more important than that—"

"—more important than that," emphasized Ingram, "is the two

years and half million dollars it would take to develop the procedure, let alone do the experiment in the animal laboratory. The ICU is a great place for clinical research, Burleson, but not without a lot of homework. A lot of good researchers drown by jumping into the clinical deep water before they can swim."

"I'm sure you're right," said Burleson, "but if it were me I'd want someone to give it a try. I mean, it's got to be worth a try."

"What would you want done, if it were you, Dan?" asked Ingram, serious but leaning back in his chair.

"C4, total quad?"

Ingram nodded.

"A brain with no body. Just like a solitary head rolling around. Only the ability to see and hear and smell and think great thoughts and read great books, with no connections. Like a head on a shelf. Like a computer with emotions. Sort of alive . . ."

"Totally alive by anyone's definition."

Adams squinted and sighed, thinking out loud. "Depends on the level."

"If it were T12?"

"T12—wheelchair bound, but working from the waist up. I could live with that."

"C7?"

"C7. Motorized wheelchair with a neck brace, thumb, and finger. Maybe."

"C4?"

"C4. Like Rizzo." He paused, idly taping his fork on the uneaten eggs he'd left on his plate. "I'd rather be dead."

"So would I," said Ingram.

They sat silent, imagining the concept of a bodiless head.

"Then why are we still treating Rizzo?" asked Burleson, with a sincerity that revealed his naiveté.

"Because, Randy, we can't impose our value judgments on our patients. Besides, maybe you'll get Gordon Murray's operation to work," Said Ingram. They all chuckled, even Mac, all feeling that a little heavy conversation goes a long way after a night without sleep. Ingram rose, picking up his tray. "If the two of you would kindly finish rounds without me, I'll talk to Anne . . . to Mrs. Jones. Mac, I know you're off duty, but could you arrange to have me paged at 8:15?"

"With pleasure, Donald."

* * * *

The morning nursing report had recently finished and a smoky haze still hung in the air in the nurses' lounge on 9 North. The name had recently been changed to Team Conference Room in the spirit of modern nursing, but it still looked, smelled, and acted like the nurses' lounge—overflowing ashtrays, the aroma of street shoes and bag lunches emanating from the row of lockers, old copies of the American Journal of Nursing and new copies of Cosmopolitan—the coupons clipped out—cluttering the Formica table, one quarter of a cinnamon coffee cake, brought in by one of the chubby types on the night shift, still available for munching. Ingram pulled the lever on the old coffee urn, filling a Styrofoam cup with thick, burnt coffee. He remembered that Anne had taken her coffee black at L'Argent. However, that was good coffee and this was not. He added a dash of the white powder which substituted for cream. On impulse he picked a big white chrysanthemum from the bouquet on the table (retired to the nurses' lounge when left by a discharged patient).

Although the barriers remained, there was no security at the end of the hall, since the senator was still in the intensive care unit. Ingram entered the room quietly and put the coffee and the flower on the bedside table. A beam of early morning sunlight played on her face and her golden hair. For a minute he watched her sleep. She looked so relaxed after being so tense the night before. There was white downy fuzz on her cheek which he had not noticed before—he found it attractive. She must have a defect—a mole, a roll of fat, a gaping pore—to bring her back into the mere mortal category. He found none. Standing in the silence, watching her sleep, he noticed the fullness deep in his chest, the acceleration of his own pulse and breathing. Noticed it just long enough to be aware, then chided himself for letting emotion take over for a moment. With a jerk of willpower he pulled himself into more professional thoughts. He touched her cheek.

"Anne?"

A deep breath.

"Anne?"

She simply opened her eyes. No yawning, stretching, scratching or casting about for orientation. She simply opened her eyes.

"Hi Don. Any change yet?"

"Yes. I just came from the ICU. John's starting to wake up. It looks like we'll get that tube out of his throat in a few hours."

"Then everything will be okay." It came out as a statement, not a question.

"It's a little soon to say that, but so far so good."

His hand was still resting on her cheek, and she took it between her own hands. "I have such trust in you. We both do, John and I. I know he'll be alright with you looking after him."

Ingram was accustomed to this declaration of trust—all surgeons are. It is part of the complex psychology that surrounds a surgical operation, and usually comes, as it did now, in the first postoperative day along with shedding the anxiety which comes with the operation itself. "Thank you." The simple statement always acknowledged and completed the declaration and acceptance.

"No, it's more than that," she said emphatically, as if sensing that the statement which was so heartfelt to her must sound trite to him. "I know you're a great surgeon, you don't need me to tell you that. It's that I know you'll do the best for John regardless of the fact that I . . . that we are . . . that . . ."

"That we are old friends?"

"Yes. Before we called you I thought a lot about whether I would be putting you in an awkward position, or me, or John for that matter." She released his hand. He wondered if she had any of the same emotional rush he had just felt. But she gave no indication, and he concluded that he was over-reacting.

"And what did you decide?"

"I decided we could all handle it."

"Of course we can handle it. But I'm glad to have those old questions resolved. By the way, thanks for coming to dinner last Tuesday. I wasn't sure what to expect. I hope I didn't overdo it."

"To tell the truth, I almost canceled twice. But I'm so glad I didn't.

You didn't overdo it, you were very gracious. And you are right. It's good to have old questions resolved, and we handled it well. It's good to recognize it for what it was—more than recognize, cherish it for what it was. And now we can go back to real life and set it aside for another twenty years." She said this earnestly, quickly, as though she had thought this through in her own mind several times. She had taken his hand again.

"Fourteen years," he corrected her. His eyes showed just a hint of resignation. "Can we meet for dinner again in fourteen years?"

"It's a date."

The soft smile returned. Her eyelids hung heavy. "Don, could I ask you a personal question?"

"Sure."

"Can I go back to sleep?" Still smiling, eyes closed, head back on the pillow. When she awoke much later in the morning she found the cold coffee and the flower.

* * * *

Ravikrishnan was pleased. Rothstein seemed to be listening. He looked at Ravi directly when he was speaking, and even tried to talk. The fluid collecting in the plastic burette taped to the bedpost was as clear as water, and the nurse's marks on the piece of tape indicating the level showed that very little had drained during the night. Ravi continued what he had been recounting to his friend.

"And then the class went from Descartes into the functional description of the mind as free will. Campbell, that's the pre-med student, argued that what we call free will is simply a conditioned reflex. He gave a rather good example, actually. He showed that 90 percent of people—anywhere in the world—have the same religious belief that their parents have. Since all religions are equally believable, then religious beliefs should be equally distributed with no relation to the parents' belief. Then Francheski, the seminary student from Boston College, disagreed with the premise, stating that all religions are not equally believable and, in fact, there is only one correct religion which any intelligent person could accept. Of course that was a trap set by Campbell who argued if that were true then, according to Francheski, any intelligent person who had free will would profess to be a Catholic. It strengthened his argument nicely. Then Simmons argued that religious choice was a matter of education and environment and not a good example of free will, but Campbell countered that choices made on the basis of education and environment were precisely conditioned reflexes, just the point he was trying to make. Simmons is a persistent young man, though, and he insisted that choices based on learned facts—his definition of education—are the ultimate example of free will. Campbell then repeated that well-educated, intelligent people would be equally distributed among religions if free will exists, which is not the case. He had no data but everyone seemed to agree with him, at least on the lack of religious conversions which take place among educated adults. Of course this was very upsetting to the younger students, especially Horowitz, who claimed to have exercised totally free choice in his choice of religion, although by chance he settled on the same religion as his parents. It was a lively afternoon."

"Horowitz *would* say that," said Rothstein. It was the first time Rothstein had spoken since his return to the intensive care unit.

It was as if a great weight fell from Ravi's shoulders. Tears came to his eyes. But he responded calmly. "They all miss you Ben. I told them that you'll be back soon." Rothstein nodded and seemed to fall asleep.

"Excuse me, sir, I couldn't help overhearing your conversation." Father John O'Reilly was nearly back to back with Ravikrishnan, separated only by a curtain, as he sat at the bedside of Kathleen Dugan. "It sounds as though you are discussing a seminar."

"Yes we were Father O'Reilly. My friend Rothstein is a Professor of Philosophy and I am taking his seminar while he's recovering from his operation."

"Then you are at Harvard also?"

"That's right."

"Was your seminar on the freedom of will? That's what I heard in your conversation."

"The seminar is on Descartes, actually, but the title might be as you suggest." Each turned away to look at his patient. Both were sleeping.

"And what did you conclude about the freedom of the will?" asked the priest cautiously.

153

"Do we ever come to conclusion on that question?"

"We can try." Another pause. "For many years I taught philosophy at Boston College. Philosophy and theology."

"Really?" Ravi's interest went from gentlemanly to genuine.

"Yes. I'm going to step out for a cigarette. Would you join me?"

"Why yes. Our charges seem to be sleeping." The little waiting room was deserted. Father John searched his pockets for a Camel filter while Ravikrishnan deliberately stuffed Sobranie's Bulkan (white can) into an old, well-caked Dunhill. "I taught a course called, 'The Will of Man and the Will of God.' We used a lot of Descartes."

"And did you come to a conclusion?" asked Ravi, as the intellectual's version of a little joke.

"I did, personally. I found it difficult to teach after I became convinced of the answers."

"The teacher is intended to know the answers."

"Yes of course. Especially a Jesuit. But I became more of a priest and less of a teacher. I guided my students to the conclusion which I believe is right."

"Isn't that education?"

"In mathematics, yes. In music, perhaps. But in philosophy, no. I wanted each student to examine all the facts, then choose a conclusion. But I argued down the conclusions other than my own."

Ravikrishnan sensed a confession, or at least a rationalization. "And did your students learn well in your class?"

"I thought so. My students thought so. But my chairman thought not. All my graduate students wrote theses about why the church was right and everything else was wrong. It's ironic, don't you think, that the Catholic chairman of a Catholic department should find that offensive?" Ravi did not answer. "At any rate, I was reassigned to the post of parish priest at St. Cecilia's—at my request, mind you."

"It sounds like that was a wise request."

"It sounds like the Irish martyr in me. But in fact it's been very good. I'm a much better parish priest than I was a teacher." They sat in silence for a moment, Father John looking like he had just come out of the confessional.

"Can a mind exist without a brain?"

"I beg your pardon?" said Father John, who had been reflecting on more personal matters.

"You said that you studied the mind of man and the mind of God." (The shift of semantic gear between the 'will' and the 'mind' was made by both without further comment.) "I'm asking you where does one find the mind?"

"The simple answer to your question is that the mind is in the brain and the mind can not exist without the brain, but I would prefer to talk about the soul which, in my definition, includes the processes of personal intellectual functioning—that is to say the mind—and a larger part of divine energy which adds emotion and response and sensation and faith and substance to the mind. The mind is transient, the soul immortal. Loved by God. Part of God."

"God has emotions then?"

"Yes."

"And experiences love for each human being?"

"Yes."

"And hears prayers and decides between good and evil and intervenes in natural events on occasion?"

"So I believe."

"God has thoughts then?"

"Yes."

"Then God must have a brain."

"That doesn't exactly follow. We can't take our concept of anatomy and physiology and expand it to assume that God has the same characteristics."

"But you teach that man is made in God's image."

"That's an allegorical poem. The image of God's soul, yes. But anatomy, I don't know, I don't care even."

"But you've just made your argument by attributing a whole variety of human characteristics to God. Love, you cited, and value judgments and listening and doing. Can you be anthropomorphic in one category and not another?"

"I believe what I choose to believe, because I believe it is right. More importantly, generations of wise and thoughtful men have thought about these questions and come to the same conclusion. We,

155

we humans that is, we are driven to have answers and explanations for events we can see but do not understand." O'Reilly realized he was lecturing to a man who did this for a living, but the passion of his rhetoric continued. "The concept of grand infinite energy or spirit is universal. I call it God. From there the details fall into place. It may be unscientific, even irrational, but is supported by a leap of faith based on all the facts I can gather." More silence.

"Were your parents Catholic?"

"Why yes." They both chuckled. "Your student would appear to be right based on a sample of one."

"A sample of two," said Ravi, pointing to himself, More chuckling. The feeling was that of mutual respect.

"Do you go to football games Ravi?"

"On occasion."

"Then I must tell you a funny story. Several years ago Yale came to play Boston College but they didn't bring the Yale band—I don't even know if there is a Yale band. Anyway, at half-time four students with brass instruments came on the field and another student provided the announcements. They formed a square, a circle, and a triangle and a straight line and played a little music. It was a wonderful spoof. Finally, the announcer declared, 'And now the Yale band forms the mind of God' and one student stood alone in the middle of the field. Of course the Jesuits thought it was hilarious—most of them anyway."

"The point being that the mind of God can be whatever you wish it to be."

"The point being that the mind of God is what you know it to be."

* * * *

Randy Burleson ached for sleep. His nervous energy had carried him through most of Grand Rounds, then he had two hours of scut to run afterwards and the students were on vacation. He kept himself awake by standing up while he wrote his orders. It was Saturday, and he thought about the bed as he started IVs and removed Foley catheters. He weaned the senator down on the ventilator, but left him intubated, following instructions from Adams and Ingram. He could almost smell the bed when his beeper went off with a page from the emergency room.

The ER had a patient with an acute back. A patient of Dr. Emerson, one of the private neurosurgeons who was on the golf course and had told his patient to come to the emergency room for admission. Just what Burleson needed. He was angry enough at Dr. Emerson to stay awake through the history and physical and to document that the paraspinous muscles were like bricks, but there was no sign of nerve root involvement. The patient complained about not seeing Dr. Emerson, complained about the bed, complained about the food (in anticipation), and asked for a private room. Burleson promised to see what he could do, ordered 10 mg of morphine for the patient, and decided to swing through the ICU one more time to preclude any phone calls which might interrupt his sleep.

The senator was stable and gesturing at the endotracheal tube. Rothstein's CSF pressure was low and the fluid drainage was minimal. Kathleen Dugan was attempting to sip a milkshake offered by the nurse. Rizzo was coughing violently, causing the buzzer on the ventilator to sound off loudly. Flint stood calmly in the corner of the cubicle where the senator lay.

Burleson sat on the low rolling stool to write a progress note, but soon his head drifted forward and each word he wrote trailed off down the page before the last letter was accomplished. He awoke to the feeling of firm hands kneading the muscles of his lower neck, expert thumbs relieving the strain on his rhomboids. In the middle of his back he felt the unmistakable push of a female pelvis. "If this is a dream I don't want to wake up," he mumbled, feeling the tension drain away.

"You looked like your head was going to fall off." The voice belonged to Kay Lawson. "Your back is really tight." He tipped his head back until it rested on her soft chest. She didn't seem to mind. He looked up and found her smiling. She moved her massage to the front of his shoulders, pushing his head further into the pleasant pillow.

"Can you talk and rub at the same time?"

"I can do almost anything and rub at the same time."

"Great. What are you doing here on Saturday Kay? Shouldn't you be at a football game or something like that?"

"No, I'm on call for anesthesia. I'll be here until eight o'clock. The OR is quiet, the ER is empty, so I came up here to check on our famous patient from yesterday. Then I saw you trying to dislocate your cervical spine."

"Damn lucky for me," he said. "Just don't stop."

"It's your lucky day Burleson. I've got all afternoon with nothing to do and you need a proper back rub." He tilted his head up again to see the look on her face. She was still smiling.

"Well look, I could stretch out on that gurney over there . . ." She slipped her hand inside his scrub shirt, her fingers caressing his right nipple.

"Burleson, what's your room number in the Crow's Nest?"

"Jesus, Kay." A gentle tugging on the hairs of his chest. He wondered if he could safely stand up. "Four-ten."

"I'll be there in ten minutes. Now finish your note." He put a period where he had stopped writing, scribbled his name and stood up, holding his white coat in front of him.

"Jesus, Kay, are you serious?"

"Nine minutes." He took the elevator to the first floor and nearly ran the quarter mile to the old part of the old hospital where the residents' quarters were. He ran up the stairs and made an attempt to tidy things up, sticking the Playboy in a lower drawer and piling dirty clothes in the closet. He looked at his watch, and tried to decide between changing the sheets and shaving. He opted for the latter, clattering across the hall, pulling off his scrub shirt. He cut himself twice, brushed his teeth, rubbed on some deodorant, and tried, unsuccessfully, to urinate. When he crossed the hall to his room she was in the bed, her scrub dress and a few other garments folded on his desk. She pushed the sheet down to her waist and stretched. He swallowed hard, frozen to the floor.

"Kay, are you sure about this? I mean, shouldn't we have a couple of dates or something? This can lead to big-time commitment. And Dan Adams is my chief. Isn't he . . . ?"

"Dr. Dan Adams is just a good friend who happens to have another date tonight," she said with a touch of bitterness. "And don't take yourself too seriously. You're just a good intern. You've been working your ass off and you just won the Longwood Hospital morale award. Now get out of that scrub suit." She sat on the edge of the bed to hurry him along.

"Jesus, what a body," he said, mostly to himself as he moved to join her on the bed. He eased her on to her back, and tried to make as much skin contact as possible, touching fingers to fingers and toes to toes.

In a few minutes, when the surge of hormones and heavy breathing reached force five, she said, "Wait a minute, wait a minute. The back rub comes first."

"Jesus, Kay whatever you say. I can't believe this, I cannot believe this," mumbling into the pillow as she slid out from under him and straddled his thighs. She began with his ears, then his scalp, brushing over the middle of his back as she leaned forward. "Oh yeah. I cannot believe this."

"This is just the beginning, Burleson." She murmured, tongue in his ear.

That was the last he heard. Much later, he remembered a sort of semi-stuporous nightmare in which a beautiful, naked woman repeatedly tried to awaken him, or at least arouse him, but sleep was too dear and he failed on both counts.

At 4:30 her beeper went off and she left to anesthetize a boy with a ruptured spleen, feeling entirely unsatisfied. Burleson woke up at 1:00 am. When he put the events of the previous day together he hastily paged the anesthetist on call. Jeffrey Banks answered. He didn't know where Kay Lawson was, undoubtedly gone home. Burleson cursed himself, noticed hunger, but fell asleep again before he could do anything about it.

CHAPTER 13

Matthew Rizzo Jr. was only beginning to put thoughts into words, but he recognized the sensation of hunger and recognized when a wet diaper was getting cold and sticky. He responded, instinctively, with the universal sign of discomfort, turning rather purple at the end of each wail as he shook his little fist and ran out of expiratory air.

"Carol, I think Matt needs to be changed." More wailing. The late afternoon sun had set and the street lights came on automatically. There they sat, the three of them, in the little living room in Natick, sighing, looking out of the window, and at the clock. They had done a lot of that in the last week. More wailing.

"Carol, I think little Matt needs to be changed."

"I heard you the first time, Mom." Silence, then more wailing. Finally the older woman put down her knitting, having come to the end of a row. Groaning and sighing as if it were a great effort, and casting a disapproving glance at her daughter-in-law, she hoisted her heavy body up the stairs one by one. In time the wailing stopped abruptly.

"She used to change Matt ten times a night. Never let the boy cry." James Rizzo was tall and thin with a poorly-trimmed little mustache and a blinking tick which began every time he spoke. He sat in the chair facing the television, continuously arranging the lace doilies on the arms. The television was not turned on. The room became darker. "Never let the boy cry. My she loved that little boy. He was a good boy, Matt. He was a fine young man."

"He still is, Dad. You've started talking about him in the past tense." Carol sat at the old oak dining room table in the next room. She sat on a straight-backed chair with a needlepoint seat that her mother-in-law had made long ago. She turned the pages in a magazine aimlessly, although the room was nearly dark.

"I know Carol, but it won't be long, will it? I mean—how long can a boy live with all those machines and a broken neck?" The tick became faster. With more groaning and sighing Ida Rizzo lowered herself back into the living room. "The boy was wet," she said rather triumphantly.

"I was saying, Ida, that we should face up to the fact that Matty's gone, or going to be. He can't talk to us, he can't move. It's just not fair Ida, it's not fair."

"Don't start in again Jim. You mustn't say things like that. You saw him today. And he knows exactly what is going on and Dr. Adams said that eventually he could sit up in a wheelchair. He might even be able to work one of those electric things with his thumb. Dr. Adams said that." She knitted another row furiously, her voice tight, trying in vain to hold back the tears that seemed to be coming even more frequently with each passing day.

"Can we please just stop having this conversation?" Carol pushed the magazine away and put her elbows on the table. "Matt's brain is alive. He's the same sweet Matt he always was. He needs us more than ever. It's been over a week. Let's stop saying it's not fair. No one said it was going to be fair." Silence, save the clicking of knitting needles. They hurt together, they argued. They needed each other, they couldn't stand each other. They wanted him better, they wanted him exuberant and running and playing with his little boy. They wanted him dead, although they didn't say it. They wanted him any way except the way he was. They couldn't stand it any more but there was no alternative.

"It's just not fair," James said again.

"Let's do something," said Carol. "We can't just sit here another night. We have to get our minds on something else. Let's go down and get some pizza."

"We did that last night."

"Let's go to the mall. We could walk around the mall."

"The mall's closed in half an hour."

"Then let's go to a movie. Come on, we're all going to a movie."

"Past little Matt's bedtime."

"Nonsense. He can sleep in tomorrow just like we can. Come on, we're going to a movie." She stood up with resolution and bounded up the stairs.

"Don't be hard on the girl, Ida. She feels just as bad as we do."

Clicking of knitting needles.

"The little boy was very wet." She tugged on the ball of yarn. "Stop playing with that doily. I can't help thinking if Matt had never met her . . ."

"None of that Ida." Blinking furiously. "We'll not hear any of that." Soon Carol reappeared with little Matt in a little jacket and a little hat.

"Gamma, Gamma." The presence of the little boy seemed to ease the atmosphere. Ida put her knitting in the plastic bag and pulled herself upright.

"Come to Gamma, Matt. I guess we're going to a movie."

* * * *

Like most surgical chief residents, Dan Adams couldn't go near the hospital without visiting his recent post-op patients. So he parked in the "no parking" slot next to the dumpster behind the hospital and advised his date that he would be back in just a minute. His date was a slender, austere, neurology fellow who played the oboe and read Emily Dickinson. Riding up the elevator, Adams wished he had arranged a date that was less cerebral and more palpable. He took the direct approach to the ICU, hoping to see Carol Rizzo in the waiting room, but the waiting room was empty.

The senator looked much as he did when Adams and Ingram had left him several hours before. After the endotracheal tube was removed he coughed and moaned a few times, but never really responded. Tonight he was still the same. His vital sign sheet showed that his heart, lungs, and kidneys were working well. His Glasgow Coma Score, recorded by the nurse in the line of the chart marked "Neuro" was nine. Flint sat at the bedside and leaned forward as Adams approached. Adams ignored him, nodded to the nurse, and shook the senator by the shoulder, calling his name. Bradford groaned and shrugged as if to push Adams's hand off his shoulder. This was repeated twice with the same result.

"What is your opinion, Dr. Adams?" asked Flint.

"Status quo, Mr. Flint. Actually this is about par for the course for this type of operation. He may wake up in a few hours or a few days. It's hard to tell."

"Thank you, then, I'll just stay here."

"Suit yourself."

The ventriculostomy tube coming out of Rothstein's head had been clamped since noon. Adams moved the drainage bag level with the patient and took the clamp off. The fluid accumulated very slowly in the bag. He was pleased. Rothstein, who appeared to be sleeping, now stirred and looked from side to side.

"Adams."

"Yes Professor."

"John Quincy Adams. Samuel Adams. Ansel Adams."

"Dan Adams, Professor."

"Quincy, Braintree, Plymouth, Falmouth." Rothstein was staring ahead, and turning his head from side to side, grasping at Adams's sleeve.

"It's okay Professor. You're having a dream. Everything is okay. It's Saturday night and you're doing fine." Adams held his hand while talking so that Rothstein could concentrate on what he was saying.

"Yes, I was confused. Today is Saturday . . . Saturday . . ." He returned, apparently, to sleep.

At Matt Rizzo's bedside, Sally was alternately injecting and aspirating fluid with a large syringe attached to his nasogastric tube. The fluid went in clear and came out looking like rosé wine with small chunks of tar. A half-empty bag of blood was dripping slowly into the IV. "That's the second unit," said Sally, anticipating his question. "Bleeding has almost stopped, though." She held up the full syringe for Adams to examine. It was almost clear. Matt was sleeping.

"Have you seen Mrs. Rizzo?" asked Adams.

"Which one Dr. Adams? His mother of his wife?" she asked with a sarcastic smile. Dan Adams was the most eligible bachelor in the hospital, and the ICU nurses noticed when he took an interest in any young lady.

"I was asking about his wife," he said, blushing slightly. "I wanted to bring her up to date about the bleeding," he added, unnecessarily.

"I'll tell her when she comes in. Should I page you?"

"No, thanks, I'll see her in the morning."

Mary Dugan was sitting at Kathleen's bedside, holding her hand, as she always did. Dan recognized Michael Dugan but not the other young man in the green blazer. "Good evening, Dr. Adams. This is our son Pat. Pat, this is one of Kathleen's doctors." Pat was taller than Michael—probably six feet six inches—with white skin behind his ears providing evidence that his marine-short haircut was newly acquired. "Pat plays football for Dartmouth." Michael Dugan couldn't resist the show of paternal pride. "They played Boston U this afternoon, and he came over to see his little sister."

"And she's doing much better, don't you think so Dr. Adams?" asked Mary Dugan.

"She's certainly better than she was a few days ago." It was an honest statement. Pat Dugan, who had last seen his sister a month ago in the full flower of life, could only nod. Now, propped by pillows into a slouching position, her eyes slowly scanned from side to side without stopping to focus, even as they spoke of her. She didn't look very good to Pat.

"How did it go?"

"What?"

"Your football game—how did it go?"

"Oh—we won. Won by two points."

"Pat scored the winning touchdown." Michael Dugan looked fondly at his big son. "Took a screen pass on the thirty and carried it all the way in. Heck of a run."

"Congratulations," said Adams, impressed.

"Doesn't seem very important now." Huge young hands holding on to the end of the bed for support.

Adams thought about Kathleen Dugan as he descended the back staircase to the parking lot. There was something about her that bothered him. Not her scanning gaze or her lack of speech. Not her mild fever. It must have been her face. The right side of her face seemed to droop a little more than the left. He made a mental note to check it again in the morning. Just now his asthenic date was still waiting in the car.

CHAPTER 14

"He's not waking up. He looks like he is having a dream." Anne Bradford had been sitting at her husband's bedside ever since they brought him back from the ICU. Initially he had looked at her and it seemed as if he had tried to say her name, but that was two hours ago and he had shown no other outward sign of recognition since. She called his name regularly at first but with no response, and now sat just watching him. She addressed her observation to Flint, who sat by the foot of the bed. Her tone suggested to Flint that she was worried, as he was.

"Yes he does. A bad dream, I'd say." Flint had noticed Bradford's pattern of behavior before Anne Bradford mentioned it. The senator appeared to be sleeping calmly with eyes closed, taking long, measured breaths. Then, at irregular intervals, he began to breathe rapidly. Moving his lips, then his mouth, then his whole face in a series of twitches and grimaces, then chewing and grinding his rear teeth together. Finally, he opened his eyes and stared straight ahead, mouthing some inaudible words. After a period of several minutes he sighed and became relaxed and appeared to be sleeping again.

"John. John, it's Anne. Honey, can you hear me?" She squeezed his hand and arm. "John, it's Sunday morning. You're waking up. Hon?" He opened his eyes and looked toward her, mouthed some words without sound, and fell back on the pillow.

"Has he said anything at all to you?"

"Nothing yet," said Flint. "Sometimes it looks like he is trying, as he did just now, but he hasn't really said anything." She slumped back in the chair and looked away. "Mrs. Bradford," said Flint in a gentle voice that she had not heard from him before. "Dr. Adams said that's not unusual. Brain swelling. Temporary."

She looked up. His expression was almost soft. He looked quickly away from her wide-eyed, open stare, and back at the senator.

"Temporary," he said with a kindly nod.

"Let's hope it gets better soon Mr. Flint."

Bradford started the rapid breathing again. Anne stood up and walked to the window, her back to Flint. But not before he saw the tears in her eyes.

* * * *

The waves were cresting at eight feet and the wind was blowing so hard that it drove the foam straight out like horizontal rain. The spray beat into his eyes, soaked his clothes despite the oilskins, and froze his fingers to the cold metal wheel. With only a storm jib flying he was making six knots, pounding into the chop. In Bradford's mind's eye every detail of the old boat and every detail around the 360-degree horizon were equally clear. Each wave knocked the bow over and pushed the lee rail into the water so that he had to compensate on each succeeding swell, requiring constant attention to the helm and the compass. The sea looked exactly the same in every direction, angry and gray, waves rushing toward some undefined destination, falling over each other to get ahead; heavy, unpleasant rows of clouds rolling under each other in the same direction, mimicking the waves. The sound of wood on wood as joints that were once glued and screwed shifted under the strain. The sound of rain and spray tattooing an irregular cadence on the hood of his oilskin. The sound of the steel cables resonating in the gale, the little jib cracking as it luffed coming up the swell, and the incessant slapping of the main halyard, now slack with the sail tied down around the boom. On the next pitch a crack and a twang as one of the wires in the braided cable on the forestay let go. The boat shuddered and recovered. The wire coiled up behind the sail where he could see it. He watched the forestay with the next pitch and roll but it held fast. He knew it was only a matter of time. He called below for help, but no one answered.

There was a man standing in the companionway who ignored him. Suddenly, Anne was at his side, calmly calling his name and squeezing his hand. He tried to tell her to hold the wheel so he could go forward to drop the jib, but she could not hear above the howl of the wind. She just kept calling his name. The man in the companionway was speaking to Anne but not to him. Another wire in the forestay gave way with a snap. Bradford somehow knew that he had experienced this before and, strangely, he felt no fear, no dread, and no panic. He was only interested in the observation that if the forestay broke, he would be dismasted and adrift. He decided to loose the jib sheet, and as he did the line flailed about the cockpit, whipping him across the back and face and cutting his hands, until it finally pulled out of the block and tangled on the lifeline. Let free in the gale, the old jib thrashed violently and in minutes was torn in a series of strips, flying its pennants of desperation from the remnants of the forestay.

When the storm was at its worst, the man standing in the companionway came forward, followed by two other men from the cabin. Suddenly a bright light was shining in his eyes, held by one of the men. It was so bright he could not make them out, although their voices were familiar. They talked to each other but not to him. The light became brighter. He tried to look away but could not. Dr. Banks told him to look at a spot on the wall while the source of the light began to click and move back and forth. Banks was talking about the need for some special sort of X-rays. The office was cold and austere with white walls and a white tile floor and stainless steel cabinet filled with stainless steel examining devices. He had definitely been here before. Every detail was familiar, even the eye chart on the back of the door. Despite the bright light in his eye he could read the next to last line on the eye chart. E S T A U. The face of the nurse was friendly. She wore oversized glasses with wire frames and small rhinestones set in the lower corner of the glass. The entire examination was exactly as he had remembered it except the last time it had been accompanied by a sense of foreboding and worry. Now there was no emotion attached to it. It was simply a series of events. As Dr. Banks clicked down on his other eye he read the eye chart aloud.

* * * *

When Adams and Burleson appeared on their rounds, Anne Bradford was still looking out the window. The charge nurse came with them, anxious for an update on the status of her very important patient. While Burleson read aloud from the vital sign sheet Adams raised the senator's eyelids and turned his head from side to side. He directed the light from a small flashlight into each pupil, noting that the reaction was somewhat slower than he expected. As Burleson completed the list of medications, Adams focused on the optic disc with his ophthalmoscope. One disc margin was slightly blurred but it looked better than it had earlier in the morning in ICU. Adams was pleased. The charge nurse, standing opposite Adams, addressed a rhetorical question to the senator. "When the doctors are through with rounds we'll have to get you shaved and cleaned up won't we?"

"E S T A U," responded the senator.

＊＊＊＊

"Mrs. Rizzo?" Both of the women in the ICU waiting room stood as Ingram addressed the younger one. His face must have showed confusion.

"We're both Mrs. Rizzo," explained Carol. "This is Matt's mother. Ida, this is Dr. Ingram."

"It's so nice to meet you, doctor. I've heard so much about you."

He smiled and asked them to sit down, sensing some tension between them, in addition to the standard ICU apprehension.

"Matt's doing fairly well." He came directly to the point. "It's been almost two weeks and his level remains at C5. It's very unlikely that any further recovery will occur."

"Does that mean he'll never be able to walk again?" asked Ida Rizzo, as if this were somehow new information. She asked the same question every day.

Carol answered. "Yes Mom," trying to cover the irritation in her voice. "It means that he can move his shoulders and one thumb. It means he's permanently paralyzed and can't feel anything below his neck."

"Is that right, Dr. Ingram?" Ida actually turned her head away during her daughter-in-law's explanation, as if she refused to hear it.

"Yes Mrs. Rizzo, I'm afraid that's right. He'll probably be able to operate an electric wheelchair though, and eventually he'll probably be

170

able to sit up a good bit of the time."

Despite the tears in her eyes she sat up straighter and shifted her bulky frame to the front of the chair. "Matt has a very strong will, doctor. I don't know about medicine but I do know that Matt wants to get up and walk around and if anyone can do it, he can do it. I've read about cases like that. Matt has a very strong will." She lifted her chin and clutched at the knitting in her lap.

"I'm sure he does, Mrs. Rizzo. And he's going to need a very strong will to continue his recovery."

She seemed satisfied, but still unconvinced.

"How about the GI bleeding?" asked Carol, directly.

"He's had some blood from his tube intermittently. When his intestine wakes up from the spinal injury we'll be able to start feeding him and I think the bleeding will resolve."

"He had two units of transfusion last night."

She was better informed than Ingram but he did not register his surprise. "I didn't know that, but I'm not surprised," he said. "He may need a few more before we're out of this acute phase."

"What's causing the bleeding?"

"Probably just irritation from the nasogastric tube, as I said. Or it might be some stress gastritis, or even a duodenal ulcer. The treatment is the same in any case. We're giving him antacids and some medication to prevent him from making stomach acid."

"Tagamet?"

"Yes."

"Is there some limit to the number of transfusions, or some plan for operation?" Carol knew all the right questions and also knew that Ingram was the proper source of policy information.

"Don't be silly Carol," said Ida. "Everyone at church gave blood and all the people at Jim's shop said they would give blood too. We can get plenty of blood for Matt."

Ingram reassured her. "Of course we can Mrs. Rizzo. It's not a question of the amount of blood for transfusion. Carol's really asking when we'd consider doing an operation to stop the bleeding, and she's anticipating the next step." He turned back to Carol. "We've asked Dr. Hawkins from General Surgery to see Matt. He'll probably want to look down there with a gastroscope. Dr. Hawkins and his team will be the ones making the decision about operation for bleeding. Of course we hope that won't be necessary."

"You mean, Dr. Ingram, that the general surgeons will give us advice about the GI bleeding, and operate if necessary. Matt and I will make the decisions."

"Of course, Carol. That's exactly what I mean."

* * * *

As Ingram left the waiting room in the ICU an orchestral piece of music that was unmistakably John Williams came from the small television mounted on the wall. Rolling graphics proclaimed the NBC Nightly News. He took the stairs to 9 North, and went from room to room, examining incisions, talking to families, discussing discharge plans and pain medication.

Ben Rothstein was making steady progress. He was sleeping when Ingram entered, so he reviewed the vital sign sheet and nurse's notes. Satisfied, he left the professor undisturbed.

Kathleen Dugan's room was empty except for the girl herself, propped up in the bed. She turned when he called her name. Definite recognition. She actually smiled and tried a few words. Mostly unintelligible but "doctor" was among them.

"That's right Kathleen. Each day gets a little better, doesn't it?" No response from the girl, now gaunt of face and drooling.

The television across from Kathleen's bed was on. Adams had a theory that constant audio and visual stimulation improved the rate of recovery from closed head injuries. Ingram had seen enough patients improve to think there might be something to it. Last month a young biker uttered his first words after three weeks of coma, "Bud Lite." The NBC News was still running.

" . . . and when we return, our Boston correspondent has some clues in the case of the disappearing senator." John Williams's theme in the background, leading to a Chevrolet commercial. The last few words grabbed Ingram's attention and he stood still, absentmindedly holding Kathleen's hand, waiting for the commercial to end. Tom

Brokaw returned with introductory remarks and cut to an earnest young reporter standing outside Longwood Hospital.

"It has been almost two weeks since anyone has seen or heard from Senator John Bradford. The Senate Select Committee on Central American Affairs, which is chaired by Mr. Bradford, has been in recess since the famous senator apparently became ill during a national television program. The senator's office merely says that he is in good health and working on committee material somewhere in the Caribbean. However rumors have been growing that the senator was hospitalized some weeks ago, and there is a suggestion that the senator might be here in the prestigious Longwood Hospital in Boston. Hospital officials deny any knowledge of the senator, and a check of the hospital patient list shows no John Bradford. With me tonight is Maureen Doherty, a nurse's aide at the Longwood Hospital." The camera view pulled back to include a nervous-looking girl. She was anxious, twisting strands of red hair with pudgy fingers. The hair, the fingers, and the crucifix around her neck all indicated South Boston. The reporter brought the microphone to her mouth. "Miss Doherty, is Senator Bradford a patient here at the Longwood Hospital?"

"I think he might be."

"Uh . . . Miss Doherty, we were told that you had seen Senator Bradford here in the hospital." The reporter suddenly looked anxious.

"I'm naught shua. I said I seen Mrs. Bradford heah quite a lot. I recognized her from the papers."

"I see. Well . . . Miss Doherty . . ."

"Can I say hello to my boyfriend? He might be watching."

The screen cut to Tom Brokaw looking angry. "Thank you, Bruce, for that interesting report. I'm sure you'll keep us informed as it develops. And now, turning to the Middle East . . ."

Ingram's mouth went dry as he absorbed the information. He had heard about the calls from the press. Soon they would all be in the spotlight.

Kathleen tugged at his hand.

"What is it Kathleen?"

"Chevy. Chevy doctor." She tried a smile.

CHAPTER 15

Alex Hawkins looked like an orthopod. He was a big man. Not tall, but burly—hard and cylindrical from his shoulders to his knees with short pudgy fingers extending from his meaty hands, which were the same size as his wrists, which were the same size as his forearms. No matter how he dressed he always looked as if his shirt was too tight at the neck, and no matter how often he shaved he always looked like he needed a shave. He did not have an air of intimidation like some big men because his sensitive blue eyes gave him a gentle aura. Almost every breath he took was audible and the harder he concentrated, the louder the breathing. The residents secretly called him the locomotive. He was a very good general surgeon, but he looked more like an orthopod.

He arrived in the ICU after eight o'clock on Thursday night, picked up the chart, and asked the ward clerk to page Burleson. He riffled the progress notes until he came to Ingram's distinctive black pen printing. In a few concise sentences this told him all that he needed to know. He leafed through the laboratory data and found a signed consent form for endoscopy witnessed by Adams. When Burleson answered, Hawkins asked him to stop by the OR to pick up the endoscopy cart and meet him in the ICU.

When Burleson arrived, Hawkins was bending over, talking to Matt Rizzo. Hawkins had played his share of football and seen more than his share of paraplegics. Most people in the hospital talked around Matt's problem. Hawkins was very straightforward, and Matt found that reassuring.

" . . . sure one hell of a tough break. I tore my knee up playing ball. Had to delay starting medical school. 'Course that seems minor compared to your problem. Tell you what though—you're in the right profession. Paras make good teachers. Just last year I operated on a girl who graduated from Bridgewater. Teaches high school in Milford. Drives her own car, has an electric wheelchair, they say she's a hell of a teacher. So in a sense, you're lucky there." Rizzo nodded and looked reassured.

"Now Matt, I'm pushing on your belly a little bit. I know you can't feel it but tell me if you get any funny feelings like wanting to toss up your cookies or anything like that." Rizzo shook his head, indicating negative. Burleson had come to the bedside. "Hello Randy. I'm glad you're working late tonight. Did you get the endoscopy cart?"

"Yes sir. All set."

"Matt and I were just talking about his injury. Hell of a tough break." Then a sigh. "When a para gets peritonitis or has a bleed or a bowel perforation—any abdominal problem—they can usually tell you there is something wrong in their belly. Nausea, sweating, hypertension some times. People get that feeling when you tug on the peritoneum fixing a hernia under spinal. Know what I mean Randy?"

"Yes sir."

"Good." He turned back to Rizzo, "Matt we're going to take a look down in your stomach to see where this bleeding is coming from. We'll pump you full of Valium so you won't care how it feels." Rizzo nodded and Hawkins signaled the nurse who emptied a syringe into the IV line. Soon Rizzo smiled, and his eyes closed. Hawkins put a bite block with a hole in it between his teeth.

"We did a lot of these together in July, didn't we Randy? Good, then you drive and I'll push." Burleson looked into the eye piece and maneuvered a slight hook on the end of the large black endoscope. Hawkins guided it into Matt's throat. "Now just swallow Matt, that's a boy. Keep swallowing. That's a boy. Look okay Burleson? Okay? Keep swallowing. Good stuff, good stuff."

"We just passed into the stomach," said Burleson. "I saw the EG junction then everything turned red." By irrigating the nasogastric tube and the lumen on the endoscope they cleared several large clots and finally could see most of the gastric mucosa.

"What do you think Randy?"

"Looks okay to me."

"Looks good to me too. Let's see if we can get through the pylorus. Here, let me drive a minute and you watch through the teaching head. "Burleson was amazed how deftly Hawkins's pudgy fingers maneuvered the wheels. Almost immediately the pylorus was in view and a few seconds later they were in the duodenum. The lens ran green with bile, which they suctioned off.

"Wow," said Burleson.

"Double wow. Those are two mighty big ulcers for being just a few days old. See the sharp edges and the white base. This one . . . are you with me Burleson? . . . This one's on the lateral wall but this one . . ." He changed the view by twisting one of the dials. "This one is straight posterior. Not bleeding at the moment. Let's rough it up a little bit." He maneuvered the scope directly over the ulcer. Only a small ooze appeared at the rough edge of the mucosa. Burleson thought this was a risky maneuver, considering the huge artery which ran under the base of the ulcer. As if he could read Burleson's mind, Hawkins said, "Better know right now if it's eroded into that artery, Burleson. It'd be easier to fix it now than at three o'clock in the morning. Looks okay though."

He handed the scope back to Burleson who looked at the rest of the duodenum then backed the scope out all the way. Hawkins leaned over in front of Rizzo again.

"Matt, we found the cause of the problem. You've got a little ulcer down there, which is not too surprising for a young fellow in your condition. We can usually treat those pretty well with some medications, but if it bleeds much more we may have to do an operation to stop it. Understand?" Rizzo nodded and mouthed some words. Hawkins studied him for a while and finally said, "Can't quite make it out. Try again. Here Randy, you're used to talking to Matt. What's he saying?"

"Tooah?" Rizzo shook his head and tried again. "Tellwa?" Rizzo nodded. "Tell my wife?" Rizzo nodded again.

"Will do," said Hawkins. "I'm going to give her a call right now." Rizzo relaxed again. "Tell you what, a little of that Valium every few hours would do wonders for your ulcer. Know what I mean Randy?"

While Burleson wrote a note in the chart Hawkins pulled up to the telephone at the nurse's desk. He had the phone number written on a little card, but sat, elbows on the desk, staring at Rizzo across the room for thirty seconds, breathing very loudly.

"Poor kid." He picked up the phone and dialed the number.

* * * *

Even Flint looked tired and frustrated. He allowed himself time to sleep and some time away from the hospital now, leaving a Boston policeman in Bradford's room in his absence. Over a week since the operation and Bradford showed no signs of cognition, no intelligence, no emotion even. Like a smart frog or a dumb monkey, he could spit, bite, twitch, scratch, kick, slobber, sputter, seize, and sulk. He could glare, sleep, cry, watch a single object for an hour or look into nothingness for a day. His ankles and wrists were chafed by the heavy leather restraints, but when he was constrained to bed by the Posey belt alone, he kicked the nurses and threw feces around the room. His hands were bound into large gauze and tape mittens, but whenever he freed two digits which would appose he would masturbate or pull out his nasogastric feeding tube which was his only link to sustenance, and difficult to replace. When Anne or the nurses tried to feed him he spit the food out as fast as they put it in. He went days without intelligible utterance, but occasionally shouted out long disjointed memory seizures which had begun with childhood events but were now getting closer to the present. It was this situation which kept Flint looking frustrated and tired.

The memory seizures occurred without much warning. Usually they were preceded by a period of sleep, followed by grinding of teeth, then looking intently at objects in the room—particularly people—then the torrent of words—disjointed conversations, directions, verbal salad—then a perfectly intact paragraph, then maddening reiteration of the same word or syllable, some times for hours, until he lapsed again into sleep. Flint was worried about what Bradford might say. The nurses were worried about how it was said, indicating the potential for real mid-brain violence if he worked free from the leather restraints (which he did regularly). When the IVs were still in, a quick barbiturate-induced sleep ended the outbursts, but now there was no easy access, and no baseline level of Thorazine or Haldol seemed to control the outbursts. So they settled on IM injections of Nembutal. The dose needed to quiet him was larger every day. It took at least ten minutes for the Nembutal to have an effect, and when the shouting was particularly loud or vulgar, Flint, or one of the orderlies, or sometimes Anne, would hold a towel over his mouth to muffle the sound, carefully to avoid being bitten.

Flint had just put down the towel when Ingram came in.

"What is he saying today? Does it make any sense?"

"He was burning a jungle in Vietnam for awhile, then campaigning in Woonsocket. How long do you think this will last? The press, the office staff and other senators, the rest of his family. They're giving us a lot of pressure."

"Hard to say," said Ingram, as they both watched the remnants of the senator run some mental gauntlet of sucking and chewing. So far the papers seemed to be satisfied with the comatose explanation.

"Sooner or later some nurse's aide or housekeeper is going to talk to the press. I think it's time we move out of here to someplace that's more . . . secure."

"Like Water Reed or Bethesda Naval?" asked Ingram cautiously.

"I was thinking more of a little five-bed facility in the Virginia countryside. Out past Dulles."

"It would be hard for me to look after him there, and hard to bring him back and forth."

"Oh we can find a neurosurgeon to look in on him down there, if that's necessary." Flint said this without bitterness or malice. Ingram stood straighter, and addressed Flint. "Since, as you have pointed out, you are not in my profession, it probably never occurred to you that I am professionally and emotionally committed to the care of this patient, whatever that means and however long it takes. Now is not the time to send Bradford to some institution—much less to some other neurosurgeon. Later perhaps, but not now."

Flint was about to comment when a familiar voice came from behind him.

"Mr. Flint, we're certainly not going to transfer John out of this hospital. His blood pressure and pulse may be fine but his mind is critically ill and we're not moving one inch until he's well . . . or . . . until Dr. Ingram says he's as well as he's going to be." Her firm statement faltered a little at the end.

179

Ingram was pleased to hear her voice. They had dropped the formalities in front of Flint. He took her hand. "Hello Anne."

"Anne!" from the creature in the bed. "Anne Harrington. Climb on you bitch, climb on you fucker. You bitch, you fucky bitch." He continued shouting, audible halfway down the hall. Anne, who had heard this tirade several times before during the last week, tried to quiet him, hands on his bare chest, tears in her eyes.

Flint applied the folded towel, more roughly than usual. "Please be careful, Mrs. Bradford. Please let me do this. I'm sorry you have to hear this. He doesn't mean it."

Ingram noticed Flint's haste. And something like genuine warmth in his voice.

"You bitch, you fucker, you . . ." muffled obscenities under the towel. Eventually the shouting was silenced.

"As I was saying," began Flint, "there is a very secure sort of a . . . hospital in a little town that's not on any of your maps. Dr. Ingram, you know how I respect you, how we all do. But if you remember our discussions before the operation—"

"Not yet, Mr. Flint," interrupted Anne. The tears were gone from her eyes. She turned to Ingram. "Could you give me a ride when you're through with your rounds? I have to get out of here."

"I'm through now."

They walked the hall, the elevator, and the lobby in silence. Ingram was trying to imagine what Anne was thinking. Despite sighs and shaking heads, neither spoke for half an hour as they drove.

It was unusually warm for mid-October and the late afternoon sun dripped from the golden leaves of maples on Storrow Drive and glared into their eyes as they turned west on the Massachusetts turnpike. It warmed their spirits but made vision difficult. He turned north on 128 and they were in Tewksberry, sun at their back, before she asked where they were going.

"Marblehead. I have to put the boat to bed for the winter. Okay?"

"Fine."

The sun had long since disappeared and the eastern horizon was well into the dark blue phase of twilight as they made their way down the narrow floating pier, past the sign that said "Private—Owners

180

Only," past the tugs and the lobster boats and the working fisherman boats closer to shore, past the carefully coiled spring line of a three-masted schooner, and into the gently rolling cockpit of the big sloop. She held a flashlight as he freed the small lock from the companionway, pushed back the hatch cover, and flipped on the switches. He started to go below but paused to watch her inspect the ship, still amused and amazed by the self-confident attitude which came so naturally to her and yet was still so surprising to him. She walked forward, noting the position of the winches and the halyards, checking the jib sheets and the sail itself which was rolled on the forestay, onto the bowsprit to look at the masthead, back down the starboard side, glancing at the tell-tale on the back stay, and a long look past the stern, past the dinghy, past the string of red buoys, still faintly visible in the afterglow, and beyond. Finally she lowered herself into the main cabin where he was putting cans of food and bottles of beverages into a box.

"I hope you didn't drag me all the way up here to help you pack up your galley. Let's go sailing."

He paused, grinned, and began returning the bottles to the secure food lockers.

"There's a locker in the aft cabin. Wear the heavy sweater. It'll be cold out on the ocean."

By the time she reappeared on deck in jeans and boat shoes and sweater and slicker he had started the diesel and hauled aboard the shore lines. "These were in a locker. They must have been Emily's," she said, indicating the clothes.

"You look good in those."

Without needing direction she pulled the dinghy close to the stern as he backed the boat into the channel and klunked the gear shift forward, then she played out the line as the big boat rumbled toward the jetty. She stood beside him at the wheel, warmish easterly rattling the halyards, family of ducks working their way past the bow, harvest moon glow just beginning to appear on the horizon. Time for a thoughtful moment. She put her hand over his on the steering wheel.

"I'm a nurse, you know. I've handled much worse hallucinations than that."

Ingram was surprised. "How did you know I was worrying about you and not the patient?"

"You feel badly about John, but that's clinical. You were feeling personal about me back there in the hospital. And thank you for caring, but you needn't worry. I've been there."

"Not with your own husband."

"No, you're right. But thanks for caring. I'm okay." She gave him a little kiss on the cheek.

"Now Captain, are we going to sail or are we just going to putt around Marblehead Harbor like some lousy stinkpot?"

"Just steer the damn boat, mate, and button yer lip."

She headed for the first floating can while Ingram took off the mainsail cover and raised the sail, winching up the last few feet. He unfurled the big jib by hauling on the starboard sheet, but the breeze was right on their nose and they opted to motor and flap, preferring the mechanized expediency of gaining the open sea quickly rather than the purist series of tacks out of the harbor. She went below and returned in time with large mugs of coffee, a box of stale crackers, and a large chunk of hard cheese. As they passed the last channel marker he bore off to the south, close-hauled the main, and the Genoa billowed out, bringing the lee rail close to the water. She sat on the lee side of the cockpit, which quietly pleased him, waited until the heading appeared right for the trim of the sails and the boat settled into its groove, then she turned off the engine. After a minute she said, "There's no sound like it."

"Like turning off the engine under sail?"

She nodded.

"You're right, there's nothing like it." They listened as the sea slid past the boat, chunking on the windward bow, gurgling into eddies and whirlpools far astern. Stays cracked as they reached tension. Spreaders groaned. Somewhere below, heavy timbers and fiberglass joints acknowledged and accepted the load, like a brace of horses leaning into the traces. They listened and sailed until the first cup of coffee was gone and the moon itself could be seen, laying a silvery trail off the port bow. He went below to get heavier jackets, the chart, and another cup of coffee. She stayed at the wheel and he sat close to her on the windward side. They watched the lights ashore.

"He's not going to get any better, is he?" She said it lightly, looking up at the wind indicator at the top of the mast.

"Too soon to say."

"But it's unlikely."

"Very unlikely."

"I keep waiting for some sign that he's in there. At first I thought I saw him sometimes, in his eyes—you could see into his soul through his eyes—but not anymore. His mind, his wit, his personality—they're gone. Where did they go? Is his soul gone too? I can't see it; I can't feel it."

"He must have infracted his other frontal lobe. And, we had quite a lot of bleeding and a long period of hypotension. I worried about some of the feeding vessels to his thalamus."

"Not anatomically. Actually. Spiritually. Where is he? I can see his body. It looks the same. I can touch his face. I could kiss his mouth. But where is he? You knew him. You liked him."

"I like him very much."

"Well, I loved him. Damn it Don, I've loved him with my heart and my brain and my pelvis and my gut and he loved me. Where is he Don? He's not in that poor man lying in the hospital bed. Damn it Don. I just miss him so much." She buried her face in her hands, suddenly sobbing hard.

The boat started to round up and he rose to take the wheel. "I'm sorry," she said between sobs. He put an arm around her shoulder which she did not decline, but neither did she respond. She just looked away, crying really hard for the first time, Ingram trying to hold her with one hand and keep the ship on course with the other. The breeze was easing a little. The sail glowed with moonlight. Whenever he thought about it Ingram could see the torrent of blood where he had burned a hole in Bradford's artery. He had trained himself not to hurt—to take responsibility but not blame—to rationalize that he did what he did as well as anyone in the world could do it—the ego of the surgeon, and who would want it otherwise? But he hurt now, in a way that few people know. Not because of her anguish—she'd survive. Not because she loved her husband more than him—his ego wasn't that big. Not because he had a bad result which was visible to anyone who walked into that depressing hospital room. He hurt because he too loved the man—if respect and admiration and the coequal meeting of minds can be given that appellation—and he was the one who had killed him. He knew where John Bradford was. On glass slides. Floating in a bottle in the Path Lab. Sucked up with the borders of the tumor, discarded by some OR helper down a stainless steel drain ultimately into the deep cold depths of the Boston sewer system. Rotting inside his own calvarium, the chemicals that were John Bradford were providing the leisurely lunch for a legion of macrophages. He was taking the blame as well as the responsibility. He recognized the feeling. The sobbing stopped and he wiped her face.

"We'd better come about," he said eventually, gently.

She nodded, and then went through the routine with ease, precisely, as if they had been doing it for a lifetime.

Speaking not a word they settled the boat into a nice reach toward the blinking light outside Marblehead Harbor. They stood together behind the wheel for warmth, for comfort, for safety, for gathering of the spilled emotions. They dropped the main halfway into the run down the channel and came in, slowly furling the jib. The combination of the dying wind and the calm harbor and the ever smaller corner of exposed sail brought the momentum of the heavy boat under control and they drifted—so slowly—right into the slip leaning gently into the big tire on the pier, without ever interrupting the night sounds with the engine.

The aft cabin was the quickest to warm with the heater, and after everything was made fast they sat in the dark on the aft cabin bed, still bundled in rubber pants and sweaters, watching the moon beams reflect from the water through the transom windows onto the ceiling of the little cabin.

"I'm sorry I got so emotional," she said finally. "John's not going to recover. I know that. I'm just trying to work through it. It's hard to know where to go next." She raised her head and looked into his face through the dim light, holding it between her hands. "Thanks for helping. I'm very lucky to have you." She drew him closer, burying her head on his neck, and sighed. He pulled her very tight with both arms around her chest, riding up on the emotional swell—one, two minutes—until the powerful wave eased him down. She leaned back, pensive, watching his eyes. Ingram stood and pulled back the quilt. "Let's stay on board tonight. It's too late to try to pack all this up and drive back to Boston. I'll sleep in the forward cabin. There's a sleeping bag in there. Things always seem to have practical answers in the morning."

The sleeping bag was old and musty but the bed was comfortable. In the morning he would pack the loose gear and make arrangements for winter storage. Rivulets of water rustled against the hull beside his head. Tide going out, he thought. In the morning he would make what was left of the coffee, maybe the cocoa too, then they'd stop for lunch in Gloucester at the little lobster shack with the red picnic tables. Lobster and cole slaw. He thought she called him once. He listened very intently for several minutes but he heard nothing more. Then a foghorn. Must have been a foghorn. In the morning he would call to check on his post-ops. He would remind Adams to put the disk on the schedule first on Tuesday so that no one could cancel the craniotomy. In the morning there would be plenty of practical things to do.

CHAPTER 16

There were no neurosurgical cases scheduled for Monday morning, so Adams and Burleson and the students made leisurely rounds at eight o'clock. The ICU was half empty, awaiting the big elective cases from the operating room. Rizzo had stopped bleeding and appeared to be sleeping. Their other neuro ICU patients had all been transferred back to 9 North.

Professor Rothstein was sitting up in bed, eating breakfast from the tray in front of him. Scrambled eggs dribbled down his chin onto his chest and the tray was awash with spilled orange juice, but he seemed in remarkably good spirits. "Good morning, Dr. Adams. As you can see I'm having a little difficulty coordinating this morning. It seems I keep trying to put my scrambled eggs in my ear. But my headache's gone and breakfast tastes good, when I can get it into my mouth."

"That's because we were tugging on your cerebellum, professor. You won't always mistake your ear for your mouth."

"Oh I know. I'm doing much better today than yesterday. But best of all, my mind is clear this morning."

"Yes, I noticed."

"It's such a remarkable sensation. Like awakening from a bad dream. Or actually returning from the dead. I've been told it's Monday."

"That's right."

"That it's two weeks since my operation, but I remember very little of the last week. Headaches. Visits with Ravikrishnan. Waking up twice in the ICU. But all is good this morning. Parts of my brain are still asleep. Last night I couldn't remember any word that began with the letter F. I noticed that I couldn't say the word meaning rapidly or quickly, then I couldn't describe to the nurse an ice cream drink with

187

milk, then I couldn't identify this eating utensil." He held up a fork. "That's when I realized that I was blanking the letter F, when the nurse told me the name of this utensil. You see I still don't quite have it. What is this again?"

"That's a fork, professor."

"Words are so important. The logical positivists argue that the whole of human knowledge and experience centers on the words, rather than the other way around. Do you know Wittgenstein?"

"Yes. We studied Wittgenstein in a logic class."

"Well Wittgenstein was . . ." he was obviously searching for a word, "was . . . was very interested to the point of obsession—what would you call that?"

"Fascinated."

"Fascinated—yes—an F word." He smiled and continued, "Wittgenstein was fascinated with the abstraction represented by words. It's purely human, you know. He used this very example. This utensil," he held up the fork, "when we say this word or read it or hear it—what's the word again?"

"Fork."

"Yes, when we say 'fork' we can all visualize an eating utensil which can be held in one hand with prongs and a curve to it and we can eventually visualize an entire concept of forkness. Wittgenstein used this very example which I have described a hundred times in my classes but never thought about it in such detail as I have this morning. I have a clear concept of what this is and how to use it and how to describe it to others but that part of my brain which has this word stored in memory is not yet . . . not quite . . . not operational?"

"Functional?"

"Yes, thank you, functional. But I'm pleased, almost exuberant as you can see, that my mind is returning bit by bit, as you and Dr. Ingram said it would. So if I can only learn to control my hand, I can use this pronged eating utensil to put my . . . to direct this combination of eggs and bacon and stale toast . . ."

"Food?"

"If I can only use this utensil to get the food in my mouth, then I shall survive quite nicely."

They saw the other patients on that side of the hall and, leaving the senator for last, stopped in Kathleen Dugan's room. The nurse was coming out as they were going in. She looked concerned. "This girl doesn't look too good to me. They just transferred her down from ICU last night. They said she was sleeping all night on report, but I can't rouse her at all this morning. Has she been like that?"

"We'll see," said Adams. Kathleen was breathing but that was her only activity. Her limbs were flaccid. Her eyes were closed, and didn't move when Burleson raised her eyelids and moved her head from side to side. She showed no response at all to pain. Her vital sign sheet showed only progressively slowing respiration. No medications which might cause sedation. Her pupils were mid-point. The right one responded slowly to light but the left did not.

"What's the problem?" asked one of the students.

"Don't know yet," said Adams, irritated. "Sometimes a closed head injury looks good for a few days and then falls apart again. Sort of an ATN of the brain." He clicked down on her left eye with his ophthalmoscope. "This disc is choked." He turned to the nurse. "Miss, can you get us an IV setup and some Decadron?" She left. "Burleson, get us an ICU bed. And see if you can find Dr. Ingram."

* * * *

In 1672 Josiah Smithson and his two sturdy sons spent the summer building a dam across the creek which was later called the Sudbury River, in order to create a millpond to provide the power for the water wheel and the grinding wheels of the Smithson Mill, which was in turn used to convert to flour and meal the wheat and corn, which was grown with ever increasing success by the second-generation Americans who cleared and farmed the fertile land one day's journey from the harbor. Clear mountain water, which should have run directly to the ocean, now meandered into meadows and woodlands a mile or two upstream from the dam. A shallow marsh resulted with islands and banks of beech and hickory to which the squirrels and chipmunks retreated, leaving the new wetland for the beavers and the ducks. When a hot late harvest afternoon was followed by a cold clear morning, the shallow pond exhaled a billow of mist which hung above the surface as high as the shorter balsams. A mother mallard and her nearly grown offspring swam by, giving the optical illusion of gliding through the thick air rather than on the water.

Ingram could have driven to Fitchburg more efficiently on one of the major highways, but he intentionally took a series of back roads so that he could savor the full flavor of New England autumn. When he rounded the little curve at the bottom of a hill northwest of Sudbury a bank of mist ten feet high hung over the marsh, glowing golden from the sun behind him. A gentle easterly blew puffs of mist from the surface as if from a dozen chimneys. A pair of ducks broke the surface of the mist as he slowed to cross the narrow bridge.

Like most of his older colleagues, Ingram had stopped giving lectures at small community hospitals, happy to leave the rubber chicken, disinterested compulsory audience, broken slide projector, would-you-mind-seeing-a-patient-with activities to his younger colleagues. But he always accepted the yearly invitation from Fitchburg. Partly because the chief of surgery who had to assemble the list of speakers was a former classmate and an old friend; partly because the only neurosurgeon in north central Massachusetts would be there (a former navy jet pilot who lived with a former flower child in a three-hundred-year-old farm house and rode the neurosurgical circuit from Lunenburg to Peterborough at very high speeds in very expensive Italian sports cars); and partly because it gave him the opportunity to wander through rural New England for a few hours, and to converse with himself. That opportunity had been more important when Emily was alive and the children were young because it had really been the only time he had solely to himself—away from patients, telephones, family, and friends. Now his house afforded that every day, but there was still something satisfying about the thought that he could continue driving for hours or days if he wished, the commander of his own destiny.

He stopped in front of the Unitarian Church facing the common in North Amesbury to change a tape. The Mahler Eighth was lovely, but too heavy for the day. The town square in North Amesbury was a prototypic New England town square with white churches and white town hall and white prominent citizen's home all facing each other across the green. Leaded panes and black shutters and bright brass handles added

190

to the air of formality, permanence, and eloquence. The scene needed music of elegance. Looking through the glove compartment he discovered that his choices were Brubeck, Mozart, and the Strauss last songs. All elegant, but he settled for the Mozart horn concerto.

He checked to be sure his slides were in his briefcase (he brought the talk on head trauma), and glanced at the time. Two hours to cover the last twenty-five miles. He turned off the two-lane blacktop onto an unnamed country road which aimed generally west. Despite the brilliance of the morning and the music, the somber undertone to his thoughts was John Bradford.

In a short time, and in a partly professional way, the two men had become friends. Bradford had the same aura of genuine, intelligent concern in person as he radiated in public. His ready laugh and sense of perspective were pleasantly surprising to Ingram who generally found politicians (and lawyers in general for that matter) pompous or narrow—boring in either case. It was now clear that whatever combination of wit, perception, candor, compassion, and sense of moral value that had combined to make the personality of John Bradford had vanished in the operating room. It remained to be seen what combination of memory, new experience, enhancement, modulation, and central coordinator would emerge. The concept of a central coordinator was not unique to Ingram, but he found it the most convenient way to describe and discuss the activities of the mind. In this metaphor (he considered all of psychology and philosophy as metaphor) the central coordinator was the conscious self, positioned between the input coming in at thousands of bits per second, and the memory banks, in which were stored trillions of bits of information, duplicated and cross-referenced in a system which was orders of magnitude more complex than any computer yet manufactured. The central coordinator monitored the input, put most of it on automatic pilot, filed some in the appropriate places, and—most important—controlled the output of the system in a manner which was uniquely human. It enhanced some responses, inhibited others, colored some with emotion, and converted new input, banked memory, and modulation into concepts (forkness), then to language (fork), then to conscious or subconscious thoughts, vocal processes, or written symbols of the language representing the thought and the concept. In the metaphor, the coordinator does all of these things simultaneously, while watching itself in action. So that a man could drive a car, enjoy the color of the trees, listen to a full orchestra coming from electronic gadgets which were not an orchestra, all the while thinking about the lost mind of a lost friend while also thinking about thinking about driving a car.

The central coordinator in Bradford's brain—if it still existed intact or in pieces—would be like the mayor trying to run North Amesbury after the town hall was hit by a tornado. A huge tangle of wires in the basement of the town hall. A crowd of citizens demanding attention on the common. Most of the records and directions missing. The telephone company intact down the street but no way to connect to it. The police and the ruffians, ministers and the housewives, the businessmen and the customers, the teachers and the students are all there, but in the confusion no one can remember which is which or who should do what. Suppose the old mayor is dead. A new mayor can connect wire to wire, but without the directions, a connection might turn on the street lights, or sound a siren, or unlock the jail. Meanwhile the bell in the steeple clangs away without control and in the train station the controls send unintelligible signals.

With other patients, Kathleen Dugan or Matt Rizzo, for example, the damage was done by someone else. Ingram's job was simply to prevent further damage and facilitate the recovery process—whatever course that might take. But when the damage occurred during an elective operation, the feeling was never quite the same. To be sure, Ingram had not placed the tumor there, had not caused the cells to grow, had not sought out this patient and suggested that he have his head opened. In fact the patient had found him, had asked him to remove the tumor, realizing the risks, had entered into the episode just as consciously as Kathleen Dugan crossing the street or Matt Rizzo running down the sideline. But it was never quite the same when the patient started whole and ended up less than whole. Ingram knew that every surgeon lives with this thought, and it is the very ability to have this thought and put it aside that makes it possible to operate the next day. But a lifetime of accumulation of such thoughts must be handled by the central coordinator, in conversation, in dreams, and in private thoughts while driving down country roads.

With John Bradford there were several extenuating circumstances that needed special thought and eventual resolution. First there would soon be the media to deal with. It was now generally known that Bradford was in Longwood Hospital (an X-ray technician had received a fifty-dollar story fee from *The Globe*). Soon there would be press releases prepared by partially informed hospital spokesmen. Press conferences. Nurses and orderlies interviewed by brazen television reporters, and neurosurgeons from Houston or Los Angeles, explaining in four and a half minutes on the Today Show why the operation should have been done differently. Then there would be other family members. Bradford's parents lived in Providence and had not been informed, at his request. There were brothers and cousins. And an ex-wife. Then all the Beacon Hill and the Washington connections, some close friends, more political acquaintances, even more political opportunists. Who fills the seat of a United States senator? What constitutes being disabled? Who would advise the governor that the senator was disabled?

He wondered what the governor would do when he realized that the person represented by John Bradford was not at all the person elected by the citizenry of Rhode Island. Well, somehow the government would get along. After all there are ninety-nine other senators and world events will be what they will be, regardless of the existence of John Bradford. Still, there had been events in his memory and mind—and perhaps still were—that may shape the events that become history. Ingram thought it a little strange that he had not heard from the senator's office, or the president's office, or whoever it was that worries about continuing the events of government and bureaucracy. He concluded that they must be communicating through Flint.

Oh yes, Flint.

Coming down a hill on the dirt road he passed into a grove of maple trees which grew together over his head, forming a yellow and red canopy that reflected the light but put the road in shadows. He slowed the car and drove slowly through the sugarbush, enjoying the suddenly cooler air and the brilliance overhead. The dense crown of maples prevented growth on the floor of the little forest so the mush-rooms and the fern which grew up through the decaying leaves gave the appearance of a landscaped park—no trash dumps or beer cans here. The road wound up the hill on the other side of the sugarbush, where luxuriant sumac grew and, giving a crimson fringe to the maple grove. Sumac, that woody weed, was interesting to Ingram because it appeared to be so useless. It couldn't be eaten, burned, or used for building. It didn't support animals or birds. Not even insects. But if its only purpose was to provide that crimson color for two weeks every fall, the rest of the life cycle was worth it.

Since the operation, Flint had become even more attentive to Bradford's behavior. Watching carefully, listening, questioning. The equivalent of nervousness in anyone else. Flint remained enigmatic to Ingram. Was Flint really a bodyguard to protect Bradford's political future? Not that, Ingram decided, because Bradford's political future was over, and it was obvious to everyone. He wondered how a man like Flint thought—so dedicated to his task yet so apparently indif-ferent, so interested in intellectual pursuit yet so apparently serious. Did he ever laugh? Had he ever sat with the senator and joked over tall tales of governmental or international intrigue, the way men do to keep perspective in their lives? What did he think of the hospital system, curious nurses, the residents? Of Ingram, or Anne Bradford?

Oh yes, Anne.

The road ended on the east side of the Shirley Reservoir. Reflecting the sky, the water in the small pond was deep blue with black cats' paws dancing across it at the whim of the westerly breeze. Clumps of white birches in front of the dark hemlocks added a very different second movement to the symphony of color. Seeing that he still had plenty of time, he found his way around the north side of the pond, pausing to watch a pair of swans drifting in a little bay beside a deserted wooden dock. Summer cottages here, mixed in with year-round residents occupying tiny houses with tarpaper walls and corru-gated aluminum roofs, stacks of firewood and partially disassembled trucks and chicken coops in the backyards.

Anne Bradford had begun to fill the empty spots in his conscious experience. Waking from sleep, walking through hospital corridors, driving automatically down city streets and this country lane. Triggered by dozens of little events, when there was no other purposeful activity which required full command of his thought process, he had begun to experience a free-floating warm and satisfying feeling which inevitably materialized into some aspect of Anne. Even in dreams, usually with sexual overtones and frustrated by some witness or unsolicited chaperone. Three times he had tried unsuccessfully to work at a chapter on memory localization which was more than a month past due, but was unable to concentrate as she kept displacing the first paragraph in his mind. Well, he hated writing chapters anyway.

Did she have the same thoughts? Or more importantly, if she had the same thoughts, how would they deal with it? No, how would he deal with it? Since the romance—he had come to think of it as such—remained purely personal and socially acceptable as long as it remained unspoken, unrecognized, and unfulfilled. Best left that way. Not that he needed more complications in his life just now. Certainly not that Anne should proceed from fantasy to romance to affair to whatever. She seemed more concerned and consumed with John Bradford as his recovery progressed—or didn't progress. Yes, best left alone. And yet . . .

Down the main street now, through the two traffic lights. Past the hardware where nails were still displayed in metal bins and screws were kept in their proper boxes in little cabinets with the size of the screw displayed on the door. Past Haskala's Department Store where the back-to-school sale was now over and down-filled vests hung in the window and Mr. Haskala worried about the loss of business to the shopping mall on the edge of town. Past the public library and the school and the Lutheran Church, up the hill and into the macadam-covered hospital parking lot.

* * * *

"Dr. Ingram's office."

"Miss Lewis, this is Dan Adams. I need to talk to Dr. Ingram for a few minutes."

"Dr. Adams, Dr. Ingram is not available. I'll be glad to have him call you back. Is there a message I may give him?"

"No, I really needed to talk to him right away. It's about one of our patients who's going sour."

"I'm afraid he's not available. And as I explained to young Dr. Burleson a few minutes ago . . ."

"Excuse me Miss Lewis, but we've tried his beeper and his home but we haven't been able to find him."

"Well I'm not surprised Dr. Adams. He's on his way to Fitchburg to give a lecture. I have already left Dr. Burleson's message with the hospital in Fitchburg but until he arrives there's simply no way to make contact. So I will have him call you when . . ."

"I'm afraid that will be too late Miss Lewis. Who's covering for Dr. Ingram?"

"I believe Dr. Emerson is in town."

A pause on both ends of the telephone line.

"Well I guess I'll try and call him."

"Dr. Adams?"

"Yes Miss Lewis."

"Which patient is it and what is the problem?"

"It's Kathy Dugan, the high school girl with the head injury."

"The policeman's daughter?"

"Yes that's the one. She's lost consciousness and blown one pupil. Her intracranial pressure is elevated."

"Dr. Adams, when did you start your chief residency?"

"In July Miss Lewis."

"Well Dr. Adams, what needs to be done for Miss Dugan?"

"She needs a stat CT scan and possibly a decompressive craniotomy depending on what that shows."

"If Dr. Ingram were here I'm sure he would ask if you know how to get all that organized and underway. Can you do that?"

"Yes."

"Then, if Dr. Ingram were here, I'm sure he'd say 'do it.'"

"Right."

The phone clicked dead. She returned to the mail. From her desk she could see the framed photographs of chief residents in neurosurgery extending back to 1922. She had known them all since Victor Hall, 1949. Many famous and not so famous neurosurgeons looked down on her daily, including Donald Ingram, 1972. Each of these famous men had, at one time, been a boy. The telephone rang again.

"Dr. Ingram's office."

"Miss Lewis?"

"Yes Dr. Adams."

"Thanks a lot. You're a sweetheart."

"Thank you Dr. Adams."

Click.

* * * *

Sickness or not, there was still laundry to do. Family crisis or not, there was still cooking and dishes and grocery shopping. Hospital visits or not there were still closets to clean and carpets to sweep. Actually, it kept her mind off Kathleen for the first few days, and now that Kathleen was improving she could attend to the details she had left undone last week. In fact, Kathleen had shown such improvement by the end of the weekend that Mary Dugan had planned to spend all of Monday morning cleaning and shopping and having a mini-celebration. So she was alone, and unprepared, for the telephone call from Dr. Adams. Trembling, she dressed quickly. Unable to find Michael at the station office she called St. Cecilia's and asked Father O'Reilly to meet her at the hospital.

She caught a glimpse of herself, reflected in the stainless steel plate in the elevator. No makeup, disheveled, and scared. No matter. On 9 North the ward clerk was on a break, the charge nurse was in a meeting, so she went directly to Kathleen's room.

The bed was empty! Father O'Reilly sat in the dark corner in an attitude of prayer.

"Oh no! Oh mother of God. Father John is she . . . ?"

"No, no Mary. She's gone to X-ray. Ease yourself now." She slumped, sobbing, to his shoulder and he held her close in a paternal, priestly sort of way.

"I'm sorry Father. I'm so scared."

"I know. We're all scared. Dr. Adams asked us to page him when you arrived. He's down in X-ray with Kathleen. He said something about an operation."

"I know, he told me on the telephone. Where's Dr. Ingram?"

"I'm sure he's close by." The ward clerk paged Adams, had a brief conversation, and directed them to the surgery waiting area on the second floor. In that room, full of extremely anxious people trying to look calm, they met a receptionist who ushered them into a small side room. Four chairs, a lamp, and a Monet print. Soon Adams and Burleson appeared in operating room regalia, Burleson carrying a clipboard with an ominous single paper on it. To Mary Dugan, Adams looked calm and reassured. To John O'Reilly, he looked rather young.

"Kathleen took a turn for the worse last night. The CT scan shows that there's a large blood clot pressing on her brain. It's been there since the accident, and it was small at first but now it's a major problem. We need to operate to remove the blood clot right away. You need to sign this form for us. Do you have any questions?"

"I'd like to reach my husband. How urgent is this Dr. Adams?"

"We need to get started right away. Either Dr. Burleson or I will talk to your husband as soon as he arrives. But we shouldn't delay."

"Is Dr. Ingram here? I'd like to talk to him."

"Unfortunately he's giving a lecture in the central part of the state. He'll be back soon and he knows . . . He would agree with the urgency of this operation."

"I just don't know."

"This is so sudden for Mrs. Dugan, particularly after Kathleen looked so good yesterday," O'Reilly spoke softly. "Just how bad is her condition now?"

"Comatose. Unresponsive except to pain. Decerebrate. Showing the signs of pressure from the blood clot."

"Two on a scale of ten?"

Adams was surprised, then remembered that O'Reilly had attended their clinical research conference. "Closer to 1.6." A brief smile for O'Reilly. "It is important that we start right away."

"The doctor's right Mary. I'm sure Michael would want us to proceed. He'll be along soon."

"Alright. Where do I sign?" She took the clipboard, noting that the few blank spaces were filled in with "bleeding, infection, permanent brain damage, restrictions—none." "I should have this form memorized by now." She signed her name. Burleson retrieved the clipboard.

"Thank you. Wait in the waiting room. We'll keep you posted." Adams left abruptly. Burleson lagged behind and took Father O'Reilly back into the consultation room after Mary Dugan was as settled as she would be.

"Father O'Reilly, could I ask you a question about biomedical ethics?"

"Ethics are ethics Dr. Burleson. I'd be glad to help if I can."

"I'm a Catholic, so killing someone is a sin."

"It is whether you're a Catholic or not."

"I know, I was just trying to give you my background. Anyway, my question is this. Suppose I have a patient who has an incurable condition." O'Reilly nodded, waiting. "Now the patient develops a life-threatening complication. Treatable, but life-threatening." O'Reilly nods again. "If I intentionally fail to treat the complication and the patient dies, have I killed the patient?"

O'Reilly sat back in his chair and paused. "This is not a simple question and there is no simple answer. Is the patient terminal?"

"How do you define terminal?"

"Death from the original condition is imminent and inevitable. End stage cancer for example."

"No. Not terminal by that definition."

"Too bad. I mean the church's position with regard to terminal patients is straightforward, at least as I interpret it. Neither God nor the pope nor common sense would expect us to prolong the act of dying. Withholding treatment from a terminal patient, under some circumstances, is the kind and proper thing to do. Good doctors know that."

"Then there are circumstances in which allowing the patient to die by withholding treatment is not killing the patient."

"Of course, of course."

"But how about my patient—my hypothetical patient. The condition is not terminal, by your definition."

"A condition such as . . . ?"

"Quadriplegia."

"Oh. The Rizzo boy." Stated, eyebrows raised for verification.

"Yes." A longer pause, O'Reilly pushing one shoe against the other, deep in thought.

"First of all," he began slowly and deliberately, "there are legal issues and hospital policy issues. And then there are the wishes of the family . . . In all these issues the wishes of the patient come first. A patient can choose his doctor, or choose not to have a hospital or a doctor. There are some recent cases which are important. A woman with multiple sclerosis, for example, refused treatment and the court supported her contention against a hospital which insisted on having her fed."

"I can deal with those problems. I am asking your advice about the personal, ethical issue. The issue for me."

"The moral issue of withholding treatment so that a patient will die?"

"Exactly."

"A patient who does not have a terminal condition? A competent patient whose mind is sound?"

Burleson nodded in agreement, "A sound mind with no functional body. Like the patient you described with multiple sclerosis."

"If such a patient asked you to kill him, and you did—by an injection or some similar means—that would be killing. Murder. Sinful. Sinful in the church and illegal in the society."

"That's not what I asked."

"I know, I know. I'm trying to make some logical steps. Now if the patient refused sustenance—food or intravenous feeding—it would be your obligation to comply with the patient's wishes and when the patient died—of dehydration or starvation—I cannot imagine that you would be held responsible, either legally or morally. Between the patient and the church, that's a different matter. Is that suicide or not? It would require some more thought."

"And now to my question."

"Yes. The patient develops a life-threatening complication and refuses treatment with the intent of dying. It seems to me that your obligation is clear. Your first duty is to respect the wishes of your patient. After all, the patient has contracted with you; you're not

200

assigned to him for life. Your first obligation is clearly to serve the patient as he wishes. What does the Rizzo boy want?"

"I don't know. I haven't asked him."

The priest tried not to look shocked. "Surely you've discussed something. About his prognosis? About his new complication?"

"It's not as simple as that. First of all there are other doctors and family members involved. It's not up to me to make the final decisions. But I have to carry them out."

"A priest can understand that very well."

"And second, we hardly ever do that. I mean, I've only been an intern for three months now, but I've never seen the attending offer death—or no treatment—as an option. We always assume that patients want to live and go on from there."

"That's just a matter of experience—or your own inexperience. Those discussions are never easy. They're conducted in private, not in committee. You'll have many of those private discussions. That's an important part of your responsibility, helping people decide about dying."

"I suppose. But I'm committed to preserving life. I'm a doctor. Who wants to play God?"

Now the priest chuckled and put a kindly hand on the young man's shoulder. "Don't flatter yourself or your colleagues, Burleson. Nobody plays God. You can't determine whether someone will live or die. Occasionally how and when, but not whether. And if you use some common sense in helping the patient decide how and when, both God and the patient will thank you." Burleson's beeper sounded, followed by the message, "Dr. Burleson report to the OR Room 3."

"That's Kathleen Dugan. I'd better hurry. Thank you Father. I think you answered my question. They should teach this stuff in medical school." He left abruptly.

"They should indeed."

* * * *

Ingram was still tying his mask behind his head as he pushed the door open into Room 3. "What are you finding in there Dan?"

Dan Adams spoke without looking away from the spot of white

201

light in front of him. "This girl developed a symptomatic subdural early this morning. I thought we should move right ahead." He didn't say "I hope it's alright," although this was implied.

"That's why you're the chief resident. That is one hell of a subdural." He examined the small sequential images presented on X-ray-sized celluloid on the view box. Mentally, he traced the outlines of the large mass, some liquid, some solid, pushing out against the skull and in against the brain. It seemed only a few years ago when they would have had to rely on an arteriogram, or even subtle differences in physical findings, to make this diagnosis. Now it was so simple. Engineering technology and biology, interdependent to make progress in the field of medicine. Interesting too how these twenty little computer-generated gray and white pictures—each representing a single plane cross-sectional view of the head (as if a frozen cadaver had been crosscut in thin sections by a band saw which, in fact, was how the anatomy was prepared for study in medical school)—how these images, when presented sequentially and examined visually came to represent in the mind's eye of the observer a three-dimensional image corresponding exactly with the three-dimensional image over which Adams was running his finger at present. Ingram was fascinated by the fact that the simulation process, although taken totally for granted, was one which is infinitely more complex than the generation of these images by the computer.

"We found a lot of clot. It came out in two big pieces. Now I'm just cleaning up a little debris. The brain's coming up already." On the back table Jimmy had spread out a green towel and the two large chunks of organized clot were placed on it, looking like fresh liver,

Ingram moved close behind Burleson to get a better look into the field. He was satisfied. "Anything else going on?" His question was directed to Adams, but Burleson had been doing a good job, and Adams recognized an opportunity for his intern to get some recognition. He signaled to Burleson with a nod.

"Everyone else is doing well," said Burleson, taking the hint. "Rothstein is more alert every day. Mr. Jones is unchanged. We discharged the two discs yesterday. We admitted a four-year-old with a glioma that's on the schedule for tomorrow."

"Jamie Harrison."

"Yes, Jamie Harrison. And—oh, I forgot to tell you—we 'scoped Matt Rizzo last night. Dr. Hawkins and I. He has a posterior duodenal ulcer. There was no more bleeding overnight."

Silence except for the slurp of the sucker.

"That's worrisome."

More silence.

"Dr. Ingram. Have you . . . I mean, shouldn't we . . . ask Matt Rizzo how aggressive he wants us to be? If that ulcer bleeds he'll need an operation. But he'll still be quadriplegic. Sooner or later a urinary infection, or a decubitus with osteomyelitis, or pneumonia, or some other thing will happen. Shouldn't we discuss the options with him?"

"That's a perceptive question Burleson. Actually, I've already done that with Matt and his wife. They want us to give it the whole shot."

"Retract over here Burleson." It was Adams's way of telling Burleson that he had once again overstepped his bounds. With relief, Burleson realized that Ingram didn't seem offended.

"You have to be careful though. Considerate is a better word. Families and patients don't have any background to make medical decisions. It's unkind to force them into choices for which they have no background. Should we use dialysis? Should we apply CPR if the heart stops? Should we use radiation or chemotherapy or both? Patients can't make those decisions. They rely on you to make the decision and advise them. You have to decide what you think is best before you have the discussion with the family, because they will surely ask you to help them."

"So you decided that we should operate if Rizzo starts bleeding again?" A nudge from Adams.

"Not quite. I told them that if the bleeding continued it might get to the point where Matt's heart would stop. Then I waited. They know the prognosis for the quadriplegia, at least Carol does. They have the options laid out. I didn't direct them because in this case I'm not sure which is the best alternative. They clearly wanted to do everything, despite the prognosis. So we went on to discuss the methods of treating the bleeding. The next time around, the next complication, it might be different."

"Well Burleson, should we put the bone flap back in or not?" The question came from Adams who wanted to get Burleson on a different subject. There followed a conversation related to brain swelling and the merits of different methods of decompression. Observing that Adams had the situation well in hand, Ingram prepared to leave.

"Dan, I don't need to scrub in, do I?"

"No sir."

"I'll stop to talk to the family." He left the room but stuck his head back in the door. "Oh, Dan. You did a good job."

Ingram met with the Dugans and Father O'Reilly, all of whom were much relieved by his message. He talked with the family of Jamie Harris and visited the ICU. He visited with Rothstein, who was reading the F section of the dictionary, trying to refill, or at least recall, that section of his memory, gleefully, as if he were discovering exciting new facts with each turn of the page. Finally to the end of the hall and Bradford's room.

* * * *

Except for the healing incision surrounded by a two-week stubble on his head, the man in the bed certainly looked like the young senator from Rhode Island. Ingram read the vital sign sheet and called his name, and received an empty stare in response. He went through a more careful examination than he usually did at this early stage in the postoperative course. He flicked the fingernail of Bradford's middle finger. His thumb responded. He scratched the bottom of his feet and his big toe turned down. He tapped at the insertion of various tendons with appropriate reflex responses. He pressed hard on each eyebrow (where bruises would not show if he pressed too hard) and Bradford pulled away and grimaced, all of his muscles apparently working appropriately. He checked the pupils, turned the head from side to side, gently irritated the corneas and the back of his throat, all with appropriate responses. Almost by habit he directed Bradford to squeeze his fingers and, to his surprise, he did. Rather slowly and not too firmly, but definitely a grasp. The same on both sides. He lifted Bradford's arm from the bed and held it straight in the air with a directive to hold it there. The first time his hand fell on his own face, but the next time

204

Bradford could hold his arm extended. First the right then the left. No tremor. Encouraged, Ingram directed Bradford to look at his flashlight and moved it slowly from side to side. Although his stare was blank and he appeared not to focus, his eyes tracked the moving light. Any neuroscientist knows that responding to commands is a significant abstraction and requires a lot of intact brain with motor tracts and functioning synapses and memory encoded and recalled in language.

"Touch the light." No response. "Touch the light John." Several major abstractions and some reasoning required now. Bradford reached up, slowly at first, then slapped at the flashlight, knocking it from Ingram's hand. Still the blank stare.

Ingram picked up the flashlight, excited now. Perhaps someone was at home after all. He held up two fingers.

"How many fingers John?" No response. He repeated the question, shaking Bradford by the shoulder at the same time, lips moving, then jaw, finally a spitting sound, tongue behind teeth.

"T . . . T . . . Tu . . . Tu . . . Two."

"How many now?"

"Four."

"John who am I? What's my name? John, look at me. What's my name?"

"Two. Two, four, six, eight, ten. Two, four, eight, sixteen, thirty-two, sixty-four." He was looking at Ingram, speaking thickly but urgently.

"Every now and then, you get the impression of function. Just now and then." Flint was standing at the foot of the bed.

"Yes, Mr. Flint. Some fragments of memory come to the surface from time to time."

"It's a long way from Senator Bradford. I wonder what he's thinking—if he's thinking."

* * * *

The sensation of a full bladder came from the balloon on the catheter, but the neurons in his hypothalamus did not make that differentiation. So the sensation that appeared in his mind was merely that of a full bladder, and instantly he searched the files for a learned

205

reaction. What came up was the full bladder he experienced on February 9, 1948, when, at 2:30 in the afternoon, standing in front of the rest of the third grade class at the Eisenhower School in Pawtucket, his bladder had been overly full. The teacher was Mr. Donaldson. His first male teacher, and he had the reputation of being very strict. Mr. Donaldson called his name and asked him to recite the multiplication tables. He didn't start, trying to think of a way to explain the fact that his bladder was too full to think about multiplication. Mr. Donaldson was angry and took off his shoes and socks and scratched his feet. The boys in the class pulled at his fingernails, and the girls started taking off his clothes, while Mr. Donaldson began to hit him with a hammer, demanding the elements of arithmetic. His bladder bursting, and him standing naked in front of the class, the boys giggling and the girls gawking. Mr. Donaldson shined a bright light in his eyes, teasing him, and inviting him to punch out the light. He tried, and finally succeeded, crashing the spotlight to the floor. Now Mr. Donaldson was holding up two fingers. It didn't look like Mr. Donaldson anymore, it was someone else. Someone with a better feeling about him. No matter, his bladder was still too full. Two fingers he shouted. Could he pee now? The principal came in looking over Donaldson's shoulder. The principal was a woman, Mrs. Johnson, who always dressed in men's suits with ruffled blouses and had a small watch hanging from a pendant on the lapel of the suit—no matter the principal was watching too. Four fingers. Two four six. Two four six eight. The principal commented that Johnny finally started reciting. Finally he reached down to clamp himself off, bending over, but too late, as the warm urine sprayed into his underwear, running down his leg and dripping on the floor in a little circle beneath his short pants which had miraculously re-appeared. The boys laughed so hard they were falling out of their seats. Girls too. Mr. Donaldson looked reassuring, told him he could go to the bathroom, but too late of course. So he shouted the worst words he could think of at the age of eight at Mr. Donaldson, at the principal—warm urine now cooling in his left shoe, sock soaked.

"Pee, pee, pee. Piss, piss, piss. You asshole. You flaming asshole. Piss, piss, piss."

Ingram and Flint were both startled, but Ingram wasn't particularly surprised.

"Don't be shocked Mr. Flint. You're never sure what will come out as the brain wakes up."

"That's exactly what I'm worried about," said Flint.

"Two four six. Piss on you. Piss on you asshole." Bradford had managed to grab the Foley catheter and jerked it back and forth, swinging with the other hand at Ingram. Ingram pushed the nurse call button which was answered immediately through the intercom. "Ask Colleen to bring me a syringe of Nembutal please."

CHAPTER 17

"This is irrational. More than irrational. It is preposterous. I just spent a week of time and untold numbers of dollars in your Physical Therapy Department practicing walking and now I'm told I must exit the hospital in a wheelchair." Rothstein was complaining to Adams, who was walking beside him toward the elevators on the ninth floor.

"Don't blame me Professor, it's hospital policy. They worry that you might fall down on your way to the door and sue the hospital." Gray tweed sport coat, tattersall-patterned shirt, nearly new cordovan loafers, suede cap. Only the maroon ascot differentiated him from a professor of law, say, or economics. A miraculous transformation. Clothing makes the difference between a person and a patient. Clothing and demeanor.

"If it's hospital policy, then why don't they send a proper hospital attendant to drive this thing?"

Ravikrishnan, carefully pushing the wheelchair, smiled. "It's a very high-priced chauffeur you have today, sahib." They chuckled aloud together, a raspy rumbling guttural Yiddish and a high-pitched nasal proper Hindi. Like old little boys. Discharged from the hospital—like summer vacation after the fifth grade; like landing safely after a pitching, rolling airplane ride; like Scrooge having peered into the grave prematurely, awakening on Christmas morning with time to replay and revise. They stopped at the nurses' station where Rothstein signed a paper and received a brown paper bag of medications—the penultimate step. Soon he would be at the hospital door, in Ravi's car, sitting in his own chair, in his own study, in his own house, master of his own . . . he still had trouble with F words . . . destiny, then.

"Dr. Ingram won't be in this morning, but I spoke to him on the telephone. He asked me to wish you well and remind you to come back to see us in the office in a week. All the instructions are in the bag along with your Dilantin and some pain pills. Are you all set?" To Adams the discharge of Ben Rothstein provided him a bed for tomorrow's craniotomy. Discharges also served as a way of keeping score. When he dictated the chart that afternoon, Adams would remove the five-by-seven card with the hospital-stamped name and number in the upper-right-hand corner and the cryptic notes in meticulous small handwriting, move it from the pile in his right-hand coat pocket to the pile on his desk. Then, at the end of the month, after totaling the score, he would combine it with the other October cards in a rubber-banded packet to be stuffed in the back of a file drawer, from which it would be pulled for examination three more times: two years later when applying for the Neurosurgery Boards; ten years later when trying to remember the name of the philosophy professor with the pineal tumor; forty-five years later when his son, discarding boxes of personal effects, paused to riffle through the stack of cards marked October 1986 before throwing them into a plastic bag.

"Thank you, Dr. Adams. Please thank young Dr. Burleson when you see him. I'm told the two of you saved my life." Adams had forgotten about the ventriculostomy and Burleson had rotated onto the Urology Service.

"You're welcome Professor Rothstein." The handshake—such a formal gesture between gentlemen—completed the sojourn from primal patient dependency to civilization. "We never save lives. We just prolong the experience. See you next week." He waited by the nursing station until the elevator doors closed. Another discharge. A new admission on the way.

* * * *

The designation on the hospital name tag pinned to the pocket of the white lab coat said "Blood Bank Technician." The white lab coat was too small, and the bare wrists of the tall boy stuck out for several inches as he manipulated the fast rewind button on the Walkman. The white lab coat covered a black t-shirt which advertised the message,

"Jaco Pastorius Word of Mouth Tour 1983." The boy's head nodded rhythmically in response to music which, although pumped directly through the earphones, could be heard across the room. He was a student at Berklee School of Music, doing his homework, and picking up a few dollars as a helper in the Longwood Hospital Blood Bank. The real blood bank technician on the night shift had suffered a flat tire on route 128 and was not expected for another hour, but the boy didn't worry. The blood bank was usually quiet in the middle of the night and besides, he'd already had two months experience and, in fact, had completed all the cross matches for the morning OR schedule. So he jammed hard with Weather Report on the last two choruses of Birdland, and didn't notice the telephone ringing until the blinking red light caught his attention.

When he finally snatched off the earphones and picked up the telephone, the ward clerk in the intensive care unit berated him for not answering, then asked for two units of blood for Matthew Rizzo. The boy hung up, plugged back into his Walkman, and checked the refrigerator. No blood for Rizzo. He checked the blood samples in the test tube rack and found Rizzo, but the sample was thirty-six hours old. He returned to the telephone and transmitted this message to the ward clerk in the ICU. Minutes later Randy Burleson was on the telephone.

"Look, I need blood for Matthew Rizzo stat. Can't you just match him to the sample that's down there?"

"Can't do it, this sample is over twenty-four hours old and besides he's been transfused since this sample was drawn. It says here in the Blood Bank Guidelines—"

"Never mind. What's his blood type?"

"AB negative."

"Then get five units of AB negative. I'll take it without the cross match. I'll send someone down right away."

"Can't do it. I only have four units of AB negative and they're cross matched for an open heart tomorrow. Besides you can only take one unit at a time. That's the regulation."

"Listen buddy. Regulations or not, I'm going to be down there in four minutes and I want those four units of AB negative and four units of O negative ready to go. Got it?"

The boy turned off the Walkman, which had been playing into his neck during the telephone conversation. In a quandary, he walked from the refrigerator to the procedure book to the telephone and back to the refrigerator. Finally, he picked up the telephone and dialed the number of the blood bank supervisor. Busy. He looked through the procedure book with steadily rising anxiety. He dialed the supervisor's number again and it was still ringing when Burleson appeared.

The front of Burleson's scrub suit was soaked in blood, still wet and dripping down the side. Burleson had a determined, frantic expression that bespoke potential violence. Seeing no blood on the counter, Burleson directed a malevolent look at the boy, opened the refrigerator door, and scooped up four units of O negative blood.

"Come on. You can't do that! I've got to report you for this. You can't do that." The boy knew better than to stand in Burleson's way. Bags of blood cradled in his arms, Burleson left the blood bank and ran down the hall to the waiting elevator.

Alex Hawkins arrived in the ICU just after Burleson had left for the blood bank. Hair mussed and eyes puffy, he assessed the situation in seconds. The blood was an inch deep on the Stryker frame, dripping over the edge and settling into large puddles on the floor. The nurse threw a blanket on the puddle so that she could step closer to Matt to suction his mouth. To Hawkins, Matt looked dead. He had a white, waxy, cadaveric appearance and did not move except for the motion produced by the ventilator. However, when Hawkins took his wrist to feel the pulse he opened his mouth, turned his head slightly, and vomited another pint of blood, along with the nasogastric tube which had been used, ineffectively, to drain the blood from his stomach. The blood, although fresh and red with thick maroon clots, appeared to be very watery. Ringer's solution was running wide open into both IVs.

"Where's Dr. Burleson? This patient is exsanguinating."

"He went down to the blood bank to get the blood. There was some problem about cross matching."

"Can you hear a blood pressure? There's no pulse over here."

"Only with the Doppler. The pressure was fifty systolic a few minutes ago."

Burleson burst into the room carrying his precious units of blood, followed by Adams who had been summoned by the charge nurse.

"How's he doing?" asked Burleson of Hawkins, as he handed one unit of blood to the nurse and spiked another himself, replacing the lactated Ringer's solution and squeezing the plastic blood bag.

"Aren't we going to check the numbers on this blood?" asked the nurse.

"After it's in," said Hawkins. "I hope there's more coming. I can't feel a pulse anywhere."

"I hope so too. The jerk in the blood bank wasn't even going to give me these."

Ten minutes later when the last of the second unit of blood dripped in and two more were hanging, there was still no pulse. Rizzo felt cold to the touch and had not moved spontaneously since Hawkins arrived. Hawkins had called the general surgery resident and the OR, and was making arrangements to move to the elevator. A small tank of oxygen was cracked open and attached to the ambu bag. IVs were gathered together on a single pole. The nurse disconnected the EKG leads from the monitor and attached them to the portable monitor.

"There must be something wrong with this monitor. All I get is a straight line. The batteries must be dead."

"If the batteries were dead you couldn't see anything. Try another lead."

"Nothing on this one. Or on this one."

"What's his pressure?" Agonizing seconds while the nurse inflated the cuff and listened with the Doppler probe.

"I can't hear anything. You listen." More seconds.

"I can't hear anything either. I think he's arrested. Let's hook back up to the wall monitor. Get a regular EKG machine."

"Hold on. Let me in there." Adams pushed the others aside and began pushing on Rizzo's sternum with the heel of his hand. Electrical complexes registered on the oscilloscope, accompanying each thrust. "This monitor's fine. He's just in diastolic arrest. Keep ventilating. Burleson, try to get some blood gases. Can you feel a pulse now? Let's get some epi drawn up. Get the stat cart over here."

Immediately but calmly, without disturbing too many of the other nervous patients, the veteran ICU team pursued the familiar exercise of cardiac resuscitation. The Stryker frame, which had been inched toward the door, was pushed back into the cubicle and the curtains were drawn. Respiratory therapists, the EKG technician with a machine, a sleepy anesthesiologist, and a curious general surgery resident who had been waiting in the OR all appeared in minutes. Most stood around the bedside ready to help, watching, playing out the twentieth-century version of the dance of death. Powerful drugs, enough to wake a bear from hibernation, were pumped into the IV lines. Two liters of a starch solution ran in, dropping Rizzo's temperature even further, as Burleson cursed the blood bank. Periodically Adams stepped back, looking miraculously unharried and fresh—staring at the EKG tracing. Periodically some rhythmical electrical activity occurred, but no pulse was felt and after several seconds the line became flat again.

"What happened? Did he just bleed out?" the general surgery resident asked of Hawkins, who was standing back from the immediate action.

"He bled out from the posterior ulcer. I think they got a little behind him this afternoon and this extra bleed just tipped him over."

"What's his basic problem?"

"Quadriplegia from a football accident. C5."

"C5? Then what the hell are we doing this for?" The question intended for Hawkins happened to come during an instant in the proceedings when everything else was silent. Everyone turned toward the general surgery resident.

"What kind of a question is that?" exploded Burleson. "Here we've been busting our ass for weeks for this kid and you waltz in and ask—"

"Never mind Randy, it's not important," said Adams, pulling him back to the patient. "It's a question that somebody ought to ask at every arrest. Give another amp of bicarb." He returned to the rhythmic pumping. The thought voiced by the resident rattled around in everybody's mind. Finally Adams said, "We'll give him two more amps of bicarb and one amp of epi and continue this for three more minutes. If we're not getting anywhere, we'll quit. Okay with every-body?" There were no responses. After three minutes by the bedside clock, Adams straightened up and stretched his back. There were six rapid heart beats, then another, then another, then another, then nothing. "That's it," said Adams. "Eleven forty six. Thanks for the effort everybody. You can't resuscitate an empty heart."

11:46. At 10:30 he had been a human being, sharing a joke with Burleson and asking for a drink of water. At 11:10 the nurse had noticed that he was sweating and pale. At 11:12 he vomited 800 cc's of blood. At 11:45 he was being fortified with every weapon the Longwood Hospital had against its ancient enemy. At 11:46 Matthew Rizzo was officially declared a corpse. As always in the ICU, the tran-sition from patient to corpse occurred very quickly, and the mental adjustment of the staff was almost as fast. The technician and the charge nurse and the anesthesia resident and the respiratory therapists gathered up their gear and disappeared to clean the weapons for the next battle. The medicine resident, who had four yards of EKG paper in his hand, started to ask if anyone wanted it, thought better of it, and dropped it in the trash. With murmured words, sighs, shaking of heads, and hands on the shoulders—the touching is an important part of the ritual—the tenseness between Burleson and the general surgery resident were resolved and the resident left, as did Hawkins, leaving Adams and Burleson sitting at the nursing station. Irrepressible what-ifs boiled up in Burleson's mind. Adams could tell he was anxious, and feeling responsible.

"Randy. Sometimes people bleed out from ulcers. Even quads. Don't take it personally."

"Yes. Thanks," was all that Burleson could trust himself to ver-balize. Even so, his voice quavered.

"Tell you what. If you do the paperwork, I'll call the family."

Burleson was grateful, but all he could manage was a nod.

CHAPTER 18

Flint watched her get off the elevator, check in at the nursing station, and come resolutely down the hall. He had stopped confronting her a week ago. Tonight he greeted her softly. "Good evening Mrs. Bradford," he nodded with deference. "It is so nice to see you."

"Why thank you Mr. Flint." She detected his look of boredom vanishing. "At least I can come and go. You must be getting weary of your assignment."

"I must admit I did not expect to be here for three weeks. But if it's difficult for me it must be very difficult for you. I admire your perseverance, and your optimism."

"Thank you again Mr. Flint." She was surprised by his comment—not by his perception, but that he had said it. "You are very thoughtful."

Flint acknowledged her compliment with a nod and said, "I don't think you want to go in there tonight Mrs. Bradford. It's worse than usual."

"Thanks for the warning. Would you come with me?"

For different reasons both Anne and James Flint had come to fear and detest the shreds of mental activity that now represented John Bradford. Flint, because his assignment now seemed mindless and futile, but there was no way of confirming whether or not the crucial information he was protecting was still in Bradford's brain. Anne, because the body that had been her husband no longer included his soul. "Yes, I'll go in with you if you like." He had observed the pain and fear in Anne's face when she visited her husband lately. Because they were forced to face a common problem, Anne felt they had come to a common understanding, even a friendship. By agreement she had dealt with John's family and non-political friends. Flint, through an impersonal hospital spokesman, had dealt with the government and its minions. Together they had concocted the press release which had run in the *Globe* and the other national newspapers. "Senator John Bradford in coma. Not expected to live."

"Yes, I'll go in with you if you like," he said gently, and stepped aside, holding the curtain open, so she could enter before him.

He was sleeping. A heavy canvas vest was attached by straps to the bed. The bedside table had been moved out of his reach. Softly, Anne touched his forehead. "John? Honey?"

He opened his eyes, looked through her but not at her, chewed and mouthed some silent words.

"John. What are you saying?" More chewing, then suddenly he reached up, grabbing her hair with one hand.

"John, let go, John." He pulled her head down to his chest, then jammed her nose into his crotch. Gurgling sounds came from his throat. His hips bounced on the thin mattress. "John," her voice muffled as he pushed up into her face.

Flint moved quickly, but even as he grabbed the senator's wrist, Bradford's grip grew tighter on Anne's hair. He jerked her head up and down, cutting her lip. She shouted in pain.

"Suck, bitch! Suck bitch!" he yelled.

"Enough, you bastard," said Flint through gritted teeth, his face red with fury. He reached for Bradford's trachea and pushed hard. The voice stopped. Bradford struggled violently but silently, and released Anne who fell back, gasping. Flint waited as Bradford turned blue, then purple, then stopped moving. Anne was shaking, wiping sweat and blood from her face. Her expression of anger and revulsion was replaced by one of shock when she looked back and saw Flint still standing above Bradford, his large hand pressed to the senator's neck. John was not struggling anymore. Flint's expression was cold and unemotional. She realized that Flint would continue until John was dead. She put her hand on Flint's arm and shook her head no.

Flint released his grasp. Bradford coughed and wheezed, breathing with audible stridor, trying to feel his own throat. When they could see that he was alive, they left the room. In the corridor, Anne noted that Flint was shaking too.

"Thank you, Mr. Flint. You warned me. I should have been more careful."

"It was my fault. I am very sorry," said Flint. Anne thought she saw tears in his eyes, which she assumed were brought on by anger and exertion.

"I think I'll just go. Goodnight." As she walked away the thought occurred to her for the first time. To herself she muttered, "This has to end," softly, but overheard by Mr. Flint.

* * * *

"I've never been to one of these before."

When the emotional whirligig slowed, when the urge to vomit and the urge to laugh subsided, when the horror gave way to fascination, when he felt the need for routine, viable reality, Kevin Tracey leaned over to the Bridgewater State teammate next to him and whispered, "I've never even been to a funeral home before."

His friend simply nodded, indicating either a dispassionate familiarity with the rituals of the dead or the inability to control his voice. Several members of the football team were sitting in the next-to-last row of cold, uncomfortable, metal folding chairs, which, through chips and scratches, revealed their history of being stacked and re-stacked hundreds of times. His chair creaked as he set it straighter, getting a better look at the profile of Matt Rizzo lying in the coffin at the front of the little room. He felt strangely guilty about the act of looking. The room was too warm and had a sweet, flowery smell— almost unbearably sweet with lots of rose scent and more than a hint of formaldehyde which only the very experienced nose might detect. There were a dozen bouquets—maybe fifteen—arranged below and behind the coffin, making it appear to be floating on a bed of flowers. Half of them were made of silk and came with the use of the room. Kevin didn't know that, and wouldn't have cared anyway, as he watched the dead body, almost expecting it to move.

Carol knew about the fake flowers. Sitting in the front row with little Matt on one side and Matt's parents on the other, she looked at the flowers intently, trying to identify the real ones and the fake ones, concentrating on that to keep her mind from the ultimate reality of the moment.

The chapel of the Halloran Funeral Home had been the living room of what was once a grand old home near the town square in Natick. The former parlor—across the broad, oak-floored, staircased foyer—was now designated the "Sunset Viewing Room." Through the lace curtains covering the double doors into the hallway, Kevin could see a serious-looking man in a dark suit directing occasional bereaved viewers from the coat rack to the Sunset Room. The small-paned windows at the back end of the former living room had at one time looked out over the expansive lawn of the estate. But the grass had given way to parking lot and the end of the room was hung with an expensive-looking velvet curtain, in the center of the curtain was hung an enlarged inspirational photographic print, illuminated by a spotlight on the ceiling, and provided at no extra charge. The photograph was that of a country lane in winter, bare branches hanging heavy with snow, hoof prints and sleigh runners in the foreground, warm lights and smoking chimneys beckoning from the little town in the valley below, just at dusk. This photograph was selected from the six other choices by James Rizzo, to settle an argument between his wife—who favored the likeness of Jesus in the garden—and Carol who, if she had to make a choice, preferred the lake and moonlight with the paddler resting in the foreground and the campfire glowing on the other shore. The Hammond organ—for there is no other sound like it—was played by Mary Halloran herself (twenty dollars an hour), and she was currently softly but persistently working her way through "Blessed Be Thy Tie That Binds" at maximum tremolo. Carol thought harder about the flowers.

As he absorbed the novelty of his surroundings, Kevin realized that it was the first time he had ever seen a dead body. He had heard somehow that Matt would look peaceful, as if he were sleeping. But that had not prepared him for the powder, and the hand with the wedding ring, and satin upholstery in the casket. He had known for a few days about Matt's death. Known long enough to come to his own resolution, and to call Carol, and to collect for a gift of flowers from the football team. But he was not prepared to sit in the little audience, listening to the organ, smelling the sickeningly sweet flowers, and watch the face of his friend—well, his friend's body—lying like some giant doll. He expected rather, that the whole experience would have been more religious and less fantastic. Yes, that was it. The whole thing suddenly seemed fantastic to Kevin Tracey. This little group of people were all sitting here having similar thoughts, looking at a dead body. He had learned in catechism classes that the soul departs the body at the moment of death. He hoped that Matt had confessed and been administered the last rites of the Church on that last fateful day. He knew that Matt's soul was floating out there somewhere, in the company of angels, drawn to the bosom of the Holy Mother and the Saints and the Son of God himself, and watching the proceedings in this little room. But it required more than a little imagination, looking at the made-up waxy corpse in the blue suit and the blue tie under an eggshell white satin cover—with its young wife and its little child and its fretful parents sitting by—it took more than a little imagination to picture that the invisible soul sitting in the clouds would be thinking and feeling and joking around with the spirits, as Matt would have been. Kevin tried to imagine a mechanism by which Matthew Rizzo would be having thoughts and feelings and conversations with its fellow spirits. It was more plausible in the abstract.

Kevin had readily accepted the concept of the soul and immortality and the inevitable sojourn through purgatory and the miracle of forgiveness and the opportunity to sit at the hand of God. Just as he accepted the importance of the sacred relics and the sanctity of the saints, and the unique ability of God to listen to personal prayers, and the eating of fish on Friday (well, they changed that one when he was a little boy). Those thoughts were calming, stabilizing in the abstract. But just now he wondered how the memory of Carol Rizzo's brown eyes, and football Saturdays, and family gatherings, could be occurring in the soul of Matt Rizzo as he watched the little proceedings. How could they occur when the brain in which those memories had been stored was lying in front of him, pickled with formaldehyde. He should have asked the Father that question in catechism class. He was sure there was an appropriate answer. He had just never asked. He turned to the coach, sitting next to him.

"Hey coach," in a soft whisper, "why is that . . . Do you think that Matt . . ." The coach had been enmeshed in his own thought, and turned, tears in his eyes.

Kevin could not formulate the question. "Never mind," he said.

Now Reverend Pulasky, who had arrived a little late and was ushered to the oak-veneer lectern by Mr. Halloran himself, was saying that he never had the opportunity to know Matt, but he had recently met the Rizzo family and he was sure that Matt must have been a wonderful person. He explained that God had a reason for calling home each of His promising creatures, even young fathers, even the only children of loving families, and some day, when we are all (or most of us) united in heaven we'll look back on this event which seems so tragic to us today, and realize how it fit into God's great scheme of things.

Reverend Pulasky spoke for only ten minutes, including the official pronouncements, recited in a monotone, hand and fingers raised in the direction of the corpse, as if Matt were in there listening. Reverend Pulasky had another funeral and two weddings this afternoon and took his leave before the others, pressing hands with the family members, squeezing the cheek of the brave little lad sitting next to his young mother, and pocketing the envelope passed to him by Mr. Halloran with discreet solemnity. As Mary Halloran played something of her own choosing in a very melodramatic key (it was derived from the Franck D Minor Symphony), and after Mr. Halloran had announced that the graveside ceremony would be limited to the immediate family only, Kevin arose with the other mourners. The plan was for everyone to leave the room and assemble on the sidewalk next to the line of grim, black Cadillacs parked at the curb, serving as a silent barrier to the busy traffic on route 9. Then the six members of the football team who were to be pallbearers would be called back in to carry the casket from the little room to the back of the hearse. (Mr. Halloran had learned long before that the actual closure and sealing of the casket was an act too visible, too final, for some unstable family members to witness, and the attendant commotion often upset mourners in the other parlor.) That was the plan, but Kevin lingered, waiting until the family, then the football team, then the Hallorans had left the room. He walked up to the casket and looked intently at the face of his friend. The face looked, indeed, peaceful. The incongruity of personal thoughts by Matt Rizzo on high, related to the empty cranial vault of the corpse slipped to the category of trivia. The emotional exercise of looking at the clay and remembering the vibrancy of life had its effect on Kevin Tracey. "Matt?" he whispered. "Matt?" He reached out and squeezed the dead fingers. They were stiff and cold and his grip left a dent in the embalmed tissue as if it were putty.

* * * *

October in New England. The opening of bow season for deer in New Hampshire. The time to start preparing ski lifts in earnest. Peak of color season. Goodbye Red Sox, hello Bruins. A day to pull boats, store lawn chairs, put on storm windows, and split wood left to dry and season since July. October to Dan Adams meant a new intern. A monthly ritual of long rounds, repeated speeches and introductions—familiar to every chief resident. The new intern was Diane Harris. Harris was from the University of Minnesota. She was diminutive, rather plain, very quiet. To his own surprise, he wished for Burleson. Burleson who began so green but wound up so helpful. This occurred to Adams as they finished rounds late in the evening, waiting for the new intern to catch up from room to room.

Dan Adams was more than a little chauvinistic, even for a surgeon. He learned from her that after internship she was headed into orthopedics. This wispy little girl in orthopedics! Adams couldn't fathom it. Still, girls rarely got into surgical residencies at the Longwood. And when they did they were usually much better residents than their male counterparts. Hoping for this advantage of natural selection, Adams bit his tongue and withheld judgment on Diane Harris. They entered the last room on 9 North.

"Hello Mrs. Dugan. Hello Kathleen. You look terrific tonight."

"Hello Dr. Adams," beamed Mary Dugan. "Yes she certainly does. Ever since your operation last Friday she has been doing much better. Say hello to Dr. Adams, Kathleen."

223

Kathleen reached toward him with one hand, rolling her head from side to side on the pillow and contorting her lips in a series of grimaces, making incredible effort. "Haaroo. Haaroo dookaa." She smiled after this effort, clearly proud of herself.

"Hello Kathleen. Yes you are making wonderful progress."

"Haaroo dookaa." She smiled—a grotesque, slobbering smile.

"Mrs. Dugan, we have some new faces today. This is Dr. Harris who will be taking Dr. Burleson's place." They nodded acknowledgment. "And this is John and this is Gary. They're the students that will be with us this month." More nodding. "Of course I'll still be around, and Dr. Ingram."

"Where's Dr. Burleson? We all liked him so much, didn't we Kathleen?"

"He's still around. I'm sure he'll be in to see you from time to time. He's just gone on to another service this month." He turned to the diminutive intern. "You have some big shoes to fill, Dr. Harris. Dr. Burleson had some private patients, like Kathleen here." He detected just an instant of reactive fire in her gaze, but all she said was, "Yes, sir." Adams hoped for a little more zip. Perhaps she took a while to warm up. Well, she might as well warm up on some good intern work.

"Dr. Harris, Kathleen is ready to start on some PT, so make sure she gets down there tomorrow. Make sure she gets Henry. No one else will do. Henry's great for closed-head patients. She needs a hematocrit tomorrow morning. Check her discs twice a day. Book a CAT scan for next week. We can cancel it if we don't need it. And get her skin staples out on Thursday." Harris was writing these directions in the service notebook. "Goodnight Mrs. Dugan. We'll see you in the morning. Goodnight Kathleen."

As they left the room she was still trying to write in the notebook and walk at the same time. "Look, Diane. What services have you been on so far?"

She spoke so softly he could hardly hear. "I started on children's orthopedics, and ER, and endoscopy. This is my first busy rotation." She tried a little smile, looking nervous.

"Yes. Well, the first lesson is we can't wait for you to write all this stuff down on rounds. Pay attention, remember it, then write it down when we're through. Okay?"

"Yes, sir."

"Good. Then see if you can remember this. That trauma patient in the ICU needs a central line and some TPN started tonight. Give him mannitol to keep his ICP under fifteen. The craniotomy in 914 needs a Dilantin level and the patient in 916 needs an LP tonight. Be sure to get cells and protein and look at it yourself under the microscope. Then tomorrow morning she needs a full set of labs. Be sure to look under the dressing on the laminectomy from today. Emerson is a stickler about that. And John Jones—the VIP guy down the hall with all the security who was raving around when we were in there— he's more than two weeks post-op and not eating worth a damn. He needs to go back on tube feedings tonight."

"How do I do that?"

Intentionally, Adams looked exasperated. "Put a feeding tube through his nose and into his stomach—you know, a nasogastric tube. Then order some tube feedings. Blenderized hospital diet, start with fifty cc's an hour, check some residuals now and then. Don't tell me I'm going to have to be the intern on the service too."

"No sir."

225

CHAPTER 19

It was not a coincidence that Jack and Marian's Sandwich Shop and Deli was located within a block of Temple Beth El in Brookline. And it was good food, not good luck, which had brought consistent success to the little restaurant over the last forty years. "Good location, good food, you can buy it; good service, you have to work at it." So said Jack himself and so it was recited to all the employees at Jack and Marian's. Rachel Schwartz was working at it, working hard. She was beginning her second year as a weekend waitress at Jack and Marian's and she was good. As a political science major at Brandeis, her weekdays were filled with intense discussion, long boring lectures, and scholarly papers gleaned from dusty tomes. The waitressing job provided not only income but also a tether to hard world reality. Waitressing at Jack and Marian's provided the opportunity to do that in an atmosphere where excellence was expected and rewarded. Excellence and artistry can be recognized in a Rueben sandwich just as much as a Rueben's painting, Rachel thought.

Rachel was popular with the regular customers because she remembered their names and how they liked their coffee. Popular with the other waitresses because she was never late and never pompous (although they knew she was a college girl). Popular with the manager because she was a mensch. Popular with the boys in the kitchen because she was uncommonly pleasant for a pretty girl, and traded ribald double-entendres one for one (sure I like tongue sandwich, but only if it's well done).

The crowd had been heavy, even for a Saturday night, and Rachel was working four booths and four tables. By ten o'clock she reduced the load of plates she carried on one arm from three to two. She brought two cups of coffee and a thick slice of blueberry cheesecake (two forks) to the Goldbergs before he asked for it. "Tank you Rachel dollinck." The hostess who seated the serious goyem couple at the next table was saying, "And this is Rachel, she'll be your waitress tonight." The woman looked vaguely familiar.

"May I bring you some coffee?"

"Please," from the man.

"Later thanks," from the woman.

Quietly and efficiently Rachel picked up the plates and cups from the adjacent table, leaving the two-dollar tip for the busboy. She overheard bits of their conversation. "... not really very hungry ... menus are new and the prices are higher but everything else looks the same and smells the same ... keep thinking of John with those restraints and that look ... good night's sleep ..."

When the evenings got boring, Rachel would entertain herself by imagining the social circumstances of her patrons. This couple—well mannered, fortyish, perceptive—seemed serious and distracted. She brought the coffee, along with a crock of soft whipped butter and a basket of steaming, black rye bread folded in a white linen napkin. " ... too soon to say. In another week, maybe two, we'll have a better idea. Oh thank you, miss. That bread smells good." The conversation stopped while Rachel poured the coffee.

"Have you two been to Jack and Marian's before?"

A hesitation while each waited for the other to speak. The woman smiled and winked at the man, barely perceptibly. "Yes, many years ago," she said.

"Well the food is as good as ever. The soup tonight is onion, baked with mozzarella cheese and dark rye croutons. The specials are the roast beef, fresh scallops in a white sherry sauce, and a puree of smoked trout served with endive. I'll be back for your order in a few minutes." Rachel noticed that the woman had a large diamond ring and a wedding band, but there was something about their polite demeanor which made her think that they were not married to each other. Still, she thought she had heard them discussing a sick child. Perhaps they were normally outwardly formal to each other. She took the order, and when she returned with the food they were touching hands across the little table, self-consciously withdrawing as she approached. Definitely not married to each other. The woman continued talking as Rachel settled the smoked trout in front of her. " . . . so glad we came here. I'm so glad to get out of that hospital. I don't know how you tolerate it year after year. Thank you miss. This looks lovely."

"The hospital is not a bad place. It's just the frustration and the sense of impotence that bothers you. And your blood sugar's low. Eat already, you'll feel better." He gestured with his hand, fingertips apposed. She smiled at him, warmly now.

Rachel was pleased with herself. She had melted into the environment, no longer an outsider to impede the conversation. She busied herself with her other customers, getting the special hot mustard for the man at table forty and a draft of Carlings (still served in a pilsner glass) for the man at forty-two.

"Flint still wants to transfer John to a hospital closer to Washington." No response. "I think Flint is getting suspicious."

"Flint is suspicious of everything. That's his business."

"Suspicious of us, I mean."

"I have learned there's more to Flint than meets the eye. And if he's suspicious—about us, I mean—he wouldn't care. He's not given to value judgments."

"Yes, I've learned to like the mysterious Flint too. Nevertheless, we shouldn't be out in public like this. Try some of this trout, it's terrific."

Dill was the underlying aroma at Jack and Marian's. Dill and brine, and a little garlic—pickles really. That was the basic aroma. Then superimposed on the baseline olfaction was the salty, smoky presence of lox, modulated by coffee—not burned coffee but good coffee—and the smell of cream cheese and cheesecake and hanging dried salamis and occasionally cigar smoke. Not a good cigar like a Macanudo and not a cheap cigar like a Whiteowl, but a comfortable bar-mitzvah-type of cigar, like a Gold Label or an A&C. It was an A&C that Mr. Goldberg was lighting up now. An A&C Grenadier with a dark natural wrapper, and in the growing era of no-smoking zones it seemed the good and right thing to do. Seemed good and smelled like her grandfather to Rachel, who, for a moment, brought to consciousness a very similar deli in the Bronx where she and grandfather Aaron—bald head with

white fringe above a broad belly and brown and white wingtips—
would go (on occasion, after her grandmother died) for a bagel or a
piece of cheesecake, after which he smoked a cigar. Cigar smoke folded
in with the salmon and the rye bread. And the dill.

The smoke didn't seem to bother the couple but the food had
warmed their common cold spot. When Rachel brought more coffee
(they declined the cheesecake) the woman's hand was covering his on
the tabletop as if to show the world (represented by Rachel) that they
shared an affection so special that it was acceptable to put it on display. At least in a small way. To this waitress who was part of the environment at Jack and Marian's.

"When John gets better I'm going to bring him here," the woman
was saying to the man, but clearly loud enough for Rachel to hear.

"I hope you do," volunteered Rachel, playing out her guess. "Is
John your son?"

An awkward pause, since the conversants had not expected the
question. The hands withdrew. They looked at each other, each
starting and stopping in speech.

"John is my . . . patient." "Husband . . ." they answered simultaneously.

"My husband John recently had an operation done by . . ." she
began earnestly, realizing that she was blushing violently. " . . . his surgeon is this man, who also happens to be . . ." Anne faltered, unable
to suppress a grin at her own disquietude.

"You see, this lady's husband is a patient of mine, and it just happens that she and I are old friends who . . ." Rachel saw that the
woman was laughing silently now, with a hand over her mouth to
avoid being impolite. The man had turned a deeper shade of red than
she. At first the sight of her laughing had made the man a little angry.
"You see we, she and I (gesturing), used to be friends. We used to
come here—where . . . Well, we're still friends, actually. It's just
that . . ." The humor of the situation was infectious. Watching her
forehead turn red and her eyes dance with mischief, he had to stop to
suppress a chuckle. He coughed into his napkin. The woman took a
deep breath and regained some control, and turned back to Rachel
who was still holding the coffee and looked bewildered.

"This is quite serious actually. My husband had a brain tumor and Dr. Ingram here . . ." She covered her mouth and her shoulders shook again. Another deep breath. "Dr. Ingram took it out . . . It really isn't the least bit funny . . ." She collapsed onto the side of the booth, holding her napkin fully over her face now and unable to hold back the tears of laughter. Rachel started to back away, but the man addressed her.

"He's doing better and we're both a little tired and—" he seemed back in control now, but avoided looking at the woman, looking instead a little too directly at Rachel. "And we were hungry, and like old friends, we decided to visit this old place. The food was very good, just like you said it used to be. That is, it used to be very good, and you said it would be good, and it was, and thank you very much miss. Could we have a check please?" He was biting his lip, watching the woman, still laughing, out of the corner of his eye.

Rachel, who couldn't imagine anything humorous about brain tumors and certainly didn't understand the disjointed explanation, beat a hasty retreat, even though the check pad was in her pocket, realizing she was at first included, and then intruding into some emotionally charged experience. She totaled the bill while watching the couple who were both wiping away tears from their eyes, and signaling to each other not to talk lest they continue to make some sort of a scene. When Rachel returned with the bill they were quite composed, murmured thank yous, and left a ten-dollar tip as if, she felt, to buy her conspiratorial silence. They stood at the cash register as he paid the check, apparently composed, with only the dimples in her cheeks showing her effort to suppress a recurring grin. The man waved briefly at Rachel as they were leaving, making her feel less embarrassed, and she maneuvered to the front of the deli after they left, to catch a glimpse of them crossing the street, arms around each other, talking and gesturing and laughing so hard they could not walk straight.

* * * *

"Now watch my finger."

"We should be getting good at this game Dr. Ingram; we've certainly had enough practice." Ingram smiled and moved his index finger far to the right, then far to the left. Rothstein's gaze followed easily, without nystagmus.

"The practice must be paying off. You're doing perfectly. How are the headaches?"

"Everyday, a little better. A minor inconvenience."

"Balance?"

"Sometimes a little dizzy. Not bad."

"Next game." Without the need for further instruction Rothstein closed his eyes, extended his arms, and brought the tip of his index finger to his nose. First the right, then the left.

"Just right. You know the rest." Rothstein got up from the table and stood on the floor, feet together, put his hands at his sides and closed his eyes. Ingram pushed him gently from the front, from the back, side to side. With the last push Rothstein seemed to be falling, opened his eyes and moved his feet.

"Not bad. Better than last time," said Ingram. Rothstein steadied himself on the examining table, obviously pleased with his own performance.

"Since I'm doing so well, Dr. Ingram, when can I go back to teaching my classes?"

"When you've dressed, stop in my office. We'll talk about it."

Ingram welcomed the chance to talk with the famous professor of philosophy, and intentionally scheduled him at the end of his clinic to allow plenty of time. Minutes later Rothstein was at the door to his office. "My friend Dr. Ravikrishnan is also my chauffeur these days. Can he join us?"

"By all means. I'm pleased to see that you're not driving yet."

"I insist that he follow doctor's orders," said Ravikrishnan. "I think he'd be out on the squash court if I didn't watch him carefully."

"It's true," said Rothstein. "So please tell my friend that I can return to teaching."

"Not yet Professor. It's only been about four weeks since—"

"Four weeks and three days. And I feel just . . ." An anguished look crossed his face as he searched for the word. "I feel just . . . just wonderful."

"Still having trouble with the F words I see."

"Not always. It's getting better. It helps to think of them as PH words. But I find it very . . . very . . ."

"Frustrating?"

"Yes, that too, although the word I was looking for was 'exasperating.' Sometimes it's hard to tell my postoperative deficit from the inevitable approach of senility."

Ingram chuckled. "It's obvious that you don't have to worry about senility Professor, but I think your students would benefit from your entire vocabulary, including the F words. And your balance still has a long way to go. You should wait until next semester."

"Just what I said," said Ravikrishnan. "Besides, I'm teaching his seminar and I wouldn't leave it now for anything."

"What's the topic?"

"Descartes. At least that's the way it's listed in the catalog. It's more of a general discussion of the concept of mind."

"Dr. Ingram here is quite a student of Descartes, Ravi. He thinks that if we read between the lines of the Discourses we will find Descartes was actually a mechanist not a spiritualist. Isn't that right Doctor?"

"Why yes. I'm surprised that you would remember."

"Of course I remember. It's an extremely perceptive concept. Tell Ravi about your idea." Ingram felt at once honored and embarrassed to be discussing the intention of Descartes with his modern-day biographers. He could imagine himself listening as Rothstein suggested new a surgical approach to the optic chiasm. He watched their faces as he explained, sensing more tolerance than enlightenment. It was a good discussion, though, and Ravikrishnan became progressively more interested.

"And where do you think, Doctor, that the soul can be found? Surely if my friend here can lose and regain the words that begin with F, or if my grandmother can suddenly lose the function of her left leg and arm, there must be some cluster of cells which we could isolate and characterize and stimulate or ablate. If not the pineal gland, where then?"

"Of course you're asking about my personal search for the grail," said Ingram after a pause, leaning forward. "It comes now to the definition of soul, which I would say starts with value judgments, which in turn requires memory, selective control of memory, and behavior based on those memory patterns. That puts the soul, I suppose, in the frontal lobes, but it's probably not a cluster of cells but rather a network extending throughout that part of the brain. It's like standing at the post office and saying 'where's the postal system?' or standing in the middle of Oxford and asking 'where's the university?'"

Rothstein winked at Ravikrishnan, who looked surprised at the use of an analogy familiar to philosophers. "He reads Ryle," he smiled.

Ravikrishnan pressed for more answers. "Is it possible to live without the frontal lobes?"

"Yes."

"Does that ever happen?"

"Without one frontal lobe, quite commonly. There was a time when we disconnected one frontal lobe as a cure for violent schizophrenia."

"And what happened to those patients? Did it work?"

"It certainly calmed them down. Intellectual and motor function remains intact but the emotions are gone. Love and hate, pleasure and pain, excitement and disgust, fear. Awe. It's all gone."

"Half the soul is gone," commented Ravikrishnan.

"Yes. Intellect without emotion. The visceral behavior side of value judgment memory. Gone."

"And if both frontal lobes are removed?"

Ingram paused, realizing that Ravi had anticipated the hypothesis of his research. "Then the intellectual half goes too. I have such a patient in the hospital right now."

"And did you know the patient before this happened? Has his personality changed?"

"I knew him only a short time but I came to know him very well." Ingram was talking softly, as if to himself. "He was a man of wit and understanding. A friend. He became a friend." He paused again, then looked up at the two men. "And he is gone. There is a body lying in his bed which behaves like a lower animal. It can say some human words at random but it's less functional than a dog or a horse." The room was silent as Ingram sank deep in his own thoughts.

Finally Rothstein said, "That's what scared me having this operation. I had an overwhelming . . . f . . . fear that I would lose some element of reason. The F words I can do without. The headaches I can tolerate. But to wake up a different person, or no person." He shuddered perceptibly. "Well I'm grateful for your skill."

Ingram had regained his usual composure. "In your case, Professor, we were nowhere near the frontal lobes. I was much more worried about your sense of hearing and balance than your soul. You seemed to be doing very well without your pineal gland, just to support my own theory of Descartes' treatise. And you lost the F words when all that pressure developed in your brain after the operation. Do you remember that?"

"No, f . . . f . . . luckily I do not. I seemed to have lost about a week of time, along with one section of my vocabulary."

Ingram was still thinking about his soulless patient. "Professor Rothstein, before the operation you told me that you would rather be dead than living without your mental function. Did you mean that?"

"Of course I meant it. I hope you took me seriously."

"Yes and no. Many intelligent people say something like that, but few people understand the spectrum or the implications. For example, you've lost the F words—temporarily no doubt—but certainly you would rather be here than dead."

"Quite so. And I'm sure I could tolerate being partially paralyzed or deaf or blind. But the ability to reason, the ability to appreciate, to share such . . . f . . ." He held out his hands towards the other men, "Such comradeship. I would most certainly rather be dead. It worries me now to hear that you misjudged my sincerity."

"Not your sincerity at all Professor, but perhaps your understanding. Besides, what I promised was not to pursue extraordinary life-saving measures if your mind was affected. I couldn't assure that you would die. Quite the contrary, in fact. Most patients with severe brain injury don't die. At least in the visceral vegetative sense."

"Like the patient you described to us?" asked Ravikrishnan.

"Yes. Exactly like that patient."

"Well if that had been me, Dr. Ingram . . ." and he leaned forward, touching him on the hand, smiling to indicate a non-critical empathy,

235

"and I sense you are asking my opinion as a recent participant in this process. If that were me, I would hope desperately that you would find some way—legalities notwithstanding—some way to make me . . . at peace. That was my understanding of the promise I extracted from you before I agreed to have you venture inside my head."

They sat quietly for almost a minute.

"Thank you Professor, that's what I wanted to know."

* * * *

Without consciously intending it, Ingram saw John Bradford less and less. In the morning the OR took priority. In the afternoon there were meetings and other sicker patients. On weekends there were conferences, or leaves to rake, or grants to write. His subconscious could manufacture an infinite list of reasons. So instead of three times daily his visits to the end room on 9 North now decreased to twice, or once, or occasionally none at all. Ingram knew, but never wanted to acknowledge, how that happens with terminal or bad-outcome patients—a subconscious dilemma usually won by the less painful course. Ingram recognized it in the residents—warned them against it, in fact. Now, although he recognized it in himself, he let it happen. He had done what he could. There were hard decisions to be made—but there was always a reason to put them off. So he came less frequently. Except for evening rounds.

In the evening Anne would be there. She came less often too. Ingram assumed that it was for the same reasons of helplessness and denial. She spent her days visiting friends, reading, writing to family, keeping up the public charade.

The John Bradford she knew was gone—she knew it, even if no one else seemed ready to admit it. She had cried and grieved and realized some inner peace over it. Visiting the viable body of her late husband—she had come to think of it thus—was like visiting a living grave. A reminder of what had been, without hope for what might be. She could deal with it that way and—like visiting a grave—usually calm acceptance dominated overflowing emotion. He was obviously going to need chronic care. In an institution? At home? Would this be her wifely

236

duty over decades? There are decisions to make, but the first of them belonged to others. So she came less frequently, except in the evening.

At first it was always spontaneous. Ingram and the team at the end of rounds. Anne waiting for information, then fearing information, then not asking. Days shorter. Nights colder. A ride home was practical. Although his admiration and affection grew steadily, Ingram kept their interaction polite. An acceptable contact. A quiet friendly personal time when Ingram could be both doctor and friend. A time when Anne could be both friend and grieving widow. A time to laugh and cry in private. A time to grow close. Occasionally, then often, then every night for the last week. It wasn't verbalized or planned. But it was no longer by chance.

Anne noticed that Flint was looking out for her. Bradford always seemed to get his calming Nembutal injection just before she came. When they approached the bed Flint stood between her and the patient until he was sure it was safe. Once he complimented her on her recent hair cut, which even John would not have noticed. And he always mentioned if Ingram had been in, or when he was expected.

Ingram often drove her to The Towers, and more frequently the ride home included dinner, once a concert (it seemed too public), once a movie. The subject of John Bradford came up regularly at the bedside, of course, but rarely in their private conversation. And they carefully avoided discussing the future, concentrating instead on his children, her parents, his patients and research, her career, now on hold. They seemed to share every preference in books and music, art and nature. One Saturday evening, in semi-disguise, they went to Durgin Park and a Bruins game. One Sunday afternoon they drove to Concord and walked hand-in-hand around Walden Pond. One Tuesday, responding to impulse, they pulled into the parking lot at Lars Anderson Park and snuggled as best they could in the MG as they watched kids cavorting in the playground. The following night they were back at Jack and Marian's sharing a sandwich. "Tomorrow I'm going to San Diego to a neurosurgical meeting. Want to come?" She could tell he wasn't serious.

"Sure. Let's call a press conference."

"I know. Impractical." They sipped at coffee.

"Don, sooner or later we need to discuss the future."

"That's practical. We might not like it, but it's practical."

"Don, you've been so careful not to bring it up. But we might as well say it. I've become so close to you. I don't want to lose this again."

For an instant Ingram almost cried. It was the first time she had let him glance into her soul. And, yes, she had been feeling what he was feeling.

"Anne, I'm so . . . Do you really . . ." With a surgeon's instincts he quietly calmed himself, sure that he had misinterpreted her intent. "What did you have in mind?" he asked carefully.

"Just that we have to talk about the future. There are so many options and possibilities—all very complicated."

"I know, but every possibility begins with John."

"That's right, but he's been the same for weeks. He's not going to get any better is he?"

"No." He had admitted this to himself a week ago.

"So the John Bradford we knew is gone. Dead for all practical purposes. As you say, the possibilities begin with the fate of that creature in the bed, and I have some responsibility there. But it's a sense of duty, not love. In my mind I'm not bound by any vows I made with John, because John no longer exists. Just like you are not bound by any vows to Emily. Can you understand that?"

"Yes. You've settled the most important part of the discussion in your mind—what's right and wrong, faithful and unfaithful. But there are so many other issues: legalities, public perception, scores of other people, and practicalities of life. Not to mention that John Bradford might be dead to you and me, but not to the rest of the world."

"That's why we have to talk."

"Okay, when?"

"Is the invitation for cognac in your library still open?"

"Of course. But tonight I . . ."

"Not tonight. When will you return?"

"Saturday."

"Saturday, then. Dinner and discussion. Is your cognac any good?"

"You'll be the judge."

CHAPTER 20

They came in through the kitchen, and put the two just-purchased bags of groceries on the butcher block island in the middle of the big warm room. Brass pans hung from a big brass ring, all hanging from the beams on the ceiling above the chopping block. Some dishes in the sink. Blue and white tiles showing windmills and sailing ships laminated into the brick wall behind the sink. Dark green ivy—looking dry and unattended—cascading down from a brass pot hanging from the ceiling next to the sink.

"This is very nice. Your plant needs watering." Without invitation and without needing directions she opened the cupboard over the built-in oven where there was a brass watering can with a long spout. She filled it at the sink, without commenting on the dirty dishes and, standing on tiptoe with a hand on his shoulder for balance, watered the ivy. Her long neck, stretched out that way, was irresistible. He kissed it gently, and felt her shiver.

"There," putting down the watering can on the countertop. "Must I start cooking immediately or do I get the tour first?"

"The tour's expensive."

"I'll work it out . . . In the kitchen of course."

He led her to the library first. The library had been the living room in the original house. Big bay windows on each side, brick fireplace at the end. Bay windows looking east toward Boston and west toward the sunset, that window glowing gold just now. Walls covered with shelves of very dark wood, filled with books of every description. The dark wood and the crimson carpet and the black leather chairs would have given the room a very heavy feeling, were it not for the fact that the small window frames were painted satiny white, along with the window sills and the doors and the ceiling and the cabinet to

239

the side of the fireplace which he now opened. With the push of a few buttons a warm consuming melody filled the room—all strings—gentle and secure somehow matching the sunset.

"Dvorak." She plopped down in the Eames chair, feeling the texture of the leather, shoes kicked off, feet on the footstool. "I was expecting Chopin."

"I was planning Chopin—later. You have to earn it . . . in the kitchen."

"No pain no gain. Some resident told me that once." She scanned the bookshelves, settling on two feet of volumes on sailing and the sea. "You know, we have the same sailing books in our library. There are so many things here that I'd like to read."

"He handed her a large Waterford crystal glass with two fingers of an amber liquid in it, and clinked his glass against hers. "To hours in my library." She swirled and sniffed.

"Ah, but this isn't cognac."

"That comes later too."

Effortlessly she came up out of the chair to touch glasses again. "As long promised, with the Chopin and the fire in the fireplace. After the tour. After I cook dinner?"

"After dinner."

"So on with the tour, tour guide."

On to the small living room, the original parlor, but still with a fireplace. Bare oak floors stained dark with modern walnut furniture (modern in 1967, but rather timeless). Hallway to the family room with pictures and proclamations in black frames.

"This must be James's high school picture. And this is . . . Janet?"

"Right, Janet's high school picture—last year."

"I recognize your boat? Such nice lines. And here the kids again. This must be a few years ago. And this must be Emily."

"Uh hum," sipping scotch.

"Oh Don, she's lovely. I never saw her, you know. All these years I just imagined what she looked like. What I wanted her to look like, I suppose. I had her shorter, sort of chubby, with curly hair and a round face. Instead she's just . . . lovely." She traced Emily's image on the glass, as if it would engender some kind of communication, making it alright.

"Yes, she was."

The family room was, well, the family room. And the dining room was austere as, somehow, dining rooms in old New England houses are expected to be. In the foyer he paused, hand on the dark wooden banister set on white railing.

"Does the tour go upstairs now?"

"Later. With the Chopin and the cognac after . . ."

"After I make dinner. You are hungry."

He sat on one of the dinette chairs and watched, fascinated, as she took command of the kitchen. She gave him a knife, a bowl and vegetables from one of the bags, instructing him to make a salad. By the time he finished chopping and stirring there were sourdough rolls in the oven, butter melting for the sauce béarnaise, and two small filets soaking, however briefly, in two inches of red wine. By the time he uncorked the wine (a chalky Monterey Vineyards Cabernet) she had prepared an hors d'oeuvre of crab meat and cream cheese and had time to sit down at the kitchen table.

"Don, I know I said we should discuss John and the future, but I don't want to spoil a wonderful evening. You have to know how I feel. You are such a good friend, and I am trying to push the realities and the impossible dilemmas to the back of my mind, but this is just playing house. We could talk about the future but it would just be pretending. I'm grieving so hard inside for the man I loved, and I'm pretending that I don't think about it."

"I know that. If it helps to pretend or if it helps to cry, I'm just glad to be able to help."

"I've done my crying, and it does help to pretend, I was just beginning to feel rather guilty."

"Don't worry. We can stop pretending whenever you want."

"No, I don't feel at all guilty about John, I worry about misleading you." Her hands on the sides of his face, earnestly. "John Bradford has been dead since the operation. How long has it been?"

"Over a month."

"It seems like a year. I miss him terribly, particularly when I see that tormented animal that's living in what used to be his body. But John is gone and he won't be back." Holding her face also, now he wiped her tears with his thumb. "It's so good to have you to lean on now. But I don't know what the future will bring. I wouldn't want you to mistake mourning and pretending for . . ."

A long silence, an exchange of emotion, mind to mind, through the eyes, which superseded simple language. Gentle smiles. The tears had stopped, and he kissed away the residue. "Let's pretend . . ." he said, finally, "to have supper."

Laughing then, she hugged him awkwardly as they sat knee to knee on the dinette chairs, kissed him and stuffed a crab meat-laden cracker into his mouth, returning to the stove where the aroma of butter and tarragon steamed up from the frying pan.

The steaks were too good to be pan fried, but it was quick and they tasted good. The salad was satisfactory, the wine excellent. The conversation, in fact, settled on the wine and wineries and wine collections, then ambled on to the food and the music, avoiding both the pathos of John Bradford and the ethos of the rest of the evening. The bottle of cabernet was two-thirds empty and the glow had returned to the eyes of Anne Bradford. "And now," she said when the dishes were cleared and the wine was corked, "have we earned the much-discussed cognac in the library?"

"I hope my cognac . . . meets your expectations."

"There's only one way to find out," leading him into the library.

Anne curled into a big leather chair, her bare feet tucked under her. Although the cognac was mutually understood to be a metaphor, it seemed the right thing to do to play it through. He did, indeed, have a bottle of Camus Grande Champagne that had been decanted from cask to bottle on a warm summer evening in the south of France in 1935. This particular bottle had been ignored by the German officers who occupied the chateau, confiscated by an American lieutenant who carried it to Paris, then to London, then to Boston, where it had slept in the corner of an old foot locker for a generation until the former lieutenant, now a president of a large company, remembered it as a unique gift for the neurosurgeon who had relieved his sciatica. The essence of a French sunset, captured for fifty years, glowed golden in the Waterford goblets. Sitting beside her on the couch, the feel of soft leather against his back, slowly and deliberately he reached out and, with a single finger, touched her fingertip, entwined her fingers, squeezed as hard as she did until—warm, fed, brandied, and heady with anticipation—their arms trembled. Minutes they sat, looking at how their hands fit together, then to each other's eyes, then back to the hands with a small embarrassed smile, each having the same thought. In time the tape conveying the Chopin clicked to a close and the silence demanded conversation.

Putting the empty brandy glasses on the floor he asked, "How are you?"

"Happy. Content. No, more than content, fulfilled. Excited, trembling inside. And a little scared."

"Me too," looking at their hands. "Look Anne, I don't want to make you feel uncomfortable. I can take you home whenever . . ."

"I'm scared nervous, not scared frightened." The sparkling mischievous look which he had come to look for. "I have given this fourteen years of thought, and I'm as comfortable as a girl can be with her clothes on."

Laughing, he stood abruptly, still holding her hand, and led her to the music cabinet. "Alright then, what shall be the appropriate music to make love by?"

"Here in the library?" she giggled. "Scott Joplin."

"There are speakers upstairs in the bedroom."

"Ah hah, I might have known. Then something very . . . lush."

"Schubert."

"More contemporary."

"Stan Kenton, ballad style."

"More grandiose."

"Richard Strauss."

"With singing."

"Mahler Fourth?" He took a record from the shelf. Gently she put it back.

"No," she said, running her finger across the rack of tapes and selecting one. "Something much longer." Without letting go of her hand he inserted the cassette—Nabuco: The complete opera—into the machine and led her to the stairs.

On the landing halfway up the stairs he paused, suddenly struck by the reality of it all. "Isn't this amazing. Amazing and ironic. After all these years wondering how it would be and then—"

"Dr. Ingram," finger over his lips, pushing against his body until he met the wall, "there is a time to be analytical and a time to be quiet." She licked his lips—twice—thrice—and entered into a kiss so ravenous that his knees might have given way, were it not for the fact that she was still pressing him into the wall. Soon his hands found the smooth skin of her back under her sweater. She seemed to purr as he explored the supple muscles along her spine, reaching the back of her neck without encountering any other garments.

"Hmm!"

"Hmm?" as in, what did you expect?

"Hmm!" as in pleasant agreement, tracing the full width of her back with both hands.

"Hmm?!" as there was a new resistance to push against. All of this wordless conversation proceeding as the kiss continued. At length they reached what seemed to be mutual agreement on a stopping point.

"You're absolutely right. Too analytical." They attempted simultaneous kissing and stair climbing—barely successfully—and between the two of them had his shirt off by the time they reached the bedroom.

The harvest moon illuminated the bedroom just enough. The big bed was covered with just a sheet—turned down—and the picture of Emily was safe in a drawer—he had done that a week ago. But he felt a little awkward at the obvious next step. She kissed him, gently now.

"Where's the bathroom?" He pointed, indicating a direction out the door and down the hall. "I'll be right back." She took his shirt and left. He shucked the rest of his clothes and slid under the sheet, trying not to appear too eager, and listening to the Verdi, which was perfect.

Soon she was standing at the foot of the bed, wearing his shirt, hair down, smiling at him. "Did you arrange the moonlight too?" deliberately releasing one button at a time.

"I'll be glad to take . . ." He lost his voice as the shirt fell to the floor. Slowly she pulled the covering sheet entirely from the bed, and crawled over his feet, knees, and chest, suspending herself over him and, remarkably, not touching him. " . . . to take credit for it," he whispered.

"Then I thank you," whispering very close to him. "It's just right." She settled into him, with the mutual sensation of warmth and coolness, rough and smooth, pressure and hollow, hard and soft, which feels like no other feeling. A feeling to be cherished and savored for several minutes then adjusted, reapplied, and savored again, as if each of the infinite permutations of skin contact would provide a new and better sensation to be tasted and enjoyed. A remarkable feeling, really, being at that high emotional plateau at the end of an entire enticing preparation, finding it good, and expecting that it will get better, like surveying the mountain range from the base camp before making the run for the summit.

In time the writhing search for new skin contact led to wetter, more delicate tissues, and as that union was made he pulled back from the hollow of her neck to watch her face, finding her smiling and watching him. For an hour they explored nuances of anatomy and sensation, each trying to send the other beyond the bounds of pleasure, each thinking how natural it all seemed, as if no time had gone by. The experience at the summit was spectacular.

Almost every hour Ingram awoke, disoriented, then pleasantly surprised at her presence in his bed. The first time she was awake, propped on her elbow smiling at him. The next time she was sleeping, nestled into the hollow of his shoulder, their legs intertwined. Thereafter they were settled in, back to belly like spoons in a drawer. He took delight in falling asleep then awakening to find her there, caressing the soft spots in the darkness. At 5:05, he noted from the luminescent clock at the bedside, he reached out and she was not there. Forcing himself to become more awake, he realized that she was far across the bed, shaking.

"Anne, are you okay?" he pulled himself close to her and she sniffed.

"Yes, fine. I thought you were asleep."

"I was, but I missed you." Reaching over, he realized that her face was awash with tears and she was sobbing.

"Anne, what's the matter?" Drawing her closer to him.

"It's nothing. Tears of joy." She pulled closer as if to reassure him. He waited a long time, thinking, until the sobbing had subsided.

"Is it John?"

"Yes," in a soft voice.

"Oh Anne. I'm sorry. I should have—"

"Don't be sorry," raising up to look at him. "I'm certainly not sorry. Not for myself and not for that wretched creature in the hospital. It's just the opposite in fact. You and I are so fortunate to have what we have. It's just that John Bradford's dead and I miss him." A soft smile but eyes wet with tears again. "Okay?"

"I should have realized." She settled back onto his chest and they held tightly to each other. "I'm sorry."

"Don't be sorry. Be happy for us." He held her until she fell asleep, remembering long, lonely nights after Emily died. Anne was right. It was warm, loving bodies that would seem to help melt the grief. Just before he fell asleep he realized that, although they discussed John Bradford as dead, there was a very viable person of that name lying in a bed a few miles away.

* * * *

When she finally awoke the room was full of sunlight. On the wall hung a large framed poster from the Boston Museum of Art advertising a Monet exhibit, and featuring a young woman with a parasol, standing in a field with a child, slightly blurred as if the wind which blew her skirt briefly blurred the vision of the observer. "Lovely," she thought to herself. "Very feminine. It must remind him of Emily." She closed her eyes, not to return to sleep but to bring the last night into perspective. Ingram was sleeping beside her, one hand lying loosely on her hip.

Earlier, while it was still dark, the clock radio had blared briefly— the choir of the First Presbyterian Church of Wellesley singing "Stand Up, Stand Up for Jesus," fervently taking advantage of the half hour of public service time offered at 6:00 a.m. by WGBH. Ingram had slapped it into silence after "Lift high his royal banner," hoping she had not awakened. She had feigned sleep while he quietly slipped out of bed, visited the bathroom, and climbed back under the covers. He was not ready to think about the implications of her presence in his bed, only to enjoy the warmth of it, so he was pleased that she still slept. He had kissed her softly on the neck, though, and she remembered that first as she sorted through her mind for orientation. She opened her eyes again, sunlight bright enough to illuminate small specks of dust in the air, refracted into beams by the small panes of glass in the French doors, and made golden by the curtains and the yellow roses in the wallpaper and the creamy color of the parasol in the Monet. Very feminine. She had not seen the Monet or the wallpaper the night before, and with the sunlight she suddenly realized that these were not just his images of Emily. This had been Emily herself.

Emily had hung this print, not him. Her wallpaper. Her bed with the huge down quilt covered, like the bolster pillows tossed to the floor the night before, with a blue and white floral design. Emily's husband, friend, and lover. Ingram stirred and she moved his hand, feeling just a little selfish. She was not the only one seeking to share the load of emotional baggage.

Carefully she slipped out the bed—Emily's bed—well, his and Emily's bed—the sight of her own naked body in the mirrored closet doors surprised her initially, then pleased her. More weighty considerations aside, it had been one hell of a sexual event. Smiling again, she twisted, stretched, and strained to awaken her joints and ligaments. A gush of warm fluid leaked down her thigh. Still smiling, she picked up his shirt from the foot of the bed, found the bathroom, and was soon in the shower. No sign of Emily here.

There was only one toothbrush which she used without hesitation, recalling reading that this particular shared intimacy differentiated those in love from mere sexual partners. She used the toothbrush longer than necessary, brushed her hair with the only brush she could find, rubbed on some of his deodorant and put on his shirt. Feeling euphoric, almost giddy, she even winked at herself in the mirror.

On the way to the kitchen she paused at the wall of family photographs in the hallway. Last night Emily's photograph had seemed to bring an ominous presence. An aura of memory which she imagined as bittersweet for Ingram, an aura which she had actively ignored, pushing herself to the center of his attention. She had rationalized that memories painful to him would be best left undisturbed. Now she realized that subconsciously she had felt competition, comparison, a little jealously perhaps, maybe even guilt. But this morning that feeling was gone. She traced Emily's features on the photograph with her finger. To her surprise, she noted that she felt affection, not jealously. She saw her pictured at the helm of their sailboat. She felt respect, not intimidation. Judging from the apparent age of the children in the photograph she deduced that the last photos were taken three or four years ago. Did she suffer in that last year? Did she endure the ravages of chemotherapy? Did the children remember her in misery or in the merriment of these photographs?

Passing into the kitchen she saw her presence in the cookbooks, in the old African Violet plant, in the telephone numbers on now-yellowed bits of paper thumbtacked years ago beside the refrigerator. She felt a strange camaraderie., not competition. If comparison was inevitable then she compared well, even to memories polished by time. If the man's love for her grew from his life with Emily, this morning it was flattering, not threatening. And if her love for him . . . the realization made her stop short in her search for the coffee . . . indeed, she loved the man.

She cleaned the grounds from the night before from the Melior pot and ground new coffee. Lacking fresh bagels or smoked salmon or even eggs, she settled for a frozen Sara Lee pecan roll she found in the freezer. Their grocery shopping had included only the makings of one grand dinner. Shopping for breakfast would have seemed presumptuous.

While the water was boiling and the pecan roll was warming she opened the front door just enough to retrieve the *Globe* and the *New York Times* from the edge of the porch, quickly because she was not completely covered by the tails of his shirt. She went into the library, picked up the brandy glasses, and perused the records and tapes looking for something romantic and glorious. She selected a tape of excerpts from Rigoletto and mounted it into the player, set the switch for infinite repeating, but did not activate "play" until all was ready. When she had gathered the coffee cake and the orange juice and the napkins, she poured the boiling water over the french roast, started the music, and carried the tray up to the bedroom. Sunlight and grand opera filled the room and he was smiling.

"I love the smell of Verdi in the morning."

"Mixed metaphor," she said, handing him the orange juice in a Waterford crystal goblet. "Maybe you need to see a neurosurgeon."

"Don't trust 'em. I'm strictly Christian Science." He drank half the orange juice, then handed the goblet to her. "God you're beautiful."

"Thank you sir." As she took the glass a few drops fell into the hairs on his chest. "And you look good enough to eat." She licked up the spilled orange juice slowly.

"The juice is terrific. I can hardly wait to make crumbs with the coffee cake."

"Fortunately for you, I'm good at crumbs."

"You're good at everything," and he set the glass on the bedside table and pulled her close. "In the middle of the night you were crying," he said softly. "I had decided this was a bad mistake, under the circumstances. I've been trying to think of the right way to apologize." She put a finger over his lips to silence him.

"Last night I was thinking about John and feeling sorry for myself. This morning I woke up thinking of Emily and how you loved her and how you deal with it. It made me feel pretty special. And it helped me to understand how I could love John, or the memory of John, and still . . ." She sat up to be able to look at him. " . . . and still love you." The Verdi swelled to a crescendo as if on cue, leading them across an emotional bridge.

"And what are your intentions?" he asked.

The question took her by surprise. "To keep up appearances. To work through the practical difficulties. To find an acceptable way to spend time . . ."

"No, no, no," he was laughing. "I mean your immediate intentions. A question stimulated by the seductive way you're unbuttoning that shirt." She chuckled with him at the way her mind had run to the more serious issues.

"My immediate intention is to make love to you with Verdian intensity," finishing the last button and shedding the shirt, "and to bring you over the top at the end of the quartet."

"The quartet is forty minutes from now."

"Forty-five."

She was right.

CHAPTER 21

Henry Kazanjan was not certified. He thought about it only occasionally, during the annual salary discussion and whenever a new therapist was added to the staff. The new therapists were all female nowadays—well-scrubbed, bright-eyed, athletic-looking, younger-than-his-daughter graduates in fresh white dresses with little blue and gold cloth emblems stating "Certified Physical Therapist." Thirty-one years ago, when he began at the Longwood Hospital as a cast technician, he had had plans to be a veterinarian. But he was very good at casts, and kind when cutting them off, and careful with the withered yellow limbs, flaked with dead skin as he eased them out of the smelly Webril, and gentle with the patients trying their first tremulous steps or mastering the art of crutch walking. The salary was good in those early days, especially when former orthopedic residents, gone to practice in Newton or Framingham or Nashua, would send their patients with frozen shoulders or unextendable knees or painful backs to Henry for whatever magic it was that he could work on them. Nowadays there were administrators and managers and clinical specialists for cerebral palsy only, and occupational therapists who did all the hands, and even MD specialists and residents, if you please, in Physical Medicine and Rehabilitation who walked through the big treatment room in the morning and the afternoon, looking at charts, bending stiff joints, saying "Good, good," and rendering a professional fee. Henry recognized all of these changes as progress, and they still called him for the most difficult cases. But he was never certified.

Henry sat on the edge of one of the heavy tables, and, grasping the edge of the table with both hands, lifted himself up and into a sitting version of a handstand, his usual habit while waiting for time to pass.

Indeed he looked like a gymnast, not just his muscular torso and slender hips but also his white t-shirt and white pants—renewed daily—and white shoes always freshly shined. He had tried the official PT uniform when the hospital began to supply them ten years ago, but he found them confining and a little frilly for his taste. Now, balancing on the heels of his hand, waiting for Kathleen Dugan. Soon she appeared, joggling to the side of the wheelchair, pushed with indifferent roughness by a sullen transporter who, having deposited her charge in the PT exercise room, exited quickly to smoke a cigarette on the back stairs.

Kathleen had been coming to PT for two weeks and was assigned to Henry at the request of Dr. Adams. He made a little vault to the floor and, brushing at both sides of his graying bushy mustache, he greeted his patient and moved her back to a central position in the wheelchair, fluffing the pillow and smoothing her hair.

"Hello Kathleen. How lovely you look this morning. And where's that charming mother of yours today?" She must have been a very pretty girl, before the accident, thought Henry, who had developed the ability to imagine her fifteen pounds heavier, with sparkling Irish eyes and a winsome smile. As it was, her spindly legs protruded at unfeminine angles from the brief hospital gown, knobby knees leading to atrophic calves into over-sized high-top white basketball shoes. Spidery arms led to hands in her lap, opposed back of wrist to back of wrist, to spastic fingers extended on each hand. The auburn hair had been made somewhat attractive by the efforts of the nurses on 9—not an easy task considering that half of her skull had been shaved a month before. Her eyes were roaming, dull and lifeless. Clefts that might have been freckled dimples now constantly moving with her drooling, sucking, tonguing grimace. She smiled in response to Henry's greeting—he could tell it was a smile—and reached her arms up toward him, having learned what was coming next.

"Haawou," she said with apparent great concentration.

"Hello who, Kathleen?"

"Haawou Hernree." She smiled again. He was pleased. It was unquestionably "Henry" as best she could articulate it. He put her arms around his thick neck and scooped her up into his grasp as if she were a two-year-old. She giggled and said again, "Haawou Hernree."

He settled her carefully on the therapy table, put a pillow behind her head, and started to work the overnight stiffness out of the joints, stretching ligaments and kneading tendons, readjusting the hospital gown to cover her auburn-haired crotch, momentarily angry at the ninth-floor nurses for forgetting, once again, to put her in pajama pants and tops. Throughout the range of motion exercises he maintained a constant conversation in a soft, pleasing, voice, pausing for her to attempt response and beginning again, discussing her joints, her mother, her progress, never impatient, most important never talking down to her, or talking too loudly as inexperienced people do to the handicapped. When her legs and arms were as supple as they were going to be, he took her through some active exercise, playing little games (How high can you reach? Well, I believe that's higher than last week). And assisting her when she reached the point of ligamentous limitation. He sat her on the edge of the table, the flimsy gown pulled apart in the back, exposing the skinny remains of once voluptuous buttock. Across the room, an old man learning to use a large-handled fork with his left hand stopped in mid motion, remembering the warm feel of an eighteen-year-old girl's back. Cursing to himself, Henry left her perched on the edge of the table and went to the men's locker room for a set of small scrub pants. She giggled as he put them on her. As he tied the drawstring, a tall burly man in a business suit approached them.

"Mr. Kazanjan?"

"Henry, please. You must be Captain Dugan. It's good to meet you. Kathleen's making some fine progress."

"So I hear." He caressed her cheek and kissed her forehead.

"Haawou Daddy. I kawaa."

"What's that darlin'?"

"I kawaa. Kawaa." Michael Dugan looked at Henry, bewildered, tears filling the corners of his big eyes, which seemed to happen every time he could not understand Kathleen.

"She says she can walk, Captain. Okay my dear, let's show off for your daddy." He cinched a heavy canvas belt around her waist. Henry carried her the ten feet to the parallel bars and set her down carefully, supporting her all the while, placing her hands on the bars. And then, standing behind her, he grasped the back of the belt in one strong hand and put the other gently on her shoulder. Kathleen was excited, bouncing and grimacing faster than before, needing no encouragement to place one foot in front of the other. She seemed to think she was going somewhere, but making no progress aside from the bouncing movement. Henry spoke, prodded, reminded, touched, directed her to look at her feet one at a time, encouraged, and praised. Very slowly—about thirty seconds per step—she moved ahead between the bars. In a few minutes, sweating, crying, and laughing, the steps started coming closer together, awkwardly dragging the outer edge of the big gym shoes forward. Some times she forgot which foot was next. Some times she sagged back or forward, supported by Henry's strong hand on the waistband. Eventually she was singing, or shouting in a tonal voice, syllables that even her father could understand as "Look daddy, I can walk." The other therapists and patients in the big room, most of whom had a two-week perspective on this performance, shouted encouragement and applauded.

By the time she reached the end of the parallel bars her legs were giving way with every step. "Moreee wallkaa, mooree walkaa," she said, but Henry put her back in the wheelchair.

"Enough for today my dear. Your legs are tired. Besides we have to draw some more of those nice pictures remember?" Michael Dugan had been crying freely, and dabbed at his round ruddy face with a handkerchief. "See Captain. Isn't that something. Great progress, great progress."

"Mr. Kazanjan . . . Henry . . . Could we talk for a minute?" They settled into practical but uncomfortable chairs in a corner of the room. "You say this is progress. And it is," hand on his arm for quick reassurance, "it is progress and I'm so grateful for your effort and your skill. Don't get me wrong," coughing in an attempt at control of his uncertain voice. "But what are we doing here? Two months ago this girl was working out with the boys' soccer team. The *boys'* soccer team. She has all A's in high school. Never got a B. Never got an A minus. And she could sing, oh Lord she could sing. And beautiful . . ." whispering, voice failed now, "beauti . . ." stopped again, pulling out his thick cop's wallet with thick shaky hands, pulling out a color photograph and handing it to Henry, giving up on the conversation, big face and the big thick hands, back turned to the scrawny girl across the room.

"Beautiful indeed," acknowledged Henry, noting the mischievous green eyes, the freckles and dimples, the luxuriant dark gold hair falling past broad shoulders onto the curving ample expanses of the green sweater. She was even prettier than even he had imagined. "Very beautiful."

Michael Dugan had regained his composure, sniffed, snorted, blew. "Seven thirty a.m., September seven, she goes off to school—this wonderful daughter—I kiss her goodbye. Seven forty-six a.m. some jerk in a truck just runs her down. Runs her down," smashing heavy fist into heavy palm. "In an instant my daughter's gone. Just like that. And the days, and the weeks, then her mother, God bless her, and the waiting. Up in that ICU—it's a circus up there. Wonderful people, you understand, but it's a circus. Waiting to see where she is, our daughter, where has she gone. And here we are this morning. Don't get me wrong. Don't get me wrong Henry. But it would be better if she had died. She wouldn't want to live this way, my daughter. What are we talking here? Years at the Shattuck? Mass Mental? I could handle her dying Henry. I could have handled that, but I can't deal with this," gesturing over his shoulder across the room. "I can't deal with it, remembering her," taking back the photograph, lovingly. "What are we doing here?"

Henry Kazanjan did a little handstand on the heavy chair then lowered himself down, as he did when he was thinking. He had been through this conversation many times. Burned patients, stroked patients, paraplegic patients, grieving children, grieving parents, angry families, loving fathers who in one awful memorable instant, realize that the fight for life is over, and won! No more intensive care unit, no more waiting for the telephone to ring in the middle of the night. No more carnival stars, no brass-band bioengineering gadgets. No more super nurses, no more twice-a-day bulletins from the doctor. No more doctor at all for days at a time, no more flowers and cards and long distance phone calls. Technological victory over death! And now the crowd's gone home, the lights in the arena are dim, the last janitor has swept up the last popcorn, the gaudy rides, the ferocious animals, clowns and superheroes are packed up and trucked up and the intensive carnival has moved on, leaving a lonely little family in the middle of a lonely, dusty, weedy vacant lot having won and there's the prize. Surprise. The moment comes looking in a mirror by chance, watching the expression of a friend, worse yet a stranger in a supermarket, worse yet looking at the residue of your own wife, your own child. After the crying and the vomiting and the depression and the anger, then comes the unloading. The first conversation with the first medical establishment figure who will listen. The first taste of the sour berries on the unending hedgerow of bitterness. It seemed to happen to Henry Kazanjan a lot. He rose up on his hands again, looking at the captain, looking at the picture.

"You're right, Captain. What's more dear to a man than the memory of a lost child? Especially a lovely daughter. Lovely." He took the photograph again, looked, and handed it back. "It would be better if she were dead. In my job I see it. Just yesterday I had a boy in here paralyzed from the neck down. Better off dead. Three years now he's been that way. His mother brings him in every month. Better off dead. Well, take that fellow over there," pointing with his eyebrows to the elderly, poorly shaven man obviously paralyzed on one side trying to manipulate the large-handled fork. "Once a bank president. Had a stroke. Can't talk. He'd be better off dead. Just last week his son said those very words to me. Better off dead. Look at that little boy," indicating a patient newly arrived on a stretcher. "Sixty percent burns. Hands and face. Look at those scars Captain. Been here for four months. We're making braces for him. Why are we doing this? I ask myself. Better off dead the poor little guy."

Michael Dugan expected platitudes. Expected an argument. Wanted an argument. Wanted more of the brass band, however out of tune, that supported him through those early weeks. He looked at the drooling, vacant bank president, jello on his johnny. He looked at the little boy, hideous as he chatted away with one of the younger therapists.

Henry continued. "It's not fair Captain. Why, I see the unfairness of it every day. It's just not fair—well, who said life's fair anyway, eh captain? But it doesn't seem fair. Did you ever ask yourself whatever happened to the man after the good samaritan left?"

"How's that?" Michael Dugan was still focused on the little burn patient, who seemed inappropriately happy.

"The man in the gutter. Beset and beaten by thieves. You know the man. After the good samaritan dumped him off and went on his way. What happened to him?"

"I . . . I don't remember."

"Of course you don't. God didn't tell us. On to the next chapter. That's the way the book goes. Leaving some poor, banged-up, half-witted cripple who'd be better off dead. It's not fair to him, I tell you Captain, and it's not fair to you—well who said life is fair anyway?" Pausing, rising up on his hands, giving the bewildered captain time to spin around in his mind.

"It must be hard in your business Captain. I mean life and death, the good and the bad and the criminals and the innocent people hurt. Oh I don't envy your job. No sir. Now in my business I see it now and then. Nothing like you do I'm sure, but it's never easy, is it Captain? Take this bank president here. He's gonna have to eat left handed. Gonna have to learn to talk all over again. Gonna need a brace to walk most likely. All that big retirement plan going into medical bills. Wife has to feed him. Wife has to change his clothes. Son says he'd be better off dead. Some days I wonder what I'm doing here myself, Captain. As you must wonder some times. I'm sure you do." Michael Dugan looked at the bank president. He didn't look quite as bad as he had on initial examination.

"Of course the young ones can fool you some times. Especially the thinking part. Why that little boy over there couldn't say a word two months ago. The boy with the burns. I thought he'd be better off dead. Surely I did. Now he's such a chatterbox. I can't get him to be quiet to fix his braces. He jabbers away so much some days I wish he were dead." Shocked look from the captain and the first smile from Henry. "Well not really I suppose. He's a cute little bugger. But those scars, I don't know Captain, I think you may be right. But the young ones, sometimes they'll surprise you. Now take Kathleen over there." He was careful not to say "your daughter Kathleen." "Trying to talk the way she does. God it's pathetic you know? Lord, she can only say ten or twenty words and not very well at that. That's all she's learned in two weeks is ten to twenty words."

"She said 'daddy' today, and 'walk.'"

"Well you're right she did, Captain. I guess that's better than nothing. And she did walk through those parallel bars. Well I guess you really couldn't call it walking, but she gave it a try. Spunky thing, she wanted to do it again. It might be too soon to tell about her." Deliberately not looking at the big man, he watched the activity across the room, brushing at his mustache with the backs of his fingers. Michael Dugan sighed and blew again. He put the photograph back in his thick cop's wallet. Overcoat in hand, he walked across the room and squatted down in front of Kathleen to be at her level.

"Daddy. I kawaa. I kawaa today." "Today" was clear and crisp and she focused on him with one eye.

"I know darlin'. I saw you walk. Mr. Kazanjan helped you and you walked very well."

"Hernree."

"Yes Henry. And tomorrow you'll walk some more."

"This afternoon she'll walk some more," said Henry, coming up behind him.

"Look darlin', it's only October. On St. Patrick's Day, I'll have you walk with me right down the middle of Commonwealth Avenue." She definitely smiled. For an instant the grimacing stopped and freckles and the dimples and the perfect teeth flashed through that familiar expression, just for an instant. The big man stood up and turned to Henry, putting both hands on his shoulders, looking into his wise brown eyes, trying to formulate a statement, trying to distill his drained psyche into a dram of sense, still trying to catch the bits of mind fluff, blowing around his brain like milkweed seeds across a vacant lot.

"St. Patrick's Day. Isn't that an Armenian holiday?" Henry took him by the arm and led him toward the door. He knew the father would be embarrassed and would want to push through this next phase by himself. Out in his car, in his office, or in the men's john down the hall. "Well, I'll tell you what. We'll walk down Commonwealth Avenue all three of us, arm in arm. St. Patrick's Day, hell, we'll run down Commonwealth Avenue. We'll need your help of course."

Outside the door the big cop turned again, trying to bring some conclusion, some gratitude to this kindly man.

"Now Captain," in his matter-of-fact business voice, "I've met your wife several times these last two weeks and it's a great pleasure to meet you, sir. You've a fine family there. A man could be proud of that. Yes, proud of that. Now I know you're busy and I have lots to do myself, so, begging your pardon, I'll just get back to work." Without waiting for a response he left him there, the big man with big hands and a big heart, groping for words in the hospital hallway.

* * * *

"Good evening Mrs. Bradford."

Anne Bradford could never tell what Miss Lewis was thinking. Prim and proper remnant of a different Bostonian generation. Crisp and dry as a Vermont lawyer, authoritative as a clipper ship captain, straight as the columns on the Atheneum, she was old New England personified. Her father and his father before him had owned the Lewis Cordage Company, and there had been no bigger or more important purveyor of rope on the Eastern seaboard. She had grown up in an elegant home on Louisburg Square, had attended the finest girls' school, had spent summers down east at their camp on Cranberry Island, and had made the Grand Tour with her aunt after her eighteenth birthday. Her brothers, the ones that did not stay with the company, were lawyers. She had wanted to be a doctor but her father would hear none of it. A proper Beacon Hill girl became a nurse, or a secretary and married a doctor, for God's sake. So become a secretary she did, and her father, remembering her goal and considering himself quite paternally considerate, got her a job at the Longwood Hospital. That was in 1947.

"Why good evening Miss Lewis. You're working late tonight." Anne Bradford had delayed coming to Ingram's office until Miss Lewis would be gone, or so she thought. It wasn't that she didn't like Miss Lewis—she did. At least she didn't dislike her. But she made her feel uncomfortable, particularly on this Monday evening. "Is Dr. Ingram in?" She glanced nervously at the half-open door to Ingram's office, then back to Miss Lewis, then down at her shoes, sensing that she must look as guilty as she felt.

"Yes. But he's on the telephone. Would you like to have a seat Mrs. Bradford?" Miss Lewis nodded toward the black Windsor chair with a Harvard emblem, in gold, on the back. Through her wire-rimmed spectacles, she looked at Anne as she moved, sat, shifted, and fidgeted. It seemed to Anne Bradford that she stared for several seconds, a cool, proper, puritanical gaze.

"She knows," she thought to herself. "How could she know? Does it show that much?" She sighed and smoothed her skirt, trying to sit up straight and look nonchalant, like an errant seventh grader under the ministerial stare of a dictatorial teacher. Miss Lewis returned to the papers on her desk.

It wasn't just Miss Lewis. Actually the whole day had been a manic combination of lighter-than-air euphoria alternating with a fear of discovery that bordered on panic. Left to herself, awakening this morning, over a solitary lunch, walking along the Fenway, she couldn't stop smiling. Music—Verdi usually—played constantly in her inner ear. She looked at every clock, counting hours until she would see him again. And then, reality. Mr. Duffy the doorman had asked about her weekend. How did he know? The nurse at John's bedside seemed strangely aloof this morning. Enigmatic Flint commented only that Bradford seemed to be worse, and pushed her again to transfer him to Virginia. Of course he knew. He must know. And now Miss Lewis, who acted like Ingram's mother anyway, knowing instantly why she had come to Ingram's office at this late hour. Waiting for her, in fact.

"Anne! Come in, come in." He bounded through the door and stopped short, not expecting Miss Lewis. "I was just on the phone to . . . It was a long distance call and . . ." She watched him go through the same adolescent adjustment, explaining things that weren't necessary, trying to conceal his obvious glee, glancing at Miss Lewis. Anne suppressed the urge to laugh. His demeanor squirmed back to its usual role. "Thank you for coming. We should discuss your husband's condition. Mr. Flint is suggesting transferring him again. Please come in." Stifling a giggle she moved to the inner office. "Miss Lewis you're working late tonight."

"I'm leaving now, Dr. Ingram. Thank you." Did she smile? Perhaps a little. He closed the door.

Anne was laughing, silently, but hard enough to bring tears. She put her finger over his lips before he started to speak, then he joined in the suppressed chuckle.

"What's so damn funny?" he whispered.

"You are. We are. You look like I feel. You look like your mother just found your love letters."

"I feel like my mother just found a Playboy under my bed." He pulled her close and held her so tightly that her feet came off the ground. "I kept thinking about you all day."

"Me too. But then I kept imagining that everybody knew about last weekend."

"Like Miss Lewis?" They moved to the leather couch.

"Especially Miss Lewis. I don't think she likes me."

"She loves you. Everyone loves you. But she might not understand . . . the circumstances."

"Nobody would understand, Don. I'm not sure I understand. I go from being as giddy as a teenager to seizures of fear and conscience. Can you imagine the uproar if this ever got out? The . . . the families. The hospital people. The Washington people."

"The press."

"The press of course." She paused, squeezing his hand, realizing that her own hand had gone cold. A long sigh. A short smile and another long sigh. "We need to deal with this. We need to talk."

"So talk."

"Come on. You know what I mean. Here we are, head over heels all over again, acting like kids, copulating like—like rabbits."

"Making love is the proper euphemism I believe." He was caressing her ear and seemed to be ignoring her words.

"Making love," taking his hand from her ear, kissing it, then holding it between hers, "like there's no tomorrow. But there is a tomorrow, and all these people, and your career, and John's career. Well, the way John's career will be remembered. It may seem comical, Don, but it's serious."

"I know. I've been thinking the same thing all day. One minute I want to announce that we've fallen in love and the next I'm wondering who might have seen us. On balance, you have to admit it's a great feeling."

"The greatest." Squeezing hands, warm now. "So what are we going to do?"

A loud knock on the door, then it opened immediately. They jumped back, releasing the grasp, and tried, unsuccessfully, to look composed. Dan Adams stuck his head in, then retracted, then reappeared in a few seconds.

"Excuse me sir. I thought you were alone. Hello ma'am." Adams looked more unsettled than they did.

"Come in Dan. We were just discussing the senator. How do things look today? I haven't been up there yet."

"Uh . . . no change, really. Uh . . . Dr. Ingram the glioma we did this morning—Mr. Foster?—he's developed a big bleed under his flap and I think we should take him back. He's okay but it's as big as a grapefruit."

"Okay, Dan. Set it up and let me know when you're ready to go."

"We can go now, but Mrs. Foster wants to talk to you, and Mr. Foster won't sign the consent 'til you come by."

"Okay. I'll meet you in Recovery in five minutes."

"Thanks. Sorry to bother you." He said it to both of them, still blushing, and closed the door behind him. A long silence followed. Finally she said, "See what I mean?"

"Yes. You're right. There aren't any good options."

She stood and kissed him gently on the forehead. "Take care of Mr. Foster. Settle down young Dr. Adams. Call me when you get home."

"Shall I pick you up for a late supper?"

"Maybe . . . No . . . I don't know. Call me first. We need to talk without touching."

The hematoma was quickly drained. Later, he called. They talked. But rather than resolution it merely deepened the dilemma.

He slept fitfully. His promises to Bradford and conversations with Rothstein kept appearing in semi-dreams and semiconscious thoughts. His bed still smelled of Anne. The next day he yawned through three uneventful cases, leaving most of the last one to Adams while he sat in his office, staring, yawning, and staring. In the evening he went to 9 East, expecting to see Anne, but she was not there. Instead Bradford was raving obscenities and Flint suggested a transfer again.

Midway through another restless night, the solution came to him. He sat upright and considered all the implications—discounting problems, evolving the steps, repairing the raveled sleeve of care. Sleep was sweet.

* * * *

Leaving Ingram's office, Anne decided to visit John's room one more time before returning to her apartment. Maybe watching his torment would help her make some decisions. Maybe Flint would have a good solution. Flint, once so aloof, seemed so kind to her now. But Flint was not there, only the Boston policeman who greeted her respectfully as he opened the door to John's room. As soon as she entered Bradford started screaming obscenities. He had been incontinent again and the bed was smeared with shit. He had worked one hand free from the restraints and threw a handful at her, splattering both Anne and the policeman in the face.

"God damnit!" exclaimed the cop. "Oh, I'm sorry ma'am," he wiped his eyes and glared at Bradford, who was gathering another handful. Anne was frozen, aghast. The cop pulled her out of the room and closed the door. They could still hear him screaming. The cop called the nurse, then found a towel and awkwardly tried to clean Anne's face and blouse.

A nurse who had been through this before brought two large male orderlies, held a blanket in front of her, and entered the room. The blanket protected them from the next hurled missile. The orderlies pinned Bradford's arms and covered his face with a towel, carefully avoiding being spit on or bitten. These rages now happened so frequently that the nursing staff kept three syringes of Nembutal in a cabinet above the sink. The angry nurse took one and injected its contents into Bradford's thigh, not too gently and without an alcohol swab. In ten minutes Bradford slumped back and fell asleep. Anne watched through the open door.

"I'm sorry Mrs. Bradford," said the nurse, who had returned to her professional composure. The hospital had long since given up on trying for anonymity. "Let me get a basin to clean you up."

"No thinks, Rita. I've wiped most of it off. I'll just say goodnight to John and clean up at home." The staff had all developed real affection—not just admiration—for their patient's wife. She had accepted the horrible facts with such grace and elegance. The nurse and orderlies left, almost bowing to her, and closed the door. She walked over to the bed where Bradford, hands now restrained again, was snoring. She made no attempt to wake him, nor did she show any sign of affection or even recognition, now that the door was closed. The empty syringe with the orange "Nembutal" sticker was lying by the sink; the nurse had forgotten it. A nurse on some other shift would refill it with two cc's from the bottle at the nursing station, arm it with a new needle, and replace it in the cabinet with the other Nembutal syringes. (The pharmacist had objected vigorously to the practice of keeping syringes loaded with Nembutal in the room. But he relented when the head nurse demonstrated the urgency and frequency of the problem, the security, and the prominence of the patient.)

Anne washed her hands at the sink and noticed some residual smears on her face, reflected in the mirror. Instinctively she reached into her purse for some tissues, then changed her mind, deciding that the hospital towels would be more useful. As she started to close her purse, Anne felt the epi pens. Because of John's allergy to nuts, she always carried two epinephrine pens—syringes loaded with one cc of highly concentrated adrenaline—in her purse. She had actually used one five years ago when he had an anaphylactic reaction to nuts in a salad at a barbecue. It had caused incredible sweating, fast pulse, and high blood pressure, but an ER doctor said that it had saved his life.

Ingram had mentioned one time that her husband had a weak artery in his brain. That there was risk of the artery rupturing. Before she could suppress it, Anne vividly imagined herself bending over the slumbering animal in the bed, injecting the epi pen. She imagined the symptoms, the sudden rupture of the vessel. "Stop," she whispered to herself. But to her amazement, she did not feel guilt. She felt quite cool-headed. Well, it was impractical. Too obvious, with her alone in the room, and the evidence in her hand, and a cop outside the door. Worse than that, it would be just plain murder. She dismissed the thought, and found herself incredulous that she would even think it. Well, it might not have an effect. The artery might not rupture after all. Even so, it did not seem like murder. It seemed like an act of love.

She sighed as she sat at the bedside, cleaning up with a damp towel, surprised at the wandering of her own mind. She looked intently at the empty Nembutal syringe. Suppose she filled it from the epi pens. Suppose she wiped it, and put it back in the cabinet with the other two Nembutal syringes. Suppose another nurse—tomorrow or the next day—picked it up when John was screaming, and Anne was out of the hospital. In his rages, he had a fast pulse anyway. She rebuked herself for the thought. And yet . . .

Later, as she left, she passed Flint reading in his anteroom. "I heard about the episode tonight," he said, coming to her side. "I'm sincerely sorry for you. For your husband and you. This can't go on much longer." She recognized the concern and affection in his face, which he showed only to her. Impulsively she reached up and kissed him briefly on the cheek. "Thank you Mr. Flint. Good night."

CHAPTER 22

Once he decided to do it, he was overwhelmingly impatient to have it over. The tedious, exhausting mental work was all in the decision, and as soon as the cloudy dilemma resolved, the whole issue became so clear as to be over, except for the doing. He had gone to Bradford's room three times that day: tentative, dry-mouthed, filled with the ironic angst of it all the first time, only to find someone else there—not part of the plan, a frustration. Of course, his appearance aroused no suspicion, and he did something official and left. Now, between the evening and night shift, he tried the door again.

Once he decided why it should be done, it became acceptable, reasonable, a matter of moral right. Passionate personal commitment over frigid societal law. After all, Bradford, when he was intact and thinking clearly, had asked him to intervene. Had implored him to act on common sense. Had gained from him the promise of quality of life. Ingram had promised him to prevent the dehumanized condition in which he now existed. As soon as he decided to do it he remembered why to do it—all these precise rationalizations. Best for Bradford by far. Best for the state and the country. Best for anguished family. Best for parents. Best for Anne. Well, he hadn't asked her, he didn't have to, it was clear. He entered the dark room and looked around. Bradford in the bed apparently asleep. Flint was gone. The Boston cop was sitting inside the door. He checked Ingram's name against the list. Ingram asked him to wait outside and he left.

Once he knew why to do it, how was simply a practicality. He had, on many occasions, hastened the inevitable process of dying for his patients. Without anguished bedside drama, without overly dramatic, hand-wringing family conferences, without Ethics Committees and court orders. Like any doctor who faces mortality head on, he considered it his duty as a physician to know when to quit and how to quit on behalf of his patients. With more perception than most of his colleagues, he knew that he could only affect how and when life ran out, never whether. When death was imminent and inevitable, then he saw his job as facilitating how and when, not prolonging the agony. He had done it many times, and all in good conscience. Sometimes his role had been passive—turning down the fluids, avoiding the ventilator, not using the mannitol infusion. Other times he had encouraged death more actively—turning up the morphine drip for a cancer patient, or continuing the potassium infusion after the onset of renal failure. In the name of good medicine he had done it many times in terminal patients.

Bradford was not terminal.

Not terminal, not comatose, not even physically ill. Just crazy. Mindless. In agony, worse than the pain of any relentless cancer gnawing on nerves and marrow. Agonizing, painful, but not terminal. He let himself reflect on this fact. A matter of semantics he rationalized. John Bradford the man was already dead. Anne was right. The fact that his heart pumped on, and he digested food, and had incessant, lurid and random thoughts was a mistake of nature assisted by modern technology. He should be dead. If he were here, able to consult and consent, he would agree. It was Ingram's doing, in many ways, hence his responsibility for the undoing. How to do it was simply a practicality.

It was, however, a major practicality since there was no life support system, no intravenous line, no simple medication to be supplemented or withdrawn. And surely there would be an autopsy—even an argument over whether the autopsy should proceed here or in Washington. And his own staff to account to. Crazy people don't just turn up their toes and die. There were always people in the room. Flint, if no one else, but nurses and housekeepers and Anne and residents. So the how of it was a major practicality.

Once he was mentally past the when and why, thoughts of how did not seem to him to be premeditation of murder. Technically that was what it was, of course, and somewhere in his brain an amber light was flashing irksome discontent. But his sense of moral right overwhelmed his understanding of the words themselves. Just words, after all. So, as he thought of those drugs which would not be detected by toxicological screening, or physical methods which left no bruise or puncture mark, it was a medical decision, certainly not a criminal decision. Barbiturates, hypnotics, and narcotics, all measurable. And justifiable, perhaps, for extremes of agitation, but certain to be measured. Curare, cyanide, carbon monoxide, electrocution, now that would be murder. Potassium—no intravenous access. What would be the natural cause of death for such a creature? Starvation? No, quite the opposite. Bradford was on tube feedings. Seizures? Probably. Seizures—and vomiting—and aspirating. The natural history. An act of God. It was not only practical, it was natural. Pre-destined—any good Presbyterian would agree. He simply decided to allow the natural history to run its course. God had spoken for John Bradford, calling him home. Home tonight.

Bradford was not talking tonight, just looking around. Ingram walked around the bed, tightening the leather restraints holding Bradford down. Half of the liter bag containing tube feeding formula had run into Bradford's stomach over the last several hours. Ingram removed the tubing from the metering pump and let the remaining fluid run wide open. The next bag of tube feeding formula was lying on the table. He took from his pocket a full bottle of ipecac and added it to the formula. Having run through the exercise a dozen times in his mind, it was remarkably easy. He squeezed the bag to mix in the emetic and waited impatiently for the last few ounces of the first bag to run in. The plan was simple. By the time the second bag had run in Ingram would be in the lobby or the cafeteria. Bradford would vomit, aspirate, and suffocate, held in position by the heavy restraints.

He realized that his hands were shaking for the first time in twenty years.

Now the first bag was empty and he prepared to attach the second, with its lethal ingredients. Once again his hand shook. He paused. Eastman had always told him that if a surgeon's hands were shaking he shouldn't be doing the operation. "If the patient trusts you to operate on his brain he deserves a surgeon with total confidence." Ingram had excused from the OR many a resident who had a little tremor. Did he lack confidence? The reason for lack of confidence is uncertainty over what to do. He stepped back from the bedside holding the tube feeding bag, still holding the empty ipecac bottle in the other hand.

What the hell was he doing?

Killing a patient. Overtly killing a patient. The reality of it suddenly settled in. People had seen him with Anne—many people. What would they think? What would Flint think? What would Flint do? What would Eastman advise him to do? What would he tell his residents to do? The decision was clear. Don't do it. Not tonight. Maybe not ever. His hands had stopped shaking. He started toward the sink to dispose of the concoction in his hands when the door opened.

"Evening rounds Dr. Ingram?" It was Flint. Ingram froze, his hands suddenly shaking again. Flint picked up the empty brown bottle from the bedside table and read the label. He looked at Ingram, still holding the plastic bag of feeding formula. "So you've decided to do away with the senator. I wondered how long it would take you. Tube feeding, vomiting, restraints, sedation, aspiration, death. Not very direct, but a reasonable plan."

"I . . . " Ingram stammered, fighting for self control, "I was just about to throw this in the sink. I'm sure this looks incriminating . . ."

"Why don't you just let us transfer him to that little hospital in Virginia? Believe me, it will have the same result. Get him out of your life."

"Because it's my responsibility. I really don't expect you to understand that. John is still my patient. I brought him to this point. It's my responsibility to see it through. What's more, I made him a promise as a friend."

"I know. He told me."

"Then he told you that I promised not to persist with heroic life support measures. But as you can see it's not as simple as that. The only life support measures are food and water. The John Bradford that we knew is effectively dead, but this body can go on vegetating for months—years. Whether he's here or in Virginia or in some private nursing home. He had a brilliant career. He shouldn't be remembered that way. He wouldn't want this. I don't want this for him. And—" He stopped abruptly.

"And then there's Anne Bradford to think about." Ingram started to object, trying to look offended. Flint held up his hand as if to stay any response. "I like Anne Bradford very much. I like you, Dr. Ingram. I liked John Bradford when he was with us. I'm not being judgmental. I'm just a little surprised that you brought yourself to this." He held up the ipecac bottle, then put it in his pocket. "Officer! Come in here please."

Ingram slumped, feeling his career and life running to his shoes. No matter that he intended to abort the lethal feeding at the last minute. The incriminating evidence was in his hands. Flint was compelled to act the bodyguard after all. The policeman bustled into the room.

"Thank you, officer," said Flint, looking from Bradford to Ingram to the officer and back again. "Would you kindly check the restraints on our patient here? It seems our conversation has upset him and he is acting up again." The policeman examined the heavy leather straps on Bradford's ankles and wrists. Bradford scanned past the policeman with his vacant look, grabbed his fingers strongly when he tightened the wrist strap, and spat in his face when the burly cop bent over the bed to check the other wrist. The policeman jumped back, stifling a curse and wiping his face with his sleeve.

"Thank you officer. Dr. Ingram was just leaving. Why don't you go have a cup of coffee? I'll watch the senator until the night nurse comes on."

"Thank you Mr. Flint, I will. Frankly I don't know how you stand it day after day." He walked to the door. "Are you coming, doctor?"

"Why . . . yes." Ingram had watched Flint's performance dumb-founded. He put the bag on the sink and walked quickly to the door. Bradford was straining to sit up. He appeared to be watching.

"You know Dr. Ingram," said Flint, "on the day we met here in this room you told me to stick to my business and you would stick to yours. I believe you were right. Why don't you take the officer down and buy him a cup of coffee. I'll see you tomorrow." He closed the door, leaving Ingram and the policeman in the hallway.

Flint poured the ipecac loaded feeding down the sink and rinsed out the bag. Ipecac has an odor. He walked to the bed without a moment's hesitation. Bradford's eyes suddenly focused on Flint's face, and he almost smiled. He started screaming random words, including "yes! yes!" Flint opened the cabinet and selected a Nembutal syringe, hesitated, and put it back. Bradford spit at him and screamed louder. Flint picked up the folded towel and silenced the screaming.

Before returning to his room Flint stopped at the nursing station, helped himself to some orange juice from the nourishment refrigerator, and commented to the charge nurse that the tube feeding had run in and the patient had been agitated but now was sleeping quietly. The charge nurse was pleased because the floor was busy, she was short staffed, and she could leave the senator's vital signs for the night shift.

* * * *

When the phone rang at 11:45 Ingram was in bed sleeping. The events of the evening had left him drained and exhausted. He awoke fully with the first ring, as he always did, and waited for the third ring so that he would be coherent. "Hello. Dr. Ingram."

"Chief, it's Dan. Senator Bradford coded. The arrest team is up here, but he's dead."

"What?" Now Flint's last remark made sense. Or was it just a coincidence?

"The night nurse found him dead in bed about . . . thirty minutes ago. They called a code and called me. I was in the ICU. We've been pumping on him for quite awhile but he's cold and mottled. He even has some rigor. I'm going to call it, but I wanted to talk to you first."

"What happened?" Ingram's mouth was dry and the tremor had returned. "Did he aspirate?" He tried to sound calm and clinical.

"No sign of it. I suppose he had a pulmonary embolism or arrhythmia. I'm going to stop the resuscitation. Okay?"

"Sure. There's . . . There wasn't much to resuscitate anyway. From what you say it sounds like he's been dead for a while."

"The nurses' notes say that you made rounds about eight o'clock, then he was reported sleeping at nine. That was the last note. When the night shift nurse came in to check he was dead." The conversation stopped temporarily while Adams directed the arrest team to desist. The night nurse had fifteen years of experience. She had already assembled a stack of washcloths and towels and sent the aide for a plastic shroud. "There's really no need for you to come in. Would you like to call . . . the family . . . or should I?"

"Oh I'll call Mrs. Bradford, Dan. Thanks anyway. Have you seen Mr. Flint?"

"Yes, he's here. He came in during the code. I guess he was sleeping next door."

"Well, thanks for your effort. I'll call Mrs. Bradford."

"Do you need her phone number? I'll get the chart."

"No thanks. I have it."

* * * *

He sat on the edge of the bed for several minutes piecing together the sequence of events. Maybe it was an embolism. Or an arrhythmia. Or an intracranial bleed. Possible. Damned unlikely. Probably vomited and aspirated. The nurse probably hung that last fatal bag of feeding formula. Probably vomited just enough to suffocate and arrest. And Flint had the ipecac bottle in his pocket. The drained, sinking feeling returned. But wait a minute. If Flint were going to expose him, he would have given the evidence to the Boston policeman right on the spot. But he hadn't. In fact, he had sent Ingram and the policeman off together having established that Bradford was very much alive. Perhaps Flint had hung the lethal bag of feeding. Or perhaps Flint had dispatched him in some other way. Or perhaps he just had a pulmonary embolism. In any case, the body of John Bradford was now as dead as his soul. He dialed the number.

"Anne? This is Don. I have some hard news for you." He could have said "John's dead." He could have said a lot of things. He could have been more compassionate, more friendly, more scientific, more direct, but what came out was the pat phraseology he had used in this circumstance for twenty years. "John was found dead in bed a little while ago. He was okay earlier this evening and was dead when the night nurse came on. He must have had a pulmonary embolism or an arrhythmia. The arrest team worked on him for awhile but . . . they couldn't get his heart beating again. So John . . . a few minutes ago . . . John passed away." As soon as he said it he felt awkward with the old-fashioned term. It was part of the routine. A euphemism which always seemed a little softer for most families. There was a silence; there always was.

"John's dead?"

"That's right Anne."

"What happened?" she asked, quickly.

"I don't know. I'm not in the hospital. Dan Adams just called and said the night shift nurse found him dead."

"Was he having one of his rages?"

"I don't know."

"Did they give him Nembutal?"

"I don't think so. Flint saw him last."

She was silent for what seemed like a long time.

"Then this nightmare is over?"

He was relieved. She was taking it well. Of course, he should have known. She didn't care about more details, not yet. Only that it was over. "The personal nightmare, yes. The public part will be different— I mean the next week or two."

"I can handle that. And I'll call John's family and the Senate office. Do I have to come there? Is there anything I have to do now?"

"All you have to do is designate a funeral home. They'll take care of all the details. You can do that tomorrow. There's no rush. And we need your written permission to do an autopsy. I'm sure the government will expect to have one done."

"Mr. Flint already has the permission."

"What?"

"Before the operation both John and I signed a power of attorney authorizing Flint to dispose of any . . . remains. We signed a lot of other forms too. He said it was routine. John didn't care and I certainly don't care. We planned for cremation anyway."

"Okay," said Ingram, realizing again how thorough Flint had been.

"Don? Did you see him tonight? Did he say anything?"

"I saw him. He was about the same. He didn't say anything at all."

"He never improved at all, did he? He never even knew we were there?" Composed as she was, like any other family, she needed reassurance.

"That's right Anne. His mind has been gone since the operation. As hard as this is tonight, it's probably a blessing." The old terminology slipped out again. It was such an automatic platitude. But it helped.

"Yes. It's a blessing," she repeated. More silence. "Was anyone there? Did he suffer?"

"He must have died . . . in his sleep." Here they were, speaking of Bradford as if he had sensation and feelings. Part of the ritual. Play it out. "He just died in his sleep. No suffering."

"That's good." Another pause. "How do you think it happened?"

Now the silence was on his end. There were so many possible answers. All of them too complex for a telephone conversation. Some of them she might already know. Some of them . . . well, some day perhaps. "I don't know. Would you like me to come over there?" She sighed so loudly it was audible as static through the telephone. "Don, I'd like to see you, but . . . I'd like . . . Maybe I'm making this too dramatic, but I think it would be best if we didn't see each other at all. Not for quite a while anyway. There's going to be a lot to do, and I have a lot of things to sort out."

"I understand. And I agree."

* * * *

A mighty fortress is our God,
A bulwark never failing.

Crimson robed and white collared, standing forward to reach double forte without straining, one collective eye on the large congregation and one on the music director who was trying to be unobtrusive, all forty-eight members of the St. Andrews Episcopal Church choir sang the first throaty stanza in unison. It was a trademark of Bryson Filmore, the music director. First stanza always sung in unison. The last four bars were repeated by the solo organ leading into the second stanza in full four-part harmony. It had an Episcopalian feel to it—austere but substantial beginning, prelude to the rich chords and chromatics which enriched the soul and caused goosebumps on the more musically sensitive parishioners. This approach to hymn singing occurred not only on Sunday mornings, but at vespers and sunrise services, even at funerals in mid-afternoon, like today. Stained-glass windows and granite archways ascending five stories above the stone floor deflected and reverberated the sound so it seemed that the very angels and armies of God provided the echo at the end of each phrase.

Our helper He amidst the flood,
Of mortal ills prevailing.

The church had not been this full of people, standing, singing, voices co-mingled with the choir, since last Easter. Reverend Thompson was more than a little nervous, partly because of the occasion and partly because the archbishop from Washington was standing next to him. He noticed that the archbishop was not singing, but rather examining some notes on a small card that he held in the palm of his hand, presenting an attitude of grave meditation. Baskets, wreaths, and garlands of flowers of every description filled the nave, covered the altar, and draped the front of both pulpits. From the front to the back of the church, amidst the congregation of serious-looking men with white hair and women in black veils, nephews and nieces fidgeting, parents and brothers working at self-control, through the politically elite and the everyday citizens of Boston and Rhode Island, he saw a dozen Secret Service agents who had been in the church since early morning. At the front of the church, before the kneeling rail, was presented the shining black coffin, brass rails gleaming, flag draped deliberately over its lower half, surrounded by so many deep red flowers that it seemed to be floating on the delicate blossoms.

Doth ask who it may be?
Christ Jesus it is he.
Lord Sabbath his name
From age to age the same.
On earth is not his e-e-e-qual.

The organist, knowing that this was not the usual hometown congregation and suspecting, correctly, that the extra four-bar interlude before the second stanza would take most by surprise, attacked the interlude with force and divergent chromatic runs, feet and fingers flying, taking all but the regulars by surprise with its gloriosity, and launching everyone, with the leadership of the choir, into a stirring, martial, second stanza.

Did we in our own strength confide,
Our striving would be losing.

James Flint stood in a dark alcove in the back of the church, favorably impressed by the improvisation of the organist and the acoustics of the sanctuary. He did not attend funerals, as a rule, and was here only at the request of the director to report on the presence of any unusual foreign guests. The worship service, he observed, was exactly that. Somehow he had expected something different for the funeral of a senator, but the hymns were posted by number on a little board in front of the church, there was a prelude and a postulate, an invocation and a benediction, a reading of scripture and a closing hymn, all sandwiched around a sermon to be delivered by the archbishop which even had a title derived from the opening hymn "Our helper He amidst the flood." All of this printed up in old English characters on heavy stock programs, looking rather like the folded menus presented to the guests at state dinners. After the opening hymn, as the large crowd settled into the hard pews, Reverend Thompson mounted the pulpit and entered directly into a fervent prayer of invocation, hands gripping the edges of the lectern, eyes so tightly closed that he had deep vertical furrows above his nose, head lifted in the direction of the circular window high in the back of the church, and beyond.

Reverend Thompson explained to the Heavenly Father the sad reason for the assembly, outlining just a few of the highlights of the career of the young senator cut down too soon (in case the Heavenly Father or members of the congregation or television audience were not fully aware), quickly acknowledged that the Heavenly Father must have had some perfectly good reason in His Grand Plan for summoning the senator at the very apogee of his career, and beseeching Him to be, very personally, within and among the grieving family, friends, and mourners here gathered this afternoon. The request was so carefully articulated that Flint actually glanced up to the high window, but saw nothing unusual. From his position he could see Anne Bradford, looking calm and straight ahead, sitting next to a distinguished couple he knew to be the elder Bradfords. The press of Boston and the world had commented many times in the past three days on her calm and stately demeanor, hiding what must be consuming grief. Flint knew that the official death of Bradford had brought an end rather than a beginning to her grief, but even he was impressed by her regal public performance. She appeared to be looking directly at the passionate Reverend Thompson; she had actually focused intently on a white chrysanthemum just below the lectern, and decided to concentrate on it throughout the service, blocking out any other thoughts which might, suddenly, interrupt her automatic composure. Flint considered it an excellent performance. By association he scanned the congregation for Ingram, but did not see him.

Four pairs of tall, young marines in dress blues with white gloves faced each other across the coffin, standing at precise attention throughout the service. Anne had had little to say about the ceremony. The senator's office staff, the Chief of Protocol from the White House, the Commandant of Marine Corps, the archbishop, John's parents, each had a personal view of what John Bradford would have wanted. St. Andrews in the Back Bay was a compromise between the little church in Pawtucket, favored by Bradford's parents, and the National Cathedral in Washington, pushed hard by the Secret Service and the Washington staff. That was the only decision she made. The rest of it, well, John didn't care and she didn't care. "Funerals are for survivors. Do whatever you want," he had told her months before. "Just one thing—have them sing 'Just a Closer Walk With Thee' at the end of the service. You know the old spiritual. Maybe Ray Charles would even come to sing it. No tempo. Rubato. Acappella. Just slow and gravelly and prayerful." She knew he meant it as a little joke, and when they could not find "A Closer Walk" in the Episcopal hymnal, she let it drop.

They were through another hymn, the scripture, and well into the archbishop's not-too-cleverly-drawn analogy between Bradford at the helm of his boat and his Senate committee and Christ calming turbulent waters. The psychology of religion had always been fascinating to Flint, and this vivid demonstration was particularly interesting. Hundreds of people, silently watching a box which held the embalmed carcass that had been John Bradford, listening to an authoritarian cleric declare that God, through Christ, had his hand on the very tiller of human experience, and needed an able-bodied mate to stand a difficult watch. Hundreds of people hearing this metaphorical speculation delivered as a series of facts, and maybe even believing that it must be so. Marines standing on guard over the metal box of bones and meat, when they should more properly be sitting on a beach, or on a boat, or in a bar reflecting, personally and privately, about the life of a former marine, drawing some lesson and example from the memory. It was not so much the ritual of parading the body, and rendering respect, and trying to fathom the ultimate meaning of life. He knew more than most about the grieving process and the psychological work of survivors. It was the pomposity of it all that Flint could not tolerate. The sanctifying and sacramentalizing of simple acts which gnaw at the guts of every man. It was the sheer audacity of feigned understanding—the solemn servitude of the ritual. Now he remembered why he avoided funerals. He felt compelled to leave the church, but there was a crowd standing around the door. He stood still, and tuned it out.

Quickly enough the whole affair was over. The marines hoisted the casket to their shoulders and walked slowly down the aisle and out of the church as the choir sang a medley of "Amazing Grace" and "Let the Lower Lights Keep Burning" requested by Bradford's mother, who was a Methodist. The simple melodies had an honest poignancy that tugged at the hearts of the mourners in a way that no highly refined rhetoric ever could. Anne, then the family, then the closest friends from the front pews followed the procession down the aisle, and they gathered briefly on the pavement of Copley Square— roped off for the occasion—before departing for the Mt. Auburn Cemetery crematorium where only the immediate family would gather for the completion of the ritual. Still calm and composed, Anne accepted murmured comments and condolences from friends and heads of state, friends and senators, relatives, and cabinet members. When she saw Ingram on the periphery of the crowd she excused herself and moved toward him, followed at a discreet distance by the Secret Service escorts.

"I didn't think you'd come."

"I just arrived, hoping to see you. I'm not much for funerals."

"Neither am I." The cautious smile. "I'm sorry I haven't called you. I've been so busy with all these arrangements."

"I understand." The funeral director was looking for her, anxious to start the procession. "When are you going back to Washington?"

"In a few hours."

"Oh." He looked away, then back at her. "Should I call you?"

"I don't know. I have a lot to do and a lot to think about." She focused on his eyes, trying to see into his mind. "Someday I'm going to ask you about John's death. Right now, I'm not sure I want to know."

"The autopsy showed intracranial bleeding."

"I know, but there are other questions." Now the funeral director was at her side, with the Secret Service agent.

"Excuse me, Mrs. Bradford. We're all waiting for you."

"Of course." Removing her glove, she held out her hand to Ingram.

"Thank you again Dr. Ingram." Very proper and formal. "All of the family is very grateful to you. Especially me." Steady eyes, which he could not read.

"You're very welcome."

She walked to the long black limousine and closed the door, never looking back. Ingram watched the last of the cars disappear over the hill. He waited as the barricades were taken up and traffic resumed across the busy square. Watching where the little queue of black cars had disappeared, he stood for minutes, deep in thought.

Well. He had set out to do the right thing for Bradford. What he had promised actually. A little more than he had promised. But the right thing for all of them. If she didn't realize that now, she might in time.

He turned toward the parking garage, nearly running into Flint.

"Elegant lady," said Flint, who had been watching the last limousine disappear. "Remarkable, elegant lady." His eyes shifted to Ingram.

"As you say, Mr. Flint." They shared a look of understanding, even friendship.

"Mr. Flint, somehow I didn't expect to see you here. You disappeared so quickly after . . . after the senator died. We have some things to settle."

"We have nothing to settle, Dr. Ingram, except to say that you have my respect. Not many people do. Did you see the report of the autopsy? The pathologist from Walter Reed said that there was fresh bleeding in the head."

"There were some areas where we stripped the anterior cerebral pretty clean. It may have blown out if he strained or raised his blood pressure. There were no other findings."

"Well in any case I think that will be listed as the cause of death. We will both get a full report of course." They walked across Copley Square, nearing the underground parking lot.

"Goodbye Dr. Ingram. I'll not be seeing you again."

"I'm sorry to hear that Mr. Flint. I was beginning to enjoy our conversations. Surely you'll be back on some other official business. Perhaps we could get together more . . . socially."

"I would have liked that. I would like to know how you resolve the anatomy and physiology of the mind-body problem."

"Our recent experience would lead me to believe that we agree on that discussion. But you speak in the past tense."

"Yes. James Flint has disappeared. You won't find any records of such a person in the government. And I'll be on a new assignment. But I'll watch for your publications in *Brain Research*. I've added it to my reading list." A little smile, unusual for the taciturn Flint. They paused, as they had reached an intersection where each would go a different way.

"Then I shall have to write very carefully, knowing that somewhere a very perceptive friend is watching for the pearl of truth amidst the old oysters of research."

"You'll know when you have it. You'll know before I read it." The sun was gone behind the higher buildings now, and a cool November wind shuffled leaves and papers between their feet. It did not occur to either of them to shake hands; a look into the eyes was sufficient closure to this particular crossing of paths.

"Know it in my soul?" With a sly, skeptical grin.

"In your mind. Soul if you add emotion to it. From the peace of mind you achieve, knowing it's right, and the goodness that comes from peace of mind."

"I can see you've been there."

Flint nodded slightly, not in acknowledgment but in salutation. "Please say goodbye to Mrs. Bradford for me." He turned, and walked across the street, leaving Ingram to descend the stairs into the garage.

CHAPTER 23

Every April, on the misty morning that follows the first warm, short night of spring, the soft tips of light-green leaves emerge from the bare branches of the maples that rim Jamaica Pond. Hundreds of trees, thousands of downy tufts, like a huge chorus of children singing of woodlands and meadows, fairness and purity, and flowers in the spring.

In the woods behind the Rizzo house in Natick, where the land dipped low and melted snow formed a swampy pond in a grove of second-growth oaks, the chorus was that of a thousand invisible baby frogs—spring peepers they used to call them. The incessant, high-pitched chirping, which would be annoying when sung by locusts on hot nights in July, was as pleasant as an animal noise can be, coming, as it did, with wild daffodils and robins and wrens and the first walk in the woods without a heavy coat. They scuffed through a mat of last year's leaves, the three of them, and the smell of earth was in the air. Little Matt ran ahead. He knew the way to the pond. Carol and her father-in-law followed, more slowly, inhaling the warm essence of the new season. It was her first visit back since Matt died and she had moved to San Diego, and it was going well. Even Ida admitted that it was going well.

Little Matt recognized Grandma and Grandpa Rizzo at the airport. That was the first good thing. Of course she had coached him, and showed him pictures, and read their letters, and he was programmed to be joyous. But joyous he was, and it had started the visit off well. They had said a hundred times if they said it once, how much little Matt looked like his father had looked at that age. Months ago it would have irritated her, but now it was tolerable—almost pleasant to hear, considering that the boy might be like his father would have been at twenty-two or thirty-five. She had that—they all had that—and it was a consoling thought that helped to ease many a might-have-been memory.

They could speak about Matt now. Speak about him without crying, and without hurting and without wishing that they hadn't brought it up. Just the opposite, in fact.

"Matt loved these woods," she said, kicking at the leaves. "He brought me here last spring to listen to the peepers."

"That's nice to know. We used to walk back here when he was a little boy—about like little Matt there—but I never realized it was special to him. That's nice to know." James Rizzo had grown even thinner, as Ida had grown chubbier, since the tragedy. Carol was the same. James had always thought of her as attractive, but months in the southern California sun and the tincture of time had made her downright beautiful in his eyes.

When they reached the little pond Carol ran forward to prevent the boy from getting into the water. She had become very protective, already deciding that he would certainly not play football, probably not any contact sports whatsoever. Grandpa Rizzo (it pleased him to think of himself that way) knelt down in the damp leaves, then scooped up water in a jar and looked for tadpoles. He showed little Matt a squirrel's nest and a sparrow and a jack-in-the-pulpit and a blue jay feather. Twenty years seemed as no time, and for a moment he expected the little boy to actually be his son. The wistful look, the full flood of memory, came and went quickly, although Carol saw and felt compassion for the older man.

When they returned to the house Ida had a bouquet of daffodils and irises arranged on the lace tablecloth in the center of the big oak table. A picture of Matt, and of his and Carol's wedding picture, and a picture of little Matt were displayed prominently on the mantle. They couldn't handle it at Christmas, but when Ida had put the valentine from little Matt on the mantle, Jim had replaced the pictures back to their usual places, and it felt good. At dinner—little Matt sitting on three telephone books and spilling occasionally—talk turned to the bitter time in the hospital. It was the first time that they had been able to discuss it, and it went well. They wondered about the other patients they had come to know, especially the Dugan family. There had been some reference to Captain Dugan in the paper just a month ago.

A week after Matt died Carol had received a letter from Dr. Ingram and Dr. Adams expressing sympathy, briefly describing the autopsy findings, and offering to be available to the family. She had thought of this, on occasion. When the trip back to Massachusetts was finally set, thoughts of the quiet, confident Dr. Adams appeared in her mind without warning more and more frequently. The letter had been folded and filed away, but she retrieved it to read the last paragraph. Several times. "We were impressed with the personal yet professional under-standing which you brought to this difficult situation. I sincerely hope we will have the opportunity to meet again under better circumstances. Please contact me personally if there is anything I can do for you, or for the Rizzo family." The letter was signed by both neurosurgeons, but the initials in the corner indicated that it had been dictated by Daniel Adams. Was the personal pronoun intentional? Did she read into it more than was intended? There was a telephone number in the letter and she resolved to call Dan Adams in the morning. Just to thank him for his care during Matt's illness. In the morning she would call.

After dinner and a half hour of his first instruction in the fine art of baseball in the backyard, little Matt was ready for bed. Grandma Rizzo, at her request, took him up the stairs, got him into his pajamas, and tucked him in the big bed—(much bigger than his crib at home. As big as mommy's bed)—the bed with the sailboat sheets in the Wonderful Room. The Wonderful Room, as he would come to think of it over the next ten years, had wondrous trophies with statuettes of baseball players and football players, pennants and programs, and photographs of the 1970 Bruins and the 1968 Patriots when the franchise was new, and the Natick High football team, class of '81. It had a desk with sharp pencils and a stereo and a bookcase with the life story of Bobby Orr. It had a big chest of drawers full of old Cub Scout uniforms and hockey jerseys and athletic shoes of six different varieties and sweatshirts with names that became important years later. It had a BB gun and a .22 rifle in the back corner of the closet where he was not intended to look. It had a lock on the door. Not like his room at home where Mother could walk in at any time. No, the Wonderful Room had an actual lock right on the door. And it had a smell about it. A combination of an old hockey bag in the closet that went unopened for many years and a bottle of Old Spice aftershave which very gradually eked its fragrance. The smell caused a pleasant, even dreamy feeling whenever he noticed it, sometimes in association with a vague mental image of his father, although in later years he remembered only the pictures, not the person. It was a Wonderful Room reserved only for him when they came to visit Boston.

* * * *

Just like every April, there were twenty visitors to hear Rothstein on the mind-body problem. Two from France, one from Stockholm, his friend from Columbia, two students from Oberlin, and a smattering of others. They came to audit two weeks of a freshman philosophy class at Harvard. To hear the famous Rothstein. The lecture moved to a larger auditorium, and the blasé freshmen wondered why seniors and graduate students and unidentified visitors took the time to attend this class which, for them, was simply another compulsory dull three hours of humanities credit. Most of the visitors knew that Rothstein had been ill and only recently returned to the lectern. He looked much better than they expected.

He entered through the side door, slightly late, so that all the seats would be full and the side conversations finished. In the larger auditorium the desks went up several levels toward the back, making a little stage out of the lectern. Well, it was always good theater for him anyway. As he came in, heavy briefcase at his side, some of the graduate students began to applaud, then the visitors, then the bewildered freshmen were standing on their feet applauding although they knew not why. Rothstein was surprised and pleased. He actually made a little bow. As the class returned to their seats he put two books on the table: Descartes (the first French edition of *Meditations on First Philosophy*) and Ryle (an autographed copy of *Concept of Mind*, personally inscribed).

"Today we begin a series of six lectures on what is commonly called the mind-body problem. Immediately we recognize a series of words used improperly. It's not a problem, it's more a phenomenon. We can be more specific than 'body' for we know that the phenomenon we wish to discuss occurs in the brain, even in specific parts of the brain. And the mind—well, there are as many definitions as there are authors who undertake to define it—but if we accept the definition of personal awareness of self (which would satisfy both Descartes and Ryle), then we can more accurately title these discussions as the phenomenon of the conscious self studying itself studying itself, if you can follow that. The ability to do this is a uniquely human event, so far as we know. It is, according to many thinkers including Descartes, at the very basis of existence. I think, therefore I am.

"The 'problem' is this: It is said, or at least hoped, by many intelligent people that man has an immortal soul, representing some combination of the collective energy of the universe and some very specific thoughts and memories of one individual. That immortal soul, we would like to believe, continues to exist after the death of the brain. It has personal thoughts and wishes and value judgments and memory and self-examination, therefore it exists as the soul of a person. This is the doctrine of the Christian faith, the Moslem faith, the Jewish faith, essentially all the religions. Religion exists, in fact, primarily because humans must have an answer to this problem. The doctrine was not only the dogma of the church, but the law of the land for centuries, including when René Descartes wrote this monumental book." He held the book up and looked around the room. "That created a problem for Descartes. If he accepted this explanation of the soul (and he believed it himself), then the problem was to rationalize that concept with the very real observation that when the brain is dead, or parts of it are removed, the person appears to have no soul or mind—and therefore cannot exist. Explanations for this dilemma have been advanced by thinkers since the beginning of written language, but the best modern expression is in Descartes. He proposed what is now called the Cartesian argument—that the brain is inhabited for a time by a spirit or ghost which provides the very means to think these thoughts, but vacates that venue at the time of death, maintaining its innate spirit and ability to think. Ryle would say that this reasoning is simply a giant category mistake." He held up the other book. "Mistaking concepts of religion for concepts of physiology, and vice versa.

"This year I am going to depart from my usual format and begin with proof that at least part of Descartes argument is wrong.. My proof is here." He produced from his briefcase a small clear glass bottle full of a clear liquid, with a small round lump floating around the bottom of the jar. He placed it carefully in the middle of the big table.

"In support of his theory, Descartes stated that he had found the resting place of the soul. It was in the pineal gland—the only unpaired structure in the brain. He was very definite about it. Well, here you see my own pineal gland, removed several months ago. My own ability to contemplate—both the analytical and the emotional parts of that process—that ability seems to me to be perfectly intact. Therefore, unless my soul cleverly stepped aside when this snippet of tissue was removed, Descartes was completely wrong and if he was wrong with this dogmatic statement, is not the rest of his discourse totally discounted?"

The clarity of his speech, the simplicity of his explanation, and the sheer theater of this demonstration seemed to seize the audience—the stuff that stories to grandchildren are made of. He paused a moment to let it filter down.

"This year I will explore with you a different interpretation of the writings of Descartes on mind and body. He did not make a category mistake, he simply lacked some categories. Science and religion were only one category. God, afterlife, spirituality were the unquestioned truth. The facts of mind, body, and soul had to fit into the axiom. It was easier then than it would be now. Mind and body and spirit communicated by humors that flowed through the pineal body. Why not? At the time of physical death the ghost leaves the machine the way it came, as humors and vapors. Once you accept the axiom, the logic follows."

He paused, holding up the specimen jar and contemplating the ball of tissue. The audience stirred, and seemed to lean forward together. Those who had heard the lectures before looked at each other, and felt for pens in their pockets. "Today the discussion is the same but the perception is reversed. Now we know about electricity, membrane potentials, neurons, synapses, and neurotransmitters. We know where and how the brain controls speech, motion, pain, breathing, thousands and thousands of functions. Scientific facts have become the axiom. We have to rethink philosophy "in the flesh" as some have said. We understand the body. We are beginning to understand the mind. So we are trying to make our spiritual observations fit the axiom. Some would say that to postulate more than the cold facts is simply wishful thinking and religious faith is an optimistic wishful thought. Some would say that the religious explanations are self-obvious and Descartes had the right concept all along. Some, like my friend Ravikrishnan there in the first row, would say that energy is energy, and only complicated by the idea that the energy has a mind and should be described and worshipped. I do not know the answer. In fact I have become fascinated that we must have an answer. Does the brain include a group of cells that makes up answers for events we do not understand? Perhaps. The mind on one hand and the body on another, and the world on yet another.

We will not answer the problem, nor fully describe the phenomenon, mind you, and we will have more questions than answers at the end of these six lectures than we do this morning. But it brings another dimension to the discussion of the self considering itself personally and privately, then offering a different self as a public image.

"Now you recognize that we are walking in the house of dualism, which actually begins with Plato, so let us return to that touchstone to begin the discussion."

* * * *

There were four morning masses at St. Cecilia's on Easter Sunday. By the beginning of the fourth one, the acolytes were losing interest. Even Father John O'Reilly found the liturgy, however beautiful a story, a little tedious. He scanned the crowd while reciting in Latin. Three-quarters full. He had not seen old Mrs. McGildry—just as well, the dear. He had not seen the Debasios or the Shaunaseys. No matter. But he had not seen the Dugans. Last service and he had not yet seen the Dugans.

289

The day was perfect for an Easter Sunday. All morning long bright sunlight gleamed through the stained-glass window in front of the church, illuminating the inspiring face of Christ with a special glow. The window had been designed with that in mind, made in Italy and brought to Brookline at the turn of the century. Catholics came from all over New England to see it, especially in the spring, especially on Easter Sunday. Father John liked the window because it depicted the ascension, rather than the crucifixion, which was the norm in most of the cathedrals. It placed the proper emphasis in the allegory. There were, after all, hundreds of martyrs who died for principle. But only one who rose from the dead to sit in heaven. Not quite accurate, actually, for we all rise from the dead, as our souls, and depart this earth. But only one who did that in body as well as spirit. To prove a point. That's what made this particular religious allegory so very special. And he was pleased that the window in St. Cecilia's showed this most miraculous of events.

He referred to this in his message. The topic was "Miracles." He discussed spring, really, and the rebirth of the earth, the growth of trees and plants and flowers, the return of birds and warmth and sun. Miraculous. He discussed the labor of man. The sowing of seed and cultivation of crops and harvest of the sea. Miraculous. And he discussed rebirth of the soul. The meaning of life so simply explained, the rules so straightforward. The visible appearance of the Lord himself on Easter Sunday after being dead. Rebirth. Miraculous.

The big doors in the back of the church opened for a moment. Two, three, then six figures filed in, stepping softly so as not to interrupt the service. Cautiously they approached the aisle, kneeling briefly at the appropriate place. O'Reilly paused in his discussion, trying to see into the dark back of the church. He waited so long that other parishioners turned to look. A murmur began at the back and moved to the front. Then Father John did something very unusual.

"Is that the Dugan family standing in the back of the church?"

"It is Father," came Michael Dugan's strong voice.

"Then please come forward. There are seats for you right in the front. Please come." He held out his arms.

Deliberately, self-consciously, proudly, the Dugan family came down the center aisle. All the congregation watching. Father O'Reilly, interrupting the whole Easter mass just for them—just for her, really. The big captain and the slender girl came first. She, holding his arm but walking very independently, head back, smiling at friends and at her father. Reaching out, on occasion, to the end of a pew for additional support. The rest of the family, beaming, following in behind. They filed into the front pew and sat in front of O'Reilly.

"Kathleen, may I say how very glad we all are, every one of us, to have you join us this morning." The girl smiled her famous smile. "We were just speaking of miracles. I believe you've just said it for us."

The organ swelled, joined by the voices of the choir, reverberating through the top of the sanctuary. There at the railing, the face of Christ beaming down, voices of angels in the belfry, kneeling for the sacrament, a man could feel the hand of God.

* * * *

On a Friday afternoon in May a nearly finished chief resident can start to taste the end of it. Like trail horses trotting to the barn, there's rest and security and satisfaction just ahead. The tenth reunion of his college graduating class was planned in June. Most of his classmates were successful investment counselors or law partners or full professors. Adams was earning twenty-five thousand a year, said "yes sir" and "no sir," and worked from six a.m. to midnight on a good day. But the end was in sight and the feeling led to a sense of confidence and freedom that tasted good. Ingram seemed to read his mind.

"How are your plans coming for next year?" he asked, as they tugged the fascia together with heavy Dexon sutures.

"Coming very well chief," laying down knots with no wasted motion. "They wanted me to start in July but I told them I couldn't get there until mid-August. I'm going to finish that paper on carpal tunnels and take a little time off. I'm going to drive across the country and spend a week camping in Rocky Mountain Park. Maybe stop in San Diego for a day or two."

"Carol Rizzo was in town last month. She came into the office to say hello. Did you see her?" Ingram smiled behind his mask. He knew from Miss Lewis that Adams and Carol had left the office together.

"Yes, yes I did. She lives in San Diego you know." Adams was smiling also, realizing once again that Ingram was very human.

"Sounds like fun. What are they paying assistant professors at UCLA these days?"

"Eighty thousand to start. It seems dishonest somehow, taking all that money for having so much fun. The neurosurgeons do half of the carotids there, you know. And I get my own lab. Not a big one, but it's a start."

"Good for you Dan, you deserve it. And listen—take a lot of clinical time at first. Get yourself well-established in the OR. You'll be able to catch up in the lab. You don't want to get the reputation of being a rat doctor."

"Yes sir." They smiled at each other, preparing staples for the skin. They had had this conversation before, only once or twice, but enough for Adams to benefit from Ingram's advice.

"I'm going out of town again this weekend Dan. Is there anyone I have to see tomorrow morning?"

"There's a boy named David Dodd that came in last night. A motorcycle injury from Framingham. He was brain-dead when he got here and he's being qualified as a donor. You might want to see his parents. Then there's the girl from Michigan with the temporal lobe seizures."

"Janet DeBoer."

"Yes that's the one. Her monitoring electrodes are working fine. We should have all the data by the time you get back from your trip. She's on the schedule in a week and a half. Her mother wants to see you. Then there's the L-5 disk from Wednesday. The Egyptian guy in 914. He's doing well. He seems a little spooky."

"Yes. He was referred by Mr. Flint. Remember the marshal who was here during the Bradford case last fall? He sends me a patient every now and then. They come from all over the world, and he uses a different name every time. Very mysterious, Mr. Flint."

"Yes I remember." They finished putting in the staples, laid on some sterile four-by-eight gauze dressings and peeled off the drapes. "If he calls you about anyone from southern California, I'll be in business, looking for patients in August," said Adams.

"I'll remember."

CHAPTER 24

After seventy-seven winters, spring still brought renaissance for Ian McClaren, but in recent years this was related more to the relief of his arthritis than any spiritual reawakening. Nowadays he took active notice when his hip was not painful, rather than the opposite. Today was such a day. It was also the day of the Red Sox home opener which, since both his gait and his mind were enjoying a day of juvenescence, he decided to attend. He rewarded himself with two pats of butter in his oatmeal, thanked the serving girl who was barely awake, and walked without a limp to his table, where Ingram was already sitting.

"Good morning Mac. A white shirt this morning! Now that's a sure sign of spring."

"Aye it is Donald. My guud wife, God rest her soul, would have nothing else after Easter, so it's a habit I've had a long time now, don't you know." He spooned into the sticky oatmeal, applying just enough pressure to come up with the right proportion of gelatinous goo, milk from the outside of the bowl and melted butter from its center. "Are you going on another trip Donald?"

Ingram chuckled aloud. Mac knew this from the census sheet and the preliminary operating schedule. He was always right.

"Not an official trip. I'm just taking a week off." The old man paused, spoon hanging mid-air, but did not comment. "I'm doing some early season sailing." As if further explanation were necessary. "I had the boat put in last week and I'm going to tune it up. Might sail all the way down to Bar Harbor."

"Be careful Donald. It can blow up out there this time of year." The old man could not resist fatherly advice, but was quietly pleased. He knew that, since the death of his wife, Ingram had rarely taken off a day, not to mention a week. He noticed that Ingram looked more relaxed this spring than he had for years. The highs and lows of life for Donald Ingram came as international acclaim and personal tragedy. For Ian McClaren they came as a white shirt and a painful hip. Such is the nature of aging. But the median tone for both, the average hum of life, was only a major third apart, to be sung today in Fenway Park and Marblehead Harbor.

He decided that, since he had officially declared himself on vacation, he would skip Grand Rounds. He went to the pediatric floor first, explaining discharge plans to the family of a baby with a meningocele. Then to Rehab and General Surgery to see the trauma patients they had been following. Then to 9 North.

The distinguished man with the Egyptian English accent was sitting on the edge of the bed, trying to adjust his IV. "It's been two days since your operation. I think we can just get that out of there," said Ingram, removing the tape, pulling the plastic needle, and showing his patient how to keep pressure on the vein with his thumb. "I'm going to be gone next week, but Dr. Adams will take good care of you. You should be ready to leave the hospital on Monday. How do you feel?"

"Wonderful. Free of pain. Look, I can raise my toe." He had been practicing for two days, delighted with the gradual return of muscle function. "Mr. Steele told me that you were excellent. I'm very glad I came here."

"Mr. Steele?"

"Yes. The man who referred me to you. From Beirut. I brought you his letter."

"Oh yes. I knew him by a different name."

"I understand. Thank you again."

Janet DeBoer's mother was in the room, and she stood nervously when Ingram came in. In a strange hospital, in a strange city, staying at the Holiday Inn, all that was unsettling enough. Then the operation and the big head dressing and the cable of wires hanging from it like a pigtail. Very unsettling. Sensing this, Ingram tried to ease her concern.

"Janet is doing very well Mrs. DeBoer. Everything is going exactly as planned. I'm sure all of this dressing looks a little frightening to you, and all the testing this next week can be rather exhausting. But it's all very important in order to solve Jeanette's problem. Look at it this way, in a month or so this will all be over and she should be back to normal."

"No more seizures?"

"The chances are very good that there will be no more seizures once we have taken out part of the temporal lobe."

"You didn't take any out at the operation yesterday?" asked Mrs. DeBoer. Ingram had already explained this twice, but remained patient.

"No Mom." Dopey as she was from medication and the recent operation, Janet could still become intolerant of her mother's confusion. "The operation yesterday was just to put in some wires for testing. So Dr. Ingram will know what to take out. Isn't that right?"

"Exactly."

The older woman seemed flustered, and returned to the little list of questions she had compiled during the night.

"All this electrical testing—won't it be painful?"

"No, but it will cause some of Janet's hallucinations. That's why we're doing it. But it won't hurt." Carefully, he felt under the head dressing for swelling, finding none. "I'm going to be gone for a week. Dr. Adams will direct the testing. I'll be back to talk to you more about the operation—it's a week from Tuesday."

"They won't operate 'til you're here, will they? I mean, they'll let me know, won't they?"

"Yes Mrs. DeBoer. We'll have plenty of time to talk again before the operation."

Backstairs to the ICU and David Dodd. The curtains were drawn around the bed, to shield his parents during their final farewell. A transporter from the operating room, looking impatient, waited with an empty gurney near the door. Poor timing, thought Ingram, who had left the ICU until last, hoping that this particular scene would be played out. Soon enough the Dodds came out, she crying, he struggling hard for control, self-consciously working at a strong masculine image until they got out the door. Seeing Ingram, they paused and the transporter detoured around them into the cubicle. Ingram led them into the hall.

"I'm glad you agreed to the organ donation. Four people will live because of it, but this is a difficult time to try to make decisions."

"Dr. Wilson explained it very well. He said that David died two days ago in the accident. This is more like an autopsy than an operation. He let us talk to a kidney transplant patient. It was very helpful."

"His kidneys are going to stay here in Boston," sniffling but steady, Mrs. Dodd had regained her voice. "His liver is going to someone in Pittsburgh. That's why the delay. They're waiting for someone from Pittsburgh to come. They're actually flying here right now. And his heart . . . David's heart . . ." Back to sobbing, she couldn't finish the sentence.

" . . . is going to New York City." This thought finally overwhelmed Mr. Dodd who turned his head toward the wall. Ingram mumbled condolences again and left. There was no point in further conversation. It had been the father's idea to buy the motorcycle; Mrs. Dodd had been against it. He had had visions of using it himself on occasion, an ironic twist on the dad-can-I-use-the-car scenario; she had argued that a motorcycle led to motorcycle people, a fast crowd, loose women, drinking and drugs. He had envisioned the two of them fixing it, shining it, riding tandem on a camping trip to the White Mountains or a quick jaunt to the Cape; she had imagined the force involved when an unrestrained, unprotected boy's body traveling fifty miles per hour meets a mail truck or a bridge abutment or the trunk of an old red oak tree. They would have this argument again every day for the rest of their lives. Never out loud, always in the inner self only. She would never say "It's your fault," not once. But she would think it, looking at him as the dirt fell on the casket. Crying with him as they took down pennants and boxed boy's clothes months later, bitter with him on every would-have-been birthday. Hating him, in a secret way, twenty years later when he had a stroke and imposed on her the burden of care. Now, however, they needed each other, sobbing in the hallway. But it would never be the same.

* * * *

With more provisions and gear than he could carry in the MG, Ingram took the rarely used Ford station wagon. The keys were still on Emily's key ring. It being Saturday afternoon, he tuned in the opera on the radio rather than playing a tape. The Met season was over and

296

the Chicago Lyric Opera was presenting the Magic Flute. Glorious Mozart and a ridiculous story, but who cared about the story. Random thoughts brought him back frequently to David Dodd. Liver to Pittsburgh, heart to New York, what the hell. Boston academia had really blown it on transplantation. After starting the whole thing, after laying the cornerstone, after surveying all the scientific turf they just sat back and decided—for reasons no one could remember now—at committee meetings run by associate deans and hospital administrators at nine o'clock in the morning when surgeons were busy in the OR—decided that transplantation was too expensive, too difficult, too gimmicky, too close to the borderline of ethics, too surgical, too practical, too applied, so they gave up. Four boat lengths ahead at the first mark and they just sailed off the course. Well, that was Boston academics. They had done the same to neurosurgery after Cushing. It shouldn't be a surprise. In fact, he didn't really care. He shrugged it off, but still feeling irritated he picked up the tape recorder he had brought along to dictate a chapter for a student-level textbook and dictated instead a letter to the editor at Duke, declining with regrets, and suggesting a few other very well-qualified (younger, hungrier, academic-climbing) neurosurgeons. What an easy stroke. In five minutes he saved himself five days of precious time. It was getting easier.

He could see only two sailboats resting in the water as he began the winding drive from the hill down into the cove. The early morning sunshine had given away to gray clouds, then dark clouds, and a misty rain dappled the calm water inside the jetty. He waved to the marina manager, took the duffel bags which he could carry easily, and walked down the hinged stairway to the floating pier, warm rain and salt air and the deck-like rise and fall of the pier adding to his anticipation. The teak and bright work were newly cleaned and the mooring lines were neatly coiled—all handiwork of the boatyard manager. Instinctively, he felt for his keys, but the lock on the companionway hatch was open, and the sliding boards which were the door were stacked on a cockpit seat. The propane stove was off, but there was definitely the aroma of coffee. He felt the coffee pot with the back of his fingers. It was warm. Quietly, he put the duffel bags on the seat and tiptoed to the forward cabin. No one there.

There was a light on in the aft cabin. Anne was lying in the middle of the big bed, sleeping, dressed in jeans and a heavy white sweater. Ingram sat on the edge of the bed, watching her, looking for some minor fault, finding none. She opened her eyes.

"Hello Dr. Ingram. I lay down here to read and I guess I fell asleep. Are you here to stay?"

"I'm here for a week."

"The skipper tells me that this ship is headed down east. Are you assigned to this cabin?"

"I made special arrangements with the skipper to share this cabin with the beautiful and mysterious widow Bradford."

"The widow Bradford has decided that six months of public mourning is enough."

"Are you sure? A little mystery sweetens the anticipation."

"Donald Ingram, you continue to surprise me," she said, pulling him back onto the bed, under the down cover, for the rain had brought a chill to the air. "There really is the soul of a romantic buried in that stuffy scientific body of yours."

"If that is true, which I would never admit, then I challenge you to find it—anatomically I mean."

She chuckled confidence. "Oh, I can find it."

COMMENTS FROM THE AUTHOR

This book was inspired by daily encounters with the interaction of mind, body, soul, clinical facts, and supernatural beliefs during a career in surgery and critical care. The events are set in Boston, and the characters and story are purely fictional. However, many readers will recognize fictional versions of Boston hospitals, physicians, hospital staff, restaurants, and geography.

I am grateful to the physicians, staff, patients, and residents of the Peter Bent Brigham Hospital in the 1960s, who are represented as prototypes in this book. Readers who were there will recognize admiration for surgeons Francis Moore and Donald Matson, both deceased. Many of my friends and patients contributed to the story through their personal dealings with love, life, and death.

Neuroscientists and neurosurgeons Michael Gazzaniga, Bernard Agranoff, Julian Hoff, and William Chandler provided helpful review of the manuscript. Philosophers James Wichterman and Carl Cohen brought thoughtful analysis and practical corrections to the book.

The manuscript was prepared (and wisely edited) by Phyllis McLelland. Emily Jacobson of Curtis Brown, Ltd. reviewed the manuscript and offered essential modifications. Marian Nelson of Nelson Publishing and Marketing inspired moving from manuscript to publication, and brought her skill to the editing and preparation of the book.

Finally, I am indebted to editor Sarah Hart for her perceptive analysis of content, style, and plot, which brought synthesis to diverse components of the book.

ABOUT THE AUTHOR

Robert Bartlett is Professor Emeritus of Surgery at the University of Michigan. His clinical career included general surgery, trauma, and life-support systems. He was central to the development of critical care medicine that evolved during the last three decades. His laboratory and clinical research in cardiopulmonary physiology and artificial organs have been recognized with many awards including election to the Institute of Medicine of the National Academy of Sciences. He authored twelve medical monographs and texts.

Dr. Bartlett's first novel, *The Salem Syndrome*, addressed personal and sociological value judgments in the setting of a family accused of child abuse. *Piece of Mind* is his second novel.